Compline

The Lake District Trilogy 2

ALLAN JONES

THE LAKE DISTRICT TRILOGY

Canons
Compline

THE CATRIN SAYER MYSTERIES

The Chinese Sailor
The Scottish Colourist
The Falmouth Model
The Carnforth Double
The Powys Deacon
The Stratford Hunter
The Thornham Copyist
The Chiswick Chauffeur
The Pinewood Gardener
The Tavistock Lieutenant

All novels are released as ebooks
and as Kindle Direct Publishing paperbacks

CONTENTS

Prologue. Maryport   1

PART 1. Birkby   3

1   Jumper   4

2   Toronto   12

3   Barricade Tapes   18

4   Applethwaite   27

5   Maryport   43

6   Gossip   53

7   Denominations   58

8   Chan   66

9   St Mary's   75

10   Kulis   90

11   Doreen   101

12   Carlisle   111

13   Haverigg   121

14   Valerie   133

15   Nichols   140

16   Chaplain   149

17   Conference   156

18   Bradford   162

19   Hospital   174

20   Rehearsals   179

     PART 2. Compline   189

21   Funeral   190

22   Trumpet   195

23   Stephanie   204

24   Decisions   212

25   Secret   218

26   Champagne   225

27   Mettler   235

28   Compline   242

29   Arrest   253

     PART 3. Aftermath   259

30   Retraction   260

31   Sunday   270

32   IOPC   274

33   Azikiwe   282

34   Sill   295

35	Bail	301
36	'Mid-Morning'	307
37	Solway	319
38	Beardsley	325
39	Fielding	330
40	Luhar	340
	Epilogue. Windows	345
	Notes	353
	About the Author	355

Compline

Also known as Complin, Night Prayer, or the Prayers at the End of the Day, is the final church service (or office) of the day in the Christian tradition of canonical hours. *Wikipedia*

PROLOGUE. MARYPORT

June 5, 2008.

Dennis Lewis changed into the tan-coloured, casual jacket as soon as he was out of sight of his school. After folding his maroon school blazer neatly to fit his backpack, he closed the zip and assessed it. Now it was a bit bulkier than normal, but workable. He wouldn't arrive looking like a hillwalker, lost in Carlisle. Removing his school tie and tucking it into a side pocket, he thought he was suitably dressed for the important discussion ahead.

He had been told they would meet before Compline. Dennis didn't have data on his mobile phone, as his mum wouldn't allow it, worried about the cost. That was a little embarrassing at his age. But he connected by wi-fi at the station before catching the train from Maryport, to do a quick check. Compline was the night service, the one following Evensong, he learned. Something like that, anyway. He closed the browser, switched off his phone and boarded the train.

As someone whose family attended a Methodist church, he knew nothing about that service; it was a Catholic or a monastery sort of thing, it seemed. Still, whatever it was, he would get to meet someone who could advise him what to do.

On the train ride east to Carlisle, across the top of Cumbria, he rehearsed again what he wanted to say. His approach, he decided, should be the same as his own embarrassment at age nine, after breaking the window of a neighbouring house with a ball and not owning up to it. The neighbours were suspicious, and he was in fear of being found out. A week later, he told his father. Once he had been to see the neighbour, made his apology and offered to pay the cost from his meagre savings account, he sat down with his dad.

They talked about how the feeling of guilt was worse than the confession of the deed. That things were best dealt with in the open. How people would understand and forgive; not condone but forgive.

He had looked up his venue on the internet and made notes on where to go when the train arrived. It was a short walk, but he would take it easy, as he wanted to arrive calm and presentable. It mattered. Afterwards, he would call home and explain his absence. His mother would understand, even if his dad gave him merry hell again.

Dennis Lewis, just past his fifteenth birthday, walked out of Carlisle train station and impulsively gave a twenty pence piece to a street person begging outside. The old man glanced at him, then at the coin, and gave him a smile and a nod. In the evening light, no-one else noticed. In fact, no-one really noticed him leave Maryport earlier.

The rough sleeper would never hear about the search focused on Maryport for the missing teenager. Dennis would not be seen alive again.

PART 1

Birkby

1 JUMPER

The daytime community police team based in Keswick, Cumbria consisted of one sergeant and three constables, supplemented from territorial command units during the holiday periods. They were meant to be locally visible officers, dealing with everything from minor traffic issues, petty crimes, and the seasonal tourists in the Lake District getting lost or drunk. Like other community teams in the smaller towns in Cumbria, they put a human face to the largely anonymous police infrastructure in the county.

The old police station in Keswick, a listed building, was permanently closed, a monument to the past. The community team worked from the 'Police Base'; rooms hived off at the Town Hall on the corner of Main Street. Given the size of Keswick, they were also probably the first officers on scene at any local incident, unless a territorial command unit happened to be nearby. From Main Street, it was only five minutes to just about anywhere in the town.

On a wet, blustery afternoon in October, Community Sergeant Harriet Calder stopped her police car behind its twin near the top of Stanger Street. She jammed her uniform cap a bit tighter and pulled her rainjacket collar closer to her neck as she emerged; a tall, slim woman in her forties.

Constable Pam Keston, shorter and rotund, and a big probationer constable, Keith Clarke, on training with Keston, were standing there keeping people back. Their eyes were partly on the crowd and on the wet, slate roof of the nearby house. A young man was standing, straddling the peak of a dormer window. A little further along the street sat an empty ambulance, silent, with its lights flashing.

Harriet's other community constable, Patrick Harris, was in his assigned vehicle, approaching with lights and sirens flashing from the other direction, down the hill.

Calder said into her radio, "Patrick, cut the noise and block the top end; no one to enter, but make sure they ambulance can get out."

She turned to Pam. "Paramedics inside still? Are they ready to leave?"

"They are with the girl, yes. It's pretty bad. She has a knife wound to the abdomen. They'll be out with her as soon as they can, but…"

Her eyes focused again on the roof. The tall man, looking even taller from their perspective, was looking down and crying.

"… they are worried he'll jump if he sees her."

And land on them and the stretcher, thought Harriet. I would be, too.

She asked, "Did he leave the knife in, or pull it out?"

To an onlooker, that would be a strange question, but Keston was with it. "Still in. They supported it in place, but she has lost a lot of blood."

Over the radio, the despatcher told them that two more

police units were now between two and eleven minutes away, and a crisis negotiator was setting out from the Cumbria Police headquarters in Penrith.

"We haven't time," said Harriet, to herself. Then, to Clarke, "Get me the megaphone, then drive that ambulance down the alley at the side, out of sight. Pam, you go in and tell them to move her out the back way when they are ready."

As her team members moved, Calder stared up at the face of the man, Archie Lynn, in his late teens. The last time she recalled seeing Lynn was during a school visit, a talk about road safety, well over five years ago. And the only reason that came to mind was because his mother worked at the tourist centre, and they had occasional contact.

She needed to get closer, get his attention and make eye contact. Clarke passed the megaphone to her and ran to the ambulance, to move it as instructed. Calder climbed on the bonnet of Keston's police car, denting it. Then she moved to stand on its roof and turned to face the house, looking up.

She switched on the megaphone. "Archie, it's Sergeant Calder. Don't look down, look over at me, please. You are wobbling as it is with the wind. Remember me?"

She lowered the megaphone, showing her full face.

He looked down at her, twenty feet separating their head heights, with Calder about fifteen feet in front of him.

He yelled, "Up and down ladders are my living now, Sergeant. Yes, I remember you. You're a fixture here, like the bloody clock at the town hall."

He had been drinking, Pam had said. His voice was slurred.

"Can you get down please, Archie; unaided, do you think? I could nip up and help you back through the window. Or just sit down on the roof until the ladder gets here."

It was sod's law that the fire department was responding to a road accident on the bypass. She had been monitoring that at the base when the news of a knifing and a jumper came in.

He laughed. "I can be down in a sec; literally. Head fucking first."

Then he sobbed. "She'd been screwing him for nearly a year. Can you believe it? My Julie with my best mate. And me; I had no idea."

Harriet sounded sympathetic. "I can see how it hurts you... and the anger. But you left the knife in, thank goodness. It makes it easier for the medics to sort it out."

He shook his head in silent denial. "I stuck her deep. No chance."

"There's always a chance, Archie. Honestly, there is."

In the corner of her eye, Harriet saw two more police cars, lights flashing, entering Stanger Street and the sound of a fire engine in the distance. Then the ambulance with the knife victim suddenly reversed out of the alley, flashing its lights and siren briefly before turning and driving up the hill, heading to the hospital.

Harriet pressed on, forcing Archie's attention back to her. "More damage is done as the knife comes out usually, you see. The doctors will be very careful. You need to get down so we can check on her, let you in to see her, to apologise and sort it all out. We can't do that if you are down on the ground with a broken back, can we? You know ladders, you say. That's probably what will happen, won't it? And you want that, don't you; for you and your girlfriend to work it out?"

"Too late."

"No, it's never too late. I'm sure that your mum would

tell you the same thing. She looks for the positive in everything, doesn't she?"

Harriet was clutching at straws now, recalling the mother's cheery comments in passing conversation, about weather or life. She hoped that it was true, and not simply a forced cheeriness for the workplace.

As the first two territorial command officers moved nearer, Calder held out her hand, warning them to stop. Her eyes were on Archie's, locking his gaze. For a moment it was all in the balance, she felt. There was no more to say without repeating herself. He would jump – and mess that up, most probably. They would need another ambulance here.

Archie said suddenly, "You'll let me see her?"

"Under arrest, yes. You'll get the chance, God willing."

If the woman pulls through. And it would happen no time soon, but she wasn't going there.

He gave a deep sigh, signalling his decision. One leg moved across the peak of the dormer, so that both feet were together. A moment's pause, holding his balance as Harriet held her breath, convinced he would jump. Then he made a controlled slide down the slates, his right hand reaching, grasping the gable trim, stopping his descent. Drunk or sober, he was good with heights, Harriet saw. Within a few seconds, he effortlessly swung back in through the window.

Waving her arm, she signaled the two officers to enter and arrest him.

Pam Keston walked slowly out of the alley. Harriet looked at her, the single shake of the head.

"I waited," she said quietly to her sergeant. "Just in case he saw me, wanted to know what was happening. They are trying, but don't bet on her making it to the hospital. It will be a miracle if she does."

As Calder eased herself off the car roof, Keston looked at her vehicle and said more loudly, "These cars are made paper-thin now. I'll have to file a damage report."

As the officers emerged with Lynn handcuffed, Harriet stood back, her face impassive. They would take him directly to Penrith. He looked at her, questioningly, but was moved on before he could speak. She couldn't say anything else to him.

The probationer, hearing his shift partner's comment about the dent in the car bonnet, opened the side door of their assigned vehicle, pulled the release, then pushed his fist firmly against the insulation beneath the dip in the metal. There was a noise and the bonnet sprung back into place.

"Easy peasy, that one," he said proudly, then looked at his sergeant'as face. "Not like your's, sarge, that was –."

Calder didn't let him finish. She shook her head and returned to her own vehicle, telling Keston and Clarke to secure the scene. She called Patrick, telling him to check on the status of the accident at the bypass and report.

A team from the Major Investigation Unit will be here soon, no doubt. The territorial unit would provide all uniform support for the MIU team, and the community officers would be out of it. It was the way it worked.

Calder was five minutes from a much-needed cup of tea and three hours until the end of the day shift. The Keswick Police Base was only open during the day. After that, Penrith handled all police calls linked to the town.

Then she had four days off, specially booked. A friend was visiting from Canada.

~~

The same afternoon, the sky twenty miles west of Keswick was clearing but still blustery, with a few clouds racing across the sky. Colin Driscoll was on a farm at Birkby, near the town of Maryport, only a mile or so from the coast. Further south, the clouds were darker, and he could see that more rain showers were on the way.

As Col approached the dead sheep, he looked for signs of its demise. It had no visible wounds, broken limbs, or other physical injury that he could see. The cause of death wasn't obvious, he mused, and with sheep, it could be anything.

There were few people and cars in sight. Further south, Col mused, groups of foreign tourists and city folk will now be trudging across the Coast-to-Coast Walk in their fancy rainwear and daypacks, scaring the sheep as they head to Yorkshire. But here it was nice and quiet. Looking at the dead ewe, he concluded that he could not blame tourists for this one.

He called the landowner, Kendal Simmonds, currently on his way to the agricultural college to give a lecture. Having a boss who was a farm owner and a college professor kept Col in full-time work in three locations, but he knew that Simmonds was a stickler for best agricultural practices.

"I'm by the little knoll in the pasture on the west side of Crosshill Farm. Yes, near that copse, checking things out in general before I start on the east pasture tomorrow."

He went over what he observed about the animal, forestalling the first obvious question. "No sign of an attack, no scuff marks of paws or bite marks. Just a trickle of blood in the saliva from the mouth. Unless it was a dog that frightened the ewe into a heart attack. But I don't think so. No tourists are around, either."

Driving and thinking, Simmonds asked about the

location, particularly for any signs of noxious weeds or dead vermin. As Col looked around, he saw nothing obvious – other than the indentation, the slight shrinkage as if the soil had subsided. It reminded him.

"It's where that ground had been dug over, when we took over the land from the Williams couple."

Simmonds considered the possibilities. "Mark the exact spot with something. I'll get the vet in to examine the carcass. Move it on to the trailer, cover it, but keep both in the field. First, move other sheep out, but don't mix them with the rest. Keep them well separated. I'll get the site dug, to see if there is anything toxic buried there. If so, it's bloody persistent, to be there all this time. It's ten years."

Col added, "Some of that sort of stuff takes ages to migrate to the surface, if it's a chemical thing."

After quickly reviewing his own actions, Col asked Mr. Simmonds if he should give Eric a ring. Between the two of them, they could get the backhoe and dig up the site to look for any drums or old pesticide bags. Eric would appreciate a day away from retirement, he knew, not to mention some ready cash.

Simmonds responded, "I want someone independent, a specialist. I'll get John Loudon's people to do it."

Loudon Associates were environmental remediation specialists, based in Carlisle.

That would cost Simmonds a bit, thought Col, but it wasn't his money. A backhoe would find any drums of old crud quickly enough.

2 TORONTO

Richards may be carrying, was Susan Carlson's thought from nowhere. This is Toronto. There are more illegal handguns under men's jackets in this city than free dinners for the needy. It alarmed her.

She sat in a visitor chair next to Jackson Richards, at an angle, both facing Dr. Consuela Ramiro, the director of Haydn House, now seated at her desk.

Haydn House was an addiction treatment centre for women located on a street near Summerhill subway station. Outside, it appeared no different from other neighbouring homes of the wealthy. Inside, it had space to treat fourteen residents, two per bedroom. The women who entered were generally fragile and jittery after detoxifying, desperate for a drink or a fix. Hopefully, by the end of their stay, they left with the skills and support system to stay clean and sober.

Jackson Richards was in his late twenties, fashionably well dressed, with more gold around his neck and fingers than Susan had seen on most women. He now looked somewhere between sullen and angry.

"I came to pick up Reanna. Now you tell me my wife has left already. Where's she gone?"

Ramiro, an older woman, appeared unperturbed by his tone or his growing anger. She expected it.

"That, we can't say, Mr. Richards, by law, and for client confidentiality. She is safe. Reanna made excellent progress here but needs other support than yourself at present to stay clean, as she transitions out."

His wife had arrived at Haydn House directly from hospital, her third addiction treatment programme in less than two years.

He shook his head in denial of the revelation. Susan knew that he expected to collect his trophy wife today, looking beautiful, cleaned up and lucid. He would be taking her to the never-ending set of cocktail parties and social gatherings in downtown Toronto, Hoggs Hollow or Forest Hill.

"I paid the damn bill; I'm the client!"

Ramiro shot back with, "Our clients are our residents during their stay, and sometimes, like Reanna, they are our clients in aftercare."

She leaned forward, making eye contact with the man, to stop his head rolling around.

"And you have been her supplier, let's be frank about it. She doesn't believe you are free of drugs, despite your written undertaking when she came in. Nor do I. Reanna is in good hands. It is her wish, her choice, on how to re-enter normal life from this treatment centre. She will be in contact with you, she said."

Ramiro sat back, a signal that the conversation was finished. "Reanna is not at Haydn House, and we can't give you any more information."

"Can you give her a message?"

"We are still working with her, as part of the continuing

care package so, yes."

"Tell her to call me today. I need to talk to her."

Please, thought Susan.

Ramiro stood. "I will do that, I promise, but it will be her choice. I wish you a good day, Mr. Richards."

And someone would be with Reanna, if she wanted, when she did.

As Susan stood also, Jackson did likewise, looking deflated. "I love her, y'know."

Ramirez nodded. "I wish you the best. Susan?"

Get rid of him, Susan understood.

"Of course."

She opened the door and Jackson Richards left without saying goodbye or thank you.

His parting shot to Susan as he left the building was, "I'll find her. She needs me."

Susan did not smile or grimace. I sure as hell hope not, she thought. Reanna stands a reasonable chance of staying clean if she stays away from you and your crowd until her coping skills are strong enough. If they ever become strong enough.

Susan had been Reanna's assigned personal counsellor during her stay and still had her own doubts on that score.

Richards was something in the entertainment sector, he had said, when they transferred his wife to Haydn. Behind the scenes, Jackson Richards was a middleman, supplying drugs to the elite not wanting to be tainted with the tawdry world of drug dealers. They got theirs from 'friends' who 'helped them'; and Jackson tried to be everyone's friend.

Reanna had collapsed at her beauty salon this last time. Later, in counselling with Susan, she admitted that she was panicking about the forthcoming Toronto International Film Festival. TIFF was a 'big business time' for Jackson, as he had lots 'friends of friends' in town and he needed her smiling face and elegant company at parties.

TIFF was over, a relief for Reanna, who still had guilt trips about letting her husband down. She was now staying with a friend, someone who had tried before to help her stay clean.

Haydn House had monied clients like Reanna, but they were the tiny minority. Most residents were not wealthy, and some were near-destitute. The basic requirement was that the guest was female and had been through at least one other alcoholism or addiction treatment program and relapsed. The minimum residence time was three weeks, but no-one stayed longer than five. It was not a sanatorium with pampering; it was a boot camp for learning to live clean and sober in a dangerous world. Some made it up the hill, others went down again. At the worst, they stopped rolling at the funeral home.

When Susan returned to Ramiro's office, Consuela pointed to the door, then the chair.

"Enough of that. You leave tonight, I just realised."

Susan responded, "Yes. Don't cancel now, please. My bags are packed, and I've finally accepted the idea."

Ramiro smirked. "Wouldn't dream of it. It took long enough to persuade you to go. It's your return that I'm thinking about now. How would you react to becoming the Continuing Care Coordinator, taking over from Olivia?"

As Carlson pondered on it, her boss continued, "New arrivals are your comfort zone and continuing care is hers. I think you see with Reanna – and others – that working with our clients as they return to the real world is at least as challenging as supporting the wrecks who come through the front door."

"You give us hell for referring to residents like that!"

Addicts arriving at Haydn House for treatment were

always to be referred to as residents.

"I do. And for swearing, if there is a resident in the vicinity. We have standards. I set them and sometimes adhere to them."

It had given Susan enough time to think. "I'll do it. It will broaden my experience, which can't hurt."

"I'll set it up. How's Miriam taking to your trip?"

Miriam Efron, a woman in her late seventies, was a former counsellor at Haydn House and the person who had brought Susan Carlson, then one of those wrecks, from the hospital to the facility ten years ago. Carlson was a first-year university student at the time.

Now she was Susan's AA sponsor.

"She's Miriam, still giving out the 'tough love' stuff and encouraging me to go. She's not doing well physically but is berating me about 'getting used to it'. Go see England again. Get a life, she told me."

Ramiro smiled. "It was meant to be, for you to stand in for me at this conference. With your comments about the Lake District and York last year, and the invitation for Haydn House to send a representative now."

Susan pulled a face. "An invitation to the executive director of Haydn House to attend and speak. You know half the key presenters attending anyway."

Consuela Ramiro was networked. Active in the politics of funding recovery centres in the province of Ontario, she was also a member of a panel on addiction treatment strategy convened by the Federal Minster of Health. The four-star general had substituted a grunt private to speak for her at the conference in the UK, Susan felt.

York University in England was hosting a four-day meeting funded by the Commonwealth Foundation, to share best practices and new developments in addiction treatment. Participants would be principally from the UK, but some international attendance was expected.

Ramiro smiled. "Time for a new face on the scene, then. Yours. But you are seeing your friend first, I recall?"

"Harriet Calder. Yes. I'll stay a couple of days there and adjust to the time change."

Her boss picked up a file, a sign she was preparing for another item in her day. "I thought you said the woman was a bit dour, I recall?"

"Dour?"

"Serious, not upbeat, the happy sort?"

Susan thought back. "Serious, yes. I did say that. She's a police officer; perhaps that's a factor. But it was a good visit last time. We get along. And…"

She hesitated.

"I'm going to take a driving lesson or two on arrival. On the wrong side of the road, for me. Then I'll hire a little car to get about. It will give me some independence."

Ramiro nodded her approval. "Make sure it's a little one. Parking is a challenge over there. And practice parallel parking."

Susan showed her surprise. "I hadn't thought of that."

Ramiro said, "Car parks cost the earth; park in the street when you get the chance. And the conference hotel will have parking, so make sure you organize a pass for it at the conference registration desk, or the hotel will stick you with a daily charge."

Susan sighed as Ramiro picked up her desk phone and pointed at the door. "I'll call Reanna Richards now, tell her how it went with her husband, and get her to call him but keep him at bay. You get out of here, and make sure you arrive at the airport good and early."

3 BARRICADE TAPES

Fortunately, the following morning, it was an environmental specialist called Hugh Thornley who did the digging at Crosshill Farm. He wanted this one completed early, as he had a tricky stage of a clean-up outside Carlisle to return to later. But John Loudon was his boss, and Professor Simmonds and John were friends. He worked it into his schedule.

Unlike Col, he understood why they had to tread gently in a potential environmental contamination site. The last thing they wanted to do was puncture any drums of illegally dumped chemicals or to burst any bags of powder.

His backhoe had a smaller bucket, which he moved carefully, lifting shallow swatches of soil. It was an expertise somewhere between the approaches of Colin Driscoll with his big backhoe and the measured pace of archeologists with trowels. Col watched, trying to hide his appreciation of the backhoe skill and his annoyance at the time this exercise was taking. Loudon Environmental even had another person just standing there, spotting for the operator.

Money for old rope, Col thought.

The sharp and experienced eye of the spotter stopped Hugh before he had completed the arc with the bucket. There was a fragment of faded tan cloth, perhaps from a bag, on the soil now in the bucket. With a long-handled brush, the spotter carefully swept the soil surface, about two feet down. He called out to shut the backhoe down and Colin and Hugh moved to join him.

The chunks of a broken grey-white line under the exposed cloth edges were not chemicals, stones, or toxic waste, they were clearly vertebrae from a human corpse, showing the high point of the spinal curvature. In accordance with his company policy, Hugh first phoned the police, not the local environmental officer.

"What do we do now?" asked Colin.

"Nothing, just wait."

Col said he had a tarp to cover the site if they wanted. "No," replied Hugh. "We do nothing now. They will even want to keep our brush, for testing, I suspect, in case of contamination. I'm phoning my boss now, who will call Mr. Simmonds."

Col looked pale, suddenly realising the implication, and vocalising his concern. "If I'd done the digging, the body would be in the big bucket."

"Or the bits would be spread across the spoil heap," said the spotter.

The A596 winds its way across Cumbria, a major east-west artery along the hills and valleys that make up the northern part of the Lake District. Around the same time as Thornley made his find in Birkby, Detective Sergeant Samantha Livermore turned on the wipers as she left the main road at the Wigton turnoff, passing over the bridge that spanned the beck. Two days ago, under a cloudy sky, she wore a new parka. With the humidity that day, she sweltered. Today she had chosen an older, three-quarter length raincoat with a hood, now pushed back. The wind had strengthened, and sleet laced the rain. She expected she would freeze if she needed to spend any significant time outside. Sammie wished the weather would decide what to do, or God would give her more sense when choosing clothes at six in the morning. God in general, she added, as a caveat. A lapsed Catholic, she was touchy on the subject.

Within ten minutes, she pulled up at the house, now cordoned off behind the barricade tape signalling the crime scene. She picked up her phone, reached into the console storage for the small tub of Vick ointment, and got out of the car. Pocketing both, she walked over to the tall, young police officer standing by the tape. He, in turn, was eyeing the smaller, stocky woman now approaching.

Sammie pulled out her warrant badge on its lanyard as she closed in, placing it around her neck and making it visible to him.

"DS Livermore, MIU."

Cumbria Constabulary Major Investigation Unit.

He nodded and raised the tape to let her enter. His face looked pale, and she caught the sour tang to his breath as she ducked under the tape.

Turning to the local officer, she asked quietly, "Were you first here, then?"

"Yes, sarge. Others are inside now."

They sent him out for fresh air, she thought. He had vomited. Inside, it must be a right mess. She reached into her other pocket, bringing out a tube of peppermints.

"Have one. Freshen the breath."

"Thanks. It's…"

He trailed off, embarrassed, as he picked a mint from the top of the tube.

She smiled. "It's OK. We all go through it. Rough in there?"

She knew there were two bodies.

He nodded vigorously. "Yes. She was peaceful, but the man... I've seen pictures, but not the real thing. DI Nolan arrived five minutes ago."

She acknowledged the information with a nod and went through the door to don the coveralls, shoe covers, and hat before reporting to her team lead.

They had adjusted to the initial horror of the scene, as they weren't just police officers but detectives, people who saw violent and tragic sights regularly. At first glance to the trained eye, the man had sedated his wife, then used a cushion to smother her. Sammie suspected he injected enough opioids to do the job within minutes, but having made the decision, he wanted to get on with it.

The gun was an Enfield No.2 thirty-eight calibre revolver from army service a century ago, one that should have been handed in during amnesties decades earlier, probably a family pass-me-down. That would have to be checked.

Once sure she was dead, he had climbed on the bed next to her, taken her left hand in his and used his right to tuck the barrel under his chin. He could shoot himself, but not his wife, Sammie mused. She saw the emaciated woman; he probably still saw the young sweetheart he married.

But conclusions like that had to wait on evidence. So far, they had only the words of the neighbour who had called 999. He told the operator he had heard a bang and was sure it was a gun of some sort.

She looked at Detective Inspector Ken Nolan, his eyes taking it all in, almost oblivious to the pathologist and the

Scene of Crimes Officers around them.

Nolan said, "The couple are James and Kirsty Yardley. The wife was terminal, in a bad state with a lot of pain, the neighbour who called it in told Roly."

DC Roland Atkinson. Roly by name and gait to his colleagues, from his characteristic walk.

He sighed. "It's too much to hope that they won't find a reportable quantity of heroin under the bed?" he asked Sammie.

The younger SOCO looked surprised.

"Relax," said Sammie to the woman. "He's just day-dreaming about transferring this one over to Organized Crime, not trying to pervert the course of justice."

She peered over the woman's shoulder at the note. It would be photographed for them now before removal to the lab, the image sent to the tablet computer Roly was now holding. Sammie caught only the last sentence, clear of the arm of the officer.

'Sorry for any trouble it causes for everyone'. Politeness in death.

She looked at the wasted body of Mrs. Yardley, the equipment around her defining a bedroom set up for hospice care. It had been transformed in seconds into a crime scene for the deaths of the patient and her primary caregiver.

Jumping to conclusions, or not, she knew in her heart how this sad story would unfold – and it wouldn't fit the bill to be transferred to the organized crime team.

Nolan's phone rang. He glanced at it, appearing ready to ignore the call, then answered.

"Yes, John?"

Sammie concluded that it was their boss, Detective Chief Inspector John Kent, head of MIU.

He listened carefully, then said, "We have only been

here a few minutes. I haven't spoken to the pathologist yet. No, nothing like that. It looks like a murder-suicide, at first blink."

Then he focused as he listened further. Sammie saw that he wasn't happy with the news. After he signed off, he said to Sammie, "You are off this one. The boss wants you out at Maryport. Another body, this one discovered buried in a field. He's over there himself now, just arrived. You head up Dearham Bridge Road, he said, about two miles, until you see the flashing lights."

Maryport was about a half-hour drive away.

Sammie looked surprised. DI Nolan's regular sergeant had two days off for a family event somewhere. Sammie couldn't recall if it was a wedding or a funeral. She had been moved temporarily to Nolan's team. With her own team leader, DI Terry Cotton, on his last day with MIU, she had been a little disappointed. She was hoping, despite less than a year as a detective sergeant, to be appointed acting lead of the other investigation unit in MIU in his absence.

As if reading her thoughts, Nolan added, "John is leading the new one himself. Newer case, I should say. It looks like the call for it came in about fifteen minutes after this one. He also said that he's sent Cotton to collect your friend Sergeant Calder in Keswick, to take her over there."

"Harriet Calder. Why her, I wonder?" she responded, taken by surprise.

Nolan was smiling. "No idea. But I'm sure Terry won't be too happy, being assigned to chauffeur a uniformed sergeant on his final day. Roly!"

He addressed Atkinson, lost in the tablet computer now. As Sammie prepared to go, and Roly paid attention, DI Nolan said, "You are acting DS on this one. Sammie's got another to attend."

Atkinson looked surprised. "Two, this morning?"

"We don't schedule them for the convenience of our resources, Roly," murmured Sammie, as she left the room.

She talked to the despatcher as she rejoined the A596, heading further west again, towards the coast.

Her mind went back to the Aster case, a year ago. She had worked with Calder on that investigation, a surprise for her, as the woman was a community sergeant in the town of Keswick. At first, she thought it was simply because MIU was shorthanded, in the height of summer. It was later that she discovered that Calder had prior experience in plainclothes work with MIU. And she had added significantly to the investigation into the death of the priest. Sammie and Harriet had worked well together.

Some months later, lunch with Harriet Calder at The George pub in Penrith was her idea, after the initial experience of her then newly appointed boss, DI Terry Cotton. He had transferred from the National Crime Agency. Cotton wasn't going to last, Sammie told her. And if he didn't, would Calder consider applying for his job? She would make a better DI for their team than anyone else Sammie currently knew.

The problem was that Harriet was also a part-time church official, a Methodist preacher. She made it clear that she had no plans to give up either her Keswick duties or her preaching, to have her life consumed day and night by homicide, missing persons, and the other joys of MIU work.

So why was John Kent having her brought out to the new investigation, she wondered? Had they set up Calder's transfer already, behind the scenes, as the replacement for Cotton?

It's a big one, she concluded, even before stopping the vehicle. Crosshill Farm stretched over a south-facing, undulating slope and, from the fancy fencing around the renovated farmhouse, was one of a spate of selloffs. The farmhouse and outbuilding, with its garden, had been separated totally from the farmland. It was far too neat all around to be a working farm.

The entrance to the crime scene was a hundred yards further along the road, into a field. Two farm workers were dealing with sheep in another pasture. A short gravel track, to allow entry for a tractor across the drainage ditch, was now guarded by an older constable.

Visible at some distance away was the pristinely white campervan with 'Crime Scene Investigation Unit' emblazoned alongside the red and yellow chevrons. It was in perfect condition, except for muddy wheels and more flecks of mud on the lower panels.

Another older, scarred vehicle of similar size belonging to the Scene of Crimes Officers was in front of it. Sammie recognized that one. This was the first time she had seen 'Norm's caff', as the new vehicle had been dubbed, long before it materialised. It arrived, she heard, the previous weekend.

Superintendent Norman Chiswell had come up with the suggestion, a vehicle decked out like a campervan, with seats and a table. And a refreshment centre. And a toilet. He had been miffed, some said, that the Joint Emergency Command Vehicles had to be shared with the Fire and Ambulance people. This would be a test of the value of a police-controlled scene command unit for MIU.

At a barricade tape for the second time this morning, she nodded at the vehicle as she spoke to the uniformed officer.

"Does it come with its own barrista; do you know?"

He smiled. "Haven't got near it yet to find out. DCI Kent is at the scene tent. You'd better suit up, not sip a cappuccino."

When she saw John Kent's face as she approached the tent covering the body, all levity evaporated from her mind. He normally looked calm, professional. Now he looked sombre, disturbed.

Seeing her approach, he said, "Sammie, I am glad you got here so quickly."

He moved away from the tent before she could enter, leading her to one side, to the shelter of a nearby tree. "How is it at the Yardley scene, in your opinion?"

"My read is that the man killed his wife, then himself. The most shocking part was not the firearm damage, bad as it was, but the state of Kirsty Yardley's body. She was emaciated."

He nodded and pursed his lips. "Poor buggers, the pair of them, if you are right. But it's not sounding a difficult one for us, messy as it is. This one, however..."

He looked at her. "It's before your time with MIU, but we think we may have found the remains of a teenage boy who disappeared from Maryport ten years ago, Dennis Lewis."

Sammie responded, "I recall it. The case comes up in reviews, but I only know the name and summary. You've sent for Harriet, Ken said. Was she part of the investigation?"

"No, she wasn't. I wish it were that simple. She was in Keswick by then. You'd better go and see the body and the evidence we found before she gets here."

4 APPLETHWAITE

Detective Inspector Terry Cotton entered Applethwaite village just north of Keswick, in the foothills of Skiddaw. He was in less than a good mood. It was his last day with MIU, and now he was playing errand boy instead of putting the finishing touches to his departure, calling some of his contacts in Leeds and glad-handing a few others around Penrith HQ.

A new case, a body found near the coast, took his boss and the rest of his own team out of the office. He worried who would do his send-off now. Perhaps Kent would ask Superintendent Chiswell to substitute.

In his short time with MIU, Terry hadn't settled. He thought the Lake District would be ideal after his stint at the UK National Crime Agency. He and his family misread themselves as much as their new surroundings. Penrith and the Lake District were fine for a holiday, but not for their lifestyle. They needed a larger city.

He pulled up outside the cottage. The address came from the relief sergeant at the Keswick police base, who knew Calder's plans for the morning. His final comment was, 'she won't be pleased, as she has a friend arriving from Canada today'.

Terry rang Calder's mobile once more. Again, it went to voicemail.

A neighbour working in the garden opposite looked at him. She asked, "Are you wanting the Askews?"

"No, Harriet Calder. I understand she is here."

"She's inside. Just knock. Vic's daughter is downstairs. Harriet will be upstairs with him."

Calder gently placed her hand over the joined, bent fingers of Victor Askew's hands, in prayer. She could feel the arthritic knuckles and hear the laboured breathing, but knew his suffering was as much emotional as physical.

"May God forgive me, Harriet."

She smiled at him. "He did that long ago, Vic. I have no doubt about that. Your problem has always been your inability to forgive yourself. We both know that."

He chuckled, a little raspy laugh that fleetingly broke his self-absorbed state of penance.

"Always the same, Harriet, telling it the way it is, the way you see it. It won't be too long until I find out meself if you are right."

Askew was bedridden, far along in stage four lung cancer.

She smiled at him. "Well, if I am wrong, send a thunderbolt or something. I'm a copper; you were one once. It's a hard job and we aren't perfect."

"If you are wrong, lass, I could be in the other place. No chance to send messages from there."

She held his hands gently. "I'm wrong about many things. But I am sure about you."

A small knock on the closed bedroom door preceded Laurel, his daughter, appearing. In her forties, she still seemed timid.

"There is a police officer here for you, Harriet, an Inspector Cotton."

Victor gave a raspy laugh again. "Work calls."

Then he coughed, choking. His daughter came over, saying, "Let's get you sitting up a little more, and your oxygen back on, to stop you gabbing."

He mumbled, "Your face, Harriet. Is he here to arrest you, or what?"

It surprised her, she admitted. And Cotton? She hadn't seen him since their meeting with John Kent after her return from Canada. That was a year ago.

"He said it's urgent," said Laurel.

"Please tell him that I'll be down in a minute. Your dad and I want a prayer together before I go."

Perhaps for the last time, Harriet thought, taking stock of the man and his condition. When she started her next set of work shifts, she would not get the chance to call in to see him. And the appearance of Cotton was ominous, as he was with MIU Somehow, she knew it would complicate her life further.

"Sorry to disturb your day off, Sergeant Calder. DCI Kent asked me to collect you and bring you to an incident scene."

"Where?"

"A field near the coast, at a place called Birkby. That's all I know at present. My team is there with DCI Kent. He asked for you specifically, as soon as possible."

Before he could say more, Harriet responded, "Could you give me a few moments more with Laurel, then I'll be all yours."

Alone, her expression said.

"Of course, I'll wait in my car."

She needed to speak to the daughter, not just walk out on her. A minute later, as she left the cottage, she approached Cotton's vehicle and pointed to her own. He lowered the window so he could hear her.

"I'll put my rainboots in your car, then, if it's a field."

She opened her car boot and took out the rubber boots, not clean, but not that dirty. As he emerged again and opened his own car boot, she saw his expression. The interior was immaculate and there was no sign of his own pair.

"I'll put them on a plastic bag," she said, mollifying him a little, rummaging for one. She always carried one or two, just in case.

As Cotton set off, he said, "I had no plans to be there. I was on my way to HQ when John called me." He did not look pleased.

If they were going to a field in Birkby, she wondered how he was going to cope in his fine city shoes.

"So, it's your last day? I didn't know. Where are you going?"

"West Yorkshire Police, to Leeds. A bigger job."

"Good for you. Still on major crime work?"

"No. A borough role, one that will broaden my experience. A big team to manage."

Where you won't get your shoes mucky, thought Harriet, uncharitably. Her mind went back to the pub lunch with Sammie Livermore before her only other meeting with the man. 'He won't last', she said. "He is like a steak and kidney pie without the filling, all flaky pastry and no substance'.

She was right, it seemed, at least about his time with MIU.

"Well, congratulations anyway."

Cotton added, "I'm a city boy really, I've come to accept. Being at Carleton Hall feels a bit like working in a stately home."

The Penrith Police Heaquarters building, located on the outskirts of the town.

Harriet smiled to herself. "Well, it is a Grade 2 listed building. I don't remember any frills or finery from when I worked there."

Cotton smiled, but said, "But you are from around here?"

Harriet responded, "Born ten miles from Keswick. Been here most of my life."

"And a sergeant in Keswick for a while, I heard. I gather that you used to be in MIU, as a DC?"

Harriet nodded. "I was. After my husband died, I went back to uniform work in Keswick. My life changed. The job is now called a community sergeant. The titles change with each reorganisation these days, but I like community policing."

Cotton smiled. "I just recalled; Sammie said after I met you last year that you are a part time preacher, a Methodist. So that's what you were doing back there, were you? Parish work. The photos inside confused me. The man you were visiting, he was a police officer once, from the photos?"

"Vic Askew. Yes, he was. I never knew him in the job, only as a member of the church. What's this call by DCI Kent all about?"

They were currently heading to Cockermouth, on the A66. She didn't want to be talking about Vic Askew with Terry Cotton on this journey.

"I'm not sure. The team was called out to a find in a field early this morning, I gather. We've been looking for a Donna Smallwood, missing, a seventeen-year-old from Salterbeck with a drug debt problem. It's not that far away.

It may be that the young woman ran into trouble, but that's speculation. DCI Kent took over the Smallwood file from me yesterday afternoon."

That would not merit calling me, though, Harriet mused.

Then she remembered the other part of the lunch discussion at The George with Sammie; she wanted Harriet to think about applying for Cotton's job, if he left. Harriet's prior experience in MIU and her strong team management skills as a shift sergeant would be ideal, Sammie thought.

Harriet had recoiled at the suggestion.

She said to Cotton, "Well, good luck to you. I hope you and your family settle well in Leeds and everything works out."

There were now two police cars, one either side of the entrance to a farm track off the Maryport Road. A police officer waved Cotton into the track and pointed to where other cars had parked near the two brightly marked vans.

MIU was well-established and set up for the long haul, Harriet saw. Further in the field, the scene tent was near a knoll, before a copse of old beech trees and oaks. The access route led there, and two plainclothes officers were emerging from the tent to meet up with other people leaving the van. They stopped and one person, a shorter stocky woman wearing her rainhood up, turned on hearing the noise of Cotton's vehicle.

Sammie, Harriet saw. She recognized the coat. Then, in the cluster of men, she saw John Kent.

Cotton parked and they got out. He walked towards the men as Harriet waited at the back of his car. Realising it, he turned, she asked, "Can I have my boots, please?"

She put them on before going any further and, from intuition rather than anything said, carried her shoes with her. She had the feeling that she wouldn't be travelling back with Terry Cotton and didn't need to lose a good pair of shoes, particularly if he was leaving the area.

In a neighbouring field, Kendal Simmonds watched the events unfolding on his land. The ewe had died of liver failure due to a tumour, the vet told Kendal. It was a coincidence. A large area of his land here was now sealed off with barricade tape, and the police presence was significant. There were cars and vans, police officers in blue coveralls and forensic people in white.

Kendal waited for news. He and his people would be interviewed at some point, he had been told. In the distance, he saw a car arrive and park, and a man and woman got out. He wondered if it was the family of the deceased. Did they bring them to an active investigation site? Surely not. Then he recognized the woman; a Mrs. Calder, who had preached from time to time over the years at both his church, Dearham Methodist, and down the road at St. Mark's in Maryport.

Kendal Simmonds was an intelligent man with a strong faith. He had lived his entire life in north-west Cumbria. But suddenly he felt a chill, a premonition he couldn't quite pin down, other than in the final words from the vet.

"I know your concern about some external factor, Kendal, but the ewe's death was not site-related; that's just coincidence or an act of God."

As his premonition crystallised, he thought it was more likely to be the latter reason. They were less than ten minutes' drive from Maryport, and his mind went back to a tragedy at St. Mark's there, in the hope that the find on his land wasn't connected.

As Harriet drew close to the huddle, DCI John Kent

turned towards her as Terry Cotton called out, "Do you need me for anything else here, sir?"

He was formal, polite, but to Harriet, she could hear the tension in the question. The only other time she had met the man, he had been fawning, if anything, over his boss. She concluded that whatever caused Cotton's move, it left a sour note between the two men, and each was making the effort to keep things on an even keel.

"Thank you, Terry. No, I'll let you get back. And I'll see you later."

Kent focused on her. "Harriet, thank you for coming. How long have you been a circuit preacher?"

Cotton took a step back. Calder, sensing he was leaving, said, "Thank you for bringing me over and best wishes."

He gave her a quick smile and said, "Thank you. The same to you, Sergeant Calder."

He turned and walked away without another word, again treading as if his major concern in life was keeping his shoes clean.

Kent's question had caught her by surprise. In their interactions in the past, John Kent had never hidden that both the Kent family and Calder were active Methodists. But he had never pushed it visibly, either.

The subdivisions of the Methodist Church District covering Cumbria were called circuits. Working alongside ordained clergy were lay preachers, with a particular set of churches and chapels they served. They either led services, gave sermons in support of the ordained minister, or provided spiritual support to their communities.

"Fifteen years this year, sir."

It was a formal question, meriting a formal answer. Her first thought, 'ask your wife' had slipped away. Carol Kent was a member of the District Committee overseeing the rotas of ordained and lay ministry in the county.

He nodded and pursed his lips. "It's not your circuit, but you were preaching at Maryport ten years ago, I believe?"

The sudden realisation of the reason for the callout hit her forcefully. She froze, her lips parting slightly. Her reaction was obvious to the cluster. Sammie Livermore hadn't spoken, but she reached out and gently held Harriet's arm, anticipating that the older officer needed steadying.

"Are you OK, Harriet?" She gave a sharp glance at Kent.

Harriet asked, her voice shaking slightly, "The body. It's not the girl with the drug problem, is it, the one that DI Cotton inferred? You've found Dennis Lewis, haven't you?"

"Why do you say that?" he responded softly, his eyes assessing her analytically.

Sammie said, "Let's get her into the van, boss."

Livermore's voice showed her concern as tears flooded Harriet Calder's eyes. Harriet's response was fragmented as she walked. "Maryport ten years ago. A body now. How could it be anything else? Particularly when you send someone to collect me on my day off."

Kent responded. "We believe so, Harriet. Sorry, I should have realised it would hit you hard. Let's get you a seat for a moment. Does this new thing have any tea or coffee yet?"

Was Norm's Caff able to live up to its nickname, he meant.

They were seated around the small table. Sammie was clucking over Harriet like a mother hen. Harriet had finished wiping her eyes and blowing her nose.

Kent pulled out an iPad.

"The main reason I wanted you over here is this. Do you recognize it?"

He was showing her an image of a crumpled sheet of paper starting to fragment. It had been placed under a glass plate and photographed. Although in several sections, and with blurred text caused by moisture and time, it was still identifiable.

Harriet stared at the screen. "It's the order of service at St. Mark's Methodist in Maryport, the month Dennis disappeared. The Lewis family attend there. I was interviewed back then, with all the members of St. Mark's. I told them I was preaching at Maryport and that I recognized Dennis's picture but, on the two occasions I had preached there before his disappearance, I hadn't spent any time with him."

He asked, "You weren't involved with him at all?"

"No."

Kent took out his pen and used the tip to point to one area with a list of dates and names.

"But you were around there as a preacher, as you said. There you are, listed as taking the service the week before Dennis disappeared."

Her name had been circled in ink.

"I'd forgotten the exact date. Bernice Lewis remembers me being there around then, she said."

"You know Dennis's mother?"

"Not back then, but over the years, yes."

"Do you preach at St. Marks often?"

"No. I am mainly south of Keswick now, the Langdale Circuit, not over on the coast. But occasionally I've stood in for someone. And Bernice and Eamon Lewis and I talk when I have done that. We always include Dennis in our prayers."

"So, you know them currently, really?"

Sammie saw that nugget of information particularly interested her boss, for some reason, but she couldn't work out why.

Harriet looked at Trent, but her mind was on the image. "A little, not well. Was this with the body?"

"Yes. It's another reason why we think it is Lewis. It was in the remnants of what appears to be a zippered inner pocket; there are zip fragments nearby. The records say that Lewis was wearing a maroon blazer when he disappeared, but there is no sign of it. He was wearing another jacket, we think. We haven't found any other items with the body and reckon that the killer – or killers – missed the zipped-up pocket."

He flicked the screen to the next image, the other side of the folded sheet. This was harder to read, as there was a stain, again from a ballpoint pen by the looks of it, in the blank area at the bottom.

"And this. Does it mean anything? I know it's some time ago."

The reverse side listed the sequence of services for the month. St. Mark's had only printed its bulletins monthly, Harriet recalled, to save money.

Written in a scrawl were the words 'Compline' and 'nun'. The computer image had been overlaid by a forensic officer, it seemed, drawing out the words from the different density of the stain, to give them clarity.

He continued, "Sammie spotted the significance of Compline and the blotchy 'nun', but there is another letter in that smudge. Forensic analysis on the lab should bring it out more clearly."

It made Harriet smile suddenly, getting Kent's implication. They both got it. She glanced at Sammie.

"Not so lapsed, after all?"

Sammie skirted the comment. "Why would a young

teenager attending a Methodist church be referring to a Roman Catholic rite and nuns? Methodists don't observe Compline, do you?"

Harriet looked lost for a moment, then said, "Compline is not part of the Methodist order of service, but neither is it only Roman Catholic. It is part of other denominations, including the more conservative practices of the Church of England and, I think, the Eastern Orthodox churches. Although, I am not sure where it fits with them. It's part of the daily office of prayers, the night service before retiring. It dates from the time of monasteries. They went to bed after dark, because they were up during the night, with the services of Lauds and Prime.

"But I'm thinking back. Perhaps that is not 'nun' but 'nunc'."

Kent asked, "What do you mean?"

"The order of the two words, for one thing. You should ask people at Maryport. I have a vague memory that someone mentioned a fundraiser, a concert of some sort, around then, but can't think where. If I remember right, it included Burgon's 'Nunc dimittis'. That was quite a popular piece then, being used in the spy series with Alec Guinness."

"Tinker, Tailor; the John le Carré story?"

"Yes, that one. But I don't recall anything in detail."

Sammie was making notes.

Kent stood. "Well, that is useful. It helps."

He was silent for a moment, clearly thinking of the next steps as he gave Harriet a long look. "I had to ask. Your name is circled and so is the word Compline. I didn't understand it; still don't, yet."

Both women waited on him, Sammie for direction and Harriet hoping to get home.

"Sammie and I are going to break the news to Dennis's parents. Not that it is him, but it may very well be. I don't want them to hear about it from others. Will you come with us? On duty, not off? Are you up to it?"

Harriet hesitated. "Susan Carlson is arriving today, from Canada. I have already had to ask a friend to meet her train, while DI Cotton drove. I should..." She stopped and closed her eyes for a moment. "But this is more important. Susan will probably just rest after the journey."

Kent gave her a surprised look. "The Aster investigation. I had forgotten that you two had become friends."

Calder looked at him. "If I can see the body first."

Kent said, "I'd rather not have any additional –."

Sammie butted in. "You want to pray, right?"

She recalled her first encounter with Calder, at Bassenthwaite Lake, at the site of the body of the Canadian priest, Duncan Aster. Calder had been nearby when the call came in and was the first officer at the scene. Sammie, temporarily in charge of the initial MIU team, had been annoyed to find her inside the barricade tape, praying; annoyed enough to insist Harriet's shoes be sent for forensic elimination.

Calder gave her a small smile. "Yes. It will mean a lot to Eamon and Bernice if I do that before I see them. And it will help me."

She looked at Kent. "I wasn't asking to be part of the investigation, John."

She was talking to him Methodist to Methodist now, she was emphasizing.

He acquiesced silently. "Not long, though. We need to do this."

To reach out to the parents. Get it done. A job which never grew easier for the members of MIU.

He added, "Suit up, then. You have not forgotten how to do that, I hope?"

John Kent smiled, turning his misunderstanding into

light relief. They needed that, they all recognized.

The pathologist was Dr. Clive Meadows. He had started working with Cumbria Police around the time Harriet had joined MIU as a detective constable. And he had a good memory. Besides, she was a twenty-year veteran; they had seen each other around. He looked up from his work as they entered the tent.

"Harriet Calder! Don't tell me you've come back to this bunch. I thought you knew better. They don't know the meaning of work shifts. They drag me out at all hours. How are you?"

"Very well, Dr. Meadows, and I see you are full of vim and vigour, as ever. No, I'm just visiting, so to speak."

The pathologist looked at the body, at one side of his position but mainly below him now, as he bent over. "That is a polite way of describing it; visiting."

She stopped talking as her eyes focused. In the harsh light of the floodlamps, she took in the trench dug alongside the decomposed body now being examined.

She said, softly, "Dear God, look at the poor boy."

It was an exclamation, not a prayer.

Harrriet leaned forward herself, careful not to get too close or touch anything. She took in the state of decay, the blackened skin fragments and residual organ tissues, the rib cage still attached to the spinal column giving an architectural structure to the awful image. It seemed as if she was staring, stunned, but as Meadows looked up at her, he could tell she was taking in the nature of the soil, the depth of the grave and the shape of the body. It was prone, with the arms folded into his chest, the legs folded up tight, so the heels were near the pelvis.

Calder asked Meadows, suddenly, "Has he been stored in a box, or a freezer, perhaps? Residual tissue analysis will reveal cellular damage from freezing, won't it?"

The pathologist said to Kent. "What we just talked about, John. Are you sure you haven't dragged her back to MIU?"

Kent ignored his question. "What makes you think that's the case, Harriet?"

"The shape. But more, it is the location, the depth. The areas around Maryport were searched quite thoroughly, I recall, back at the time. I doubt he was here then, in a newly dug grave. The surface disturbance would be visible. If I'm wrong and it was missed, someone from back then deserves reaming out. I was thinking he could have been stored and put here later, perhaps?

"But that's not why I'm here, Clive. Can an atheist give me a couple of minutes to pray? Assuming the worst, that you are still that?"

The pathologist smiled. "It's time for a visit to your wonderful modern facilities over there, and a cuppa. Don't mess up the site, now. Sally, you'll stay?"

For continuity of supervision of the site by the pathology team. The forensic assistant looked confused.

Kent said, "We are just saying a prayer before we go to see the parents."

"I'll stay," she said quietly, looking at Harriet.

As Meadows left the tent, Calder moved to stand on the stepping plate nearest to the head. Hands together in her lap, she closed her eyes and said, "Eternal rest grant unto him, O Lord, and let perpetual light shine upon him. May his soul, through your mercy, find peace and, in disturbing his mortal remains now, guide us in bringing him closer to those who love and cherish him, that in their grief, they find your strength and support, as their lost child is finally returned to them. Amen."

She led straight into the Lord's Prayer, and the others

joined in. Harriet could hear Sammie's voice and that of the young woman. As they finished and she looked at Kent she said, "Thank you."

He nodded. "Time to go."

As they moved away, he called to the forensic assistant, "Sally, I'll send that malingerer of a boss back to you. Better still, get some tea or coffee yourself, and tell him I said he should get back to work."

5 MARYPORT

Harriet rode the short distance from Birkby to Mary-port with John Kent, with Sammie following. As they set off, he said, abstractly, "You talked down this man Lynn from the roof in Keswick, I heard. Good job."

She thought for a moment. "Thank you. And his girl-friend? She made it to the hospital, I heard. That's all."

Kent nodded. "She is holding her own. It was a near thing, but she should pull through, they said this morning. It's a straightforward one for us. We have charged him with grevious assault so far. Not sure if it will go to more than that. We'll see."

Harriet said nothing. At some point she would run into Archie's mother in Keswick. At least he hadn't jumped.

Maryport was a pretty coastal town these days, thought Harriet, particularly the waterfront. In Victorian times the town had a sizeable foundry and its industrial past had lingered.

Kent said suddenly. "With the Lewis family, feel free to chip in. It may help."

His phone rang. He connected, dealing with a routine matter. Harriet wondered what he meant by his last comment, but the moment had passed.

The rain petered out as they reached the outskirts. On a day like today, with a break in the clouds and some sun on the water, Harriet wished she was taking a walk here rather than be part of the task ahead.

As John Kent turned down Church Street, they passed the large red sandstone Anglican church, St Mary's, sitting in its own grounds. He glanced at his satnav map. Harriet, catching it, said, "Left on Kirkby Street. Why don't you park at St. Mark's, on the left? We can walk up to their house. Less fuss."

They arrived at the more modest Methodist church, set between houses on either side. Harriet took in the road, with vehicles parked legally on one side, and a couple of cars parked illegally on double yellow lines nearer to the brow of the hill. Sammie drove in behind them and took the next empty parking spot.

They walked together the last few yards. Sammie glanced at her colleagues, finding it strange to be in the company of Calder again. Like herself, Kent looked impassive. Calder looked anxious. As they neared the steps to the neatly painted front door, Calder took a deep breath and, too, adopted the same expression. They were police officers, about to bring the news that the family had dreaded but also expected, waited for daily, for a decade.

On ringing the bell, it was a woman in her twenties who answered. Kent said quietly, "Are Mr. and Mrs. Lewis at home? We are police officers."

An older woman came up behind her and took in the faces at the door. In anguish, she said, "Oh, Harriet! It's Dennis, isn't it?"

One hand reached out for the bannister rail on the staircase behind her.

"Can we come in, please?" asked Kent, although Sammie was already in the doorway moving to the other side of Dennis's mother. The threshold, in both entrance and communication, had been breached.

Forty minutes later, Sammie was sitting fiddling with her teacup, ready to move forward. They had a cold case active now, a death of a teenager. That, and the other recent investigations assigned, would have all the MIU staff working hard. Glimpses of the bodies at her first stop this morning flashed back, not for the first time.

John Kent had just broken away to take a call, saying nothing but grunts and monosyllabic responses. It was Calder now, most engaged with the family.

"At least we'll get to bury him properly; that's a blessing. We always hoped he would come back, of course, but after the investigation stopped, we knew he was dead."

John Kent closed the call and jumped straight in. He said, with conviction, "We never stopped, Mrs. Lewis. The case was never closed, but we had no leads to follow."

Harriet was watching Eamon Lewis. He had said little so far. Bernice had given most of the responses, occasionally glancing at her husband, her face showing her concern.

Eamon Lewis looked at Kent. "I've very mixed feelings about you. And that Inspector Green. I hope he's not involved."

Sammie said quickly, "Inspector Green died, Mr. Lewis, nearly eight months ago. Cancer."

She had picked up on the bitter tone. Sammie had been close to Neil Green and his wife at the end. She did not want this man speaking ill of the dead.

Lewis responded, "Then God rest his soul. Between him and you, sir, you made our lives a double hell back then."

Kent looked at him, saying nothing for a moment, then responding quietly, "We had a job to do, Mr. Lewis. Time was of the essence."

The atmosphere in the room had changed. From grief and sorrow, now it had anger mixed in, visible in the face of the grieving father.

Lewis said, "We watch enough TV. We know the family are always seen as the most likely culprits. It wasn't the job you did; it was how that man Green did it."

Bernice became anxious. "Eamon, please!" She focused on Sammie. "You'll keep looking, won't you? For the person who did this. There'll be clues, perhaps?"

Sammie responded. "We have forensic officers at the site and there will be a post-mortem examination... we'll see. But as DCI Kent said, we are continuing the investigation. It was never closed."

Kent looked at Sammie and Harriet signalling that they needed to leave. He finished with, "I wanted to let you know as soon as possible of the strong possibility that we have found Dennis."

Bernice asked anxiously, "Will you want us to identify him? Can we see him? I don't –."

Know what he looks like, she meant. They all understood.

Sammie spoke up. "There's no need for a formal identification, Mrs. Lewis. We have dental records and other details. And the ability to do some DNA tests."

"But can we see him?" Eamon asked. For some reason he looked at Harriet.

She glanced at Kent. She had no say in the matter.

DCI Kent said softly, "He's not in any fit state to be seen, Mr. Lewis. The body is badly decomposed. It would be hard for you both. But we'll sort something out once we have him inside and formally identified. You can be close to him."

Bernice nodded slowly. She had focused on Calder from the start.

"Did you see him?"

"I did. And I prayed for his soul there, Bernice. And for your family, for the strength you need now."

Suddenly Bernice grabbed her husband's arm. "Will you come, Harriet? To the funeral, if Reverend Sills leads the service. Will you speak, too?"

"I'll be there if I can, yes. Of course."

She glanced at Sammie. Police officers would attend the funeral of any victim. It was procedure, their eyes mainly on the faces of the people present.

Bernice continued, "I'm glad you are part of the follow up. You'll find out what really happened? We need to know."

Harriet was caught unprepared for that statement. It was John Kent who said, "I'm sure Sergeant Calder will do what she can to help."

Eamon Lewis's final comment was, "We will help all we can, too, for Dennis. But you won't be treating us like last time, I can tell you that. I'll get a lawyer this time before you start questioning us again."

He turned his back as Bernice awkwardly accompanied them to the door.

Outside, they regrouped in the Methodist church car park.

Kent said, "It went as well as we could expect. Harriet, thank you. It helped, with you being here."

Sammie had picked up early in the home, seeing Eamon Lewis's expression, why John Kent had brought Harriet Calder along.

Kent added, "It can't be helped. Sammie, when you read the file, you will see the background. Dennis and his dad had argued the day before. We had to follow it up."

He looked at Harriet. "You have talked to them, over the years, you said."

Harriet took the implied question, pondered a little and chose not to answer. What she learned in her role as a member of the church was her business. In the end, she responded with, "Yes, and, procedure is one thing, but in my heart, I feel that neither of those parents were involved in the disappearance of their son."

Her look challenged Kent.

He came back with, "I think you are right. Neil and I came to the same conclusion, but Eamon Lewis was always a prickly character." He sighed, "With a burden on his back, his lost son, their argument, and our questioning."

Sammie asked, "What was the argument about? I take it is in the file?"

"Eamon was concerned that Dennis and his friends, on their bikes, were out and about going too far, for too long. The father was used to a tighter rein and not really letting go. It was a focal area. We concluded that the boys were just enjoying life, growing up. We found nothing to be problematic, I recall. But all that must be revisited."

Harriet was glad that she wasn't involved. She wanted to get back to Keswick, now, and catch up with Susan.

John Kent looked long and hard at the two women as he reached into his pocket for his car keys. He pulled them out, then put them back.

"One moment. Hang on."

He turned away, walking a few steps to make another call.

Sammie moved closer to Harriet and said quietly, "Thank God 'Flaky Pastry' isn't here. He would have been yakking at Eamon, making it worse."

Calder was reminded again of their lunch meeting, months ago.

"What's going on there? Cotton said it was his last day. And you could cut the atmosphere between Kent and him with a knife, I saw."

Sammie glanced at her boss, seeing he was wrapping up the call. It had been quick. "I'll tell you later."

John Kent walked back, pulling out his keys again. "I've just commandeered you, Harriet. You'll join MIU for a while as we deal with this. The media will be all over us and I am a senior officer short. You and Sammie can work together on it."

"Commandeered? You didn't ask?" was all Calder could say. She was shocked.

Kent nodded unapologetically. "I didn't want to give you the choice, or the dilemma. MIU has a missing person investigation in Salterbeck, and an apparent murder-suicide that Sammie attended this morning, and now this. Not to mention the knife attack wrap-up you know about.

"The next step on the Lewis case is to gather the forensics and review the files, see what was missed first time around. Something was, I suspect. With DI Cotton's departure, I also have to focus on a replacement. Between you two, you can handle the re-interviews of the Lewis family, as well. There is no history with them for Sammie and whatever history you have through the church, Harriet, it's got a lot more going for it than me."

Sammie gave Harriet a look, then a smile. Calder was trying to conceal her anger, she saw.

Harriet was half-listening, but also thinking of her current role in Keswick and what her direct superior would say. Inspector Robinson was responsible for the community police teams in the county.

"June Robinson agreed; just like that? I'm very surprised," she bristled.

"Robinson doesn't know yet. Superintendent Chiswell approved it. He'll let her know."

He paused. "I know it's a surprise. But are you OK with it? You'll get your Sunday mornings clear; I promise."

Calder was tall; as tall as John Kent, albeit rake thin, thought Sammie. She was glancing up at the pair, alternating between her two colleagues staring at each other, wondering what Calder would say next.

A sea breeze heading inland suddenly gained force, a gale strength gust down Kirkby Street, making each police officer turn their back, protecting their eyes from the odd raindrop and specks of dust and grit picked up by the wind. The moment passed.

Harriet found herself staring at the old Anglican church, across from the end of the street. She thought a moment then suppressed her first response.

"It's decided and out of my hands. I suspect it will help Eamon and Bernice, from their reaction."

She was not going to let John Kent off the hook that easily.

In the moment of awkward silence, Sammie asked, "Who'll lead, sir?"

"I will, but at a distance. Practically, you will, Sammie, but I expect you and Harriet to work as equals. She's got relevant experience; you've got the current MIU procedures and knowledge. Neither of you worked on it the first time, so that's two minds fresh to the investigation. And you paired well together on the Aster case, so I see no reason to do this one any differently."

His phone rang and as he looked at it prior to answering, he said, "Ken Gilles." The communications director of the Cumbria Constabulary.

He added, "The press will be on to the Lewis discovery, I expect."

As he took the call and turned away, he said, "Ken, a moment."

He covered the phone. "This find of the church notice with a reference to Compline disturbs me. Harriet, dig back in your mind and find out from others who may know what was going on back then. It may be nothing, but I don't feel it so."

He looked at Sammie as he put the phone to his ear, "Sammie, can you take Harriet home and bring her up to speed. Sorry Ken, yes, we think it is the body of Dennis Lewis. I'll…"

His voice grew fainter as he walked away, again for privacy. The women looked at each other.

Harriet suddenly called out. "Oi! I want my boots back!"

There was anger in her voice as, without breaking his conversation with Ken Gilles, Kent pressed his key fob and popped his boot lid open. Harriet walked past him, retrieved her rubber boots, and slammed the Mercedes boot lid closed. She returned to Sammie without looking at Kent.

Sammie wondered what would happen if she had yanked DCI Kent's chain like that; he would probably have put her in her place. Either he was feeling guilty about pulling Calder into the investigation, or it was that special relationship between them she had seen during the Aster case. That she was a preacher and had spoken on occasion at Penrith Methodist, where the Kent family attended services, could be a factor.

Sammie said, "Welcome back to MIU. You don't look overjoyed."

Harriet responded, "I'm not, frankly. I didn't expect

this. I've got a guest visiting for two days, all the way from Canada. I need to get home."

Sammie waited her out, just pressed her key fob to open her car doors and her own car boot.

As they exchanged glances, Calder sighed, then looked from the car which had flashed its headlights, to the distance. "Well, you lot haven't stolen my shoes this time, at least. Let's walk down here first. Have a look around."

Her eyes had returned to the large sandstone Church of England building, its tall bell tower only thirty or forty yards away. It took Sammie only a second to pick up on Calder's intent. The word handwritten on the Methodist Order of Service was 'Compline', a night service of older, longer-established religions. And yards way from the Lewis home, and the family's own church, was a building that could easily be mistaken for a small cathedral.

Calder wanted to find out more about it, and who was around when Dennis Lewis disappeared.

6 GOSSIP

They were in Sammie's vehicle, driving back through the returning rain showers. The Anglican church had not been open, and no car was parked outside.

"I was supposed to pick up Susan at Penrith Station. She arrived at Heathrow early this morning and got the train up. I had to ask my friend Kerri Sanders to do it, while I was in the car with Cotton."

Sammie had met Susan Carlson briefly, after the Aster case, at a service at St. Anselm's Church in support of the person who found Aster's body. She had subbed for Kent at the last minute, not gone voluntarily to the Anglican church.

Harriet added, "Susan's only here for two days before going to York, standing in for her boss at an addiction counsellor's conference. She will take a driving lesson or two locally and is renting a car, seeing if she can get to York without causing a pile-up."

Cumbria being a tourist area, police officers had their share of accidents caused by overseas drivers unused to driving on the left side of the road.

Trying to mollify her new partner a little, Sammie said, "At least she is taking lessons. I met her briefly at St. Anselm's that once."

Harriet continued, "It's not like we are close friends, really, but we stay in touch."

Harriet wondered why she said that. Susan was a lot younger, and Canadian. They had little in common, really. Other than, she reflected, I like the way she sees the power of God directing her life. She's not a religious person, but it seems unswervable in her.

Before she said anything more, Sammie's phone rang. She connected through the speakerphone. The voice of DC Howard Mooney came through, excited. "Hi Sarge, the Super came by. I'm on the new one, the Lewis case, with you. And I've guessed that Harriet Calder is our new DI!"

"No, I am bloody well not," said Harriet loudly. "Who said that?"

Sammie thought that Harriet must be angry, swearing. Even using just 'bloody' wasn't her at all.

A more apprehensive voice came back. "Er, he said you were joining the team. It just seemed obvious."

Sammie spoke up. "Harriet is joining us temporarily. She knows the Lewis family and has given us some useful insight into a piece of new evidence. In fact, she is probably the only one of us in good standing with the parents."

"Well, I can't be out of favour. I was in school when he went missing. Lewis and I are around the same age. And we have a newbie assigned, a Louis Chan from Carlisle. The Super said he did well in the courses."

Sammie wondered what Kent thought about these developments. "Do you have any other bright news I should hear from my boss, not you?"

Mooney's tone made it clear he knew the next item

would stir up Sammie. "Superintendent Chiswell said he's giving us consultations with Lady Yvonne for this one."

Sammie groaned. "You start on the Area Three set-up. Organize the retrieval of the Dennis Lewis case files, if someone hasn't already done that, and I want them sorted and out, ready to use, not left in boxes. Arrange desk space for Harriet and this new person. Put Harriet with me."

"No," interjected Harriet. "I'm with you and Louis Chan. Give me a desk there. Sammie is the team lead, it's a command structure, not a knitting circle."

She glared at Sammie.

Howard said, "Yes, boss." He rang off.

Sammie looked at Harriet. "What d'you think he meant by that? Yes, boss. He calls me 'Sarge'."

Harriet suppressed a smile. "He'll do what you said, I took it to mean. And what I said, too. He's sticking it to us a bit."

After a silence, Sammie said, "It's not quite my machiavellian plan, Harriet. I hoped to be working for you after Terry left. But you never did say how it sat with you, my suggestion?"

"I never gave it much more thought. I appreciated the sentiment and you raising it with me – it was a boost, I must say – but the first I heard Cotton wasn't in MIU was on the ride over with him."

Sammie nodded. "I didn't even think to give you a hint. I'm sorry."

"Don't be. The truth is, I have no plan to apply. But it's not an issue at present. Who is Lady Yvonne?"

"Dr. Yvonne Kingsley, a forensic behavioural psychologist. The superintendent's current pride and joy. She is American with a sort of posh English accent with a twang. Been over here quite a while. She does a lot of work with NCI. Terry knew her from there and jumped over John's head to get her on board. John was not amused."

"Ah, the tensions. Now I see it. Why Lady Yvonne?"

"Her cost. Someone in accounts let it be known that a three-hour consultation, during which thirty minutes is spent preening Chiswell, costs as much as a half a week's wages for a detective constable. So, aristocracy, big-wigs, hence Lady Yvonne."

She glanced at Calder. "You have got your eyes closed."

"I'm saying a quick prayer for deliverance. Is she any good?"

"She was spot on during her first one, the Tilson abduction, and Ken Nolan had his people going off at ninety degrees, in terms of profile. Her second was way off, one with Cotton and me; even he had to admit that. We will be number three."

As they neared Bassenthwaite, Harriet said, "My car is in Applethwaite, at Vic Askew's house. He's not long to go and it will be a blessing, in more ways than one."

"I hadn't thought of him in a long time. Such a sad story, him going off the rails. Did Cotton pick up on it?"

"He saw it was a former police officer, but I didn't tell him anything. I wasn't there in that capacity."

Eighteen years earlier, PC Askew had attended a car crash near Armaside, a village west of Bassenthwaite Lake. They had passed the turnoff to it just a minute earlier.

A car, clearly speeding, had knocked down a woman and her daughter at a road junction. Vic and another constable were first on scene. In the mess, Askew told the driver to sit in his car. Whatever transpired, looking at the injuries, he said something to the driver as he removed the man's car keys.

When a bystander screamed a little later, they found that the driver had cut his throat with a utility knife from his toolbox, now open on the back seat.

Vic was placed on leave during the investigation. Two months later, he was transferred away from front line policing to administrative work in headquarters. Not long afterwards, he resigned and took a job at a nursery farm, stocking plants and shrubs for a gardening chain. He had smoked himself to death, Harriet thought.

Sammie said, "I recall the little girl lost part of her leg, but the mother came out of it OK."

Harriet said, "It was Vic who never healed, really."

Sammie responded. "He never could drop the burden, could he?"

"Still can't. After all this time. I just hope before he dies, he can let go of the guilt."

Harriet asked, "What are you doing now? Do you want me in? I'd like to spend some of my supposed day off with Susan."

"Do that. We start tomorrow. Dennis has been in the ground for all this time, it's not a rush, it's a slog. Me, I'm going to see my ophthalmologist, keep the appointment this time. I need new reading glasses, I think, and its two years since they did the scans and stuff for the back of the eye. I kept cancelling."

"Good thinking. We will all have a lot of reading to do. I'll see you bright and early tomorrow, assuming Inspector Robinson doesn't send a hit team to pull me back. She'll have to find a replacement for me for a while. We are still short-handed."

7 DENOMINATIONS

Susan Carlson left the train at Penrith station, trying to recall the face of Kerri Sanders, met only once at a church service nearly a year ago.

Harriet's text apologised for being called away on a police matter. Susan hoped Sanders would recognize her, otherwise they would stand on the platform until it was sufficiently empty that it became obvious.

In fact, she had no problem. Waiting for her was a priest, complete with a light grey clerical shirt and white collar, jeans, and a corduroy jacket that had seen better days. Probably better days with the priest's father when it was new, she thought, from the style.

Reverend Chris, she recalled. He led the little service organised to help Colin Kavanagh, the alcoholic she had talked to after the Aster case.

"Ms. Carlson, welcome back to the Lake District."

She smiled, replacing the internal grimace, an automatic reaction at being in the presence of a priest.

"Thank you, Reverend – it's Chris, right? It's Susan, and I don't recall your surname."

"Willard, but it's simply Chris, please. Kerri is in the car outside with a sprained knee, unfortunately, so she can't drive. I volunteered to help her. Can I take your case?"

The slight pause before 'volunteered' told Susan that Sanders had pressed him into service, she suspected.

"Well, thank you. No, I'm fine with it. It was a bumpy flight and I appreciate both of you standing in for Harriet at short notice. I am a little tired."

Kerri Sanders, of similar age to Calder, had levered herself out of the front passenger seat and was resting against the side of the car. She beamed, as if meeting an old friend. It took Susan less than a minute to realise she would not say much, Sanders would do all the talking.

She wasn't quite correct in that hasty conclusion. Kerri Sanders would lead the conversation and ask the questions. If Harriet were now giving some poor sod the third-degree treatment in an interview room, Susan could relate to the accused rather than her English friend.

"We only saw you once at St. Anselm's, on your last visit. At the special service for Mr. Kavanagh."

"It was my first visit to England. And I'm not an Anglican."

Sanders chattered on. "But you are not a Methodist either, Harriet told me. She said you have a strong faith in God, though."

The question hung out there. Susan let it hang, leaving Kerri struggling on its rope, enjoying the silence as Sanders waited expectantly. Having met at St. Anselm's Church, Kerri Sanders had cast her as an enthusiastic churchgoer of some sort.

Willard broke it by pointing out the sign for Threlkeld Quarry and Mining Museum, talking about the history of the area. He finished by changing the subject back to her last visit.

"I hear through the Maywood couple that Colin Kavanagh is doing well. You met with him separately while you were over, I gather?"

Susan nodded. "Yes, twice during the visit. I am glad to hear that."

Kerri added, "Off the drink, Helen Maywood told me. He is holding on to his sobriety, at least."

It was tiredness that caused Susan's response, rather than letting it sail over her. It was one she used regularly with people in recovery.

"Not holding on, Kerri. Letting go. Turning things over to God. When alcoholics hold on to something, it is often a resentment of some sort. Then they end up drinking themselves stupid."

Kerri's face showed her confusion.

"I'm an addiction counsellor. I work with alcoholics and other addicts. That's my job."

Susan smiled at her, warming to the woman, then seeing the smile on Chris's face, driving.

"You knew, or guessed?"

Willard gave her a grin through the rear-view mirror. "Your prayer at the service was something of a giveaway, the extended version of the Serenity Prayer; but Harriet had also mentioned it when we were organising the service for Colin. So, yes."

Carlson's first visit to the UK had a hidden, woven link between her and Kavanagh. He had started drinking heavily after the shock of finding a body in Bassenthwaite Lake. Years earlier, the dead man, Duncan Aster, had seduced Carlson, a member of his church congregation. She was then barely of legal age. His subsequent remorse, tied to his rejection of her and the cover up of the event, led to her own spiral into alcoholism.

The complicating factor was that he was a Roman Catholic priest. She found a way out of her guilt and shame. Father Duncan Aster never did, until he walked into Bassenthwaite Lake carrying a quarrystone.

Susan's phone rang. It was Harriet, apologetic and despondent. Not only couldn't she meet her train, but she was now on the west coast, at a place called Maryport, with a family.

"Just for you; we found a body; it is their son, and I know them. Don't tell Kerri."

Susan told her it was fine, she knew her way around, she would make something to eat and have a nap or, if it was later still when Harriet got back, an early night, given the time change. They would catch up later or tomorrow morning.

"Chris and Kerri met me. Kerri has sprained her knee. But we are having a nice talk."

Catching the meaning, Harriet just said, "I am sure you are. Thanks for being so understanding."

After she closed the call, Susan said, "Harriet is now in Maryport, wherever that is. Something to do with being with a family at a difficult time. She couldn't say more."

"Who's going to look after you, then?" asked Kerri, automatically.

"We are," said Chris suddenly. "I know you are tired, but how about a light meal at the village pub after we drop off your bag and give you a chance to freshen up?"

Then he thought about what he said. "Are pubs OK, I mean?"

So, Susan saw, he knows not only that I am an addiction counsellor, but a recovered alcoholic, too. That intrigued her.

"Pubs are fine. Thank you, I would appreciate that."

Kerri insisted on buying.

It was in the Sun Inn, when Kerri limped off to the toilets that she asked.

"You know I am an addiction counsellor and a recovered alcoholic?"

The question was in the tone of voice.

He paused a moment. "Harriet didn't mention it. Your prayer in the service intrigued me. The fact that you would come over to help a stranger, as well as see Harriet... I googled Haydn House."

It was on the website. While no counsellors were named, it said that all had relevant academic qualifications and professional licenses, and each had long-standing recovery from an addiction. It emphasised that the related experience and the formal training provided the best combination for working with people early in recovery.

"I'm flattered."

He looked at her intently. "The only thing Harriet said about you was that you are a person of great faith. I could feel it when you gave the prayer at Kavanagh's service, I told her."

She looked surprised, then amused. "Feel, or hear?"

"Feel." He didn't amplify the reason or offer a further explanation.

As they looked at each other, Willard was the first to break away. He said, lightly, "Kerri wants to know every-one's religion, as you gathered. She's not a proselytiser, though, just likes to find out how different churches do things, the way they run. She is a leading light in organising things at St. Anselm's. Volunteers like her at my other churches are the reason I can cope these days."

"You have more than one church?"

"Three. Two smaller ones and St. Anselm's; a cluster

termed a benefice. There aren't enough priests, or funds, or congregants, but there are a lot of Anglican churches in Cumbria."

They saw Kerri limping back. Willard got up to help her with the chair, but she declined, standing instead, hands on the chair back.

"I'll just finish my coffee and I've paid the bill, so we can leave and get you back to Harriet's. Then you'll have a good rest, I think. Will we see you at all, during your stay? At St. Anselm's, perhaps?"

Susan smiled. "I don't think so, unfortunately. I'm staying a couple of days with Harriet then I go to York, to a conference on advances in addiction treatment. I'm not an Anglican, Kerri. I was brought up a Roman Catholic and was an active one through my teens. Now I'm not linked to any church, but I do have an unswerving faith in the goodness of God."

There, you have the answer.

Kerri pondered, thinking about it. "Don't you miss going to church, though?"

"No. I work with people who are suffering. In meetings with them and other people who help them, I often feel the presence of God in our lives. I see some people recover and others that don't; they get worse and die. I need the support of other people, like you find with Chris and the people at St. Anselm's, but no, I don't feel the need to go to church."

Willard spoke up, addressing Kerri. "God brings us all together, Kerri."

Susan said, "True enough. It is doctrine and creed which separates people, doesn't it? But you are right, I am more than ready for a sleep when I say things like that."

~~

Harriet entered her home silently, suspecting that her visitor would be in bed, asleep. She found Susan in the living room, sipping tea, reading something on her laptop. She was in her pajamas, wearing one of the dressing gowns Harriet had placed in the spare bedroom for her use.

"I slept solidly for two hours and now I am wide awake. But you look exhausted, if I may say so?"

Harriet just nodded her acceptance of the assessment.

"It's been an unexpected day, even for a police officer. A bit of a shock, really. I started with having the whole day off, to do some of my church parochial work before I met you. Then I was brought into the case of a teenager whose body turned up in a field ten years after he disappeared. Now I am dragged into the investigation, like it or not."

"Is he the one on the news I saw earlier? It mentioned Maryport and you said you were out there."

"Yes, but let's talk about you. It's good to see you."

As they caught up on life that wasn't covered in the occasional texts and emails, Harriet heated some soup, and they ate. Susan could see her friend visibly begin to relax, while Harriet could see Susan start to tire again.

Harriet went to a small basket on a shelf in the living room and brought out a spare door key, passing it over.

"You'll probably be up and awake at two in the morning. Come down and make tea or get a drink. Don't feel as if you can't do that. I'll sleep like a log. Now, with being dragged back to the MIU, I must be away to Penrith early tomorrow, I'm sorry to say.

"Gordon Ritter is coming here at ten, for your driving lesson. You have one booked in the morning and a provisional booking for tomorrow evening, around dusk, depending on how you adapt to our roads. That's the tricky time of day, with the lighting. You let him know if you want the second one at the end of the first lesson. And he has given you a good rate."

She had picked the driving instructor; she knew nearly all of them in the area.

Later, as she put her cup in the dishwasher, Susan said, "Kerri is nice, it was really good of her to collect me, even if she co-opted Chris Willard to drive."

"She is a good heart and a good friend, but she talks all the time. We became friends after Ian died. I had seen her around the village before, but she came into my life then. And you intrigued her, from the service at St. Anslem's. She has just finished being a churchwarden there, but still seems to be in and out of the church all the time. Kerri asked after you a couple of times on your return to Canada."

Susan smiled. "And she now knows I am not an Anglican or a Methodist. She does like to slot people into denominations. Chris Willard; he's different. Good night, Harriet. I'll plan on seeing you in the morning and if not, I hope tomorrow is an easier day for you."

"I hope so, too." Her voice, however, did not convey any confidence that it would be so.

A few minutes later, as she put her own cup in the dishwasher and checked the doors before switching off the lights, she suddenly wondered why Susan had said that Chris Willard was different.

8 CHAN

Sammie settled herself into Investigation Area Three as DI Ken Nolan popped into his office, adjacent. "You are leading the Lewis investigation, John said."

"In practical terms, yes. John leads it, really. I guess I have it until a new DI appears."

Ken responded, "Don't hold your breath on that being anytime soon, so run with it, I suggest. John's spread a bit thin these days.

"The Hartley couple: it was straightforward. I've got Roly doing the paperwork and Jean following up on the firearm. We will wait for forensics and the autopsies, but there is not a lot more to do. The missing girl, Smallwood, is now my case and it's more complicated; we are on an uphill slog on that one. But your investigation is the one in the news. Good luck."

With that, he was on his way.

Sammie thought, run with it. I'll do that. See where that gets me. Then the reality of Nolan's message sank in; there was no immediate replacement for Terry Cotton in the offing. She was glad he had pulled Harriet into the team, but clearly, Harriet was telling the truth when she said she wasn't considering the post.

Mooney had set up the whiteboard in the investigation area yesterday afternoon. Until forensics confirmed the identity, the body was labelled as 'Unknown Male, possibly Dennis Lewis'. The Dennis Lewis investigation records were there also, out of their storage boxes and stacked in order.

When Harriet Calder arrived, MIU was busy, a large area with police officers and support staff assigned to the different cases. It was one of the civilian staff who spoke up.

"Sergeant Calder! Reassigned? For the duration?"

The questioner, Geraldine Linnie-Morton, an information systems specialist known to all simply as Linnie, was an eight-year veteran of MIU.

"A temporary transfer, Linnie," responded Harriet, as she passed.

When John Kent pulled Harriet into the Aster case a year earlier, Linnie had been the first MIU staffer she had worked with, monitoring an interview. But the MIU team now all knew that, apart from her contribution to that enquiry, Calder had been a detective constable in MIU before most of them started work with Cumbria Police. Why she left was a mystery to most of them but, seeing her walk in, they were drawing their own conclusions.

They were sorting through the Lewis files when a uniformed officer with chinese features headed over to them. He focused on the smaller, dark-haired woman staring at him. Mooney had just picked up the assigned case line desk phone.

"DS Livermore?" He had a Liverpudlian accent. "I'm Louis, Louis Chan. I got sent –."

Harriet heard the name and turned away from the whiteboard, where she was adding information.

"Sergeant Calder, what are you doing here?"

"Same as you; just arrived."

Chan said to Sammie, "She was my shift sergeant at Keswick, the summer before last." He looked at Calder. "How are you?"

"Later, catch up later," interjected Sammie, wanting to start things off on the right foot. She was in charge, Harriet said yesterday. "This is DC Howard Mooney."

As the two men spoke to each other, Sammie asked, "Is it Louis or Louie, or what?"

Chan and Calder spoke at the same time. "It's Louis."

Sammie responded, "Then no Howie or Louie, please. You didn't change."

"No, I came over as soon as I was told and released. I'll wear plainclothes tomorrow."

Mooney butted in. "That was Dr. Meadows. He wants to do the autopsy on the body later this morning. Does that need checking with the boss?"

"No, I'll attend that, the DCI and I spoke about that last night. Harriet, do you want to come?"

Harriet was looking at the boxes and files. "No, I'm more use getting into these, becoming familiar with the earlier investigation and taking a trip down memory lane."

Harriet saw Sammie glancing between Mooney and Chan, deciding who else would be there. She said, "Take Louis, I suggest; get him into his new line of work."

"Good idea."

Calder glanced at Mooney. He didn't seem bothered by that. He had attended his share of autopsies, on the coattails of a more senior officer.

Chan looked surprised, then apprehensive. Harriet said, "It'll be fine, Louis, to get you over the hump. Sammie and

I have seen the body *in situ*. It will be different."

From what, thought Sammie. To be answered by Calder.

"Louis was first on scene at the Netherton pile-up last month, I heard. Road deaths like that would upset anyone. We are a team on an investigation here, so there is no need for hidden agendas. And on that note, Louis and Howard are to call me Harriet. Sammie is leading this one."

Both men nodded, Chan clearly relieved.

Sammie asked, "What time is the autopsy set for?"

Mooney said, "Ten-thirty."

She addressed Chan. "So, sit in on the morning briefing, but get yourself settled here first. Afterwards, come with me to the autopsy. As Harriet knows, Dr. Meadows is good with first timers. It is only when he gets to know you that he gives you hell. Right, Harriet?"

Calder smiled.

As her phone rang, Sammie answered. Others could see her face change as she focused on the call. After a few moments, she responded, "Yes, Dr. Kingsley. We will check that out. Thank you. We will see you later this afternoon."

She put the phone down.

"That was Dr. Yvonne Kingsley."

Seeing Chan's blank expression, she added. "She is a consultant, a forensic behavioural psychologist. She spoke to John, and he put her on to me. Kingsley is in a meeting in London but will arrive later. She suggests we check the bindings on the body, if possible."

She looked at Harriet. "It should be, perhaps, from what I saw."

Harriet nodded in agreement. "I saw some intact rope sections, and other fibres, yes."

Sammie gave a sigh. "Her words. 'If the knots are intact,

or their routing around the body identified, they could indicate the nature of the perpetrator. Simple knots could mean anything, just a means to secure the body. Complex or specific knots, or some sort of precise binding pattern could indicate a ritual or psychopathic element'. She will put calls into NCA and to a forensic contact at the Met who specialises in that sort of thing, see if there are any similar crimes we should know about."

Harriet saw Chan's pupils dilate slightly, showing his surprise. Like herself, yesterday he was dealing with routine small crime and other police work. At least she had the prior experience in MIU to draw on.

"A good suggestion by her," she responded, "but let's check the knots and get Dr. Meadows' feedback before we go down the Clarice Starling route."

Before he settled down with files and a desk, Louis had a private chat with Calder, Sammie noticed. She was appreciative of Harriet's effort to sort out the process for a team currently containing two sergeants and no DI, but aware that she had done that effortlessly while Sammie was still working out what to do.

She asked Harriet quietly, "What's Louis like?"

"Keen, obviously. A good officer, but on the 'a bit too serious' side. Which is better than the other way, in this job. He spent four months at Keswick, as he said, during the tourist bulge before his transfer to Carlisle. He doesn't miss much."

Sammie replied, "Then he should be an asset."

Harriet nodded. "The Kingsley suggestion was a bit of an eye-opener for him, what he may possibly be getting into."

Sammie was candid. "I've never had one with a sadistic predator; not so far, anyway. You? When you were with

MIU?"

Harriet shook her head. "Not a sadistic murder. No. We arrested a man over in Cleator Moor who gave his wife scars, cigarette burns, for her 'transgressions', as he saw it. That felt the same way. When they flashed up the photos of the damage to her, I shuddered. The abuse had gone on for years."

She paused. "He was put away. Died of a stroke in prison the following year, I heard."

It wasn't strange for Harriet Calder to be in a morning briefing, just to be in one led by DCI John Kent, in Penrith HQ. It took her back to her first days here, with a different DCI leading the team, and Harriet still excited about plainclothes work as a detective constable.

Kent's introduction of new staff was brief; the two constables reassigned, including Chan, a tech specialist standing in for Zoltan Paczynski, Linnie's boss, who was on holiday for two weeks, and 'Sergeant Harriet Calder, from the Keswick base, temporarily assisting with the Lewis investigation'.

He gave a summary of the active cases and assignments, saying he would be in a senior officer meeting for the rest of the morning. DI Nolan was to be acting lead until he got back, when he would focus on the Donna Smallwood investigation. He finished with, "Sammie, I'd like an update at 4.00 p.m. on any progress on the Lewis case, either in person, or give me a call, if either of us are still out. I think Dr. Kingsley should be around by then. If so, she will attend."

Harriet watched the exchanges of glances between other members of MIU. She got the impression that 'better Sammie than us' was the order of the day.

Louis Chan had agonised about the post-mortem from the moment Sergeant Calder had pushed him forward.

When Sammie took him to the pathology department at Cumbria Infirmary in Carlisle, he realised that while there was a strong smell of antiseptic and a faintly unpleasant smell that he couldn't quite place, there was no odour coming from the hunched and folded body lying sideways on the mortuary table. The pathology assistant and a forensic photographer were already busy with the preliminary work.

Sammie must have explained about him earlier, Chan realised, as Dr. Meadows gave him a cursory welcome, then said. "If you don't feel well at any time, don't head back to the corridor. Through there – and, if you can't make it that far, there is a bucket in the sink."

Chan nodded.

"But this boy's body is well decomposed. The challenge will be to think of him, despite the remaining flesh and skin, as a person and not something from a movie special effects group. I hope to show the person to you, and if we are lucky, find out something about how he died."

His voice was quiet and considerate. As Calder had intimated, it would be easier, he hoped, than the bodies of a mother and son thrown from an overturned vehicle at Netherton. Neither had been wearing seatbelts.

In the early stages, the photographer took shot after shot of the ropes, the knots and the freshly exposed surfaces as the folded body was carefully repositioned. The pathologist's terse comment early on, when cutting carefully around one section of the binding, was 'looks like a granny knot to me, but I was never a boy scout'. Neither Sammie nor Louis could see anything special about the bindings.

Eventually, the corpse was laid out on the table. As Dr.

Meadows probed the tissues still adhering to the skeleton, he fixed his eyes on one spot at the side of the forehead.

Moving his focus between that side and the other, he said, "He could have been hit here. But I will check this area microscopically for signs of a compression fracture. And see this area, the skin at the base of the kneecap. I'll check under the microscope, but it is looking like freezer damage. Calder saw that, too."

Sammie asked, "The forehead. A blow of some sort?"

"Perhaps. Not from anything small or capable of breaking the bone, a broader impact, part of which had a linear edge. It broke the skin, but there is a wider area of damage there also, post-mortem, I think. It could be a result of two different blows."

Chan had been paying attention and moved behind the pathologist. Meadows stopped recording and asked, "What do you see?"

He spoke up. "The cheek facets, I don't know the correct term. They aren't symmetrical, they seem wrong."

Meadows looked at him. "That's correct, the zygomatic arch. The zygomatic bones are never truly symmetrical but not, I think, as much as I see here. There is some displacement, inflicted separately from the forehead damage higher up. He took a bang, perhaps a heavy punch, it seems. That's a good catch. How are you doing?"

"Chan said, "It's fascinating; it really is."

"Well, I'm going to open the skull now, see what is left of any brain tissue and look at the inside of those areas of bone, particularly the forehead behind the bruise. Look away if it makes you queasy."

He switched the recorder back on.

It was later when Dr Meadows summarised his findings. "Even before the dental results are back, I can say it is probably Dennis Lewis. The fracture site of the left radius is exactly where his medical record said it ought to be. The skeleton is the right size and gender for him, but the dental check will confirm it. And there is enough DNA to make it absolutely sure."

He looked back at the now-covered pathology table.

"The family have waited a long time for this. You should have the dental results overnight or sooner, as I know John asked for this to be expedited."

Breaking out of his more serious, professional mood, he said to Chan with a smile, "You made it, your first autopsy."

Chan nodded. "Thank you. It has set me thinking, how he could have been hit like that."

"See," said Meadows to Sammie, "it's a good job you brought him instead of the wannabee priest of Keswick."

Sammie gave him a mock scowl. "Be careful, Clive. She used to be his shift sergeant. Word could get back. She's been seconded to the investigation by John. Kidnapped was the term she used."

"Poor Harriet, dragged out of Keswick." Meadows was smiling. "Did she swear at all?"

"Just once, when Mooney jumped to the conclusion that she was replacing Terry Cotton; she gave him both barrels. Now, don't give her a hard time."

He was walking off to get changed out of his scrubs, laughing. "I only pick on the good ones, Sammie; you know that. Which is why..."

He left it hanging.

"He picks on me," she finished. Although, she realised, he hadn't done that very much this morning. Autopsies on children and young people did that to him. She had seen it before.

9 ST MARY'S

Afterwards, Sammie decided that she would stay in the office in Penrith and prepare for the press briefing. Harriet, with Chan, would return to Maryport to talk to the parents and Dennis's sister. Mooney would go to Birkby and interview the current owners of the farmhouse, with a uniformed officer.

The press briefing was scheduled for 2.00 p.m. John Kent had already clarified that the family didn't want to be there, to be bothered by the media. A uniformed officer had been positioned in a car outside their home for the next day or so, to protect their privacy.

"Do you think they'll need a a family liaison officer?" Sammie asked Calder. "I didn't, yesterday."

"Neither did I; they are prepared for this. They have been hit hard, but they are not out of their depth. And they have plenty of support from family and friends, and people from their church. But I'll check when I see them."

As they finished the assignment plan, Calder suddenly added, "I would also like to slip off after, with Chan, and see the Anglican priest at that church nearby, a man called

Dodson. He was the rector there when Dennis went missing, I found out. See if he can shed any light on this 'Compline' thing."

Sammie nodded. Harriet said, "I'll give him a call and set it up."

Mooney added, "I googled and checked websites earlier this morning for Compline and Nunc dimittis, looking for a concert in the area around then. Closest I got was one with a choir in Bolton, nowhere near us. And that was a month later. But ten years ago, not everything got on to the internet."

"What's Nunc dimittis?" asked Louis.

Sammie responded, "A text used in a church service, sometimes spoken, or sung. Part of some evening service. The words were written on the paper found in Dennis Lewis's pocket. Ask Harriet, on the drive over."

Howard answered a telephone call. "That was quick. The dental records and the body match. It will take a bit for the written report, but they were directly on it and phoned it through."

It was the media pressure, they all knew.

Sammie suddenly said, "On second thoughts, I think I should be there as well, to give them the news, then I will head straight back here. You take your time with the Lewis family, see if anything has triggered their memories overnight. Then head off to see your priest and we can regroup."

Harriet thought that there would be many MIU car journeys covering the thirty miles between the police headquarters and the Lewis home in the next few weeks.

~~

Sammie had confirmed to the family gathered that it

was Dennis's body found at the farm. The daughter, Aileen, stood behind her dad's chair, hands on his shoulders steadying him, Harriet thought. Bernice looked lost as she took in the news, then bowed her head, saying a small, quiet prayer to herself.

The police officers waited. They knew that you don't fill in the silence with small talk.

Bernice said after a few moments, "Neither of us slept much. You can imagine. But, in a way, it is a comfort for me to have it confirmed, knowing that we can bury him now."

Bernice Lewis now seemed composed, moreso than her husband. She gave him a glance and reached out and squeezed his fingers.

She added, "With Eamon, it's brought back the anger. That stops the sleep. He went months on naps after Dennis disappeared, didn't you?"

Eamon Lewis said softly, "Aye. I did, and I may do it again. At myself, for the argument the day before, and at the person who did this. I hate sleeping tablets and that sort of thing. I think I will only sleep soundly when whoever did this is caught and tried. Then I might."

Harriet leaned forward, a move that made Eamon focus on her.

"Deal with it now, Eamon, is my advice. Talk to your doctor and to Reverend Sills, to find a way to get some peace. You all need that. The better shape you are in, the more you can help us. We are going back a long way in this investigation and need every scrap of your recollections about the days before Dennis went missing. This is going to be a slog around the detail until we make a breakthrough."

Sitting silently to one side, Louis wondered if they would ever make a breakthrough, after all this time.

Sammie gave her colleagues a knowing glance and said to the family, "I'm leaving now to prepare for the press briefing. We will do what we can to protect your privacy, as DCI Kent said."

She looked at the daughter. "Aileen, you may want to watch out for the phone calls, screen them. Some of the press can be sneaky and misleading."

Aileen looked at her. "I recall that, even though I was a girl. I think mum and I can send them packing, if you have someone outside for any that come there."

Sammie reached out and, in turn, shook Eamon and Bernice's hands. "We'll do our best on this, I promise you."

Eamon asked, "Will we be treated like last time?"

Chan felt it was an awkward question, but Sammie didn't hesitate. "We will follow the evidence and our ideas, Mr. Lewis. No-one is out of bounds, including the family, nor should they be. But Harriet is convinced you and Bernice had nothing to do with the disappearance of your son and I have a great respect for her experience as a police officer. I will leave it at that."

Eamon Lewis was a sombre, cheerless man, thought Louis. With the loss of Dennis, it wasn't a surprise.

"That's fair enough. Thank you. If I had felt that was the way when Dennis disappeared, it wouldn't be such an issue. I'm not having Bernice in tears night after night this time, not knowing whether it's the loss of Dennis or suspicions about us that is driving her crazy."

Louis realised that he wouldn't have been able to answer that question easily; yet Sergeant Livermore did so quite openly.

On the drive over, Calder had prepped him to re-interview the daughter, Aileen, who had stayed overnight with her parents. Catching Calder's eye for a second, Louis asked Aileen if she would take a few minutes to answer some questions.

"Let's go out, then."

"She needs a smoke," said Bernice.

Aileen added, "And a walk, and a latte, if you are up to it?" She eyed Chan, checking his response.

"Lead the way."

Harriet said, "And I have a few questions for you two, together."

Aileen led Chan to the Harbour Cafe, a five-minute walk away, while smoking. They talked about her parent's reaction to the news.

Inside now, Louis was working down his list. They were talking about Dennis's friends.

"Did Dennis have a girlfriend?"

Aileen Lewis gave her head a single shake. "No. Not that I know of, and I don't think he did, not a girl he was open about. And I think he had never had sex with anyone. I was going out with a boy called Robbie then, causing my mum and dad to worry about what time I was getting home and what I was up to. But Dennis, no, he was at that transitional stage."

"What do you mean?"

"He was interested in girls but bashful, a sense of the romantic rather than honest to goodness lust. I was nearly seventeen, keeping my boyfriend's hands off me one minute, all over him the next."

Louis smiled. "So, Dennis wasn't dating, but he was interested. If he was romantic, as you say, did he have anyone he thought of as a 'sweetheart' figure? A longing from afar? That sort of thing?"

Aileen thought a moment.

"It is funny you should use that term, sweetheart. He had one girl, a friend from his primary school days. They were at different schools and churches. Valerie. In fact, hang on, I saw him talking to her the morning of the day before he disappeared, in Crosby Street, at the top of our road. I just remembered that again. I told one of the officers about it at the time, during one of my interviews."

"Tell me again. I haven't had the chance to read all the files yet."

"They were talking earnestly, into serious stuff. Both were in school uniform – different schools, like I said. He liked her. They had been in the same class as kiddies and had stayed friends. He could have started fancying her, perhaps, as she was the same age but getting a figure on her."

She looked into the distance, thinking. "Valerie Krestman. She is Stephanie Krestman's sister, who was a year ahead of me. That's the name, the one I gave back then. The Krestman family moved away. And she is famous now. Valerie Carmichael, an actor."

"The one on television?"

"Same one. Small world, eh? Famous people start somewhere."

"And why did the conversation stand out in your mind, at the time?"

Aileen mused about it. "It seemed intense. The sort of expression Dennis had when he was discussing bikes with his mates. They were mad about racing bikes, the three of them. They would go on about brakes or gears like it was a major issue. Intense like that."

The 'close contacts' list was fresh in Chan's memory. "They are Barry Jordan and Charles Roswell, correct?"

She smiled. "Yes, they were good mates. Bas, Chas, and Den, the three musketeers, or worse names I used for them at times."

Chan went back a step.

"Do you – or did you – know Valerie? Did you talk to her about that meeting?"

"No. There was so much going on, the worry, the police around, it never occurred. Then the Krestman family moved, as I said. I never saw her again until she was on television."

He sipped his half-drunk latte. It had gone cold. Removing the cream moustache with his finger, he asked. "His mates, the ones he biked with. Which one was his closest friend, do you think? The sort you would share secrets with?"

"Hard to say. They were all close."

Harriet found that Bernice and Eamon had no idea about 'Compline' or 'Nunc dimittis' written on the order of service, but Bernice confirmed it was Dennis's writing, but less precise than normal.

"It looks as if he wrote it on the go, but it is his hand, I think. And I remember the order of service bulletin, of course; the week after you were here was the last service he attended. He must have liked yours, circling it."

Harriet moved on. "Eamon, I need to go back over something with you. I have read your interview reports, including those of DI Green and DCI Kent. I can see how their questions hurt you, and I don't want to do the same."

Eamon was looking wary now, waiting.

"What was it about Dennis, Chas, and Barry that specifically worried you? You talked about him being away too long, not calling in. You said you were worried, but never said why. Can you tell me now?"

She waited, focused on Eamon.

He let out a long sigh. "Green wanted me to say what mischief Dennis was involved in. And were any of them possibly gay, the word they use now. They were just boys.

It angered me."

Harriet nodded. "I know, I read the report, as I said. But I am not judging anything Dennis did and neither should any of us. He is in God's care now. Let it go. Tell me."

Eamon glanced at Bernice then focused on Harriet. "The truth is, I worried he was too innocent. Too naive. I half-wished he were up to something – not serious things, drugs and whatever – but not out in the world with his head full of... of airy, fairy things. Racing bikes, his books, those wizard stories by Rowlings.

"The three of them were full of energy and I think Chas Roswell was down to earth, moreso than Barry Jordan, but our Dennis was in a dreamland at times. It bothered me more than Bernice. She said he would grow up at his own speed."

Bernice, reminded of it, put her hand to her mouth, as tears came.

Eamon put his arm around her. "He went out in the world unprepared for the hard knocks. I was his dad; I should have done better by him. That was the basis of our arguments, including the one the day before he went missing."

It shone from him, the guilt. Harriet reached out and took his hand, squeezing it gently.

"You didn't fail him, Eamon. We are going to do our damnest to find out who did, I promise you that. I need to go, but I wish I could stay."

Harriet had other questions but sensed the couple had reached their limit. Another time. As a detective, she needed to leave them to their grief now but as she stood, looking down at them, she was torn between her chosen roles in life.

Outside, she spoke briefly to the officer on duty, then she called Louis Chan. He was just wrapping up, he said. She told him that she would wait at the entrance to the Anglican church.

Ten minutes later, they were together, entering the church grounds, seeing a car parked close to the main arched doorway of the belltower. They were a little early still for the time she had given Reverend Eric Dodson, but he was there already, it seemed.

Dodson was in his early fifties, bald on top with the remainder cut short. It reminded Harriet of the tonsure on monks. He had heavy, dark framed glasses that gave him an old-fashioned look. Even powerful prescriptions these days were more lightweight than his pair.

As she asked her questions, Chan listened, focused on the man and the interview. His assessment was that the priest's responses were measured, considered. Dodson was conscious of his own position and that he was talking to police officers.

Harriet started with his knowledge of the Lewis family and the people in the area.

"Not a lot, then. I was new at the time. I had been appointed Rector in February that year, so I had settled in a bit but hadn't been through a complete cycle. It takes time for me to get to know people."

Harriet bit back the thought that more modern glasses might help. She pressed on. "Do you remember the disappearance of Dennis Lewis?"

"Of course, very clearly. It was how I got to meet Eamon and Bernice Lewis, with their own priest, Reverend Sills, to offer our church's support and prayers. We went together with one of the members from St Mary's who also knew them.

"It was a shock to the community and to my own

parishioners. There was all the news coverage and, frankly, after the first few days, a worry that someone was targeting teenagers. I met again with the detective who interviewed me to discuss whether we needed to take special precautions of any sort. I can't recall his surname, but his first name was Ron, I think."

"DS Ronald Hammond, perhaps?"

"Hammond. That's right, now you mention it. He said that the investigation couldn't really answer that, one way or another, but we should err on the side of safety. That's what I told others who were anxious."

"Did you ever meet Dennis Lewis?"

"No. He wasn't a member of this church; I don't think I met him."

She had been taking in the office surroundings a little, noting small things, such as the A4 size appointment diary, a page for a day, open with handwritten entries including her name for the meeting time. There was no computer there, she noticed, only the one in the administrator's area.

"I'm a pen and paper man still, I'm afraid, apart from my mobile," he said, taking in her observation.

She smiled. "At least notebooks don't crash or get hacked." He was attentive too, she noted. Alert.

"Do you recall any service at the time around here that would have been described as 'Compline'?"

"Compline? It's a service with a Roman Catholic origin, the last service of the day in the canonical hours, the daily office. St Mary's, like most Anglican churches, doesn't observe it as such."

Do you hold an Evensong service?"

"No, it's far too formal for us. It's usually a cathedral service, these days." He shrugged. The world changes, his face conveyed. "And some wealthier, more traditional churches."

She asked, "More the world of Anglo-Catholics, perhaps?"

He gave her a steady look. "Just more traditional churches, I'd say, with the people willing to attend at that time. I sometimes do a spoken Evensong here, alone usually. I find it comforting; the service, the light through the stained glass."

He paused, "I see a smile hidden. You know about this subject already?"

"I'm a Methodist lay preacher. I gave a similar explanation to my colleagues. But do you know of any late services around here that could be seen as fulfilling the role of Compline: any denomination, I mean?"

He thought about it. "No." His expression was somewhere between puzzlement and query.

"How about the words, Nunc dimittis – in the context of, or around the time of Dennis's disappearance?"

He looked up, across at the wall. She recalled that there was a crucifix there, behind her; he was staring at that, thinking.

"That prayer, in the English translation, is a part of Evensong. It begins with, 'Lord, now lettest thou thy servant depart in peace according to thy word', as you are probably aware. I'm not sure of your question. The Latin text or what?"

She responded, "Anything that was linked to those words; just think as broadly as you can."

He paused again. When he spoke, there was a sense of decision in his voice. "I'm not sure of the timing, whether it was that year, or the one following. There was a choral performance. One moment."

He stood, went to the bookcase, and pulled out two of the appointment diaries. Flicking through and checking one, he closed it and did the same with the other.

"The same year and month. A performance in Carlisle at the cathedral. If I remember it right, the charity concert included Burgon's 'Nunc dimittis' in the program."

He paused. "The concert was the Thursday evening, the fifth; that's the same day Dennis disappeared, wasn't it? It was Friday when we first heard and by Sunday, we were including him and his family in our prayers."

Harriet nodded. "What do you recall about it?"

"We had two parishioners who sang in the volunteer choir put together for the event and one of them, a young woman, a girl, I should say, did the solo Burgon piece. I didn't attend, but I know she had a lovely voice."

"Do you recall her name?"

"No. But I could ask others who went there, they would remember, I am sure. My recollection is that the family moved away shortly thereafter."

Chan spoke up. "Would the surname Krestman be related?"

Harriet gave him a sharp glance. They had not had time to debrief his interview.

"Yes. That's it. I should have remembered that. The Krestman family. The daughter is called Valerie, the one with the nice voice. She is an actress, now. An actor, yes, on television."

He closed the appointment diary with a snap. "Mind you, if you are talking about the verses from the Song of Simeon, it could have been used in other venues; priories, Roman Catholic services perhaps, but that's my only recall of the possible use of 'Nunc dimittis' around that time."

Harriet was writing away. "Would any of the youth at the church around then have known Dennis Lewis?"

He shook his head. "I have no idea. Probably, though; most were local."

"How about any of them particularly troubled by

Dennis's disappearance. Did they seek support from you?"

His face charged. "If they did, it would be confidential. I couldn't discuss it. But, ten years on, I don't recall anything specific, anyway. There were discussions, mainly with parents worried about their own children."

She stood, signalling her intent to finish.

"Do you have a church historian, someone who would have any bulletins or information from that month?"

"John Eames. He is retired. Shall I call him? He lives not far away and is generally around."

"If you would, thank you."

It took only thirty seconds for the priest to reach Eames, who would come over to the church in ten minutes.

As he closed the call, Harriet said, "Reverend Dodson, thank you for your assistance. We won't take up more of your time; we will just wait for Mr. Eames and make some phone calls outside, thank you. Your church is beautiful, by the way."

He smiled. "Thank you. The beauty is the product of the congregation who care for it, thank goodness, but the heating bills are another thing entirely."

John Eames seemed happy to see them. It had taken him no more than five minutes to walk from his home to St Mary's. Fit for his age, it seemed, he led them back inside, to a room with filing cabinets.

"How can I help? Eric mentioned a Carlisle concert in 2008. It was before my time as church historian, and I didn't attend regularly then."

Harriet explained the basis for their interest in vague terms, but he caught on.

"This event took place around the time of the boy's disappearance, I take it. I don't recall the dates specifically, but I know I was away working down south that month. My wife told me about it."

He paused, then added, "She died five years ago. That's when I threw myself into church volunteer work, to fill the void."

He looked at the cabinets. "I reorganised the church records when I took over from my predecessor. So, the dates you want?"

They found three items of interest in the period. A diocesan newsletter, and two St Mary's news bulletins, one before and the other after the concert in Carlisle.

"I'll let you look at them. And we have a photocopier, should you need copies."

Harriet looked up from reading one bulletin, announcing the forthcoming concert. Chan noted her voice; carefully neutral.

"Mr. Eames, I think that this list of choir members includes your wife, a Joan Eames? Do you know any of these people who were in the choir then?"

"Some, yes. Joan knew them better, of course, particularly the sopranos."

Harriet read out, "The concert at Carlisle Cathedral in aid of Macmillan Cancer Support will be an inter-denominational mixed ensemble, chosen from volunteers across Cumbria. Participating from St Mary's choir are Ingrid Holtby and Valerie Krestman. Valerie has been selected to sing a solo, the popular 'Nunc Dimmitis' by Geoffrey Burgon, with Lyall Ingram, the trumpeter, accompanied by the choir director, Dr. Oliver Mettler, on the organ."

Eames thought back. "No. I don't recall much about that. Joan wasn't part of it. Ingrid died two years ago. I recall Valerie did that solo, though. The 'Tinker, Tailor' piece. We wanted her to do it for St Mary's later in the year, but by the autumn their family had moved."

He peered at the printed copy of the concert announcement. "Valerie is famous now, but Oliver Mettler is also well known in the north, these days, as a choir director."

She nodded, "Yes, I recall."

Her mind focused on the link; the Burgon piece, the choir, the words scrawled in the bulletin found with Dennis's body. "If we can get photocopies of these pieces, please, it would be appreciated."

While Eames did the copying, Chan took a call. He whispered, "Back by three; Dr. Kulis."

Time to meet Lady Yvonne, thought Harriet.

10 KULIS

When they arrived at Penrith headquarters, DC Howard Mooney had also returned from Crosshill Farm. He had interviewed the owners of the old farmhouse there, now a separate property. The house had been renamed Marydene. Checking with them was a priority, and it pleased Howard that Sammie entrusted the job to him and the uniformed constable, Leona Dell.

As they gathered, he thought he should speak first, but Sammie spotted a figure moving through the operations area and said, "Hang on."

She stood. "Dr. Kulis, nice to see you again." It sounded sincere, at least.

The tall, well-dressed black woman gave a beaming smile. "Thank you, Sammie, Now, I know Howard."

She looked at Chan and Calder.

Sammie replied, "Harriet and Louis, meet Dr. Yvonne Kulis."

Once they had spoken, Kulis took a breath. Sammie worried that a speech was coming. But she said, "I'll listen. After that, I would like to read the files."

As they began, John Kent walked in, moving from an update on the Smallwood investigation and said, "I'm just in time. Hold on while I get some tea."

He gave Kulis a smile and a handshake then walked off. As they waited, Kulis said to Harriet, "I gather you are clergy as well as police. An interesting mix."

Harriet said evenly, "I am a Methodist, a lay preacher, not ordained clergy, Dr. Kulis."

Kulis responded, searching her face, "It wasn't the denomination or qualification I was thinking of, but the experience and skill sets."

Sammie, seeing Kent returning, said, "Let's begin." She stood and moved to the whiteboard.

"Dennis Lewis disappeared on Thursday June 5, 2008. His last sighting, the last person he spoke to that we know of, was a boy called Philip Ryerson just outside Netherhall School at 3.35 p.m, someone from his class. Not one of his friends, just a class member who commented on an aspect of a lesson that afternoon. His statement said that there was nothing unusual about the encounter. Dennis was walking home, he thought. His backpack seemed full, was the only observation. Philip was going in the opposite direction, so didn't walk with him further.

"Dennis was dressed in his school uniform. Two days into the search, DC Toole, with his mother, go through Dennis's room once again, at DI Green's insistence, and the mother notices that a casual jacket was missing. Its absence was overlooked earlier. Mrs. Lewis told Toole, 'Dennis didn't like it and never wore it. He considered it too boring and old for him'."

She pointed to an image taken at the grave site. "That would appear to be the jacket he was wearing when found, from the remnants. There is no sign of his school blazer, his school tie, or his backpack, but the material of his pants is consistent with those he wore that day."

"His home is about a ten-minute walk from his school, mostly south-west along the main road, the A596. Birkby, where he was found, is about twice that distance the other way. Did he double back? Or get a lift from someone? Was he abducted there? We don't know."

"The fact he took a dressier jacket with him may be significant, indicating his purpose. DI Green thought it might support the idea of him running away, after the row with his dad, that he wanted to appear older. Later, DCI Kent thought it might be linked to a meeting of some sort where, perhaps, he wanted to feel or appear more grown up.

"His parents expected him home after school. Sometimes he got caught up in extracurricular activities there and forgot to text or call, so initially his absence caused no concern. It was only at supper time, with no news of him and no response to a text and two phone calls, that they began to worry and call his friends. The father went to the school to check. He then drove around Maryport streets looking for him."

She pointed to a header on the whiteboard called 'Initial Response'.

"At 7.10 p.m. they called us and at 7.20 p.m. the first report was logged. Boss, do you want to take it from there?"

John Kent spoke up as he stood, moving to the board as Sammie sat.

He sighed. "We sent over DC Rees and DC Toole initially that evening. They reported that the father had admitted he and Dennis 'had words' the previous evening, about his time spent away from home with his friends. The parents though he might possibly be rebelling, or sulking, but if so, it wasn't typical of Dennis.

"Initially, we thought he might be a runaway, as Sammie mentioned."

He paused, assessing his next words. "DC Toole found the father to be less than open about the reason for the argument with his son, and angry rather than cooperative. She called it in, and DI Neil Green drove over around 9.00 p.m.

"Neil's first thought was that Eamon Lewis was hiding something, so he became a focal point for questioning.

"By the following morning, there was no sign of Dennis and the request for tracking his mobile phone had been processed. Every signal until it was turned off was at the Maryport tower and the last contact was 3.47 p.m. No other towers east of there had contact.

"I think it was that, more than anything else, which made me upgrade the search. Teenagers don't stay off their phones that long. We started house to house calls, did a media appeal, all the usual stuff.

"There wasn't a camera on that stretch of road back then. Nor did the buses have them. Unfortunately, the CCTV at the train station had been out for four days, including that day, so we checked station cameras between Workington and Carlisle. Nothing spotted."

He paused.

"They need rechecking if the tapes are still available. I am wondering now if they looked only for a boy in school uniform, in a maroon blazer. I recall someone reporting how many school uniforms had been sighted and checked.

"But our primary focus then was Eamon. He had picked up that we were checking him out and he lost his temper with Neil while I was there. It took me and his wife and daughter to settle him down. At one point it was borderline on taking him, he was so aggressive. We didn't, but the incident soured the ongoing relationship, as Sammie and Harriet saw yesterday."

He glanced at Kulis and said, "Rather than go through the effort back then, particularly as you aren't up to speed on the files yet, we should concentrate on the new findings. For example, Sammie has already pointed out the change in jacket, and its possible significance."

The boss is conscious of Kulis's billing clock ticking, thought Sammie.

Kent surveyed the team. "Howard, the current owners at the burial site. Then Harriett and Louis, the interviews with the family."

"And the Anglican church," added Harriett.

Kent's eyebrow raised momentarily, indicating that, if she made a point of it, there was something there worth sharing.

Howard summarised his non-findings from the discussion with the couple. He ended, though, with an important observation he wanted to share.

"The impression I got was that the land surrounding the farm when the Townsend couple moved in was in a bad way; overgrown with weeds, and wild. The current owner, Kendal Simmonds, had people working at getting it back into shape over the following months, but it made me think that anyone who knew about the sale, or the condition of the land, could access the area for burying the body. Someone local, or someone involved with the original owner, perhaps?"

Kulis was writing away but nodded and said quietly, "That's a good catch."

Howard seemed pleased, as Sammie said, "Harriet; what did you find?"

Calder said, "Louis got more from the daughter than I

learned from the parents. Louis, you tell it."

Conscious of it being his first time in a briefing session in MIU, Louis gave his report carefully, sounding a little nervous. He made a point of the meeting between Valerie Carmichael and Dennis. Sammie added Carmichael's name to the growing list of people for follow-up interviews.

As he finished, Kent said, "Last but not least, Harriett. The church, the word Compline and this Nunc dimittis."

Louis listened to his former shift sergeant reprise the findings from the discussions with Reverend Dodson and John Eames. She reinforced the idea that the words 'Nunc dimittis' probably referred to the solo being performed by Dennis's friend Valerie and, if so, was that the reason he took another jacket? Had he planned to attend the concert? A plan unknown to his parents, for some reason?

Sammie said, "Perhaps the focus needs to switch to the concert, or the route between Maryport and Carlisle? There are buses and trains. Hopefully he wasn't stupid enough to just hitchhike."

Kent was absorbing it all. "We need to follow up on all those, yes. Dr. Kulis, could you give us your initial observations?"

The forensic psychologist said, "It's too early for me to profile, but two things strike me. First, the binding of the victim. I asked for those to be preserved intact. It was rope, I see, and it had cut heavily into the skin.

"Bindings reveal behavioural implications for some perpetrators. They can be complex, carefully done premortem, indicating some sort of ritual, perhaps a sadistic element of the murder. Or they can be simple knots, constraints for storage and lifting the body. In that scenario, they would probably be postmortem.

"Second, the body shape suggests a box-shaped storage, perhaps a freezer. I have seen others like this. He was young and slim but a good height and not lightweight, despite the state of his body now.

"It could indicate one or more people with a cult interest, possibly, if the bondage and the prayer ritual are linked in some macabre way. Compline is an ancient service in different religions. It includes the Nunc dimittis, so there is a linkage between the words. Aberrations of church services by cults are common enough, historically. It is a possibility."

She suddenly looked less professorial. "But I feel it is probably much more mundane, not in the appalling nature of the crime, but the rationale for the binding, as I said. In that scenario, the perpetrator could be one person, a single male or physically powerful woman who, for a motive unknown, needed the body reduced in length, kept compact, and with a lifting handle. Forensics can't say with any certainty, I expect, but the penetration of the rope into the skin may fit that. In that scenario, there could be other people involved, too, of course.

"I'll leave it there for now and give you more after reviewing the files. I would like to start that this evening and finish it tomorrow, if that works for the team."

It was Chan who spoke. "I need to read them, too, and was thinking of starting that this evening. So, I will be here."

John Kent was absorbing it, seeing the two lines of thinking; a murder with a cult link. Or a murder where the disposal of the corpse was simply a practical matter.

He took a deep breath, almost a sigh. "Harriet, you have the church angle already, so stick with that and extend it to Carlisle. Tomorrow, find out more about this concert at the cathedral from them, if you can.

"Sammie, I want you to follow up with Valerie Carmichael and this conversation observed by Dennis's sister.

Tread delicately, but no telephone or internet interview; do it in person."

Kulis nodded, seeing the logic. The probability was that a major TV actor would be busy and try to do it by phone or videolink. A police officer wants to observe the body language, the eyes and , in some cases, sense the deflection or smell the fear.

Kent focused on the younger officers. "You two work together tomorrow; the interview with the widow of the former owner of the farm site, in Blackpool – and then go back up to Birkby, interview the farm staff about their recollections when they took over the land."

He caught Sammie's expression out of the corner of his eye; she appeared a bit miffed. "OK with that, Sammie?"

"Sounds good, yes." It wasn't the allocation of work she had a problem with, but not being asked for her own proposed actions.

He stood. "Well, I'll leave you. Yvonne will want to be catching up with the files, I am sure."

Her charge meter was running, he inferred, by tone of voice. Everyone got that, including Kulis.

~~

Susan Carlson had collected her rental car in Penrith, her instructor routing the driving lesson to fit. She then played tourist a bit, driving back to Keswick, adjusting more to the roads and her vehicle. She arrived at Harriet's home mid-afternoon.

When Harriet appeared later, it was about half an hour before Susan's evening lesson. Harriet announced that Chris Willard was on his way over, he had called her on her drive home.

"Chris has a guidebook of York he doesn't need and

thought you might find it useful. He's dropping it off any minute." Susan's comment the previous evening about 'Willard being different' floated back to her, making her wonder.

When Willard arrived, Harriet offered tea, wanting a chance to unwind from the pressures of the day. Susan was bubbly with her driving success and growing confidence in being able to get around the UK.

As they talked, it was clear that her Canadian visitor was less at ease. Willard was in a dark suit today, with a black shirt contrasting with his white clerical collar. Overall, he appeared more formal and traditional than yesterday. Occasionally, Susan would appear to see the man, and sometimes a priest, it seemed to Harriet. Familiar with her friend's story from their time in Ontario together, she understood the cause of the duality.

It became clear that Chris Willard also sensed Susan's discomfort, but misread the reason. He said suddenly, "My clerical dress unsettles you, doesn't it? But it shouldn't do that, really, I hope. These are just my work clothes, as a priest. A bit formal today, for a funeral, but just work clothes."

He smiled, encouragingly. His relaxed, good mood had given him the confidence to raise the issue.

Neither woman responded. Susan pursed her lips and frowned. She had appreciated his help and company yesterday, and the gift of the guidebook, but the sudden 'I'm a priest' bit jarred in its conventionality and, to her, its condescension.

Seeing Susan's expression change, Harriet arched her eyebrows and Chris Willard caught that.

"What does that mean?" he asked, now looking lost.

Harriet responded, "That's a little presumptuous, Chris, don't you think? Like, 'said the peacock to the peahen'?"

Willard was startled by the comparison. "It's not about finery and vanity, Harriet, you know that. It's about –."

"Peacockery, like university convocations, but in a church or cathedral," rebutted Calder, smiling, pushing home the point.

He frowned. "Is there such a word as peacockery, I wonder? My dress identifies me as a priest. That I am there in the work of Christ, to help people."

"And the rest of the vestments, on high days and holidays? Come on, Chris, admit it, clerical dress is to make separate and distinct. Show me a picture of any bishop, male or female, in a mitre. Then contradict me."

Susan just watched the sparring, realising that Calder was trying to head off a more substantive response from her to Willard's original question. Well, she thought, he has dug the hole…

She interjected softly, "Yes, clerical garb does unsettle me."

Harriet went quiet, realising the issue could not be avoided, after all.

Susan's eyes were locked on Willard's face. "I work every day with women who turn to drink or drugs, and I have done that job for a more than a few years now. Whether at a recovery centre or in an AA meeting, I meet with people who are still tied to their remorse and despair. Some are also victims of sexual abuse; others are their parents or family members wracked by the mistreatment of their children. Too often, those events have been tied to either a church setting or people in your attire. So, please forgive me if I don't see your clerical collar in quite the way you do."

She took a breath, backing off, giving him a small smile. "It's nothing personal, just an involuntary reaction. If you will excuse me, I need to get ready for my driving lesson.

Gordon will be here in a few minutes. Thank you again for the book."

She stood and left the room.

Willard looked frozen for a moment, then closed his eyes, blushing. As he opened them again, Harriet was smiling. "You are a good man, Chris Willard, but sometimes…"

"With both feet," he muttered. "I'd better be going."

She stood as he did. "I didn't say, but I'm on the Lewis case at present, on transfer from the Keswick station. It's why I missed picking up Susan."

He sighed. "Dennis Lewis, the boy who went missing, the one in the news?"

She nodded. "His parents are Bernice and Eamon. Pray for them and their family, it's extremely hard on them at present."

"I'll do that. And for you. And for Susan – it is very personal for her, I think? I just realised; your link, through Father Aster."

He broke off, his eyes on the door through which Susan left, his expression conveying both his new understanding and a sense of loss.

"That would be good. Yes."

He had picked up on Susan being a victim as well as a counsellor, Harriet saw. Not that she would ever betray Susan's confidential revelations, but the involuntary reaction was not simply for the suffering of other victims. It was, as Susan was the first to admit, about herself.

Harriet knew that Carlson could not talk about that with anyone. The legal settlement between the Roman Catholic diocese in Canada and the Carlson family had secrecy provisions, with legal penalties, if broken. It is a good thing for Willard to be aware of, she reflected, so that he avoids putting his foot in it again, with Susan or others.

11 DOREEN

The following morning, Louis Chan and Howard Mooney drove to Blackpool, Lancashire. A seaside resort, today's temperatures and winds guaranteed to have any beachwalkers in winter coats, not swimwear. Their first task was to follow up there with the widow of the former owner of Crosshill Farm, Doreen Williams.

On their work plans, Calder and Livermore began the day together in the office, reviewing the reports from uniformed officers of calls made yesterday at properties near Crosshill Farm. There were relatively few of those and, ten years on, it was a long shot. Nothing new of use emerged. As Sammie and Harriet finished the review, Sammie took a call.

On putting the phone down, she said, "John and I will meet with Dr. Kulis by videoconference in a few minutes, to get her initial feedback. She will probably come here to speak at the evening debrief. Doubtlessly, Superintendent Chiswell will want to sit in, so the timing for that will be tied to his availability."

While her statement was formal, her eyes rolled briefly.

Harriet said, with a smile, "I'm heading out now – over to Carlisle."

To the cathedral, where the concert took place on the day Dennis disappeared.

Mooney had tracked Rathburn Williams' widow, Doreen, to a retirement home in Blackpool called 'Sea Vista'. It was about an hour's drive from Penrith.

When Chan and Mooney arrived there mid-morning, Louis thought that residents below the top floor of Sea Vista would need X-ray vision for the home to live up to its name. But Doreen appeared spritely compared with some others they saw there.

Louis was to lead, Sammie had said, to give him experience.

"How are you doing?" Louis asked, out of politeness. It broke the silence after the introduction.

"Better than many here, thank God. But I like Blackpool. There is always something to do, but without the labour of farm work."

As she turned into an ambassador for the place, Louis brought it back to reality, explaining their presence.

"Found on our land? The boy who disappeared. No. I can't believe it. That wouldn't have happened if Phil had been hale and active. He'd not miss something like that, I'm sure. He knew the place backwards. Oh, that makes me feel bad, for someone to do that, and on our farm."

"Phil?"

"Rathburn Philip, my husband's given names, but he was always known as Phil. Rathburn is a family name since the year dot, passed down as a blight on first sons. Your records aren't very good, are they?"

"When did Mr. Williams get ill?" They knew the date of death and the cause from the data search by support staff.

"That would be early July 2007. He had to give up work on the farm totally by the beginning of December. He became bedridden in late March the following year, the week of our wedding anniversary. Phil died on May 14, 2008."

"Who looked after the farm then?"

"No-one really. We had sold off the livestock in the autumn, all of it as soon as it was clear Phil wouldn't get better. It broke our hearts, and I think his will to continue, but it was the only way, not having any kids to take it on.

"A couple of people inquired about our plans for the place, but they came to nothing. For the last eight months, nearly, it was let go, until the paperwork closed. The severance of the farmhouse was a godsend, in terms of sale value. That Kendal Simmonds is a good man. He worked with our solicitor and the estate agent, and I ended up with enough to pay our debts and still have an annuity for retirement."

Louis was taking in her intensity, returning to those dark times.

"Phil never saw the farm at the end, as it would have been another blow to him. It was bad enough for him to feel unable to do anything. Me, I was fully occupied with him."

Howard watched and made notes as Louis carefully teased information out of Doreen Williams about people showing interest in buying the farm or wanting grazing access to the land. Each person would need to be contacted.

Louis then moved on. "And did you have regular visitors during the period Philip was ill?"

She thought about it.

"Some family, I can give you those names. An old friend, now also passed away, Henry Tingley. The nurses.

I remember only one of those, now, Jane. She was Nurse Jane Goodman. Our family doctor, Dr. Hewhitt; he is still in practice, I think. And the curate, Reverend Nichols, Shannon Nichols. Shannon was at our local church, but she stayed in pastoral care with me and Phil right through, even after she moved to Carlisle. She was so good. Regular visitors near the end were only the medical people, Henry, and Shannon."

Louis sagged inwardly. The list gave more people for him and Howard to question and perhaps visit. But DS Livermore had given them the responsibility, so he wanted to do a good job.

He looked at Howard, the look conveying the question. Anything else?

Howard asked, "Anyone visited out of the blue, unplanned, that struck you as strange?"

Doreen thought for a moment. "No. It was a farm. There's a public footpath, but that's on the other side, not in sight of the copse, from what you told me about the location. People were on the footpath quite a bit, as usual, but I have no idea about that."

Louis finished with, "Do you miss the area, the farm?", as they put their notebooks away.

"No. Without Phil, it would be too lonely. I like it here, and the walks by the sea. The sea air does me good these days."

Outside, the two detectives talked.

Louis said, "This curate, Nichols, visited the farm and she was also based around the time of his death in Carlisle, where the concert was held."

Howard said, "Give Harriet a call. Let her know. In MIU we don't take coincidences at face value."

Their next visit was two hours drive away, back in

North Cumbria, to interview the landowner who bought Crosshill Farm, everything other than the house and surrounding garden. The man, Kendal Simmonds, had the foresight to call over the two men who worked for him at the time, one now retired, the other still employed.

When questioned, Kendal replied, "The knoll at the old Crosshill Farm, near where the tree line begins. The body was found there, we know, because of a dead sheep. Other than that, I have no idea about how the boy got there. But, Col or Eric, any thoughts?"

It was Colin Driscoll, one of the hired farmworkers, who replied. He squinted, visualising it. "It was dug over when we first went there, as I reminded Mr. Simmonds when I found the dead ewe. But we never knew what Phil Williams had been doing at the spot. The soil was well settled, and weeds and grass were established on it; but I could see it had been dug. We didn't bother with it; there was too much else to do at the time."

Howard, who was leading this interview, asked, "You never went to check it out before the discovery of the ewe?"

"We were too busy. We concentrated on the grazing, and the sheep. Phil had let it go, being poorly. We had enough to do, initially, and afterwards it was just part of the landscape."

The other man, Eric, silent so far, said, "The boy was buried there, all this time. It's hard to think about it."

Colin was the more voluble one, Louis saw. Colin said, "Fields around here, there are a lot of things buried. We once found a bone while ploughing over at Greengill. From a human arm. It was probably sixteenth century, the scientists said later."

The farm workers had no recall of trespassers or visitors, nor what they were doing ten years ago, around the time of Dennis Lewis's disappearance.

Howard focused on Kendal Simmonds, to see what he could draw out of him and get a read of the man.

"We spoke to Mrs. Williams. She said you were very helpful; a 'godsend', in fact, about the sale. You didn't want the farmhouse?"

Simmonds gave some thought as to where the question was leading. "I had no practical need of the house, no. I considered buying the entire farm and severing off the property. It would mean more outlay for me then, but a lot more profit in the long run. It made business sense."

He stopped.

Howard prodded him. "But?"

"The Williams couple were very traditional farmers, not looking for growth, just holding their own financially; I know that. Been there all their married lives and never really modernised their business. I thought the right thing was for Doreen to sell the house, clear their debt, and be able to retire. I got the land at a fair price. I sleep at nights."

Eric said suddenly, "I never felt comfortable in that part, between the knoll and the trees. It's weird, I never understood why. Perhaps that was the reason."

Howard gave a glance at Louis. Time to go before they got into the supernatural aspects of detective work. Louis stood, but understood how Eric felt, for some reason. They were going there next, on the way back to Penrith, for him to see the location. Sammie had told Howard to do that, show Louis the site before things wound up there and the sheep were allowed to return.

~~

A little earlier, back in Bassenthwaite, after making herself some lunch before she left Harriet's home, Susan

Carlson was staring at her laptop, grimacing. She had spent the time after breakfast reviewing her presentation for the conference, as the thought of the session ahead where she would be a panel speaker filled her with a sense of dread.

But her unease now was tied more to her behaviour yesterday. She had called Miriam, her AA sponsor, and told her of her trip so far… and her worry bead. That was what sponsors were for.

Susan broke the silence. "I know, I know. I need to apologise."

Miriam had said nothing, just looked at her across the ocean, courtesy of the internet, while sitting in her kitchen in Toronto eating her breakfast cereal.

Over the years, Susan had seen the older woman during the day and in the middle of the night. If it were not a time zone thing, she wouldn't have called her at her breakfast time; Miriam wasn't at her most serene in the morning. Her own breakfast with Harriet had been good, but both women were aware of the limited time they had spent together, and how their plans for the two days had evaporated.

Susan added, "You haven't said anything."

Miriam shrugged. "I don't need to. You are doing all the talking."

Susan nodded. "It's nerves, I suppose, with going to this conference, and the travel over. And the jet lag."

Miriam's expression made it clear that she did not agree. It told Susan silently that she was simply making excuses.

Susan changed subjects. "What did the doctor say about the hip?"

"That it is going to be much harder for me to kick sponsees' butts when they are less than truthful with their wonderful sponsor. But with you, I will make an exception. You have the hots for this man Willard."

"I don't! I never said anything like that."

"He 'intrigued' you, you just said. And now you are upset because you took a verbal poke at him. I think you are interested in him. About time you were interested in someone but, God almighty, does it have to be another priest? Well, I can't choose for you. You can't hide away in Haydn House for ever. It's a treatment centre, not your personal nunnery."

"You shouldn't be throwing me at him! You don't like priests, or rabbis, or ..."

"I don't accept their rituals and their complicated doctrines. I never said I don't like them as people. Principles not personalities, that's our program. Now don't put the apology to Willard off. Just do it."

She stood. Susan was suddenly looking at Miriam's midriff in the awful floral dressing gown that some other sponsee had bought her two Christmases ago. Her disembodied voice came through.

"I'm off for my shower. And I'm not taking this computer in there. Call me tomorrow or the day after. Try to work your program. And drive carefully. British drivers are mad; they all think they are rally drivers. Your speech will be fine. Look down from the podium and think of everyone as friends wanting you to do well. And have a good time."

The connection broke. She knows how to turn it off, at least, Susan mused. Follow all those instructions and still have a good time. And juggle three balls in the air while I'm doing it.

Chris Willard was passing a window in St. Anselm's Church as the bright red Ford Fiesta came slowly down the track from the road. The gate, closed when no-one was there allowing only pedestrian entrance across the style, was now open.

He didn't recognise the vehicle, but as it stopped, he saw that it was Susan Carlson driving. He went out into the church entrance as she opend the door and stood.

"Hello. That's your rental car, I take it. Very nice!" It seemed safe ground, he thought, to comment on the car. She didn't acknowledge it.

"I have come to apologize for my remark yesterday afternoon. It was rude. I am sorry."

"Don't be," he replied quickly. "Do you have time for a coffee, I was just about to make one." He knew she must be about to start her epic drive to York. She ignored that, too.

"I mean, it was highly inappropriate. You only helped me. It was churlish of me."

"It's OK," he responded. Carlson was now near the bottom of the steps, looking wonderful, he thought. He added, "Then I apologise, too. Not for wearing a clerical collar, but for being presumptuous, that my interpretation should automatically be accepted by others. You correctly put me in my place on that."

He smiled. She nodded and smiled back.

"Thank you. Well, I'd better be off and follow my satnav's instructions."

Chris asked suddenly, "Will you be back, after the conference?"

"I don't plan to be, no. I return the car at Heathrow, driving down from York. Another big trip."

"Can we stay in touch?"

She smiled. "That would be nice. Yes, why not?" She pulled out her mobile. "What's your number or email?"

He gave her his email and his telephone number, as her thumbs worked away. He heard the ping on his phone.

"There, we are connected."

Susan got back in the car, suddenly looking unsure. Quickly, she started up and reversed before making a turn. She gave him one brief smile before concentrating on the driving.

He watched the glimpses of the car roof through the foliage as it drove away. Only then did he pull out his phone and check that she had, in fact, sent him her contact information. His next task was to send a response to her phone and make sure Susan Carlson was properly added to his contact list.

12 CARLISLE

Harriet Calder had visited Carlisle Cathedral precisely three times; twice in uniform (once as a Girl Guide, the second time as a police constable) and once for a wedding. The architecture impressed her, and the sense of history, but at heart she didn't like it much.

She had returned to the religion of her youth, the Methodist Church, in her late twenties after her husband became terminally ill. In her need, she found God in the little Methodist Chapel in Bassenthwaite and with it, her calling as a preacher.

Early in her re-awakening, she had visited the Methodist Central Hall in Carlisle a few times. It was near the cathedral, in Fisher Street, but had closed as a worship centre in 2005. Afterwards, it was used for events. Built in 1922, a steel structure fronted by stone, Harriet had found the hall oppressive. She liked the building even less than the cathedral.

Her grandfather, also a Methodist preacher during the era of great revivalist Methodism, had influenced her more than she would care to admit. He had been a 'small church and chapel' man. There were no vanities there, he used to say. Less, Harriet would now say, but she, too, was a small church person, happy with her worship in the churches and chapels that dotted the Cumbria landscape. Even with the summer evangelical gatherings of the Keswick Ministry on her doorstep, 'The Keswick Weeks', she took part only a little, occasionally attending the smaller, theme-specific side events.

As she approached Carlisle Cathedral, it occurred to her that the last time she had visited a similar venue was well over a year ago, in Hamilton, Ontario, the cathedral church of the diocese of Hamilton-Brant. With that came the memory of its bishop, James Azikiwe, which made her smile.

"I will pray for your ministry, sister," were his last words to her. His sister in Christ's work. Love shone out of some priests, and he was one of those.

Canon Hugh Sanderson was the Pastoral Assistant at Carlisle Cathedral. The person who answered her call earlier suggested Sanderson as the most appropriate person to speak to initially, as someone who may recall the concert in question. He was a lay person, with a long involvement in the activities of the diocese. Previously a bank employee, he was earnest, with a banker's care in his responses to her questions.

In his office, as Harriet explained her interest in the concert, he said that he had attended the event in 2008 but recalled little, other than some of the music. If she had names, he could check with others.

Harriett showed him the photocopy of the concert announcement and ran through the names, including the one just passed on to her by Louis Chan, Shannon Nichols. He knew some of the choir members and Nichols, but not

Oliver Mettler.

"I have heard him as a choir director, of course. One of note; and a first-rate organist, I say. But he is not an Anglican. He does freelance work, I think, but is primarily based at the big, new-looking church on the Bradford ring road, the Cross of the Redeemer. It's been on television, a Pentecostal or Congregationalist church, or something like that."

Harriet clued in. "You mean, it was featured on a 'Songs of Praise' programme?"

'Yes. It is a big modern building, with glass walls and a sloping roof. Very modern. Its choir is excellent."

He was looking intently at the programme. "I know that Keith Lonsdale still sings with the cathedral choir, and this person, Tracy Elmwood, is a member of the choir at All Saints', as she spent the last two years as a churchwarden there. As to the others, I will need to check other records."

"And Reverend Nichols, you said earlier?"

"Oh, Shannon, yes. We know her well. Reverend Nichols is in Solway."

Harriet asked, apparently routinely, "How would you describe her?"

Sanderson thought a moment. "You would need to speak to the Bishop, Dean, or Canon Warden for personal details on people, I am afraid. It is policy."

"I understand that. I wasn't after details, just a heads-up on the people I need to interview, that was all."

He paused.

"Shannon Nichols is lovely. She is a very dedicated priest who came into the church from a teaching career. Shannon is very interested in music – and pastoral care."

She asked, "If I could have her contact information, please? I'll try and pop over to see Reverend Nichols next."

"I can give Shannon a call now, and you can speak to

her, if you wish? For Oliver Mettler, I could only give you the contact details you can get from the website for his church."

"Thank you, I can get those myself, but I appreciate the offer for the call to Reverend Nichols and the contact information of the choir members you know. If you could send me an email with those details, it would be helpful."

Outside, Harriet left a voicemail for Sammie saying she would interview Nichols next, in about an hour. She was on the road out of Carlise when Sammie called her. Harriet needed to get back. There was a team briefing by Dr. Kulis earlier than expected.

No sooner had she closed the call with Sammie than John Kent called her.

"Harriet, feedback from a discussion I had with NCA with Dr. Kulis. She followed up on serial predators active in the area in case Dennis had some hidden relationship not found first time. She came back with one name. You and I are lined up to see a convicted former Roman Catholic priest, a Dominic McCluskey, tomorrow. He's in Haverigg now, I understand."

"He's a possible?"

"Unlikely, but they say his own abuser, a Grant Aldman, could be, in terms of fit, timing and location. McCluskey has been co-operative and talked about him. You can prep later, after the briefing with Kulis. I'm just going to talk with Ken Nolan regarding one of his suspects. See you later."

He rang off.

Haverigg was a village on the coast, at the southern tip of Cumbria. Harriet had been there several times. It was the location of an open prison, a Category D, so low-level offenders from the Keswick area served their sentences there. She was surprised that a priest convicted of abuse was being held in a Category D. Most fitted B or C status, with more secure conditions, and often segregated for their protection.

After she called Reverend Nichols to reschedule for tomorrow, Harriet set off back to Penrith. She began to see why John Kent was so annoyed at Terry Cotton. Once the behavioural psychologist was involved, Superintendent Chiswell controlled much of the agenda and timing of the MIU team involved. It never used to be this way.

But she wasn't MIU staff, then or now, Harriet reminded herself. It wasn't her problem.

~~

Sammie hurried back into their area three minutes after the set time, arriving coincidently as Dr. Kulis entered with Superintendent Chiswell. Harriet, Howard, and Louis were sitting, waiting.

Sammie said, "Let's begin."

She and Harriet exchanged glances.

Superintendent Chiswell asked her, "Where is DCI Kent?"

"He said we are to proceed, sir."

The superintendent looked annoyed as Dr. Kulis stood, ready to present. Why she stood, Harriet wasn't sure.

Chiswell said curtly, "One moment. You have put a lot of effort into this. DCI Kent should hear it. I know he is a busy man, but there are priorities. I will –."

Sammie spoke up. "DCI Kent is in the shower, then he will be on his way to the hospital, sir."

That got everyone's attention.

Chiswell asked, "Is he injured?"

"I hope not. He was interviewing a suspect in the Small-wood case with acting DS Atkinson. I was waiting for him to come out of the interview room. Apparently, the man had a nosebleed. During the interview, he started bleeding profusely just as he sneezed. DCI Kent was splattered, is the best way to put it. He and the suspect are having blood tests, following protocol."

Superintendent Chiswell said, angrily, "Why wasn't I told?"

Seeing Sammie's face, Harriet gave her head a small shake, her eyes saying, "Don't!"

She could almost hear Sammie's mind thundering out, 'You just were!'

Dr. Kulis saved the day by saying softly, "It just happened. Poor John. Hopefully, the man isn't infected with anything significant. I'll bring him up to speed later.

"I have worked your latest information into my profile. Thank you for sending me that, Sammie. You are most likely looking for a local man, local at the time to the Maryport area or, given that the body was found near the main road, local between the coast and Carlisle, or Carlisle itself. It could also be a man with a link to the concert there. He was probably acting alone. Some others close to him may be aware of or suspect his act.

"The man will be an authority figure in some way. He had access to a vehicle and probably didn't need to share that vehicle with others at the time. He knew the Williams couple possibly, or at least became aware of the window of opportunity to bury the body on the land.

"He was calm enough, with resources, to store the body somewhere between the victim's disappearance and the burial. Whatever the reason for Dennis's death, the subsequent actions were planned and calculated, and remained effective for ten years."

We know that, thought Chan.

"We discussed yesterday very briefly the issue of the

binding of the victim's body. This is a major element. Do not underestimate it. As I said then, it could indicate a planned predatory attack by a deliberate killer or an unplanned attack, with a clever, resourceful follow up. The question is, 'which one is most likely?

"The most useful indicators for me were Dennis's clothes fragments, his belt, and the rope knots. The former, and I thank the pathology and forensic people for the discussions, are entirely consistent with normal use and wear. There is no indication of removal of the pants or their awkward replacement, which could have indicated a sexual element. Residual skin fragments in the remaining buttock and genital area tissues show no sign of damage that could be linked to sado-erotic stimulation or beating.

"The knots are ordinary, not complex. Three of them were still intact. People who bind others for sado-erotic purposes become experts in ropes and knots. They select their knots carefully; it is part of the ritual. Furthermore, none of the rope fragments appear to contain residual elements of semen or another person's blood type, but that testing is still ongoing.

"I won't go into further detail on those; they will be in my report. Also included is my review of all known predatory murders involving binding or constraint in the UK during the last ten years, taken from databases I have access to, as well as your own. Nothing is a close fit. I do not see a sadistic predator to be the likely murder scenario, which leaves the unplanned attack.

"Here the words 'Compline' and 'Nunc dimittis' should be seen in a different context, not as ritual element, but perhaps as a link to the killer or the killer's environment. He killed for a purpose – to remove Dennis, or something Dennis knew which would be detrimental to him. He acted either deliberately or perhaps rashly through panic, in a location where they were undisturbed, probably a place where Dennis agreed to meet him without informing other people. After killing the boy, the person moved with care and deliberation to dispose of his body. The binding fits that, making the body more compact, more easily manipulated.

"Looking at Dennis's life, from all the interview reports, he doesn't seem to have any high-risk activities; but he was fifteen years old. Everything points to him being his age, in transition from boyhood to manhood. But no girlfriend? Was he homosexual? Did he have a secret male partner? Explore that further. Check men at his church, his school, his neighbours and, dare I say it, his father again. Something is missing there, I feel."

"The change of jacket intrigued me. He chose one he didn't particularly like, it appears, but one which could present him as being serious, more grown-up. Why? Who did he have in mind? Not his friends, or this Valerie Krestman. They had all seen him in his school uniform innumerable times. He left home in his school blazer and was found in the jacket he must have secreted from the house.

"Finally, in looking at Dennis's motivating factors – what he did and why he did them – I was struck by elements from the interview with Dennis's father by Sergeant Calder and the interview you did, DC Chan, with the sister. The impression that he was 'innocent', 'naive', 'transitional' and 'romantic' brought to my mind the concept of a knight in shining armour."

She paused.

"Knights may come across damsels in distress on the road. But they also undertake quests for them, or for close friends, or for people in authority. Perhaps his two male friends need a revisit. And, given the comment that he was in earnest conversation with this female friend described as a 'sweetheart' figure, I think Valerie Krestman needs further investigation. In fact, I see her as the most important interview subject, initially.

"I suspect that Dennis deliberately went somewhere for a reason that led to his death. It could be a coincidence that he fell victim to an as-yet unknown predatory killer, one with an interest in bondage and ropes, but my money isn't on that at all. It is on an arranged meeting tied to the words Compline and Nunc dimittis, and his purpose in going to it.

"I think that gives you some focus areas. I'll stop there and answer any questions."

Sammie responded first.

"You think that someone he knew knows more? And is either concealing it or not realising its significance."

Kulis pursed her lips. "Dennis may or may not have talked with them about his intent, but someone who knew him probably has some knowledge that is relevant, that could advance the investigation. If they are concealing it deliberately, it is not going to be easy to get them to reveal it, perhaps. But it could be that the person simply doesn't make the connection."

Louis found nothing to ask. What struck him, though, was that the profiler came to many of the same conclusions the team had discussed, but she linked them and speculated on them differently. The issue of the knots was interesting. So was her focus on Valerie Krestman. He began to see the value, despite the grumbles about cost.

After Chiswell and Yvonne Kulis left, Howard crystallised that thought more caustically than Chan had been thinking. "You know what? I don't know about Kulis being expensive, but if I had to spend this area's budget, I would probably keep her on the occasional contract and do without Norm's Caff and his interfering."

As he finished, John Kent came into view, in a new shirt with crisp folds, straight out of the box.

"I didn't hear that, Mooney. Not one word. Now, bring me up to speed. And nobody, nobody, sneeze in my presence."

Sammie summarized the feedback from the profiler.

"Anything new from today, not yet covered?" he asked.

Harriet said, "I still want to follow up further with Reverend Nichols as a priority. I'll leave it there for now."

Kent nodded.

Sammie spoke up. "I didn't mention to Dr. Kulis at this stage, but we may need to tread gently around Valerie Carmichael. I don't think I can just turn up and bang on the door."

Valerie Carmichael played the part of a hard-nosed young businesswoman in a successful ITV drama series called 'Ruston', set in Lincoln. It was in its third year. Kent knew the actor had been in several other dramas and this was her big 'breakthrough' success, but he hadn't watched the series.

"Talk to Linnie; she will pin down her agent or manager. Work through them, to make contact. It will be faster that way."

13 HAVERIGG

The following morning, Harriet turned up in their work area with a bag of fresh pastries from a well-known local bakery in Keswick. Mooney and Chan were there, but not Sammie, and dove straight in.

John Kent walked by and stopped. "Celebration time?"

Harriet responded, "In a way. My friend Susan from Canada drove from Bassenthwaite to York, the city centre, no less, on her own without a bump, a speeding ticket, getting lost, or calling me for help. She followed the satnav and gave no one the finger, she said. That makes her a better English driver than about half the people born here. I'm relieved."

She looked at Kent. "Have the spare. I forgot Sammie was having a better breakfast this morning."

Livermore was interviewing Valerie Carmichael.

Kent shook his head. "Thanks, but I won't. We need to be moving. Leave in about ten?"

Heading to Haverigg Prison, he meant.

Mooney said a few minutes later, while eyeing the spare muffin, "Thanks for this. Kids growing up, first car, leaving home; it's hard to let go, isn't it?"

Harriet said, "Don't speak with your mouth full. Otherwise, I will get Sammie to tell your mother." She knew that Sammie and Howard lived close to each other, and Sammie often gave Mooney a lift to work, picking him up at his parent's home.

John Kent drove. His Mercedes sped down the M6, its soundproofing emphasizing the silences between the cursory initial conversation elements. Harriet wondered when Kent was going to talk about the man they were interviewing. She had read the file yesterday. As they passed Thrimby, he asked, "I take it I am not yet forgiven for pulling you into the team?"

Harriet shot back, "No. Listen for trumpets from the heavens for that, not an offer of a free muffin."

Kent smiled. "I should have asked you, I know, but I thought you would say no. I apologise for the heavy-handed approach."

She said nothing for a moment, staring out the side window. Then she thawed. "Well, thank you for that, at least. It doesn't matter now. Susan's gone. And it was the right thing, for me to help break the news to Eamon and Bernice."

She paused.

"Returning to MIU stirs up a lot of emotions, John, but I want to help achieve closure for the family now."

She looked at him and he glanced at her.

"You are on board, then?"

"Yes. We should both let it go."

He nodded. "How about replacing Cotton?"

"Don't push your luck. Have you got someone else in mind?"

Kent sighed, "No, other than you. I'm looking at a

couple of people, one from Organized Crime and another from Intelligence, but they don't sit well, really; my read is that each one would use the promotion for leveraging, to move back, or up into an Area Command role as soon as they could. After my experience with hiring Cotton from outside, I'm not going to rush it."

She nodded, understanding. "MIU gets the the 'human' crimes, the family suspicious deaths, that sort of thing. It seems every young copper wants work in Organized Crime these days, taking on drug bosses and gang leaders."

He changed the subject. "What's Susan Carlson's next driving challenge?"

"Well, she's in a conference, and may drive around York a bit. The next big one is her drive afterwards, down to Heathrow, to turn in the car. But she sounds comfortable with it, at least."

He signalled and overtook a car. The driver gave them the finger as they sailed past, exemplifying Harriet's earlier comment in the office.

Kent returned to the topic of Cotton's replacement. "But I tell you this; I'm not pushing Sammie up yet; it's too soon, and she needs the time to develop." He glanced across, checking her reaction.

"Well, I agree. It's another good reason for me to be working with her at present."

Having reached a compromise, John Kent said, "Now, Dominic McCluskey, former priest, age thirty-five. He is serving a ten-year sentence and has completed four, for sexual assault of teens, male and female. He could be out on licence in a year. His base was his parish in Workington, but one of the male victims came from Maryport."

She said, "Workington's only a ten-minute drive."

"You saw the notes on his conviction. According to NCA and Kulis, he was groomed and abused by an older male, a lay person, Grant Aldman, who also lived in Workington. Aldman committed suicide as the investigation into McCluskey became known. He used pills. That was just over five years ago.

She muttered, "So the abused boy became a priest, and an abuser himself. It sometimes happens, but I struggle to understand that."

Kent pressed on. "According to NCA, Aldman was into bondage, but we need more on that from McCluskey. Aldman's suicide ended the police investigation into him."

"McCluskey is co-operative, you said. That's a plus."

He nodded. "Yes, he is talkative, open about it. Surprisingly so for a sex offender. Hence the Category D prison. He made Cat C within a year of conviction."

She was surprised. "Sounds like a model prisoner."

Kent responded, "One we treat carefully. Dr. Kulis interviewed him eight months ago on another case. She talked yesterday with the Haverigg staff psychiatrist about him for me, to update her views. Nothing has changed.

"Basically, he will come across as being open and candid, willing to help, and talk about paedophilia in clinical and personal terms. She said we could find ourselves perturbed; the conversation will appear as innocuous as discussing minor pilfering, not the horrors inflicted on children. We have to work with that, not address it head on. It is about him, even when he gives the impression it isn't so. If we confront him on that, force him to see a victim in real terms, he will shut down and leave."

Kent sighed. "That's his right. We aren't interviewing him about a potential case involving him. He has the whip hand. So, I'll lead. Chip in if you have something, but remember my interest is what he knows about his pal or other predators working the Maryport area."

She nodded, silently accepting the ground rules. "He was laicized after conviction, I assume?"

"No, he relinquished his vows while in remand. It was his choice. I don't think the church stood in his way, though."

She smiled grimly. "Don't count on it. Roman Catholics hold ordination vows as inviolable. Even when defrocked and forbidden the sacraments, a priest is still expected to obey his vows. He may have his legal rights, but I bet a fellow priest would tell him the way it is."

~~

The sign said, 'Welcome to HMP Haverigg', set in front of a mass of tall wire fences and low buildings reminiscent of the former World War II bomber training base it once was. Under leaden skies, the surrounding hills looked bleak today, Harriet thought, rather than welcoming.

Dominic McCluskey could be taken for an archetypal librarian, with bookish, academic features and a pallor. He was sizing them up, sitting across from the two detectives. In a priest's robes, he would fit into a cathedral or church setting, other than the scar on the temple and the hard, world-worn look in his eyes.

John Kent had positioned himself directly across from McCluskey, his hands together on the table, with Harriet next to him.

"We are investigating the death of Dennis Lewis, a boy who disappeared at age fifteen, from Maryport, in June 2008. His body was discovered recently, buried in a nearby farm field."

McCluskey said nothing.

Kent continued. "Grant Aldman was active in the

Workington area at the time. Was Dennis a possible target for him? I read the file, so I know Aldman wasn't reported to have killed anyone, but grooming and sexual assaults go wrong. I'm not suggesting it was premeditated."

He swung his forearms apart a little, signalling for McCluskey to say his piece.

McCluskey responded, "I recall vaguely the original news of the disappearance of a boy from Maryport, but I had forgotten the name."

He switched his gaze to Calder, assessing her, not in a sexual way, just that she was a female police officer. She returned the stare, carefully keeping her face neutral.

McCluskey said suddenly to Kent, "The only person Grant killed was himself, I feel. I don't know, but it was his mindset. He had the pills set aside for years, and he replaced them regularly as they passed their expiry date."

He looked back at Harriet. "He poked fun at me about suicide being a mortal sin. He knew I couldn't ever do that. But you'll argue that someone who would top themselves so easily wouldn't care about killing another. I just doubt it. He would have simply picked up the whisky bottle and his pills."

Harriet suddenly realised why he was glancing at her. The small gold chain necklace with the tiny cross probably caught his eye.

McCluskey continued. "Fifteen? The age was right. But Lewis wasn't a Roman Catholic, was he? Am I right?"

Kent gave a nod. "He was a Protestant, a Methodist."

"Grant only went for boys of the true faith. You are on the wrong track with him on that aspect too, I feel."

Kent asked softly, "Why only Catholics?"

The prison smile was more a grimace. "The grooming technique, to call it that. The process. You need a healthy fear of a common God."

He sat up straight, moved a little so his bodyline allowed a more direct view of Calder, whom he addressed.

"It differs from, say, a father and daughter, or father and son. There is parental leverage there. For Grant and for me, we needed other leverage. That looks like a Protestant cross. I don't think Grant would go for a Protestant. He wanted a common base to work from, not a religious dispute with a teenager."

As he was staring at her, Harriet said, "You are very open, I must say. Thank you."

"I have psychiatry professors booking appointments, bringing their students. Open and transparent, that's my mantra, these days."

He refocused on Kent, summarizing his view. "When Grant groomed me, it took weeks before there was any sexual activity. It was the same for me with my choices. That's part of the process; the hope, the fantasy. It's not a street pickup. If Lewis had been a Roman Catholic, given the proximity to Grant's home, I could see the potential, but never the outcome of killing the boy. Never. Not him, not me."

Kent continued in an even tone. "What about bondage? The NCA report says he went in for that."

McCluskey wrinkled his nose, as if the police officers were introducing a distasteful subject to a polite conversation.

"Men's ties. Used on him when he was sure of his boy, not the other way around. It's not my thing, but it's a bit like sadism and masochism, I gather; you like one or the other, not both."

"No other ligatures; handcuffs, ropes, that sort of thing?"

He stared at Kent. "No. Ties only. Old school ties, preferably. I didn't like tying him up, frankly. Can we move on?"

Harriet started slightly, sat forward. Kent looked at her. "You have a question?"

She asked, "What if the victim decides enough is enough? They choose to tell the police, or a parent, or another person?"

McCluskey looked lost, bereft even. "It doesn't happen. Read case files if you doubt me. From the outset, most victims are made to feel they are the guilty party. Grant did it that way, and I did it that way. With smaller children, which neither of us touched I will add, it is easier still; they obey instructions. With teenagers in puberty, or just through it, their nascent sex drive is made to be paramount in the relationship, and you make your own appear subordinate. That way, they feel more guilty than you from the outset; they never want to tell a soul."

Harriet's face changed, the fear showing momentarily as she thought of Susan, and the little she had learned of her abuse by Duncan Aster. But she instantly replaced it with impassiveness, trying to quell the rising anger, fearful of ruining the interview for John Kent.

But Dominic McCluskey saw it all, it seemed. Instead of anger, he chose to explain himself. "I am being honest and answering your questions, as I answer my psychiatrist, or others who come here, like you. It is the only way I can deal with it now; to be clear about who I am, what I have done, and how I felt. Still feel, I might add. It is a struggle for me."

As Kulis said, thought Harriet, it is all about him. But she could see how he chose to leave segregation, to brave it out in the general population, throwing indignation and shame back at other prisoners: 'This is me; who are you?'. She was surprised he was still standing.

Kent moved on. "What about the service of Compline

in the context of sexual abuse of a victim, and Nunc dimittis. Do they have a context?"

McCluskey looked surprised, then smiled. "Sorry, no, not to me. And not to Grant, I would think. No, not in the way you mean, anyway. 'Now, Master, you let your servant go in peace. You have fulfilled your promise. My own eyes have seen your salvation...'. The Nunc dimittis.

"I smile because I no longer have hope for peace, I have no idea of any promise, and I will never see salvation."

He sat back. "If Compline is tied in some way to Lewis's disappearance and death it wasn't linked to sexual activity like mine or Grant's. It is something else, I suspect."

He sounded as if he was finished, ready to leave; just as Harriet had a glimmer of an idea, a change of focus.

"Hypothetically speaking. Let's do it that way. And this is not about you, there is no hidden agenda here. I just want your reaction, with your experience and willingness to speak to us. You lived in Workington, right?"

"Workington, yes."

Kent was looking at her, interested, seeing the energy.

"You are on one of the bridges over the River Derwent with a friend of one of your targets. Let's say you are in 'a happy relationship'. The friend has found out and is confronting you. Would you push him off the bridge?"

McCluskey looked startled.

She continued, "He's angry at you, or trying to blackmail you, or just threatening to destroy you. One push, no-one watching, problem solved. Would you do that? Out of fear or panic or... just to keep on going. You are transparent, open, you say. Please give me your initial reaction."

She had leaned forward, closing the gap. McCluskey's eyes widened slightly, contemplating the scenario.

"Never, if I thought about it for a second, but in a panic,

at that moment, given the consequences I now live through... perhaps I would have."

He looked less composed as he sat straight in the seat again, less in control. "I hope not, and, speaking hypothetically, panic like that would not be limited to an offender like me, would it? Anyone fearing criminal exposure could do it, for any reason."

She didn't answer him, instead saying, "Thank you."

She looked at Kent who had followed her reasoning, unspoken. "Mr. McCluskey, thank you for your time."

He stood.

Dominic McCluskey stared at him. "If you have any more questions, make them soon."

Kent didn't respond, but his expression seemed to give the prisoner the motivation to answer anyway.

"I hope to start 'See-See' soon. They say it affects the memories as well as destroys the libido."

He sounded matter of fact, as if it was par for the course for a paedophile. Harriet caught on. See-see; CC; chemical castration. She knew that it was only used rarely, and the Home Office was reviewing its use anyway with sex offenders. The only regular use of the treatment in the UK these days was associated with certain types of cancer.

He suddenly reminded her of stories of monks and priests, consumed by their sense of sin, flagellating themselves in cells with braided cords. His whips were his tongue and his transparency around his crimes. But it was all about his pain, not that of his victims.

Kent turned away towards the door without any response. As Harriet turned, she asked, "Do you have a prayer book here? Are you allowed one?"

He looked at her. "I have a bible."

She turned away and followed her temporary boss. She would send him one, she decided. The man needed to pray more and parade his sins less. A cheap, secondhand prayer book, less valuable. After cigarettes, books were a hot currency in prisons. She wanted him to keep it, not trade it.

In the car heading back, she suddenly said, "How many victims did McCluskey have? I somehow missed that in the file."

She was still processing the interview, as Kulis predicted, blown away by the pedestrian, analytical nature of the discussion of teenage boys and girls targeted for sex by a priest.

Kent glanced at her, reading her face. "Four. Initially, two boys and one girl, then a little later, a fourth victim, another boy. He was open about that, too, to the psychiatrists. The fourth one gave him the scar on his head."

She thought for a moment. "I assumed he got that in prison."

"No. The boy hit him with a stone or something, immediately after the first time he was molested. Knocked McCluskey out. They were in sand dunes somewhere. His grooming and control techniques were not as sharp and convincing as he claimed just now, as the victim lashed out, revolted by what happened. Then, thankfully, the boy called the police. That's how Dominic McCluskey was caught."

Harriet changed her mind about sending a prayer book. She wanted no further contact with him.

John Kent refocused on the case. "I liked your question to him. You are thinking about a 'white knight', as Kulis suggested. Dennis was the person on the bridge over the Derwent, as you put it?"

She nodded. "Yes. Perhaps this Valerie or one of his friends is involved. With the words on the bulletin,

'Compline' and 'Nunc Dimmitis' my money currently is on Valerie."

She wondered how Sammie had fared in her breakfast interview with the television star; off camera, hopefully.

14 VALERIE

After the briefing, Sammie had Linnie contact Valerie Carmichael through her agent. She expected to be given the runaround about being busy. Surprisingly, she received total co-operation. Sammie called Carmichael right back on the number Linnie passed on to her.

When Sammie asked to meet, Carmichael responded with, "I live near Market Weighton. Can you come here, or where are you?"

The town was southeast of York.

"Penrith, at Cumbria Police Headquarters."

The actor paused a moment. "I am going up to Glasgow tomorrow for an exterior shoot and will be there for a day and a half. I can pass Penrith on the way. How early do you start?"

"When do you want?"

"Seven thirty a.m."

"You'll be up at the crack of dawn."

"Well before then. You said it was about Dennis. It's the least I can do, to help you as soon as I can. If I can. Besides, I won't be driving, someone else does that. Or you can come up to Glasgow. But you must be busy with the investigation."

She paused, "Look, can we meet somewhere other than the police station, though? Just in case I am recognized. Do you know the Appleby Manor?"

"The one in Appleby-in-Westmorland; yes."

"I know the people there. How about breakfast?"

The following morning, Sammie chose her clothes for indoors and looking good, rather than worrying about her miserable skills in choosing topcoats at present.

The country hotel was southeast of Penrith, about fifteen miles away. She had been there for a friend's wedding, with happy memories. A later visit, a dinner for two when a boyfriend dumped her, made her less interested in returning.

As she entered, wondering if the dining room would work for the interview, a staff member approached.

"Sergeant Livermore? Ms. Carmichael's people called. We have a small room set up for breakfast, in private. Ms. Carmichael suggested it. Can I take your coat?"

'The interview of a lifetime', thought Sammie: an excellent breakfast with a famous person, in privacy and comfort. A change from standing in the corner of a kitchen trying to get answers from a woman busy with babies or kids.

The staff member said quietly, "We take good care of her here. She stays sometimes and we protect her privacy."

Sammie waited in the private room, sitting in an easy chair, taking in the view of the gardens while sipping a cup of good coffee, wondering how her team were progressing. Would the boss and Harriet be sitting comfortably in Haverigg Prison this morning, cosseted? Definitely not.

Valerie Carmichael didn't arrive looking like a star, more like a plainclothes police officer who chose the wrong coat for the day. As she entered the room with a man, her driver it turned out, and a woman, her assistant, the hotel staff member fussed a bit. Valerie's initial focus was that her staff should get a good breakfast in the dining room.

Once alone, she removed her expensive Canada Goose full-length parka, losing the appearance that she was ready for an arctic trek. Sammie was torn between looking at the coat or its famous occupant.

"I'm going to be outside a lot and, given Glasgow and the winds off the Clyde, I wanted something warm."

With breakfast served and the room door shut, Sammie said, "Thank you for going out of the way to fit me in so quickly."

"Dennis and I were best friends, how could I not? How are Eamon and Bernice?"

"Doing better than I would, I think. They are holding up."

Valerie said, "We lost touch. I moved. I sent flowers and called them yesterday, but Aileen said her parents weren't up to talking to anyone at present, but she filled me in. It is understandable."

Even a famous actor, thought Sammie. She started the questions.

"What was your relationship with Dennis around the time he disappeared? We know you were friends from primary school. Was it more than that?"

Valerie looked at her, a small smile on her face. "We were good friends. Close, but not romantically so. We didn't have sex, or even fumble around, if that is the question. When we were twelve, we practised kissing together so that when we got boy and girlfriends, we could be experts. We laughed about that. It was just a good friendship."

Sammie asked, "Do you have any idea why he disappeared?"

If Valerie said no, she was going to jump straight to the meeting in the street that Aileen saw, the day before he disappeared.

"No, but you must be thinking of two days before I heard he was missing, when we met in Crosby Street. Someone probably saw us there. I am surprised no one asked about it before."

"What happened in Crosby Street?"

"He was upset. He had been told off again by his father for being out with Barry and Chas. He felt his parents were too controlling and old-fashioned, or at least his dad was. He was embarrassed when they went on bike rides, always the one to be saying they needed to get back. It depressed him.

"I told him it would get easier, reminding him of all the restrictions on me. It would take time."

Sammie was struck that there was no pause, no hesitancy in her responses.

She asked, "Do you think he ran away? Is that why he disappeared?"

"No, I don't. I thought about it afterwards, obviously, but he never said anything like that to me."

"Did he contact you anytime, after that meeting?"

"No."

Sammie had rarely had an interview where responses came as fast as she could put the questions. As she asked, and checked Valerie's facial changes with each answer, she felt the perfect interview starting to unravel, but couldn't understand why.

"Can I ask about the concert you sang at, around then?"

Valerie looked as if it was a strange question. "With the

choir. What about it?"

"You did a solo, Burgon's 'Nunc dimittis', I gather."

"I did, yes. I was nervous about that."

"Did you and Dennis talk about the choir, or about that particular work?"

The tennis match pace dropped. For a few moments there was a silence as Valerie thought about it.

"We talked about it, yes. He said he knew the tune, at least, from the Smiley Spy series. God, that man Alec Guinness was wonderful, wasn't he? A lovely actor."

Sammie kept the focus on the question. "Did Dennis attend the concert?"

"No. I didn't see him there. I didn't expect him to be there, either. If he had wanted to go, my parents would have taken him. We could have all come home together."

Sammie thought, from your responses in the last few minutes, your parents are now on our interview list. It was intuition, but she had learned to act on it.

"Let me ask again. Do you have any speculative thoughts on why Dennis disappeared? Not facts, ideas."

Carmichael thought it through. "I think he went somewhere and ran into someone or some people who were truly evil and they killed him. For him to be buried in a field, I can't see any other reason. You, more than me, know how that is, the unspeakably evil people who appear normal in our society.

"I've had a part in the past in a drama which seem to celebrate people like that, and I was glad of the money, feeling a bit shivery about the script while people on the set were joking about it all. In meeting someone in your job, I am embarrassed even to recall that because the reality is far worse, I think."

She sighed. "We were innocent teenagers. Some bastard out there killed him for no reason. Seeing as you asked."

Sammie went through a few issues of timing, meetings with Dennis prior to the one in Crosby Street and her understanding of the relationship between the three boys. Carmichael was talkative, helpful in intent, but lacked any substantive detail.

When they finished, Sammie insisted on paying for her own breakfast. The hotel gave her a bill to match the fact it was a high-end establishment. She was glad she hadn't brought Moony or Chan with her.

Valerie Carmichael paid for the other breakfasts. Sammie took a last look at Valerie's coat as she left, as Carmichael was rounding up her team. If she won a thousand pounds on the lottery, would she have the nerve to blow it on a coat like that, she wondered.

Driving back to the headquarters, Sammie mused that she wasn't an Yvonne Kulis, but the interview had started out too perfectly to be true. At no point did Carmichael show the slightest sense of unease or nervousness. It only became a normal interview when the subject of the choral solo came up and Carmichael hesitated and thought about it.

Even when the pace slowed, her face gave nothing away. Sammie couldn't remember a first interview where, confronted by a police officer, a person didn't show some level of apprehension or anxiety. Carmichael was an actor. Sammie realised that, to some degree, Valerie had been acting a part, and if so, there was possibly another set of answers, with still more to be drawn from her. But that would need delicate handling.

She called Howard Mooney. Louis and Howard had been given some routine follow-ups by phone that morning.

"Howard, I want you and Louis to talk to Linnie. Between you three, I want every member of the choir that sang in Carlisle Cathedral the night before Dennis disappeared to be identified, tracked down and interviewed about their recollections of both the night itself and the people. Particularly, was Dennis Lewis there and how did they find the behaviour of the soloist, our friend Valerie?"

15 NICHOLS

The team gathered to compare notes and update the significant elements on the whiteboard. At the end of the process, they had more names and more photographs displayed. Several items were circled in red marker.

The re-interview of Valerie Carmichael was at the top of the list. Kent had added 'damsel in distress??' to her name and 'White Knight?' to Dennis.

Below that, Shannon Nichols name came up, with links to both Crosshill Farm and the venue for the concert where Nunc Dimmitis was performed. Was there a link to the crime? Similarly, the two friends, Barry Jordan and Charles 'Chas' Roswell, were labelled with 'needing help from Dennis? Push them'.

In addition, the routine interview lists had grown; choir members, Oliver Mettler, the choir director and Lyall Ingram, the trumpet soloist, cathedral staff at the time of the concert, the other visitors to Crosshill Farm and the Krestman parents.

Kent stared at the board. "We need to prioritize. Nichols: she is yours, Harriet. You are already scheduled for her later today. Sammie, Louis, you two do the Krest-man parents. Howard, you do Jordan and Roswell with Louis; work around the Krestman couple timing. Let's pick up again after that."

He was away, into DI Nolan's office within a minute, for an update on other investigations.

Louis caught Harriet looking out of the window. "You look perturbed, Harriet. Is something wrong with the plan? Have we missed something?"

Harriet looked back, now finding all three of her colleagues examining her.

"No, it's good. I'm fine with it." After a moment, she added. "I spent the morning with a man blatantly analytical about his predatory paedophilia, that's all. I found it a little disturbing. Give me an arrest of two drunks in a bar fight in Keswick any day."

In fact, Susan Carlson and Duncan Aster had come to mind again. She picked up her phone and called Reverend Nichols to confirm the timing before she set out.

Harriet had passed the church at Newton Arlosh on the Solway Plain before, but never stopped there. Its slit windows and high, crenellated tower reminded her of the other important role a church played in medieval times, as a fortress and refuge.

Reverend Nichols said, "I love this place and its people. I was so lucky with this appointment."

They were now walking Nichol's dog together. Harriet had arrived a little earlier than planned, with little to no traffic delay, just as the priest began a quick walk with her dog. On impulse, Harriet had suggested they do it together, to give it a longer run and talk on the way.

Nichols seemed to be a happy priest. Unmarried, thirty-seven, living in a neat little cottage with her dog, a sort of terrier crossbreed, the woman was overweight and plain-looking, with a florid complexion and eyes that sparkled with life. Harriet began with questions about Rathburn Williams and his wife.

"Of course, I remember Doreen and Phil Williams! I was happy when she moved to Blackpool after Phil died, to be part of a retirement community."

After questions on timings, Harriet raised one of the points that troubled her. "It seems a long way, from Carlisle to Birkby, just to provide pastoral service to the Williams couple. Why?"

Nichols looked at her. "I was a curate in St. Kentigern's, in Aspatria, not far away from Crosshill Farm, when Phil Williams was diagnosed. I met with the couple during the early phase of his illness, the denial and false hope stage. Do you know where St. Kentigern's is?"

Harriet smiled. "I'm also a Methodist lay preacher. I've participated in services at Cornerstone Methodist near there on occasion, so yes."

Shannon seemed to warm to her. "During that period, I transferred to the cathedral staff for a year, part of my experience and training. I asked to stay with pastoral care for the William's couple through to Phil's death and the funeral because I had bonded with them, and so I could work through a complete terminal care pastoral process alone."

Harriet responded, "I can see that, yes. Did the priest at St. Kentigern's accept that?"

"He agreed, with reservations. It wasn't the normal process. When clergy leave a church, the rule is you don't continue contact with the parishioners. It is a distraction and could cause problems for a new incumbent. But Phil wasn't going to attend church anymore, being homebound. It was accepted."

Harriet could see that Shannon Nichols was stepping carefully through the issues of church politics.

"Were there any other people regularly on the farm, or hanging around, do you recall?"

"No. That was the problem. When I saw in the news that the body of the boy was found there, it gave me a shock."

She paused. "My memory of Crosshill Farm was that it was a lonely place. I grew up in the farming life, so I know some farms are like that and others, frankly, are where people are constantly around, or in and out like yo-yos. With Phil bedridden, the land was not managed at all."

"He was bedridden about the time Dennis disappeared, in early June 2008, we understand?"

She nodded, recalling the time. "For quite some time before that; he died around the same time. I attended Phil's funeral. It was really the handover point for me, to move Doreen back to the priest at St. Kentigern's."

"Any recollection of talk of trespassers, teenagers on bikes larking around, or disgruntled neighbours; that sort of thing?"

The priest shook her head. "My focus was the Williams couple. I have no memory of that sort of talk. In that situation..."

She paused, thinking. Harriet said, "I know how that goes. I have had my share of homebound parishioners; but I had to ask."

Nichols nodded, understanding. "It was all about them. That was my focus."

Harriet moved to her main other question. "You were part of the organising committee for a concert held at the cathedral around the time Dennis disappeared, an inter-faith event. Can you tell me about that?"

Nichols seemed surprised. "Is that linked, somehow?"

Harriet waited a few moments, making it clear she wasn't there to answer Nichols' questions. "We are tracing the victim's movements, as best as we can. We don't know."

Nichols responded with, "It was a fundraiser for cancer support. The idea was that by making it interfaith, we would attract a broader audience than simply one denomination. And it was successful. We raised over six thousand pounds that night.

"Four denominations participated. Anglicans, Roman Catholics, and your church, Methodists, provided most of the singers. About fifteen percent came from local other choirs – evangelicals and gospel churches.

"It was quite a large choir. No robes or that sort of thing. White dress shirt or blouse, we said, and no ties for the men. We gave every singer a sash to wear during the performance and keep as a memento. But what do you want to know?"

"Take me through the day of the concert, say from noon onwards."

Shannon stopped while thinking about it, causing an anxious look from her dog. "I was busy at the cathedral with last minute items, particularly the tables for two displays by the Foundation. The choir met at six for a final rehearsal, their first in the venue. Earlier rehearsals were at your Central Hall. They were provided with a light tea at the cathedral prior to the performance."

That surprised Harriet. "The Methodist Central Hall was closed, right? But it was being used for events, rentals."

Nichols nodded. "We got to use it for free, of course. Oliver Mettler fixed that through contacts he had. He was the choir director chosen by the committee. We had three volunteers for that job. Dr. Mettler was chosen as the biggest name – and for his performance style, I suspect."

She was smirking, then added, "Sorry. I'm not big on grandiose choir directors waving arms around."

Harriet thought back to the church historian's comment, Eames. The choir director had accompanied Carmichael and a trumpeter.

Nichols continued, "He had access to the Methodist Hall, though. Given the choir size, that made it a lot easier for rehearsals, as it didn't interfere with other activities at the cathedral."

"How well attended was the concert?"

"Very well. Over three hundred came. It was a success."

"If Dennis had attended, unless someone he knew saw him, he could have been just a face in the crowd?"

Nichols nodded. "I suspect so, yes. A lot of tickets were sold in advance but there were cash sales at a desk near the door, too. During the concert, the lights were on the choir, but were dimmed in the seating area. That would have made it harder, too. Your best bet would be to check with singers and their families from his home area or church."

"We are doing that. One of those was a soloist, Valerie Krestman, Carmichael as she is now."

They had started walking again. "Yes! The Burgon piece. She sang it well. It was a talking point afterwards. Of course, she is famous now. But at one point, just as the piece started, I thought she might freeze with stagefright. But she didn't. She started and came through wonderfully."

"As it started? Was she looking at the audience then, do you recall?"

Nichols caught on. "And seen Dennis, perhaps? No. I think she had just looked at the trumpeter and then back at Oliver Mettler, for her entry. It was the look on her face."

"Of what?"

"Fear. I'm the same sometimes with my sermons. I'll go

into the pulpit and stop, needing to recall my starting point, my opening sentence. And you? If you are a Methodist preacher?"

Harriet nodded. "Yes, I have that experience, too. But most of my circuit chapels are small, more intimate. If they have a pulpit, I generally don't use it."

Nichols laughed. "There would be some consternation here if I didn't. Most of my congregation are older people now. Creatures of habit, used to the sermon from the pulpit."

Harriet pulled from her pocket a photo of Dennis. "A long time ago, I know. But think. Do you recall seeing him the day of the concert?"

They stopped again. Shannon took a long look. "No, but that means nothing. It's mostly a blur now. I wish I had. I wish he had been there, safe with us. But no."

"Did you talk about the Williams' situation with people at the cathedral about that time?"

Nichols gave Harriet a look which said she understood the question, the possibility of a link to the crime.

"I talked with Reverend Clarke at St. Kentigern's regularly about my support for them. Other than that, no-one, I think." She paused, rethinking. "I am wrong about that. I mentioned it at a concert committee meeting. I was late and said I had been delayed in Birkby, on a farm turning into a wilderness as the farmer was terminally ill. I don't know why I explained myself, really. I suppose I was just trying to show my tardiness had a good reason behind it. Other than that, I don't recall."

Harriett deliberately took Nichols back to the concert performance for a while before asking who the other committee members were. She had been watching the dog as they walked. It reached a spot by a wall and stopped, looking at Nichols.

The priest called, "Time to turn round, Bel; we have work to do."

In talking to the dog, she was also giving Calder the sense that the return journey limited the time available for her questions. Harriet moved on from the topics of Crosshill Farm and the concert to the third issue, Compline.

"What about Compline. Does that have any meaning for you, in the context of events around then?"

"As a text or as a service?"

"In any sense?"

Nichols paused. "Not as a service. No. I sometimes include it in my daily devotions, then and now."

She looked at the police officer, who suddenly seemed to be lost in thought. "You understand?"

Harriet had been thinking of Compline as an event, a gathering, a service. Nichols had reminded her that it was also an individual process of prayer, undertaken alone. The daily office: the series of prayers that, independent of any services, a priest or person of faith may choose to perform each day.

Harriet nodded. "Thank you. Yes, I understand. Do you use the Anglo-Catholic breviary for that?"

Nichols nodded. "For my personal devotions, yes, on occasion. My church here is more traditional than modern. We have the Eucharist service on Sunday, and a Matins on Wednesday morning. It is busy with parishioner meetings of one sort or another in the week and I have a fair amount of pastoral care to occupy me."

"But Compline didn't come up in the context of the concert, or its preparations?"

Nichols looked mystified. "No. Not at all. There was no reason for it to do so."

As they neared the cottage, walking in silence for a few moments, Harriet suddenly asked, "How did you, or how do you get on with Dr. Mettler and the other committee members? Were they all men?"

It was intuitive.

"Mettler, I don't. I have no contact with him. I mean, I only worked with him for the concert. He handled the choir and the music. I was involved in the logistics and the preparations. Two other committee members were men, the fifth member was a woman, another priest, someone you might know. Reverend Shelagh Amos."

Harriet had been watching Bel's responses to her owner during the last two questions. Nichols had sounded uneasy suddenly, apologetic, and Bel had picked up on it.

The name of the other priest surprised Harriet. "Shelagh Amos, the police chaplain? I know her quite well. I get drawn into pastoral activities by her from time to time."

Nichols chuckled. "Shelagh is always good at roping people into doing things. You should talk to her perhaps."

Harriet smiled at her. "I will. Thank you for your time. You have been very helpful."

It's all in the small stuff, thought Harriet, as she headed to her car. The change in the tone of voice. Nichols had turned her head away from Harriet as she answered the question about Mettler rather than look at her, as in her responses to the previous questions.

Above all, it was Bel, the dog. She was sensitive to her owner, to her mood changes, like therapy animals. She had suddenly looked back, her posture changing as she returned to her. Nichols held her hand out and the dog licked it.

Perhaps the apparently jolly priest was not so happy with the subject of the organising committee members. Harriett needed to meet with Shelagh Amos and call in some long overdue favours.

16 CHAPLAIN

After her visit to Solway, Harriet headed back to Penrith, not to the Cumbria Police headquarters but to a red sandstone Anglican church in the centre, St. Andrew's; to its eponymous coffee shop and her unconcealed effort to bribe and corrupt a colleague of sorts.

The Reverend Shelagh Amos, now happily demoted to the role of Associate Rector at St. Andrew's after twenty years in her own parishes, was also the part-time Chaplain of the Cumbria Constabulary. Harriet had called her from her car before setting off, watching Shannon Nichols and Bel enter their home.

This was a role reversal. Over the years, Amos had 'dropped in' or fixed appointments with Harriet to draw the Keswick sergeant and preacher into one pastoral issue or another. They had become friends, two people with a similar mission in life based on the importance of their respective faiths and a common work environment, the specialized world of the Cumbria Police.

Now Harriet was going to pick her brains.

"I heard. You are in Penrith on the Lewis case. Baron Kent kidnapped you, racing away from Maryport with you thrown over the back of his white charger. I wish I had seen that."

Reverend Amos smiled, finishing a piece of the scone, and then sipping at the tea paid for by the mistreated Keswick officer. "How can I help?"

Harriet looked at her. "Don't tempt me on that one. June Robinson is spitting bullets. Use the wand of power in the DCC's office and send me home, Lady Shelagh."

Reverend Amos visited most of the police stations across Cumbria at some time or other, but worked closely with the Deputy Chief Constable.

"But failing that, how do you rate Shannon Nichols, in Solway? I just met her, as part of the investigation."

Amos knew better than to ask why.

"She's good, settled, and a sound priest. I say settled because I suspect she has no desire to move up the hierarchy in the diocese. At some point, attitudes like that always get you promoted; it's sod's law."

"Well, we can't all be voracious climbers like you, can we? Heading for bishop next, you. I can see it."

The laughter made others in the cafe stare at their table.

Harriet moved on. "She did a stint in Carlisle. That went well, she said. Been in Solway ever since. She was involved in organising a successful fundraising concert there around the time of Dennis's disappearance. As were you."

Amos looked surprised. "Yes, I was. Not as heavily involved as Shannon. She did a lot of the organisational work. I just pulled people in, to volunteer support and give money. You know me."

"I do, for my sins. I asked her about the organising committee, and she seemed evasive. I expect better of you. Tell me about them, please?"

She had turned serious; her face showed that, and Amos saw it.

"Let me recall. Oliver Mettler, as the music director. Raymond Sugden, an accountant from the MacMillan charity. Thomas Wiley, whose family attends the cathedral, monied and connected; his daughter died of cancer. Shannon and I, representing the diocese. That was the committee."

She waited for the next question.

"How did it function?"

Amos thought for a moment. "The usual way. About four or five meetings before the event, over a four-month period. The music director was chosen at the first meeting, so Mettler joined us at meeting two, the others all from the beginning."

Her face showed her query; what link did this have to the Lewis investigation? "Did Dennis go missing in Carlisle, not the coast, then? Shouldn't ask, should I?"

"No, you shouldn't. You know better. We don't know. We are just following up on everything, that's all."

Harriet continued, "It all sounded good with Shannon until I mentioned Oliver Mettler, the choir director. I sensed an evasiveness around that. I asked if they kept in touch. She was emphatic in saying they didn't."

Amos gave her a sharper look. "So, it is not about Shannon." She paused. "Mettler is a first-rate musician and works the society scene well. He is 'well-connected', as they say. Lands a lot of event contracts, so is in demand besides his work at the Cross of the Redeemer. It's a rich evangelical church in Bradford, and I suspect they pay him well. Their choir is excellent. But he is never short of other work, either."

She paused, choosing her words.

"He isn't married, I gather, and likes to turn on his

charms. But I don't think there is anything in that; scurrilous, I mean. I doubt the Cross of the Redeemer would put up with a playboy character; they are rather conservative. I only met him at a few social functions – and attended a couple of his concerts, besides the one you mentioned."

"Do you recall the Burgon piece, the Nunc dimittis?"

"Yes, the young soloist. Valerie Carmichael now; I forget what her surname was then. I've met her once since then, more recently. She is more assured these days. She was very nervous back then."

"How about the trumpeter? A Lyall Ingram?"

"Lyall is in Leeds now, with the Symphony Orchestra. Yes, he played, volunteered, I should say."

"And?"

"He's right of Attila the Hun, a very conservative Anglo-Catholic. He doesn't like women priests and would probably beat me to death with his trumpet case if your ludicrous idea of me becoming bishop was ever proposed."

"You don't like him?"

"I love everybody, Harriet. You know that. He is useful for pushing air through a brass tube."

She looked at Calder. "Do I get my thirty pieces of silver now?"

"What you gave me was worth every penny of the cup of tea and scone I bought for you; every last penny."

Amos took a deep breath. "I hope that Dennis Lewis's death isn't tied to that concert in some way. No, I am not asking. It was a good concert for a good cause."

Harriet said nothing for a moment, thinking of the Burgon work and the words found at the burial site. In some way, it was, she felt.

She said, "Well, thanks, Shelagh. I must go. Baron Kent is a slave driver, and you won't use your magic wand to free me."

Amos smiled. "Hard work is good for you, it's a Christian principle. That's what the mine owners used to tell the women and kids when they sent them into the mines with the pit ponies."

Harriet stood. "No, they didn't. They were swanning off somewhere; it was their lackeys that did that. It's why we Methodists broke away from you lot, to give people in the pit some education, so they could overthrow the owners. And the bishops who kissed their aristocratic backsides."

Amos stood, chuckling. "It's good to see you, as usual. You were visiting Vic Askew, I know. You heard he died in the night?"

Harriet nodded. "Laurel called me early this morning. He talked to her about it, alone, she said. We all knew anyway. The driver who ran over the mother and daughter asked him if he would face prison time. Vic told him that, if it was up to him, he'd be there for a very long time. The man cut his own throat at the prospect. Vic was open about it at the end. A better death."

Amos said seriously, "You will be at the Lewis funeral, and probably speaking, I hear. I will be there with the DCC and others. Cumbria Police will show their support."

She reached out and took Harriet's right hand in both of hers. "There is something right about you being on this investigation, Harriet. I feel it. Perhaps you haven't yet. But joking aside about John, I'm sure you were meant to be on this one. You will join his family in my prayers."

Harriet returned to headquarters and talked with Sammie. They pulled John Kent from another meeting and briefed him, and he called the team together.

He summarised the situation. "We have no new facts, but impressions that are starting to make some sense of what we have. The problem is, we may be speculating too much.

"Sammie gets the impression that Valerie Carmichael was concealing something about the discussions she had with Dennis the day before his disappearance. Harriet found out that the organising committee at the concert would know of the wild state of Crosshill Farm at the time from Shannon Nichols, and she felt Nichols was also holding back on something."

He focused on Howard and Louis. "Your report says that nothing came out of the interviews with one of his two close friends. Barry Jordan?"

Howard shook his head. "We think he was being straight with us. He hadn't a clue where Dennis went after school, or why. We will see the other, Roswell, this evening, at home."

Kent turned to Linnie. "We will pull in a couple of other data people. Work as a team. Focus on any CCTV records for Carlisle for the day of concert, if you can find any, looking for any signs of Dennis. Also, I want full background checks on the list of people involved in the concert, the committee, the choir members, helpers on the day. Build the picture. I want to know if anyone involved has even a whisper of a relevant criminal background, or there was any sighting of Dennis in Carlisle."

He stared at the window for a moment, the team waiting on his instructions.

"Why was Valerie so frightened at the concert? Several people said that. Was it stagefright, or what? It may go nowhere, but Harriet and Sammie, you interview the choir director and this trumpeter. Howard and Louis, you interview Roswell tonight and the Krestman parents tomorrow, see if they have anything useful."

He looked at Harriet. "You may get a second bite at

Shannon Nichols."

He stood, ready to move on, then sat down again, remembering something. "I talked with Superintendent Chiswell and Dr. Meadows. There seems little more that we can usefully achieve forensically by holding up the release of the body. I always vacillate on letting go of a body early, in case of new findings. Given the state of decomposition and that we have retained samples, we have decided to release it, pending the coroner's interim ruling on the cause of death. The family has waited a long time. I don't think it is right to delay the burial."

He surveyed the team's faces for reactions. Sammie seemed doubtful, but Harriet nodded. He focused on her. "Dennis's parents have asked you to speak at the funeral, I recall?"

Harriet responded, "Bernice did, yes. I can't really say no, although I am not sure what I can say yet."

She looked at Sammie. "I'll touch base with her myself after they are formally told they can bury Dennis, I think. When you have the go-ahead, Sammie should inform them."

Kent nodded his silent agreement and turned to go.

Mooney said, "Boss?"

Not one to keep his head below the parapet, he asked, "That means we are doing background checks on two members of the clergy, one of whom is our own police chaplain. Is that right?"

As he walked away, Kent said, "That's right, Howard. Glad to hear you were listening."

17 CONFERENCE

Susan's big moment came on the afternoon of day two of the conference in York. She was dreading it, in one sense, and happy for it to be over with, so she could enjoy the rest of the meeting. She felt she could relax a little more afterwards.

She was staying at the conference hotel, a Radisson, on the bank of the River Ouse in the centre of the city. Her little rental car was tucked away in its car park. From her room, she could see the towers of York Minster a short distance away, reminding her of her first visit with Harriet when she declined the offer to go there.

Cathedrals and churches were part of her 'baggage', she knew. The rooms and basements that AA groups met in were fine, but worship spaces and altars still made her feel uneasy.

The conference program had six breakout sessions that afternoon, three before the break, three after. The session inherited from Dr. Consuela Ramiro listed only two speakers. Susan M. Carlson, B.Sc., CCAC Certified Counsellor, seemed more pedestrian than Dr. Bruce J. Kempton-

Smith, with his long string of qualifications. It reminded her she still had three more modules to complete for her master's degree.

The session title was, 'Harm reduction or twelve-step abstinence in addiction recovery? Conflict and coherence; the views of two experienced practitioners'.

By the time Susan joined the moderator and her co-speaker on the platform, she appreciated the courtesy drape in front of the table. Not to hide her legs, but to stop them seeing her knees shaking a little. The breakout session had attracted perhaps a hundred or more participants.

Susan spoke first. She knew her subject and had accumulated considerable experience, however she always suffered from nervous tension beforehand. She delivered it with a minute left in the agenda timing, she saw, as she finished.

The moderator thanked her and pointed out that he would take questions after both presentations, then he invited Dr. Kempton-Smith to speak.

His private clinic was on the Isle of Wight, Susan had read in the programme summary. It offered 'a modern, medically-sound approach to alcohol management'. That was nirvana for a large subset of addicts; to become a social drinker, free of drugs, rather than find after the second beer they were calling their dealer, desperate for a fix.

The man began with a full-frontal attack on her speech, without notes, inferring his co-panelist represented a twelve-step mantra devised by Americans, lacking modern medical science and reliant on a thinly disguised religious foundation. He gave no elements of coherence, nor was it simply conflict, as the session title implied. He declared outright war.

Susan sat through the tirade straight-faced, burying the anger and embarrassment. She resisted a sudden urge to throw the water jug in front of her over the man. Her sponsor's advice to regard everyone as a friend certainly did not extend to her co-speaker.

Less than two minutes into the attack, the moderator muted the speaker microphone and said pleasantly, "Dr. Kempton-Smith, I would appreciate it if you would not belittle twelve-step recovery programs. This is a qualified audience. We are aware of the tenets of spiritual growth in recovery, as presented by Ms. Carlson."

He turned his gaze from the podium to the audience.

"Perhaps you could focus more on your own approach. Thank you."

The light came on the podium microphone again, as several heads in the seats nodded in agreement.

It was only a little easier then, listening to him speak. Susan found him somewhat light in detail about his psychotherapeutic program. The 'necessarily anonymous quotes' from its clients gave the impression that it worked best if you had a great deal of money and enjoyed the fresh air of Cowes in the summer months.

He finished exactly on time because his spiel was hacked off by the moderator's control of the microphone, who gave him a glare accompanied by the least sincere 'thank you' Susan had heard. More pleasantly he said, "I will now open the floor to questions."

Questions directed to Susan focused mainly on handling clients who failed to respond to twelve-step approaches. One questioner asked Kempton-Smith about his program costs, which were answered with "we work to accommodate the realities for all our clients. It is a sliding scale."

Two questions later, the moderator looked at the clock.

"I'm sorry to limit the questions, but I'm doing so now to give the two panelists a final word each, of around one minute. Then there will be the break. Dr. Kempton-Smith first."

Kempton-Smith pushed the button on his microphone. "Dealing with alcohol and other substance dependence is not simply the abstinence mantra held by AA members in old church halls or clinics employing similar methods. Modern psychology helps the patient learn about themself, to develop the skills to manage situations involving alcohol and yet avoid other addictive substances. The successful graduates of our program do not shy away from normal social situations. They can taste the wine at dinner and still reject the use of other substances."

The moderator killed his microphone and said, "And the final word, to Miss Carlson."

Susan pressed her microphone button. "There is no unique way of recovery from the disease of alcoholism or any other addiction. Our approach is not a program, it is a sharing experience, a journey of spiritual growth. It goes back to the very opening phrases of our core recovery text written decades ago. 'We of Alcoholics Anonymous are more than one hundred men and women who have recovered from a seemingly hopeless state of mind and body'. Well, that number is now many millions. For me, my clients and all those others, stopping the use of alcohol was prerequisite to saving our lives and making us more whole than we ever anticipated we could be. Thank you."

She switched the microphone light off.

The moderator said, "Thank you both. Let's give them a round of applause, in appreciation of a stimulating session. Then refreshments will be available in the usual place."

He started the applause and stood.

As the session broke up, a large woman carrying the

conference folder came up to the speaker table from the audience. She sounded Scottish to Susan.

"Thank you for your talk," she said quite loudly. "You did well. When you go home, tell Consuela that Beryl said hello. And that Bruce is still a nasty sod; a rich one, but still nasty. And yet again, he has given us no real insight."

She said it loudly enough for Kempton-Smith to look across from the person who had approached him with a question. His eyes showed his annoyance as Beryl smiled at him, daring a response.

Susan said, "I will say I have met you, Beryl, er–." She was looking at the larger text of the first name on the badge on the woman's lapel, trying to focus on the smaller text of the surname.

The moderator said, "Professor Beryl Hepplethwaite, formerly at Durham University, now in Tyne & Wear, head of the county's addiction services. Hello Beryl, nice to see you here again."

She acknowledged him and whispered to Susan, "We'll talk later. I have to go, decide what to say."

As she walked away, Susan looked at the moderator. He smiled. "Our plenary speaker, tomorrow morning."

Susan recalled the program. Yes, it was a Professor B. Hepplethwaite, with a string of qualifications and awards after her name.

He looked at the partly filled water jug and whispered, "I'm glad you resisted the temptation."

Susan felt totally drained.

Tomorrow evening, she was going to speak at 'one of those old church halls', as Kempton-Smith had referred to them. Sarah Loughry, an attendee who lived locally and yet another friend of Consuela's, had asked her to speak at her own AA group meeting in central York. That, at least, would be more familiar and safer ground. She thought it might be somewhat more healing and therapeutic than the session just completed. If Beryl and Bruce got together tomorrow morning, it might turn into a World Wrestling Federation event.

18 BRADFORD

In the team area the following morning, Linnie gave Sammie and Harriet an update on her findings about the Cross of the Redeemer before they set out for Bradford.

"It's a stand-alone evangelical church, with links to a US Foundation called Cross of the Redeemer Ministries Org. Each church operates independently, and most locations are in the USA. The Bradford and Southampton churches are their only ones in the UK."

She flipped the screen on her tablet. "The Bradford church seems to have quite a few staff, including Oliver Mettler. The CEO there is a priest, a Reverend Charles Lambert; he is from London, went to Oxford University then did his divinity degree in California. The founder in the US, a Maylon Jerry, had an annual income of just under two million dollars, as reported two years ago. He is well below the 'top fifty' in the rankings of wealthy evangelists, the poor man."

Sammie interrupted. "Don't start me off. Stick to the Bradford lot." Her fleeting thought was that Maylon Jerry would have no trouble buying a Canada Goose coat like the one Carmichael wore.

Harriet saw Sammie's expression, one she thought of as her 'I'm a lapsed Catholic' look.

Linnie continued, "Well, Oliver Mettler is or was a member of the Church of England, apparently, before he started at Church of the Redeemer. He studied at the Royal Conservatory, and he is a proud Old Blundellian."

Sammie smiled. "Are you trying to push my buttons, or what?"

Linnie gave her a smirk. "Me? No. He went to a public school in the west country, that's all. Then he did a period as an organ scholar and became a choirmaster at another public school. His career blossomed from there. He does contracts with festivals as well as work for the Bradford church."

She stopped. "And... his church is noted to be one of the top places for brassrubbers in the North of England. How about that?"

Howard squinted, thinking. "Do they still do that sort of thing? I thought nowadays it's easier to take a photo of the gravestone with your phone and use an app to make it look like a rubbing."

Sammie shook her head and looked at Harriet. "Let's get out of here."

The Cross of the Redeemer had been designed by a Scandinavian, an apparently simple rectangular church with a sloping roof from one high apex corner to the other three. The tricky bit had been the incorporation into one side of the slightly taller Grade 2 sixteenth century church tower.

As they approached it and Sammie looked for a parking spot, Harriet thought that the combination of old and new had been well done. It must have cost a mint.

Sammie said, "I was reading up. They wanted the location and had to preserve the tower and cemetery, probably for the brassrubbers that Linnie went on about."

It had a small graveyard, with ancient headstones. Inside the tower, according to a sign outside, were monumental brasses for enthusiasts to coo over. It pointed out that the church had commissioned copies of some popular brasses for that purpose, and only allowed rubbings of these, to protect the originals.

As they left the vehicle, Harriet saw some people exit from the tower, tourists carrying books and scrolls. The exit route for brass rubbers probably led through a gift shop, she concluded.

They had called ahead as they left Penrith. Harriet and Sammie kept friendly expressions on their faces as they walked towards the door.

"Smile. We are after information, not the prospect of being shown the door," Sammie said.

Harriet responded, "It's a church, so everyone is welcome."

A church volunteer showed them to Mettler's office, a little in awe or discomfort, knowing that the women were from the Cumbria Police. The furnishings there were modern and sleek, fit for a business executive.

Oliver Mettler was older than in his photos, Sammie saw. More lined. He was in his mid-forties, dark-haired still, clean-shaven, medium-height and fit. He was dressed in dark pants, a pale blue shirt, and an expensive smokey grey cardigan that Sammie immediately coveted. She was looking for something in exactly that colour.

He offered them seats at the nearby table as he stood, moving there himself. With the office door closed, Sammie announced their role as part of the team investigating the death of Dennis Lewis and began the questions.

Mettler nodded. "I saw the news. A tragedy, indeed. But how can I help?"

"Did you know, or ever meet, Dennis Lewis?"

"No, not that I am aware of; why?"

"We are just pursuing a line of enquiry. Similarly, did you know or meet a Valerie Krestman?"

Mettler smiled. "Of course. She is famous now, the actor. I met her briefly during a choral concert at Carlisle Cathedral. She had a beautiful voice and sang a solo during the concert. The combined choir was quite good overall. The basses sounded a bit off at times on the night, but I remember little else."

Sammie pulled out the photo of Dennis taken shortly before he disappeared. "Dennis Lewis and Valerie Carmichael were friends. We think that he may have gone to Carlisle to attend the concert on the day he disappeared. Take your time. Think back. Did you ever see this boy there?"

Mettler took in the image for a second or two. "No, I didn't. My focus was the choir. I have no memory of the audience at all."

Sammie moved on. "But you remember Shannon Nichols and other members of the committee, perhaps? And the trumpeter from the Burgon piece? Lyall Ingram."

"Reverend Nichols, yes, vaguely, from the committee meetings. I have worked with Lyall before that concert and after, but I know him only in a professional context. Of the others, no, unless you remind me – other than Thomas Wiley. He was one of the major sponsors, so I do recall him."

"Before the concert, you must have rehearsed, given that the choir was constituted for the purpose of the fundraiser. How many times, and where?"

His face changed, showing irritation, and his brow furrowed. "Why ever would you want to know that? I can't see the relevance."

Sammie responded evenly, "You don't have to, sir. You just need to answer the question, as best as you can."

He gave her a stare. "Rehearsals were at the Methodist Central Hall, nearby. I used it on several occasions for that purpose over the years. I lived in Alston then, before I was appointed here."

The market town of Alston is about thirty miles inland from Carlisle.

"We had two full choir rehearsals, I recall, and a session for the soloist pieces. No, I stand corrected. Two rehearsals for the Burgon work, but one for the tenor solo, the Handel 'Comfort Ye'."

"Why two for the Burgon work? With Valerie and the trumpeter, I take it?"

"Obviously because one wasn't enough. It interplays three voices, the organ, a solo treble or a soprano, and a trumpet. The timing and phrasing are trickier, and Valerie was inexperienced. I don't know where you are going with this."

Sammie switched topics. "Do you recall Crosshill Farm being mentioned by anyone during the preparations for the concert?"

He sighed, "A farm? No." He reached across to a folder lying on the table, moving it nearer to him, straightening it in line with the table edge.

Harriet had said nothing so far, and apart from watching his responses, she looked around the room and at his desk.

Suddenly she asked him, "Are you an officer of this church?"

He sat back, surprised. "I'm its music director, yes. That

is a staff post."

"Right. Are you ordained or lay? Are your church officers required to be ordained?"

His voice changed. "And what does that have to do with this investigation, may I ask? No. The music director here is a lay position. I have not taken any ordination vows, nor do I need to for my work."

Harriet smiled. "I just wondered, looking around as I came in. I also hold a lay position, in the Methodist church. What are the expectations around daily worship for your position?"

Sammie gave her a slight frown. There was something in Harriet's question other than general interest, but she wasn't quite sure what.

He pinched his lips, pausing before he gave a measured response. "I'm not having a discussion of the worship practices of this church with you. It's not relevant in any way to your investigation, is it?"

Harriet pressed on. "How would you describe your own religious affiliation?"

They could both tell he was irritated now.

Harriet added, "And it is relevant. Any question by a police officer is to be taken as relevant."

He said evenly, "More conservative than less, which fits this church well. I suppose I am more traditional again, in a sense, in terms of choral music. I'll put it this way; I am not drawn to some of the 'messy church' and related worship processes that seem increasingly popular these days. Professionally, I will work with any choir or faith, but I am entitled to my own religious views, surely?"

Harriet nodded vigorously, as if in agreement. "Of course. But you observe the Daily Office, I see. That's your breviary on the desk there. It looks well used."

Sammie hadn't spotted the book. So that was where

Harriet was heading; to the word 'Compline'.

"It is. I do. As best as I can."

"Do you regularly observe Compline?"

He now looked more angry than irritated. "A Methodist? Compline wouldn't be on your radar. I pray according to the prescribed prayers when I can. I am a busy man, not a monk in cloisters."

He glared at Harriet and turned to face Sammie. "Are there more questions? Pertinent questions, I mean."

Sammie asked, "What did you do when the concert finished? The one at Carlisle Cathedral."

He looked mystified. "Precisely, I don't recall. Thanked the choir, as I always do, chatted a little with people afterwards, then drove home. I was tired."

She beamed at him. "No more specific questions, Dr. Mettler. Does anything come to mind prompted by our chat? Anything at all you would like to tell us?"

He didn't pause. "No. Nothing. I can't even see how the questions you asked tie into your investigation. You've driven a long way for little purpose, it seems."

The police officers stood. Sammie said, "Thank you for your time. We may be in touch again."

In the car, before setting off, Sammie said simply, "And? Pushing his faith button?"

Harriett responded, "He uses the breviary. Compline could well be a daily consideration for him. How that fits, I don't know. I noticed he was increasingly polite and formal, tiring of the questions, but holding his temper until I mentioned Compline. I wonder what would happen if we pushed him hard?"

Sammie responded, "I was watching his eyes closely when he claimed he had never heard of Crosshill Farm. He started shuffling that file around. I am sure he was lying. If he had said 'only from the news' or something, I could buy it. But he deliberately lied. Mettler said we came a long way for nothing. His lying about the farm was worth it. We'll be talking to him again if I have my way, and in an interview room."

Harriet gave her a long look, then said, "Yes, boss."

As Sammie started the car, she said, "Now don't you start doing a Howard Mooney imitation. You know it should be me saying that to you!"

~~

That evening, in York, at the end of day three of her conference, Susan Carlson went off with Consuela's friend, Sarah. They walked to the location of the Alcoholics Anonymous meeting at a church off Coppergate, in the city centre. A little over half a mile away, after a day sitting in conference sessions, they decided the walk would be good. Or Sarah didn't want to experiment with a Canadian driver in the streets of York.

Sarah said, "There are meetings of recovery groups here most weekday evenings. Is it alright afterwards if I head straight home? Will you walk back, or do you want me to fix you with a ride with someone from the meeting?"

"That's not a problem. I'll walk back, I know the way now."

The meeting was not large, but it had its own ritual, as did every AA meeting, one devised by its members. There were some core common elements, but a visiting speaker had to fit into the pattern; in this case, not a podium to stand behind, but to take 'the speaker's chair' at a small table. The chair doubled as the meeting leader's position, vacated as the speaker was invited to share their story of alcoholism and recovery with the attendees.

In the silence as she sat, she looked at the room and began with, "Hello, I am Susan, from Ontario in Canada, and I am an alcoholic."

Once she qualified to be there, the rest of her story followed easily. Susan had been the guest speaker at AA meetings many times. Twenty-five minutes later, near the end, she said, "I always try to close with something for the moment, for the newcomer, as they leave."

She checked the clock; it was ten minutes to eight.

"It will soon be eight o'clock and in four hours it will be the start of a new day, a new twenty-four hours. Some of us will pass bars and pubs and restaurants on the way home. We will see the stag and hen parties wandering around and later, the people lining up to get into clubs. Some people will be merry and others already half-cut. By the early hours, a few will be legless, sitting in the street.

"But most of them aren't like you and me. They will have hangovers in the morning and put it behind them. I can't do that. You need to accept, if you are an alcoholic like me, that you can't either. We collapse on the street or elsewhere and don't get back up that easily. Some of us won't get up at all.

"We can't risk taking that first drink, but we can help each other. If you came on your own and it is going to be hard for you walking past those places, think about it.

"If you need help, ask; but remember commonsense, too. Choose wisely. And if someone asks for help, hold out the hand of friendship. Together we can get through these hours to that new day and with God's grace, start another twenty-four hours of sobriety.

"Sarah, thanks again for asking me to speak tonight."

Susan never broke away from people wanting to talk to her after speaking at a meeting. You never knew when the litany of appreciative comments for speaking was broken by the hesitant, 'What did you mean by –' or, 'I think, from what you said, I'm like you'. It is a chance to help someone, even if only to point them to another AA member locally.

Which is how, fifteen minutes later, she was walking down Coppergate with eighteen-year-old Janine Kasongo, a young black woman sporting giant earrings, a Justin Beiber jacket that had seen better days, and a bruise on her cheek.

The bruise was suspicious, Susan thought. They had enough of those sights at Haydn House. But alcoholics into the drink get bruises all the time. The floor has a habit of hitting them, or a door moving just as you walk through it.

Janine was three days sober and terrified of the thought of rehab or treatment centres. This had been her third AA meeting, and the first one she attended unaccompanied. The young woman had waited outside after the meeting broke up, smoking, until Susan was about to leave. As she started the walk back to the hotel, Janine came up to her.

"What you said was fantastic. I hope I can be like you one day."

Susan had taken in the tall, almost gangly, young woman, assessing her condition in one glance, "You can. How long?"

Janine responded, "Three days, but the first one was, you know, groggy."

"Where are you going now?"

"Home. I need to catch a bus at Clifford Street. To walk past the pubs that you talked about."

She made it a joke. Seeing through it, Susan said, "I'm walking that way, so let's talk as far as your bus stop. Did you talk to anyone else at the meeting?"

"No, I'll do it next time. I'm new."

"Did you pick up any of the literature?"

"Yes, a couple of the pamphlets."

"There's a number on the back. And another AA meeting there tomorrow night. Not the same group, but some of the same people will attend. The woman I was talking to, the big one with blonde hair, is called Sarah. If she is there tomorrow night, you approach her before the meeting. Will you do that?"

"If I can."

"Make sure you talk to someone. It's important to make the contacts to help you."

Janine suddenly said, "It's funny, I was thinking about passing the pubs as you finished talking, wondering. God, I hope one day I can be so sure of my sobriety as you sound."

Susan responded, "I didn't say that. I said, if I work at my programme, I know I can make it through another day. The fact that I have no desire to drink is wonderful, but it can change for any alcoholic in a heartbeat. I need to be as ready for that as you need to be."

They had reached the junction of Coppergate and the wider road, Clifford Street. In the near distance, across the Ouse, she saw her hotel. There was a bus stop about twenty yards away, on the other side of the road.

"Is that your stop?"

A car drove past them and came to a halt a few yards in front of the women. Janine said, "Oh, shit."

The man who got out stood between his open door and the car body. "Janine, where did you go? I told you I'd pick you up after your meeting."

Janine stood there, cowering visibly. "I can't do it, Dev. I just can't. I can't be around you and stay clean and sober. I need to come to meetings on my own and stay clear of the pub."

Dev's eyes flashed as he looked at Susan. "Who's this?"

Janine said, "Someone. We are walking. I'll get the bus home."

He glared at Susan. "Well, 'someone', whatever your name, time for you to go. Janine, get in the bloody car."

"No!"

He stepped back, slamming the driver's door shut and started to move around the front, towards them. Not as tall as Janine, he was a stocky, muscular man.

Susan said, "I think you'd better go. I will make sure Janine gets home." She thought, I'll pay for a taxi or Uber, if I need to.

"I told you to bugger off!"

As Dev moved past her, his focus was on Janine. Susan pulled her keys from her pocket and detached the body of the panic alarm from the chain. It was the first time she had used it.

She jumped with the shriek of the loud, high-pitched tone so close to her, wincing. All three of them were startled. Dev looked at Susan, swore, and punched her hard in the face.

Susan had a moment of, 'that wasn't meant to happen', before her head, hip and right hand hit the flagstones. In the next few minutes, she was never unconscious. She was disorientated and in shock, the pain growing, but aware of people around her, helping. Janine was screaming and sobbing. After that, there were police officers and an ambulance.

At one point, a bystander asked if the woman on the ground had drunk too much. Janine started screaming again, now at the bystander, and a police officer talked to her. It was in the ambulance that Susan realised she could only see out of one eye.

19 HOSPITAL

They had covered the swollen eye with a pad and bandage to stop its normal movement. Somehow, it looked the worse aspect, more ominous than the messy scrape on the other side of her forehead.

Over the years, Harriet Calder had attended her fair share of injuries, from domestics to head-on car crashes. She knew that the initial concern would be about infection and damage to the eye. Once the swelling decreased, the doctors could check on Susan's vision.

She arrived at York Hospital at one in the morning. Susan was in a cubicle in the Emergency ward, her area curtained off. It had taken Harriet two-and-a-half hours to get there once she received Susan's call.

"How do you feel?"

"Sleepy. They gave me something to make me relax. I mustn't move my head suddenly and they will keep me here tonight. They are still checking for concussion. If they have room, they will move me to a ward. But there is no sign of a bed yet."

"I know. They will check you again before discharging

you tomorrow."

Susan sighed. "I am so bloody angry. I'm not doing very well with the serenity bit."

"I'm not surprised."

"How do I look?"

"Like other beaten-up women. And the bruising will spread. Before you say it, I know you don't want anyone to see you looking like this."

She reached out and took her friend's hand and gave it a squeeze.

Susan contained her tears, but her voice reflected her bitterness. "And I can't fly home, the doctor says. Not until the swelling reduces and I can see properly. He says that my travel insurance will tell me when I can fly."

"It sounds like it was a haymaker of a punch. The man is in custody, by the way. The young woman you were with told the police. They arrested him near Derwenthorpe. He claims you frightened him with your panic alarm, so he retaliated. That won't wash in court."

Susan grimaced. "I wish it had been a pepper spray, not an alarm. Bloody laws, this place is like Canada. You can't carry anything to defend yourself."

Harriet smiled. "If it had been the spray, he would probably be in here and you'd be answering questions for the police. Janine is still sitting out in the waiting area. She won't leave."

Susan responded. "She came in for a while, in more tears than me. She's only three days sober. I told her to stay, but I needed to rest. At least she's safe at the hospital overnight. I called someone a little while ago, the woman who asked me to speak last night, Sarah. She's coming to collect her, sort her out."

"Your assailant is her boyfriend?"

"Usual story, she gives up drugs and booze. He doesn't

want to, but he won't let her change her routine. As if she will stay clean with a Pepsi in a pub while he and their friends are chugging it back and using."

Harriet said, "Well, he won't be drinking beer now. I talked with people here. Devon Adebisi already has a suspended sentence for a fight in a pub. He will be held pending a bail hearing, at least."

Susan said, "I'll miss the last day of the conference. And Haydn House will have to fill in for me next week." She looked glum again. "A mess, like I said."

Harriet gave her hand another squeeze. "Let go and let God. Remember?"

Susan nodded. "I'm trying. I keep in mind that if he had got Janine into the car, she could be dead by now. At least she has another day of recovery."

She sighed. "The car needs to be returned to the rental people, somehow. I can't drive, and I don't want to pay for another week's rental, not to mention the hotel parking fees I'll get once the conference finishes."

"Now I can fix that. Give me the keys. I'll make sure it's cleared out of any bits you left in it and sort things out with Hertz. They will collect it from the hotel and close the contract. Police officers do that sort of thing a lot and we know the process. Now, I hope you will come back and stay with me, unless you have other plans. I won't be around much, but the house is yours to rest in."

Susan smiled. "Thank you. I don't know people here well enough. Sarah asked, but… and I don't really want to stay alone at the hotel. You are busy with this case, though. Are you sure?"

Harriet nodded. "Of course, I'm sure." She was about to explain the caveat when there was a noise as people approached and the curtain was pulled back slightly.

Harriet saw a large blonde woman, with Janine behind

her, peer in.

She looked at Harriet. "I'm Sarah." Her gaze fell on Susan. "How are you doing?"

Susan smiled. "I'm on the mend slowly. This is Harriet, my friend. I'm going to stay with her."

Sarah said, "Tangling with her boyfriend, of all things. Her older brother is the only sensible one in the family, I gather. He's in the New Start group now, Janine says."

Susan said truculently, "Well, you make it two out of the family. Janine needs a sponsor who will keep her straight and not the 'hands off, call me whenever' sort. You fix it."

Sarah looked at Harriet. "Are you one of us?"

Harriet was about to reply when Susan said, "No. She's a police officer. We met in Canada. She won't give me pepper spray either."

Sarah retorted, "After yesterday evening, I wouldn't trust you alone on the streets of York with a bus ticket, never mind a can of pepper spray. If you go back to the conference, that nasty sod who spoke at your breakout session will gossip that you got drunk last night, no matter what excuse you give."

With that admonition, the big woman gave a sigh. "Apart from work miracles with this one, is there anything I can do for you? I feel really bad now, about letting you go off after the meeting."

A couple of minutes later, as Sarah and Janine were leaving, Susan said, "Janine, you get yourself a sponsor and work with her. Stay with it, stay strong And keep away from – what was he called?"

Janine said, "Devon. I will. I'm going to join tonight. I thought that after your talk last night. Now, I'm sure."

When they were alone, Harriet said, "I need to get back, unfortunately, for a meeting first thing. And I am not sure when I can get here to collect you if they keep you longer.

So, if you want to stay with me, there is a condition."

"What's that?"

"Your chauffeur will be Chris Willard. He's keen, let me say, to help."

She watched the mix of emotions on Susan's face as she thought about it.

"That's a long way. You just did it, I know. I would rather he didn't see me like this, but... thank you. How did he know?"

Harriet smiled. "I told Kerri, who was just leaving my house when you called. She called him and we three talked while I drove over here. Either you accept that offer, or Kerri says that she is coming to collect you. Her knee is up to it now, she claims. Although, between your eyesight and her knee, I very much doubt whether either of you will make it back in one piece."

Susan thought a moment. "Please tell Chris I very much appreciate his offer. I will look forward to seeing him, out of one eye."

Harriet kept a straight face. "Send him a text. I gather you two have exchanged contact information already. You can fix the timing. Now, give me those car keys."

20 REHEARSALS

The following morning, or whatever it felt to be after Harriet's broken night, the investigation team gathered, taking stock of the interviews yesterday. Howard had called in, saying he would be late, he was following up on a phone call.

Sammie asked Louis. "About what?"

"Something one of the choir members said about the concert rehearsals; he's a hoarder of stuff."

After John Kent arrived, his first comment was, "Are we making too much of this unease in Valerie Carmichael? Do we have any other lines to follow?"

Sammie responded, "Howard and Louis have interviewed his two biking pals again. We see nothing there. Other than this hunch, we are left with the unknown predator suggested by Dr. Kulis. Or, we don't have enough to say which way to go next. But the hunch is stronger, isn't it, Harriet, from our interview with Oliver Mettler?"

Kent gave Harriet a look. She seemed tired, but Sammie pressed on, not waiting for her answer. "Mettler appeared co-operative but totally vague. Harriet spotted a book on his desk, a breviary, which he confirmed he uses. Like, prayers at different times of the day, the Daily Office. Including, would you believe, Compline? And I am sure he was lying when he said he hadn't heard of Crosshill Farm."

She took in Calder's silence again. "Are you OK, Harriet?"

"I was up more than half the night. My friend Susan was attacked while walking in Coppergate, in York. I went there, to the hospital and back. She has a serious black eye and can't fly home, I gather. She's coming back here to stay with me."

She gave Kent a withering look. "Not that I will be able to spend much time with her. But yes, the Mettler interview made me feel the same way as Sammie."

Kent was deciding what to say when Howard Mooney entered, saving him the trouble.

Sammie said, "You finally made it. Anything?"

Howard smiled at her and handed over a photocopy, a couple of sheets. "A Peter Salter in Carlisle. He phoned me early this morning, which is why I went there and back before the review."

He looked at Kent and said, "The man sang in the choir and recalled nothing during the phone call yesterday, but he said he would try to find something in the things he keeps, in his spare bedroom. He did. Look."

It was a typed notice attached to the concert program, a schedule for the rehearsals.

Howard didn't wait. "Look at the soloist rehearsal entries. Two for each soloist at Mettler's home in Alston and two with the choir at the Methodist Hall. I thought all rehearsals were held at the hall. That's what Reverend Nichols said."

Sammie added, "And that's what Oliver Mettler implied yesterday."

John Kent said, "Howard, well done. I think it is terrible how your sergeant growls at you for being late. A hard worker like you. I'd complain to her boss if I were you."

He was smiling.

Mettler hadn't mentioned it in the interview. He knew Valerie Carmichael a little better than he led them to believe, Harriet concluded.

John Kent thought a moment then stood, picking up a dry marker for the whiteboard.

"We are all in the same place, I think, but let's spell it out." His hand drew lines and circles as he spoke.

"First, Dennis was buried here. He had a paper which we think links him to Carmichael's concert. One of the organizers potentially knew the location of the burial site, as she had visited the farm, and she mentioned it to others on the committee.

"Second, the recent interviews left you with the feeling that neither Carmichael, Nichols, nor Mettler were being completely open about what they knew. Third, we all seem to have bought into the idea that Dennis may have gone to Carlisle the day of the concert, even if we have no direct proof. Linnie, that's right, still?"

Linnie nodded. "No sighting. We have been through all the CCTV we have available. After all this time, though, there are too many gaps in the coverage to say either way."

Kent put the pen down. "We don't know what motivated Dennis, but Yvonne's 'knight errant' concept or, putting it more down-to-earth, Harriet's idea from the Haverigg interview, resonates with me. Dennis could have been the white knight for Carmichael and confronted someone, who then killed him. That implies something happened between her and a person involved in the event, possibly Mettler, or the trumpeter Ingram. Although it could equally be another person involved.

"My final questions are about Carmichael. Does she know what happened? Is she acting to conceal her complicity in some way? Was the damsel in distress really that?"

He looked around the group, reading the faces. "We focus, slow down on this, and dig deep. We have a half-baked possible set of events and no compelling evidence we could present – yet. I want everything you can find on Carmichael, Nichols, Ingram, and Mettler. Go back. Information on vehicles, purchases around that time and credit card information. If Dennis was kept in a freezer or cold storage, where?"

He paused.

"I'll talk with Superintendent Chiswell. Sammie, we will probably talk to Dr. Kulis again. A priest, two musicians, and a television star; they are all public figures, to differing degrees. We need to play this very carefully, but we focus first on them."

Sammie said, "The Super won't be happy."

"No, he won't."

Chan, who had been quiet while following along, said suddenly, "Can I say something? It might be way off-base?"

Sammie responded, "You are a team member. You are expected to speak up if you have an idea related to an investigation. What is it?"

"We only have the comment about the knots from Dr. Kulis that this crime is not a sado-sexual killing. I phoned Dr. Meadows. The state of the tissues they examined doesn't show the treatment of the victim one way or the other. Absence of torture in what we have doesn't exclude that as motive for the assault."

He grimaced, working out how to explain himself. "What I'm getting at is that I see the links, but if Dennis's death is tied to a predatory killer with a sadistic streak, we are totally off-base."

Kent said, "That's good, Louis. You remind us that we shouldn't rule out the unknown attacker. Profiling gives possibilities, not probabilities. But I must set priorities. As I said, we have some linkages, but no hard explanation yet. Which is why we are doing background work, not bringing them in for harder questioning."

He looked at his watch, ready to move on to another investigation within MIU. He continued, "We also have the funeral for Dennis the day after tomorrow and I want everyone there. Harriet must be present, at the request of Bernice Lewis. The rest of us are watching to see who turns up and how they react.

"The Deputy Chief Constable, the Chaplain and several other senior officers will attend, in uniform, showing support. Leave them alone unless they approach you. You are working, not hobnobbing with the powers-that-be. Go digging, but quietly."

~~

Late that afternoon, the grey skies cleared to give sun-shine, forcing the use of sun visors in the car. Although it was less than a three-hour drive, Reverend Willard had to stop at Scotch Corner Services on the A1 motorway so that Susan could go to the washroom.

She blamed, in order, the hospital stay; failing to go to the bathroom at the hotel while packing because Willard was waiting to carry her case; her medications; being near a priest; the time of day and the forces of evil.

All these things, she decided, drove her bladder to demand a stop at the busy service area. She marched off, irritated, to the washrooms, wearing her new eyepatch and with her bruises on display. She looked, she thought, like Pirate Jane.

Remove it on arrival in Bassenthwaite for an hour, then wear it until bedtime, the doctor had told her. Miriam, who had been sympathetic to her plight, would still have told her she was making excuses. Her sponsee was nervous and in Miriam's choice words, she had the hots for the man, that's all.

In the time between his arrival to collect her and Scotch Corner, they conversed politely on various topics as he drove carefully north, prior to crossing the Pennines.

As they set off again, Susan still insisted on the front passenger seat rather than sit in the back, resting. She said, out of nowhere, "I know nothing about you."

Chris glanced at her, trying to sense her mood. Having fallen flat on his face over his clerical collar pronouncement days earlier, he exercised caution.

"What would you like to know?"

Susan mulled it over. Does he have a girlfriend? How much does he like her? Does he have a sense of humour? Her most troublesome question was why she was attracted to a priest, of all people? What had he done to her?

Choosing safer ground, she asked, "Why did you become a priest?"

"I found my calling early. My parents died suddenly in a boating accident when I was nine. My grandparents raised me. My grandfather was an Anglican priest. Losing your parents, learning about loss and consequences, it felt natural for me. I love the work, the people, and that my life has purpose."

They were overtaking a slower lorry near Greta Bridge on the A66 when Chris asked, "Why are you an addiction counsellor?"

Oh no, thought Susan, I set myself up to fall into that

hole. Oh well. "I'm a recovered alcoholic; you guessed that. At university I was a nightmare on wheels when I drank. I went into a treatment centre and recovered, so I decided I could do the same job as the counsellors. And I can."

She gave him a stare; one-eyed, but still a stare.

Chris, now satisfactorily back in the slow lane, had been concentrating on his careful acceleration and deceleration while overtaking. "No, I meant why you are one now? Why do you do it? What motivates you?"

Susan responded, "That's rather personal."

Chris focused his attention on the road. Harriet had once told him that if you want someone to speak, say nothing.

A mile or so later, Susan said, "Through my drunken despair as an alcoholic, I tried to kill myself. A police officer found me. Between something he said and a woman who is still my AA sponsor today, I found a path forward, a relationship with God as I understand God, and a purpose, to help others who are like me. I still have the drive to do that."

She glanced at him, which required moving her head again. "Why the smile you are trying to hide? It's not funny. I was answering your question."

"No, I'm smiling because it's lovely to hear you say what you just said."

He glanced at her. "Apart from the fact that presumably you have a boss at the place you work, whereas I have a bishop, we seem to have similar jobs and motivations, don't we?"

Susan noticed again he was wearing a normal collared shirt. He looked quite good, she thought. She sat for a minute or so with her eyes closed. Between the bumps in the road and the effect of the pain killers, she was divided between wanting to debate that with him or close her eyes and try to nod off.

In the end, she said, "If you weren't driving, I would give you an argument on that one. But thank you for coming all the way to collect me and take me to Harriet's. I do appreciate that."

She leaned a bit, turning her head and touching his arm, squeezing it lightly.

What the hell am I doing, she thought. She would blame it on her injury and her medication if it had repercussions.

When she realised that she had, in fact, dozed off, she took in her surroundings and saw a road sign saying that Kirby Stephen and Penrith were ahead. Not too far to go to Bassenthwaite, she realised, so she had slept more than a minute or so. It both pleased and disappointed her. Harriet was probably working away in the police head-quarters somewhere ahead of her.

Chris was glancing at her as she moved. "How are you feeling?"

"Better for the sleep. My headache feels a little easier, even though I am sure the painkiller has worn off by now."

She slid open the mirror on sun visor, checking herself. The bruising was worse, more intense. She quickly pulled out a tissue and wiped the side of her mouth, some dried saliva.

"I hope I wasn't snoring."

"No; well, the odd time." The white lie was evident in the tone of voice.

He finally asked, "I'm sure you will want to rest a lot, but perhaps we could see each other again while you are here? Go out somewhere? When the eye heals, I mean."

The thought hadn't gone far from his mind all the way across the Pennines.

She gave a smile, one more whimsical than sincere, he

thought. "I'd like that, although you would be taking a risk, going out with a woman 'accursed for her beliefs', wouldn't you?"

"Who said that?" he asked, surprised.

"I'm not sure. It is number eighteen of your Articles of Religion, part of the Creeds and Solemn Declarations you are supposed to know by heart."

Her mind had gone back to Reverend Moore from Ontario, the man who had failed Duncan Aster, she felt. She had spoken at his canon disciplinary hearing. He was so different from Chris Willard.

The bright spot from that event was meeting Harriet there, and Bishop Azikiwe, and his assistant Audrey. But she had also researched what being an Anglican was, how it differed from her Roman Catholic upbringing. The religion was more loosey goosey, she felt, all over the place, with no straight answers. In reading the Anglican webpage on 'beliefs', the article she mentioned had hit her. She had pondered on it so much she could quote bits, despite the archaic language.

They also are to be had accursed that presume to say that every man shall be saved by the Law or Sect which he professeth.... For holy Scripture doth set out unto us only the Name of Jesus Christ whereby men must be saved."

Well, she was saved by an old police officer and a cranky old woman, led to a God that was still a total mystery to her, and she was comfortable with that. He could chew on that question, see if he was still interested.

Chris couldn't remember a parishioner raising issues of the Articles of Religion with him. He smiled, then said carefully, "I think I could do that, take the risk. I don't think the Articles of Religion are quite up to date."

She smiled back. "Some of your brothers in Christ may want to send you to the stake for that heresy."

"I'll take my chance with that, too. I've said far worse over the years. Being an Anglican doesn't mean leaving your mind behind when you go to church, thank God."

Was that a dig in return, knowing she was raised a Roman Catholic? Does he have a sense of humour, after all? She sat thinking for a moment or two, enjoying the feeling.

"Harriet has been so good to me, and she is very busy. You and Kerri have, as well. I'll talk to Harriet, see if I can make dinner for all of us one evening, if you are available. Just don't wear your clerical collar. I like you in that shirt."

She wanted to know if he would enjoy her cooking. She wanted to know a lot more, really.

PART 2

Compline

21 FUNERAL

St Mary's Anglican Church had kindly offered its much larger facility to the Lewis family and the congregation of St. Mark's for the funeral. Even then, it was too small. They temporarily closed parts of Church Street and Kirkby Street. People still came on foot, placing flowers at the church gates.

The entire investigation team attended the funeral, but only Harriet was doing double duty.

Among the family members, it was Aileen, his sister, who had the hardest time emotionally, at least visibly. Both Bernice and Eamon cried on seeing the coffin, but during the service they seem to be supported by its presence, and by the people there. Reverend Dodson read a lesson, but otherwise left the priest's role to Reverend Sills. The two clergymen had worked out a process that fitted.

As Sills finished his homily, he said, "Eamon and Bernice have asked our good friend Harriet Calder to say a few words. Many of you have heard her in St. Mark's over the years. She is also a police officer, as you may not be aware, and is now part of the team investigating Dennis's death."

He waited as Harriet made her way to the pulpit.

She looked at the large congregation, taking in first the pew with police uniforms and Reverend Shelagh Amos. Then she focused only on Bernice Lewis.

"Bernice asked me to say something, and part of me dreaded saying yes, as I wasn't sure what I could say. I never knew Dennis in life but have learned a lot about him. As part of the police team, I am learning more day by day. The most important discovery for me is that he loved life, his family, and his friends – and racing bikes, Bernice reminded me. He was well loved in return, and still is."

She paused. Her head rose, taking in the congregation.

"Somehow, after Dennis went missing, it was clearer for me what to say to Eamon and Bernice, to lead a prayer on the occasions I spoke at St. Mark's, a prayer for his safe-keeping and return. We did that each time I came to Mary-port, and I am sure others did the same. It was always with the hope, albeit fainter by the year, that they would be reunited."

"In one way, it is harder now, for them, and all of us, sullied by the truth of his death, as far as we know it. Somehow, it diminishes us, diminishes me, but not him. Not Dennis. Here we have certainty, for those who believe in Christ's resurrection, that Dennis is in a far better place, and that he in safe hands. In his proper burial now, we have some closure after years of questions, but Eamon and Bernice would be the first to say it is only partial closure. They are close to him physically now, but they want to understand why this happened.

"I go to work each day now, as do my colleagues, with that in our minds. It steadies us and gives us resolve. But it is a burden, too. We know we owe it to Dennis and his family to find out how and why he died and who did this awful thing to him. We will strive to determine that, to the best of our abilities.

"To most people, it would seem police officers are after retribution, searching for the person or persons who commit a crime. At the heart of it, though, as we see today, is the need to bring closure. In doing so, we hope to give answers that in the course of time will grant as much peace as possible for Eamon, Bernice, and their family, for Dennis's friends, and for this community."

She stepped back, turned, and walked down the pulpit steps as the organ began the opening chords of the next hymn.

It was outside, later. Chan had not spent much time alone with John Kent. It was intimidating.

"Sergeant Calder spoke well, sir."

Kent nodded, agreeing. "Harriet's a good preacher. She chose what to say carefully."

Chan said, "I meant, about why we are doing this, still working on it. We all talk about catching the perpetrator but, I thought it was just me, being new, that I was doing it to help the parents."

John was staring at Sammie, in the distance through the crowd, as he listened.

He replied, suddenly looking intensely at Chan, "When you lose that thought, it's probably time to be doing something else than work in MIU. What she said is right and what she didn't say is right, too. We do it to stop it happening again. The last thing we wanted today is to alarm people, but as you suggested at the last briefing, we really don't know until we catch the perpetrator."

His gaze returned to Sammie. "Who's she talking to?"

The couple were walking to the gate, so Kent and Chan

only saw then from behind. Sammie had stopped them and spoken to the woman, who shook her head abruptly as the man spoke to Sammie. They were smartly dressed, and the woman wore a veil over the hat.

"That's Valerie Carmichael. I don't know who the man is, though."

They were leaving, it seemed. A black limousine pulled forward and Carmichael and her companion entered before being driven away. Sammie walked over to Kent and Chan.

"Valerie Carmichael cried as Harriet spoke, as she talked about our efforts to find out what happened. I just asked was she alright. It was as if she forgot I had been the one who interviewed her. She looked through me and the man with her said this was not the time to talk."

She looked at John. "I was watching her. It struck me that she held it together during most of the funeral, but Harriet's reference to the search for the truth of what happened hit her hard. I tell you, boss, anywhere else and not a star, I would have her in."

~~

Shortly after nine-thirty that evening, Harriet took a call from Sammie. As the phone rang, her front door opened and Susan came in, smiling, from spending the evening with Chris Willard.

Sammie went straight to the point. "Linnie did a review of credit card expenditures for Carmichael, Mettler, and Ingram for the months around Dennis's disappearance. The day after the concert, Oliver Mettler bought a new chest freezer. It can't simply be coincidence, Harriet. I have just told John."

Harriet was stunned. As much as their work had led to

suspicions around the choir, it had been conjecture. As unlikely as it seemed, this was concrete; to her, an incriminating certainty.

"Harriet?"

"I heard. I agree. But there is still a lot of work to do now. It is circumstantial unless we can prove a link."

"We'll talk in the morning. I just wanted you prepared. Sorry it is late, but... Linnie did well."

"She did. I'll see you first thing. Goodnight."

Susan's face had changed, becoming more serious as she observed Harriet on the phone. She said, "It looks like bad news? Is it?"

Harriet shook her head. "For the investigation; no. A new piece of evidence. It is just the timing, with the funeral today. I feel a bit overwhelmed; truth be told. But you looked happy as you came in?"

I need something more positive to focus on, she thought.

Susan sat down across from her. "Miriam is right, as usual. I've fallen for Chris Willard and there is no rhyme or reason for it. He says he is deeply attracted to me, but is sounding, what's the word... reserved? Cautious? We talked a lot. I don't know what the hell I am doing. It's crazy. I'll be gone in days."

A tortured romance thought Harriet. Thank God for that to focus on. She smiled and said, "I was just about to make some hot chocolate. Do you want some?"

She said a quick prayer silently as she put the kettle on and measured the scoops of the drink mix into the mugs, a prayer for light and warmth overcoming dark terrors.

22 TRUMPET

The following morning, MIU were assigned a new suspicious death on the Kingstown Industrial Estate, in north Carlisle. DCI Kent gave it to DI Ken Nolan, taking over the Smallwood investigation himself. His comments to Sammie were succinct and, as she looked at her notes, passed on to her team in the same way.

"Howard, you will join me to reinterview Valerie's parents. Harriet you are to push the trumpeter Ingram a little more now he is back. He hardly gave us the time of day at the last interview."

Sammie was referring to Ingram's videoconference interview. The musician had been in France, playing with a group at a festival. He was brusque and something of a chauvinist. When asked about his recall of the Burgon performance, he grimaced, then looked sullen. "It's a piece for a boy chorister, a trumpet, and an organ. The voice should be a treble."

He waited a moment. "No offense."

Sammie had looked lost for a second. "You mean it should be sung by a boy, not a girl soprano?"

He sniffed. "I didn't pay much attention to the girl singing, d'you see? I was there just to play the trumpet part. Two and half minutes on the Burgon work, a couple of fanfares to accompany final verses for the choir on something else and I was out of there. It was ten years ago, as well."

They had got nothing useful out of him before he insisted that he had to leave. Harriet recalled Shelagh Amos's comment about the trumpeter: 'he is useful for pushing air through a brass tube'. She began to see why.

Sammie focused on Louis and Howard. "The boss wants you chasing down more information on the freezer, Howard, and you on Mettler's car back then, Louis."

Howard grimaced and glanced at Louis; the meaning was clear. They got the routine work.

She continued with, "Howard, he also wants you to start the next interview with our television star, and you Louis, get the first go with Oliver Mettler when we bring them in for questioning. Neither of those interviews will be routine, I assure you."

The younger officers looked at each other, surprised. Then Howard smiled. "And after, he will send in you two, the cavalry?"

Sammie nodded, looking at Harriet. "Something like that, yes. So, the message is, be completely familiar with these files and this strategy. You are in the interview seats, at least to begin. He wants a decision meeting on the path forward in three days, with Chiswell attending."

Howard looked surprised. "I thought he said slow down and go deep. Are three days enough?"

"It's what he has given us. And you go as deep as you need. And last on my list, Harriett and I are to interview Carmichael's sister."

Harriet asked, "Where is her sister. Anyone know?"

Linnie said, "I checked for Sammie; she asked a little earlier. Perth, Australia."

Louis smiled. "You won't get there and back in three days. If you want me to go..."

Linnie retorted, "You wish. Sammie, do you want me to fix up a videolink slot with her? It may be weird hours, our time." Her eyes were on Livermore.

"Please. Unless it's easier to fly Louis over there as air freight. He can hitchhike back."

She looked at the team. "Anything else? By the way, how is Susan doing now?"

Harriet responded, "Looks like she came out of the ring the loser. But no serious damage. She can see fine from the eye. Her travel medical insurance wants her to see an ophthalmologist on some list they have before they will agree to her return flight. She's doing dinner tonight, so I hope to get home."

Sammie, wanting to forestall further discussion, said, "Let's get to it, then."

~~

Harriet took a uniformed constable called Ivan Jessop with her to Harrogate, north of Leeds, to Ingram's home. She wanted someone in uniform with her; it would make clear to all present that Ingram was having police visitors. Jessop knew Harriet from her regular job, so they talked about goings-on in Keswick and Cumbria Police during most of the drive.

"You must be a glutton for punishment, working with John Kent again. But it's a good thing, at least, trying to sort out that boy's murder. What do you want me to do?"

"Just be there. If he gets a bit snotty, give him your, 'I

can have you flat on your back with one hand' look. He wasn't co-operative last time, hardly gave us the time of day."

Ivan nodded slowly. "Well, we will have to help him focus, won't we?"

They found the trumpeter at home, working in his garden, pruning roses and shrubs.

Harriet said, "Mr. Ingram, I'm following up first on a point from our earlier interview with you. You gave the impression that you were hardly aware of Valerie Krestman, as she was then. But we have information that you had two rehearsals at Dr. Mettler's home with her, then two at the Methodist Central Hall, plus the performance. Surely you have better recall?"

His eyes opened wide. "Not so. The Methodist Hall, yes, but not the earlier ones. I gave Oliver a recording, to the agreed measure – the metronome timing. Didn't I mention that? I am sorry. It wasn't a big thing, really, one piece."

Harriet suddenly had a glimmer of insight, possibly. "That means you met her first at the Methodist Hall. How did the rehearsal go?"

He shook his head. "Sorry, I don't recall." He turned back to the rose he was pruning – to find Jessop's hand crossing his and gently removing the pruning shears. His face was fixed on the musician's.

"Still a bit early for pruning some of these roses, sir, I suggest. This is a murder enquiry, so please give the detective your full attention. We have been courteous enough to come here."

Jessop's face made it clear what he would like to do. Towering above the trumpeter, he looked like he wanted to tuck the man under his arm and head back to Penrith.

Harriet said, "I want you to think back, not dismiss the

question. June 2008. Go get your calendar or whatever you may need to jog your mind. Otherwise, as the officer said, we will take you in for questioning, and I assure you there will be adequate time to focus on the concert then."

Ingram looked a little shocked. "I will go and get the score for the Burgon piece. I attach notes made for the different performances to my scores. They can be helpful next time I use a piece. There may be something there. Please come inside."

A few minutes later he looked up from the document set he was leafing through.

"I had conflicting events with the two earlier rehearsals, I now see. Oliver suggested the recording. It didn't take long; it wasn't a professional quality, just a timing piece for the rehearsal. When we had the first choir rehearsal, Valerie was word perfect, on pitch, and it went well. My notes say I stayed only half an hour. I didn't note anything for the second rehearsal.

"How would you describe her demeanor during the hall rehearsals and the performance? Do you remember?"

He nodded, finally recalling the events. "The first one went reasonably well. The second and the actual performance were at the same competency level, no improvement. Wooden, would be the description. Vocally she was sound, but she lacked expression. Oliver is a good organist as well as a choral director – he is noted for it – but it was as if Valerie was focused only on the score, not his guidance."

Harriet pulled a photo of Dennis Lewis from her file. "We also wondered, with Valerie and Dennis Lewis being friends, whether you saw him at the performance? Look at the photo carefully, please, and think back. Did you see this face among the audience during the concert?"

He did so, then said, "I never saw him during the concert or beforehand, as far as I recall."

Harriet asked, "Is there anything else you do recall?"

He paused, reflecting. "After the performance I spoke to Valerie very briefly, a courtesy. I can't recall any details. Her parents were with her. She didn't seem particularly happy, I thought. I got the impression she just wanted to go home. The girl appeared to be a – what's the phrase – shrinking violet. I was surprised later to find she had become an actor. I didn't think she had the temperament for stage or related performance work. At least, that was the way I recall it."

Harriet nodded. "Thank you. We will let you get back to your roses. We are just following up on every detail we can."

She stood and turned to go, walking to the front door. The uniformed constable took a little longer, eyeing Ingram. The trumpeter didn't like the look of him.

On the way back, Ivan Jessop said, "So Valerie was alone with this man Mettler on two occasions, was she?" His voice and eyes said it all.

Harriet said softly, "At some point, we are going to find that out. First, we need to know how she got to his home for the rehearsal. Who stayed with her, perhaps? Or not."

~~

If Sammie were to summarise the second interview with the Krestman couple, it would be 'cautious' rather than 'incriminating'. She and Howard both got the impression that some flunky hanging around their famous daughter had told them to be careful about talking to the police, rather than the parents hiding anything.

They were open about their movements and activities around the time of Dennis's disappearance. After the first interview, Mr. Krestman dug out his work appointments diary for 2008, to check.

"I put everything in there. We were just beginning the preparations for my job change. I had a lot to organize."

As they went through the questions, Sammie read his diary entries and made her own notes. The dates and times of the rehearsals at Mettler's home and the Methodist Hall were in there.

The touchy bit was revisiting the relationship between Dennis and Valerie. Sammie pushed it a bit, saying she found it hard to believe it was platonic. Was there more to it?

That made Mrs. Krestman's reticence disappear. "My daughter was innocent; a good girl, and Dennis Lewis was a lovely young man. I would have seen any signs and there weren't any. I thought about it many times since, and wish there had been, if he hadn't disappeared. They would have been a good couple. I won't have you speak ill of him or her in this house. Do you understand?"

Sammie made the right noises about 'simply following lines of enquiry'.

"Is that when Valerie showed an interest in acting?"

Calming a little, Mrs. Krestman said, "Around then. We thought she might be a singer, with that voice she had."

Mr. Krestman said more calmly, but with a steely firmness, "Nothing unsavory went on between Valerie and Dennis. We are both sure of that. You are looking in the wrong place and asking the wrong questions."

No, I'm not, thought Sammie. And I am starting to get answers I understand.

Howard suddenly spoke up. "Does Valerie still sing, do you know? Has she done any musicals? With a good voice and acting skills, it would be natural, I would think?"

Mrs. Krestman seemed mollified by the change of topic. "I thought so, too. But no, she hasn't done so. We follow all her work, of course. At the time, we just saw it as one dream changed for another. And with 'Ruston' now, she has no time for anything else."

It had struck him suddenly; she had a good singing voice but on checking her background, there were no other musical performances than the choir event.

Catching on, Sammie gave him a nod. Continue.

Howard thought that the couple would be happy talking all day about Valerie's career. But he interrupted Mrs. Krestman. "So, she stopped singing at home, that sort of thing, did she?"

"After the concert and hearing about Dennis going missing, yes. I don't think she came out of that for a good long while, really. By the time she did, she was into acting."

As they were preparing to leave, Sammie asked, "Do you mind if we borrow this diary for a few days? It will be returned, and I will give you an official receipt."

Mr. Krestman looked a little nonplussed, whereas his wife now appeared suspicious.

"I suppose so. Providing we get it back."

Sammie smiled, thanking him. It was just as well. She would have asked John Kent to get a warrant, otherwise. It would be used as evidence.

When they returned to Penrith, with Howard giving a big sigh about 'back to freezers', they found Louis had gone out, following up on cars, and Harriet was back from the interview with Ingram and just finishing a phone call.

Sammie heard her say, "Well, thank you again, Chris, I do appreciate it."

She listened a bit and broke into a smile, but her response was warm, not revealing her amusement.

"Articles of Religion? Really. Yes, that sounds like Susan. She said a fish dish. I can't guarantee to be on time tonight. I want to be, but the case comes first, at present."

Pause.

"I'll look forward to it." She smiled as she closed the call.

Sammie asked, "What's the smile about?"

"Susan; she is doing dinner for four of us tonight, including Chris Willard, the priest at St. Anselm's. She's been winding him up. I think it is a step along the path to a romance."

Sammie seemed surprised. "From what you said –."

"I know. But I take the things which make me smile when I can, in the job we have got."

Sammie said, "Howard made a good point during the interview with the parents. I'm going to give Yvonne a call on the speaker. Listen in.

They spoke to Dr. Kulis, but not for long, so it didn't cost a fortune. Kulis said, "That's a good observation, Howard. If singing that solo in the concert was tied in some way to a traumatic experience, she could have lost the impetus to sing completely; in fact, she would steer clear of any singing role deliberately."

As they finished, Linnie approached them. "You are set. A videolink with Valerie Carmichael's sister will be live in twenty minutes. It is secure, and I will monitor and record it in the background."

23 STEPHANIE

They thanked Stephanie Krestman, now Mrs. Hardacre, for accommodating them so late in her day. It had turned 10.00 p.m. in Perth.

She was dismissive about it. "This is a good time. Between nine and midnight is my quiet time. Before then, the boys are awake. Sometimes Val and I talk around now."

Sammie smiled. "What is it like having a famous sister, can I ask?"

"She's still my sis. I don't give her any room for airs and graces. Val pays for our airfares to come home and see family every other year, which is great, and for mum and dad to visit us in the intervening years. It's nice to have someone with money in the family."

Sammie took it forward.

"As our colleague mentioned, we are investigating the death of Dennis Lewis and checking with people who lived around the area at the time of his disappearance. As Valerie and Dennis were friends, we wanted to talk to you as well. We have already spoken with her and your parents."

She nodded, understanding.

"Valerie knew him, not me. I saw him, but we didn't talk much about anything, with the age difference. They had been friends since infant school."

Sammie smiled, "Yes, your sister has been very helpful. Being a busy person, she really responded to us fast. We appreciated that."

"She liked Dennis, but it was platonic. He wasn't her boyfriend at all."

Sammie nodded. "We did wonder, I must admit. We follow up on everything in this job, of course."

Stephanie waited, watching the two women sitting next to each other in an office somewhere.

"Did your sister have any other boys interested in her?"

Stephanie smiled. "Probably, from afar. She wasn't into boys yet. I was just starting; I had a crush on one. Val always wanted to know how it was going, and I was telling her to push off. But none of it became serious stuff."

Sammie nodded, accepting the message she conveyed. "She told us she and Dennis practised kissing at twelve."

Stephanie laughed. "What a hoot! She announced it at breakfast, as if she fitted it in, like an extra music lesson. Mum's look. She asked why? Valerie told her, so they would get it right when they each had a boyfriend and girlfriend later."

Her face became animated. "Dad asked her if she felt that would be Dennis. Her look! 'I wouldn't want any of the stuff I see on television to spoil my friendship with Dennis', she said seriously. We were both then grilled about our TV use, what we saw."

Sammie smiled and looked at Harriet. The glance told her the same thing; the sister was talkative and had good recall.

"Can you remember anything that might help us? The last time you saw Dennis, for example. How your sister heard about him going missing; how your family felt. Anything, no matter how small. Sometimes the details help."

"Such as? I'm not sure what it is you want?"

"Well, was Valerie hard hit by Dennis's disappearance?"

"She was devastated by it. For the week or two just before the concert she had been getting cold feet, hating doing it, which was a surprise. Afterwards, she was so upset about Dennis."

Harriet spoke up. "We heard she was a good singer and loved the choir. One line of our inquiry is to check if Dennis was in the audience that night. Whether he tried to see the concert."

Stephanie thought a moment. "Val did love the choir, yes. She was in St Mary's church choir for two years, one of their youngest members. They loved the purity of her soprano voice. Then the interfaith choir excited her. But whether it was the preparations for that concert, or singing with a trumpet playing with her, I don't know. She wasn't happy in the run-up to it. And broken-hearted afterwards."

Sammie said, "It must be hard to sing with the trumpet, the soloists having different parts."

Stephanie agreed. "It was either that or she wasn't happy with the trumpeter. He did play a bit loud."

Careful, thought Sammie. Harriet asked, "They must have practised, though. It's not an easy piece."

"Yes, they did. At the director's home. They rehearsed two or three times. Dad took her over there each time. He was always busy with things that needed doing, with the move. His sales office was in Carlisle. He dropped her off and picked her up."

"That was convenient, then. They could practice when it fitted for everyone."

"Hang on. Thinking about it, it was just the two of

them, her and the organist, the conductor. I had asked how loud the trumpet sounded in a normal room and she said, 'they adjusted the volume on the player."

Harriet gave Sammie a brief glance. Corroboration.

Sammie jumped in quickly. "Now, think back, did you see Dennis at the concert? Just in case. We are asking everyone who attended."

They were getting too close to the core issue. She needed to move Stephanie's attention elsewhere.

It was later, in the team meeting. John Kent joined them, looking worn out.

"What do we have?"

Sammie said, "All circumstantial evidence, but some new items. Corroboration that the initial rehearsals for Valerie were at Mettler's home, not in the hall, and the trumpeter wasn't there; they used a recording.

"The bad news is that his car at the time was wrecked just six weeks ago, in an accident. Louis is now checking the wrecker's yard where it ended up.

"The freezer is no longer in his possession. Ten years on, we have no more solid information than the piece of paper found with Dennis Lewis."

She paused. "At some point, we have no choice but to interview Valerie Carmichael hard and, if she lies to us, threaten to charge her with obstructing our investigation, perhaps. And if that threat falls through, it will probably give Cumbria Police a big media problem, if she goes public."

Kent literally slumped his shoulders. "It's been that sort of day. Is there anything here, apart from keeping things confidential, that gives us any time triggers?"

Sammie shrugged. "No. The more time, the more the possibility of evidence turning up; in the car, perhaps. Chan came up also with the idea of checking out pulleys."

"At Mettler's old home, in Alston?"

She nodded. "You wouldn't get a body out of a freezer without help or something like that. And Dr. Kulis' comments on the ropes comes to mind."

Kent mused on it. "Let's leave this for tomorrow. I'll set up a meeting; this team with me and Superintendent Chiswell. Sammie, I expect you, me and Chiswell, will probably see the Assistant Chief Constable afterwards. Be prepared for that. Harriet, you seem to be mulling on something?"

"Just thinking, just thinking. If I have any bright ideas, I will run them by Sammie first."

He nodded. "Let's all call it a day."

~ ~

Harriet made it home in good time for the dinner, to find Susan preparing the meal. She made them both tea and stood watching her.

"One more day, I reckon, and your face will be in full bloom. After that it will begin fade."

Susan took a long look at her friend. "I have never seen you so... burdened. Even during the canon hearings last year in Hamilton."

Harriet smiled. "That was harder for you than for me. I would like your opinion on something, though. But it may be too personal, so don't think you will offend me if you say you can't discuss it."

Susan looked up, interested.

"If you knew a woman, like you, who had been sexually assaulted as a teenager by a man, but was in total denial, appearing happy and successful, how would you reach them, get them to talk about it?"

Susan thought about it. "Do you remember my talk at the AA meeting after we met?"

"Vividly."

"I said I have a sponsee, a man, who is a recovered alcoholic, but his history was like mine. He's a psychologist who works with survivors of sexual and physical abuse. I said then that I could be his AA sponsor, but I couldn't do the job he does. So, in short, I have no experience to answer that question. Just what he told me he does."

Harriet tilted her head and waited.

"You share something about that abuse with the person, something they would never share with anyone else, that they would recognize as one of their own most hidden secrets. That you understand. Then you show them the way out, the way to recovery. That's what he does."

She sighed. "In effect, for alcoholics and addicts, that's what I do. But sexual abuse, that's a different ball game. I think I can see why you are looking so weighed down."

Harriet smiled. "I was hoping that a psychiatrist or psychologist might try. We have a consultant, a profiler, who is qualified."

"My sponsee has a doctorate in psychology; I did course units in it as well. Over time, if trust is built, it may achieve the same result, but that is a longer and less predictable process."

"Well, thank you for the insight."

"With the name Carlson, I didn't expect this! I thought it would be a Swedish dish. Harriet said your parents are of Swedish stock."

Kerri Sanders was hugging her wine glass and peering into the kitchen. The smell of seafood was associated with southern France rather than Sweden, a bouillabaisse.

"My mother learned this dish in a visit to Quebec on

their honeymoon. It became her favourite for special occasions, and she showed me how to prepare it."

From the bedroom was the faint sound of Harriet's voice. She had gone there when Sammie Livermore called her, the second time since she got home.

As the doorbell rang, Susan said, "I'll get it. Could you?"

As Kerri held the spoon and realised that Susan hadn't said what she wanted, she studied the stovetop. There didn't appear anything needing attention at present.

She returned to the living room and saw Reverend Willard smiling at her.

"Kerri, yet again, today."

Sanders decided that she wouldn't point out the trace of lipstick; it wasn't there earlier at St. Anselm's. And their faces would have given it away, anyway. Discretion was needed until she saw Harriet, at least.

Susan had put herself at the dining table with the chair closest to the kitchen, and Chris on her right side. Kerri was on her left, and she faced Harriet as they all sat down.

"I'd like to say grace," Susan said, holding out her hands.

In her situation, Kerri would have invited Reverend Chris to do that, of course, having a priest visit, but she just joined hands.

"God, we give thanks for the friendships in our life, particularly those gathered here who have helped me so much, the guidance on how to handle the challenges of each day and, above all, the gift of love. Bless the food on our table and if the garlic is too strong, can you fix it before they start eating?"

As Kerri gave a long 'amen' and opened her eyes, Susan said, "The last bit, about the garlic. I don't really ask God to fix things for me, just guide me."

As they ate and talked, Kerri kept giving Harriet a glance

which, among old friends, should have been as clear as a billboard poster. Harriet seemed to miss it each time.

As they cleared away the main course and Susan served an apple and blueberry pie she had made, 'with cream over here, not ice cream, I gather', Kerri looked at her, then at Harriet, who was suppressing a smile.

"You sod! I just realised."

Willard looked puzzled. Susan was smiling.

"You two are an item, that's obvious, and Harriet has been ignoring my glances all through dinner. Which means, Harriet, you told Susan I would be sending you semaphore signals, which I did."

Harriet was laughing. "True, but it is good news."

Susan reached out and took Chris's hand. "Good news for us, at least."

Kerri arched her eyebrows. "Even better news is that, after this pie, I'm taking Harriet for tea or a nightcap over at my place, to give you two some space for a while."

As they finished the dessert, she suddenly asked, "Will you come to St. Anselm's on Sunday, perhaps?"

Susan gave her a blank look. "If your face was like mine at present, would you go to a church on Sunday?"

Kerri gave as good as she got. "In your place, I'd go to church with him with two black eyes and on crutches. And if I were only here for a limited time, I would make the most of it, I tell you, including seeing him on Sunday, clerical garb or not. Find out what he does as well as smile at you."

24 DECISIONS

When Harriet awoke, she could sense that Susan was already up. In the kitchen she found her sipping coffee, reading something on her tablet. True to her prediction, the face was a mix of more intense colours.

"You aren't smiling; not like last night when I got back."

Susan looked at her. "It was wonderful, the dinner and after. Chris told me he had fallen for me. Men, it takes them time to talk about their feelings."

Now, as Susan was recalling it, Harriet could see that she was happy. Her face changed so rapidly with her emotions. From the first time she saw her, at the canon hearing in Ontario, she had seen her face reflect her mood changes.

"So why the expression, as I came in? You should be bouncing with joy."

"Chris said something to me. It made me think of our discussion when you came home yesterday. In fact, he said a lot of things, we both did."

She took a deep breath. "You have someone who has been through my experience, you said. If you want, I will talk to her, but only to help her, not to help the police."

Harriet showed her surprise. "Well, thank you. I wasn't asking for that, just some insight. This is not focused solely on the woman and the possible abuse; it has ramifications for the person and others, including the Cumbria Police."

She thought about it for a moment as she poured her own coffee, an idea occurring. "I could only suggest that your offer might help prepare her for our interview. Thank you for thinking about it, but perhaps you could tell me first why you offered? It's no small thing for you, either. I know that."

So, Susan told her.

Alone yesterday evening, as they kissed and held each other, Susan jumped a little with the pain. Chris realised and pulled back.

"Sorry. I just couldn't believe that you would feel like I do."

She responded, smiling, "It's a bit of an adjustment. I haven't felt like this for a long time."

Willard took her hand. "The clerical collar issue, the doctrine thing, I want to say something. Not debate it, just say it, get it off my chest, up front."

As he looked at her, more serious now, she responded, "And?"

"I worked it out, the main elements, anyway. Harriet said nothing, but the final bit came to me after I made my flippant remark about the clerical collar, when you ran out."

"I can't talk about it."

"I don't want you to, until you are ready, sometime in the future, perhaps. I just need you to accept I am a priest. Anyone who is a Christian priest has a calling, to live and act in the way Jesus Christ told us to, expects of us.

"To me, people abused by a priest have been betrayed first by a man and, for many, later by the church as an institution. When I think of it, which is not often, I admit, it sickens me. How the perpetrator can continue in the priesthood bewilders me. In this shirt, I am still a priest. When I saw you on Penrith Station platform in my clerical collar, I was a man, suddenly realising that the attractions I felt for you during Colin Kavanagh's service were still there. How I dress is irrelevant.

"If we are going any further, we must address this duality at some point, and it needs to be sooner rather than later. Otherwise, I fear it will ruin everything."

Susan seemed lost in thought for a moment.

"You are right, we need to face up to it, work things out. My part will be to deal with those feelings. Your part will be to accept that I can't speak about Duncan Aster with anyone, as there is a secrecy agreement between the institution, as you put it, and me, binding even after Duncan's death."

She saw his intensity and concern and leaned in and kissed him again, enjoying the embrace, the fact they were together, that he was serious about her – and he had been the one to bring the nagging issue of Duncan Aster's effect on her to the surface.

She said, smiling "In my program, with my God, we take things a day at time. But I promise not to take you to task over your Solemn Declarations and Creeds anymore. I will save that for James."

"James?"

"Bishop James Azikiwe, the Anglican Bishop of the Diocese of Hamilton-Brant, my buddy in Hamilton, Ontario. I told him that words like 'bishop' and 'priest' nauseated me at one time and he just smiled, understanding, saying I was like a recovered alcoholic he knew.

Ask Harriet about James, she likes him too. See, you have your bishop and I have mine."

He looked at her, somewhat stunned. "You know a bishop, and you call him your buddy, James?"

"He calls me Susan. Why not?"

As Susan explained to Harriet, she finished with, "I am over the moon and a little astonished with myself, and with Chris, but what he said about being a priest has had me thinking since four o'clock, when I woke. We talked about mission in life, his, mine and how he admires me for my work. If you have someone who is like me, like I was, I will help her if I can. I just have no idea what will happen. If it were an alcoholic or an addict, I could read it better, but there are no guarantees, even then. It is simply an offer; it's your call."

Harriet had been thinking of her own idea as she listened to Susan's explanation. Such a meeting would be extraordinary, as part of an investigation. But undertaking a hard interview with a household television personality was a looming problem, as well. They were all concerned that it could backfire badly. She wanted to run this idea by Sammie and John Kent first, and perhaps Dr. Kulis.

She picked up her coat and bag. "I will call you from the office, either way, let you know. But thank you for having the courage to offer."

~~

Superintendent Chiswell said, "I can't agree. She is not trained, not an employee. We don't even have a secrecy agreement with her."

It was Dr. Kulis who spoke up. He had brought her in for the session with the Deputy Chief Constable, given the serious implications. John Kent thought that his boss wanted to parade his prize expert again. The DCC would have final say.

Yvonne said, "Nor do you want one, a contract or an agreement. Susan Carlson is a licensed addiction counsellor in Ontario, I understand. As for any other health care professional, she cannot breach patient confidentiality, or she could lose her job. Their meeting may be held here, perhaps in this office, but it would not be a police activity at all."

"My office?"

"Well, Carmichael is a star, and this is nicer than the interview rooms or the soft room you use to talk to relatives in, isn't it?"

As he searched for another objection, she said, "This is very innovative. Suitably anonymized, it would make the professional journals. It could reflect well on the Cumbria Police. You could co-author an article, Superintendent."

Ten minutes later, they all trooped into the Deputy Chief Constable's office and Kent was given the job of explaining the plan. Chiswell had warned them that it would be a hard sell.

DCC Warren Beardsley listened. At the end, he said simply, "I recall Sergeant Calder's words at the boy's funeral. If this is what it takes, do it. An academic paper showing that Cumbria Police are innovative is appreciated, Dr. Kulis, of course, but we have parents who need answers. If it goes wrong, I'll front it. You lot just do what's needed; but do it well."

Sammie saw Chiswell's surprise, that there were no misgivings. As they walked back, she said to Harriet, "I like him, a decision maker. Always have."

Her eyes flashed across to Norm Chiswell and then looked straight ahead. Harriet didn't take the object of the glance to be the subject of the statement.

The rest of the day was taken up with preparations by the team, particularly Howard and Louis, who thought at first that they would be replaced in the interviews.

"Why?" Kent asked. "Do either of you feel you are not up to it?"

When he got no response, he said. "You will have Sammie or Harriet with you. You will be fine."

Tomorrow, Valerie Carmichael would be arriving discretely at Penrith Police Headquarters with her solicitor, to answer further questions related to the investigation into the death of Dennis Lewis. They did not tell her that, once she arrived, police officers would be positioned in Bradford, ready to bring in Oliver Mettler if the Carmichael interview was productive. In his case, there would be no option regarding when he attended.

One aspect of the preparations had Sergeant Harriet Calder and Dr. Yvonne Kulis driving separately to the Keswick Town Council car park. From there, Harriet took Kulis to her home, for the best part of an hour. When Harriet dropped the consultant off at her vehicle, she returned to Bassenthwaite.

Tomorrow was going to be a very long day.

25 SECRET

As Valerie Carmichael and her solicitor entered the police headquarters, John Kent greeted them. Felicity Murray, the solicitor, got straight to the point.

"Do you have the letter?"

He simply handed it to her. She read the document and nodded at her client.

"Thirty minutes max, no record, no observation, and the woman cannot be called as a witness. Right?"

She added, "After that, I want time with Ms. Carmichael before the interview. And a briefing from you personally, DCI Kent, before that."

As they were shown into the superintendent's office, two women, one with severe facial bruising and a taller black woman, were waiting at the meeting table.

Murray said, "I thought we were seeing one person."

Kulis replied, "You are. I am just going to explain the ground rules. My name is Dr. Yvonne Kulis, originally from the USA. I am a forensic behavioral psychologist assisting Cumbria Constabulary during the investigation into the death of Dennis Lewis. In your profession, Ms.

Carmichael, the movies call me a criminal profiler.

"This is Susan, Susan Carlson from Canada, a licensed counsellor in addiction therapy. Her field of expertise is not the issue. Her qualification is, as it means that the same confidentiality provisions apply to her as to me or any health care professional.

"Susan is visiting the UK. She was injured in York a few days ago when the male partner of a woman she was helping attacked her. That is the reason for the bruising. She is here voluntarily and unpaid. Specifically, she is not working with the police team. Susan came to stay with a friend who is a member of the investigation team, a person who knows her story. That police officer suggested to the team that Susan should meet you, given the interview about to take place.

"Second, and most important, she will share something with you. The investigation team suspects it may be relevant and helpful to you before your interview. If we are completely wrong, please don't take it out on her; talk to me afterwards, alone here. I do need to leave shortly thereafter, but I will wait to talk with you, should you wish. If we are right, listen to her very carefully indeed."

Valerie had paid attention to Dr. Kulis, but her gaze moved to Carlson and stayed there as the profiler stood and left the room, closing Norm's door behind her.

Susan cleared her throat.

"Before we begin, I have a copy of the letter you just received, and I have printed out for you, Ms. Murray, a copy of my professional license as a counsellor in Ontario, to which I have attached my business card. If I break confidentiality, I could lose my professional standing. From my viewpoint, if either of you say anything here, it stays with me alone."

She took a pause, then focused on Valerie. "I am an

addiction counsellor, working with female addicts and alcoholics, as Dr. Kulis stated. I don't know you at all, though I gather you have a TV series here."

Carmichael smiled at her. "We should be franchised in Canada."

Susan ignored it. As if she was saying nothing out of the ordinary, she continued, "When I was seventeen, I had sex with a Roman Catholic priest very unexpectedly. I admired him, and for a very short while afterwards, I wanted to be with him, dreaming that we could be together. It wasn't true. I was being abused, not loved."

It was so stark and abrupt a revelation, both Carmichael and Murray reacted. It was in their faces, but neither of them said a word.

"The outcome was that afterwards, as I began to understand that abuse, I had no coping mechanism for the despair, no way out of the pain. I ended up an alcoholic and tried to kill myself. It was a long journey back from that low point to a normal life, and from there to the qualifications and experience for my profession today."

She stopped and waited. In the silence, she watched the array of telltales being suppressed on Carmichael's face.

Valerie smiled. "I'm fascinated. Go on. As an actress, I always like character studies."

It was Murray who reacted to the gentle barb. She glanced at Carmichael, back at Susan, and then started watching her client.

Susan pressed on as if Carmichael hadn't spoken. "After we had sex; made love, I thought of it as then, we agreed that it was so special we had to keep it a secret from everyone except God. God understood and forgave us. No-one else would.

"We weren't ignorant of what we had done. I was naïve and didn't see the manipulation, but I had in my arms a most special man, a good man, a servant of God's purpose. We were, strangely enough, both very devout. We were sharing our love, our feelings with God, who would be the only one to say it wasn't a sin."

She looked at the closed door and back at Carmichael.

"In my professional world there is a joke, a truism. 'How do you know when an alcoholic or an addict is lying? The answer is, his or her lips move'. It's a truism for the struggling addict, who will lie about anything rather than admit they have a problem. Counsellors are used to it.

"They have told me nothing about why they want to talk to you, but I would be misleading you if I said that I didn't understand. Your face is picture perfect, but you are an actor, and I have dealt with enough alcoholics and addicts over the years; they, too, are actors in their own way.

"If this were a counselling session, I would decide, based on your file and previous sessions with you, whether it was time to confront some of the telltales I just saw. Police officers can do the same, I suspect, but I doubt in the interview today they will be focused on your preparedness; they have a murder investigation in progress.

"They say that this is linked to the death of Dennis Lewis, so I guess they believe you may know something valuable to that investigation, something that you are holding back. If you are like me, the thing you are hiding away in the recesses of your mind isn't to do with any knowledge of a man and his actions."

Susan saw the change in the woman, as did, she suspected, her lawyer, focused intently on her now.

"The deepest secret I held was my agreement about shame and pain with God. He would never have let me feel such heartbreak without a purpose, I decided. No-one else ever needed to know about it from me. It was my own sort of vow of silence and if I held to that, God would make it right. He would absolve me. I could appear to live a normal life.

"That was my covenant of secrecy with God. I held it through my drinking, my drugging, and my suicide attempt, long after my family and the church knew of the sex act and the betrayal of the priest's vows."

Valerie's demeanor had changed, her body stiffened. "I don't drink very much. And I don't do drugs."

Susan stood. "No. You never needed to; you became an actor. I have finished. Thank you for listening to me. Goodbye, Ms. Carmichael."

There was only one question she should stay for, Yvonne had said. Anything else, walk out. If either one asks it in some form, play it by ear.

It was Carmichael who spoke.

"Why are you helping them?"

Susan gave a small smile. "I'm not. I am a counsellor, not a police officer. The only reason I am here is to give you information that could help you, if you are like me, and if you want it. There is a way out, and I am living proof of it."

"Are you still a Roman Catholic?"

"No. I have a deep faith in God working in my life. But no, I'm not a Roman Catholic. Leaving that church wasn't easy, for me or my parents. They still are Catholics, at a different church now. But I have something that is very precious; I am at peace with myself now, and with God."

Valerie said, partly serious, partly mocking, it seemed, "So, you have no burden to carry any more."

"Not quite. Never completely. Recovery from anything isn't an overnight thing; it's ongoing. Particularly when you wake at three in the morning and it all floods back."

That comment seemed to hit home with Carmichael.

Seeing the reaction, Susan added, "But now I have a means of dealing with that, other than burying it again. I'm pretty much through it, I think. Good luck to you."

The lawyer's face showed that she too had seen the change in her client, as if an invisible shell had cracked slightly. Valerie blinked and reached into her bag for a tissue. She blew her nose hard. Her eyes were moist now but defiant, as Susan Carlson left the room.

When Susan emerged, Yvonne Kulis was standing with Louis Chan, a little distance away. He had been given the task of waiting for the door to open. He saw Carlson emerge alone and closed the door behind her. Yvonne just raised an eyebrow.

Susan nodded once but said nothing. Kingsley came across to her and simply gave her a hug. "OK? You I mean."

Susan looked at her. "Yes. I felt like I was at work. You were right about the only question to stay for. I hope it all helps."

Kulis checked her watch. "As do I. I'll wait here, to see if Murray steps out with an objection. In any case, I didn't want to leave before I was sure you were OK. I am supposed to be in Birmingham and am running late."

She paused. "I'll be really interested to see if this works. Whether or not it does, I thank you for making the effort."

She looked at Chan. "Best get Susan out of here, now."

Louis moved forward. "I'll take you to Sergeant Calder, Ms. Carlson."

He led the way to DCI Kent's empty office. Mooney, standing nearby, asked anxiously, "Did it go OK?" He was becoming nervous about his forthcoming role.

Louis winced. Susan saw Chan's expression and just smiled at Mooney. "Any chance of a cup of coffee now?"

she asked.

Susan didn't know where Harriet appeared from. All she said was, "Are you OK?"

"Fine. I just gave Yvonne the same answer; I feel like I'm at work. DC Mooney is getting me a coffee."

Harriet responded, "John and Sammie are expecting the lawyer to call for the pre-brief for the interview now. Do you want me to get someone to drive you home?"

Susan shook her head. "No, I'll wait. I don't think Carmichael will want to talk after the interview, but if she does, and wants to see me, I'd like to be available."

"Well, stay here, this could take time. Look, I'll read the likelihood of a follow-up as the interview proceeds. I can text you, let you know whether you would be better off going home. You can call Chris."

"He'll be busy. No. But I may go online later and talk with Miriam. And I am going to church on Sunday. I want to see Chris at his work."

26 CHAMPAGNE

In the interview room, once settled, and Carmichael and her solicitor had identified themselves for the recording, Howard Mooney led off. He spoke softly.

"Ms. Carmichael, as I said as we went on record, I am DC Howard Mooney. I am part of the team looking into the death of Dennis Lewis and the people responsible for his disappearance."

Valerie now looked apprehensive. Mooney appeared younger than her, or to be of similar in age. She expected some older person to ask the questions.

"You and Dennis were friends, good friends. His disappearance hit you hard, didn't it?"

"Very hard, yes."

"In a previous interview you told DS Livermore that you and Dennis were not romantically linked. Can you confirm that on record?"

"Yes, we were good friends, but we had no romantic or sexual relationship."

"When you talked to him the day before the concert, in Crosby Street, did he tell you he was planning to go to the concert?"

"No. If he had, I would have said he could come with my parents and my sister. We had room in the car."

"We think he went by train to Carlisle to do so. Did he make it to the concert?"

"I didn't see him there, no."

Carmichael was looking increasingly anxious.

Howard showed her a copy of the church order of service and explained it had been found with his body. "See here. He wrote down 'Nunc dimittis', the work. Did he ask you about that?"

"Yes, he was interested in what I was singing as a solo. I told him about it and sang the opening lines. He thought it sounded nice but was very churchy."

"On the same piece of paper is the word 'Compline'. Do you know what that's about?"

"No, I don't."

Mooney didn't challenge her on that.

"Dennis had another reason to visit Carlisle based on something you told him. What was that?"

"I never asked him to go to Carlisle. Never."

Mooney's confrontation was in an even softer voice, almost a whisper. "But he had a reason; one you gave him, perhaps unintentionally, didn't you?"

He paused and waited, glancing at Sammie, who was revealing nothing. She had told him to wait it out. To Howard, it seemed an eternity.

Looking at Carmichael now, Sammie thought it would be 'make or break' time, as they predicted. Deny it now, Valerie, and we start going uphill, with harder questions, she thought.

"He was my friend, but not my boyfriend. I didn't tell him anything, but he could read my moods and feelings. But you know about that, which is why you had this counsellor talk to me, Carlson."

Howard said gently, "You still need to tell us, though."

"About a week before the concert, he guessed I had a problem with someone. I dismissed it. I never said anything to confirm it."

Howard said, "How did Dennis react?"

"He told me if I needed help, he would always be there for me. I knew that, I said, it wasn't anything. We talked about something else then, I forget what. I consciously made myself look happier, brighter. I recall that."

"You were through it, you thought?"

"Yes."

Howard looked at her sympathetically. "And now it has all come back. And I am sorry to have to do this, but you have just seen the paper found with Dennis's body. So, we need the name of the person you were 'having a problem with', please?"

"It was Oliver Mettler, the music director. The first time, he fondled my breasts after a rehearsal."

She swallowed hard. "Can I have some water, please?"

After putting that on record, I'll buy you champagne, thought Sammie, getting a bottle of water and a plastic glass from a cabinet.

They waited patiently while she drank some. Sammie gave Howard a glance and he asked, "Was that the only time?"

"I had no idea what to do or how to deal with it. He made it seem as if it was… to be expected, which sounds crazy now, I know. I just said I couldn't have sex, that I was a still a virgin. He said he understood but he wouldn't stop. I froze. What was the question again?"

"Was that the only time?"

"No, it happened once more, during the second rehearsal at his house. Mettler fondled more then, but I would rather not go into that. Stupidly, I just closed my eyes and put up with it because I didn't want to make a scene. But we didn't have sexual intercourse. And I never touched him."

Howard asked, "Did you tell anyone?"

"No. All these years, no."

"Did Dennis know, or guess, do you think?"

The solicitor broke in.

"Don't answer that, Valerie. Supposition, officer. You should rephrase your question, please. Also, can I be clear, given the brief from DCI Kent? Are we dealing with the foundation of a sexual assault charge here? Or the death of Dennis Lewis?"

Watching in the viewing room, Kent heard Howard Mooney say very firmly, "The death of Dennis, I assure you. There may be evidence to support other charges emerging, but our focus is on Dennis."

Harriet saw Kent nod. She said, "He's doing well, John."

Howard continued, keeping the soft, gentle approach he had adopted. "You didn't discuss the experiences with anyone. Did Dennis say anything to you that indicated he thought you were being assaulted?"

"Yes, when we met in Crosby Street. He said that I still seemed depressed. I told him I just wanted to get the whole thing over with, the concert, I meant. He seemed to sense it, somehow. In Crosby Street he asked me was someone in the choir bullying me, or what was the problem."

"What did you say?"

"I denied it. Nothing was happening, I told him. The big choir event was just too much for me. On reflection, it was probably not my best acting performance; but then, I wasn't an actor."

"Now you are one, a famous actor. But not a singer, we

noted. Is that experience the reason why you don't sing now?"

Valerie gave him a long look before answering. "You are very perceptive. I stopped after the concert and, even now, get tremendously anxious at the thought of singing, even alone. It's a block of some sort."

In the viewing room, Kent said to Linnie, "Tell Sammie to tell her we are bringing in Oliver Mettler now, to interview him in connection with the death."

He picked up his mobile phone and called the team standing by near Mettler's home.

Sammie gave Howard a glance and took over. "We believe Dennis made it as far as Carlisle to meet someone there about your problem, then possibly attend the concert to hear you sing."

"Dennis went missing around Maryport, though? Not Carlisle. You asked me earlier had he come to the concert. He hadn't."

"Apparently, he never made it to the concert. Only a few people would have known of the site where Dennis's body was hidden, that it would be secluded enough to dispose of a body there. One of those people was possibly Oliver Mettler."

Sammie kept her focus on Valerie as it sank in. "We are bringing Mettler in now for interview, on suspicion of his involvement in the death of Dennis."

Valerie responded, as she realised the implication. "Dennis could have gone to talk to someone about what he suspected. I can see it now. He would go to the person in charge, to talk it through, to identify who was upsetting me."

That's what we think, too, Sammie said to herself, silently.

Valerie Carmichael had probably faked some effective

breakdown scenes in her acting career. No-one in the interview room or the viewing room thought this was acting. She fell apart, sobbing, her head in her hands. The remnants of the contents of the glass of water, caught by her arm, ran across the table.

"Interview suspended at 11.14 a.m.," said Howard.

"No, Interview terminated," said Sammie, grabbing the tissues to mop up, looking at the solicitor.

Felicity Murray said, "Is there somewhere private we can use, please? But give us a few moments alone here, first, if you would. And switch that camera off now."

Harriet went to Kent's office, where Susan was working at something on her phone.

"It might be a good idea if you hang around a bit."

Susan looked at her watch. "That didn't take very long at all. Just let me know."

As she walked back, Harriet thought that was true. Not long, but very productive. And her idea based on Susan's offer, the one that Norm had been so wary about, had paid dividends. So far.

~~

Uniformed police officers brought Oliver Mettler from his home in Bradford and placed him in an interview room in Carleton Hall, awaiting his solicitor. On arrival, Mettler asked to speak to a detective and Sammie went to see him. All he wanted, however, was to know what was happening.

Sammie told him he needed to wait on his legal counsel. It was in relation to the Dennis Lewis enquiry but, having asked for a solicitor, they were required to wait until that person arrived before the interview began.

The team had spent the intervening period absorbing

Valerie's revelations and reviewing their interview plan. Round one now was going to set out the facts and the lies; to lure him into a sense of false confidence. That was Chan, with Sammie. Round two was to rattle his cage until the door slipped open. That was assigned to Harriet and Sammie.

Kent prepared Louis Chan. "He called Arthur Fielding from Lille Associates, based at their Carlisle office, I gather. He will be very attentive to your questions, Louis, and will object immediately if they fall outside the brief given to him. Howard only got pulled up once. Stay calm and focused."

As they waited for the solicitor, DI Nolan came through the office area.

"Good luck, Sammie." He knew the plan, had given John Kent his input separately. Kent had disappeared for a minute.

"Thanks, Ken. We'll soon know."

Nolan looked at Louis, some distance away, focused on his preparations.

He said softly, "Have you noticed, John keeps pushing everyone to do tasks one level higher than we used to do? Flexible use of resources, he said."

Sammie gave him a suspicious look. "Are you thinking what is going through my head; there are changes in the works?"

He nodded. "I wouldn't be surprised."

She squinted. "You plant this on me when we are between heaven and hell on this one?"

"No, straight up. It's just a thought. We all get ones which teeter on the brink at times. I think you have done a great job on this one. John does, too."

He was so sincere she could have hugged him. But in

the office, and knowing his wife, she scrapped that idea and gave him a big smile.

A uniformed officer came into the room and told Sammie that a Mr. Fielding had arrived.

Nolan said, "Go get him, tiger."

~~

Valerie Carmichael had been moved back to Norm's office with Superintendent Chiswell attending and given a cup of coffee. The Deputy Chief Constable came in, part of the standby plan, and said kind words to the celebrity. They could see that the solicitor wanted her client out of there as soon as possible. The senior officers were patient and supportive, as this was one of the delicate phases, in terms of media and politics.

Valerie suddenly asked, "Could I speak again briefly with the woman I met first, Susan Carlson? Is she still here? She said she wasn't a police officer. And with the young officer who interviewed me, DC Mooney. And would you please stay while I do that?"

When Mooney and Susan entered, Chiswell introduced the tall, mainly bald man in uniform to Susan. Beardsley was carefully assessing her bruises. Mooney was now well out of his comfort zone wondering what he was facing, with Chiswell and Beardsley there.

Carmichael spoke to him first. "Thank you for being so considerate during your questions, DC Mooney. I have played roles in police dramas. They were never like that. You were very thoughtful. I just realised how important that can be."

Mooney replied, "I did my job, ma'am, but thank you for the recognition. It was hard for you, I know. We appreciate your help."

He looked at Superintendent Chiswell, whose series of expressions could be interpreted as, 'well done, but clear off now before you put your foot in it'. Pleading work, Howard did exactly that. His next task was out of the office, heading over to Leeds, to coordinate with the forensic team now looking at the wreckage of the Volvo that Oliver Mettler drove in 2008.

Susan stood there, waiting. Harriet hadn't appeared, she had no guidance, and here she was with Carmichael, the lawyer, and two senior police officers.

Valerie went up to her and took her hand, holding it. "Thank you for your honesty. I still can't take it in you don't even work here. There will be a path forward, as you said. The truth is out now, after all these years. I feel so embarrassed and – guilty."

Susan responded, "Get professional help, I suggest, even if you feel it to be unnecessary."

"Well, thank you again, anyway. It helped me a lot."

Valerie nodded and looked at her solicitor, her face signalling she was ready to go. She shook hands with the Deputy Chief Constable before Superintendent Chiswell, showing his gallant side, opened the door and accompanied them out.

Beardsley said, "I add my thanks to that, Ms. Carlson, on behalf of Cumbria Police. Sergeant Calder must be a good friend for you to do this."

"She is."

He nodded. "Is there anything we can do to help you?"

Susan shook her head, "No, but I need to get back to Bassenthwaite. I think Harriet is busy."

He nodded. "She's a good officer. I'll organise a car for you. Your face, does it still hurt?"

She nodded. "Particularly so if I catch the bruises on anything, a towel, or my comb. I'm just waiting for the travel insurance people to say I can fly home."

Then she realised that wasn't quite true. She needed to go home, but she didn't want to leave Chris. It was a dilemma.

DCC Beardsley gave her a stern look. "I had a word with my opposite number in York a few minutes ago. I told him I was very unhappy that a visitor to this country helping both a citizen in distress there, and now the Cumbria Police, was attacked in Coppergate. He agreed with me."

As do I, thought Susan. Looking at him, Susan didn't want to be a person who disagreed with DCC Beardsley. She got the impression that Janine's 'Dev' would be facing one of those preposterously long American-style prison sentences, probably on stale bread and cold water.

An hour later, a dark blue limousine with a small crest of the 'Cumbria Police' visible on the lower corner of the boot lid, drove smoothly into the narrow driveway to St. Anselm's Church. Susan hoped to surprise Chris, who was supposed to be there.

As she got out of the back seat, two elderly women came out of the main door, staring at her and the car.

As it drove off, one said, "Reverend Willard was called away suddenly. He has a death to attend. So, you are Susan? Kerri's been telling us about you."

The other, opening the door that had closed behind them, said, "How nice of you to come. It's terrible that you were hurt over here. Would you like a cup of tea?"

Her fellow interrogator jumped back in. "That is a nice car you arrived in. Are you a police officer, too?"

As Susan tried to extricate herself and work out how to get to Harriet's home, the questions kept coming as, no handcuffs in sight, she was led into the church.

27 METTLER

After they identified themselves on record, the first question was, "Dr. Mettler, do you have any knowledge of, or involvement in, either the disappearance or death of Dennis Lewis?"

Louis put it softly, routinely, as an interesting question, not an accusation.

Oliver Mettler looked upset, more in sorrow than anger. "No, sir, I do not. I am still coming to terms with being brought to a police station under suspicion and my home being searched. All I can say is that somewhere, I don't know how, someone has made a serious mistake."

His voice trembled a little. He was shaken, he conveyed. If this bad dream would go away, he was ready to forgive and forget.

His solicitor, Arthur Fielding, looked stoic. Eyeing Louis Chan, he seemed to convey that the slightest mistreatment of his client would have consequences. After briefing Fielding before the interview, the only comment the solicitor made was, "I hear a lot of circumstantial elements in your reasoning. You had better have tangible proof. He is a respected and talented musician, a member of staff of a church, not a criminal gang. You will treat him accordingly."

Kent said nothing. They were committed to some hard questioning, if needed. They would like factual, tangible proof, too. And if he had been a gang member, the case would be handled by a different division in Cumbria Police.

Fifteen minutes later, Louis had settled into his role. Kent observed him closely from the viewing room.

"Dr. Mettler, please tell me what you did between the hours of four and ten p.m. on the fifth of June 2008."

"That was the night of the concert. I had a light snack and went over to the cathedral early, perhaps around five or five-thirty. I ran through the annotations on my score, so they were fresh in my mind. It's pretty vague now."

Kent thought Mettler sounds good, but nothing is trackable, verifiable.

Louis pressed on. "Where did you park?"

He looked surprised. "Near the cathedral, I think."

Louis opened his file and pulled out a blurry photograph from a street camera. "Is this your car outside the Methodist Central Hall at 5.30 p.m. that day? A blue Volvo V50 estate. The plate is visible."

He looked at it. "Yes. That was my car. I don't own it now. And the Hall is only three or four minutes away on foot from the cathedral. We had the final run-through there."

Louis pulled out another piece of paper. "This is a photocopy of a record book of keys issued and returned, maintained by the Methodist Hall. Do you confirm that a key loaned to you was returned on June 11, at 3.32 p.m.?"

He studied the sheet, with his name and a signature. "Yes, I returned it a couple of days after the concert, on my way to another activity. I can't remember what."

We will return to that, thought Louis. He had his instructions. Let it slide, for now.

Sammie interrupted him. "Do you have your 2008 appointment diary anywhere?"

"Yes, of course, I used a standard desk diary back then, from W. H. Smiths. I'm not sure I have every one of them, though. Things go missing over time. And now I am all digital."

Sammie stared at him. She was sure that diary for the year had disappeared. They had found others at the house, but not the year in question. And he was already aware they had executed search warrants. He made a fuss at the time he was told, but in the interview, he didn't repeat that exercise; it was all vague co-operation.

Louis said, "Do you recall anything specific that you did over the following day or so, Mr. Mettler, without your diary to hand?"

"Dr. Mettler. I hold a doctoral degree in music." He looked annoyed.

It was a mistake, Louis's first. The young detective said, "I'm sorry. Doctor, yes."

Mettler said nothing but appeared mollified somewhat.

Kent said, "Now there is a hot button for you both, Sammie and Harriet, for later. Linnie, tell her."

Harriet, sitting next to Kent, didn't react. Sammie, sitting in the interview room, just nodded imperceptibly.

From their preparations, Harriet knew they would be through Mettler's sincere-sounding responses, the non-recall and misinformation stage of the interview, within twenty minutes at this rate. It was on to the next stage of the preliminary now, the issue of Compline.

Louis asked, "What is Compline?"

They could see the sudden tension in the man. "It's a prayer sequence, a service, in the Christian faith."

"Does the Cross of the Redeemer church have a service called Compline?"

"No. Our church services are more focused on the gospels, being an evangelical church. It is a little different to, say, Roman Catholicism or the Church of England."

Louis persisted. "But even those churches don't regularly have a service late in the evening, do they?"

Mettler responded evenly. "If you know what Compline is, why did you just ask me to explain it?"

It was his eyes, showing the annoyance building. Fielding, who had been silent so far, said quietly, "Just answer the questions, Dr. Mettler, or indicate that you will not comment."

Louis pressed on. "You have a breviary, other officers noticed. Well used. Rather than a formal service, do you say the office of Compline as part of your personal faith?"

The eyes were still angry. "My prayers are my private matter. No comment."

Louis saw Mettler was waiting for the next question. He knows where we are going now. Calder would take that one up later; the issues of his prayers around the time Dennis was killed.

Sammie, spoke up. "Let's move to Valerie Krestman, Now Valerie Carmichael. Louis?"

She nodded at Louis.

He asked, "How would you describe your interactions with Valerie, as a soloist at that concert?"

"We performed well together, with the trumpeter."

"How long did you spend together? Not at the concert; beforehand."

Mettler thought about it, searching back, he conveyed. "The rehearsal each time was about thirty or forty minutes. A singer gets tired. Her father dropped her off and collected her. He had other things to do, I recall."

Louis asked, "When you were interviewed previously at your church, you made no mention of the earlier rehearsals, and that they were at your former home. Why?"

"Because I didn't think about them at the time, obviously."

There was a sudden irritation showing, in his voice and face.

Louis pressed the point. "But you now remember those rehearsals, don't you?"

"Dragging me here and making accusations, well... yes. Bits."

The solicitor interjected, "Is this line of questions related to your investigation into the death of Dennis Lewis? Or is this leading to an allegation of a relationship between my client and Valerie Krestman?"

Louis looked to Sammie for guidance. Sammie said, shortly, "They overlap. To both. But as you raised the issue, Mr. Fielding, I must now ask Dr. Mettler the question. Did you have a sexual interaction of any sort with Valerie Krestman?"

The solicitor's hand went to the file in front of him, beside his notebook, and started to open it. Then he stopped and shook his head. "Dr. Mettler is here in relation to an allegation of his involvement in the death of Dennis Lewis. That was the pre-brief I received. It is already confusing enough for my client. I want a break to resolve this with DCI Kent, if necessary, and be briefed further about any sexual assault allegation. Dr. Mettler, you should not answer any questions regarding Valerie Carmichael at this point, is my advice to you."

Mettler nodded and addressed Sammie Livermore. "I think the answer I must give, Sergeant, is 'no comment'."

He looked at the camera, his face unreadable.

Arthur Fielding added, "And I want to know which

allegation, if there are two, we plan to deal with first."

In the viewing room, John Kent said to Linnie, "Tell Sammie to take a break."

As they regrouped, Chan, Kent, Livermore and Calder, John Kent said to Louis, "Well done. Nearly an hour of leading the interview and you were steady, despite his non-answers."

Louis said, "Thank you. But I don't think I made very much progress. And I apologise for my slip-up on 'Doctor'. It annoyed him prematurely."

Sammie smiled at him as Kent said, "Don't be. It gave the first crack in Mettler's front to us."

She added, "No, it was good. We are getting a read of him. I see Fielding's strategy, but I'm worried now about focusing on Valerie."

"Exactly," said Kent, softly. "We have until tomorrow morning before we are required to release him. Fielding will certainly push for him to be allowed home tonight, which I will deny. It is going to be hard to request an extension without hard facts. If most of this afternoon is taken up with the issue of his inappropriate relationship with Valerie, we will lose a lot of momentum. Harriet, what do you think he is going to do on Valerie's claims?"

Before she could answer, Chan said, "I saw Fielding start to reach for something, a slip of paper, old paper. Then he closed his file again."

Harriet said, "Good catch. I was going to say, he has something he plans to table, a note of some sort from Mettler. Perhaps it records a claim that Valerie made advances to him, which he rejected. It could be that sort of thing, and degenerate into a 'he says, she says' bout."

John sighed. "That will drag it out further still. I can see it."

He paused. "We stop phase one now. Sammie, you and Harriet go in next and hit him with the sequence of events and what we have. Depending on how it goes, I will let you know whether to pause at any point or go for broke. I want Mettler knocked off that comfortable pedestal we have had him on. See what that brings."

He looked at the clock. "Five minutes. I will meet now with Fielding and agree to his request, saying we will deal with the issue of Valerie Carmichael's claims separately. If you see it going down, if you need to use it, throw it in and I'll deal also with that complaint afterwards."

As he walked off, Sammie's parting comment was, "I just hope the search teams come up with something concrete."

Louis asked Sammie, "Should I go now, and join Howard and help out?"

"No. Observe. This is not likely to drag on. Watch and learn."

Kent nodded his agreement from the door.

Harriet sat preparing herself, knowing it was going to get rough. She thought back to being with Eamon and Bernice, the promise she made to them in Maryport, to do the best she could to identify the person who killed their son. It helped her resolve.

28 COMPLINE

When they entered the interview room, Harriet sat across from Oliver Mettler and Sammie retook her seat opposite Fielding.

Both men looked prepared.

As the recording began, Sammie asked, "Dr. Mettler, what happened to your bike? You don't have one anymore."

He seemed surprised.

"I sold it two years ago. I gave up cycling, with knee problems."

"You owned a road bike, I gather. A fair-weather cyclist, were you?"

Get right in his face, John Kent had told her. Sammie needed no encouragement on that score.

"I rode my bicycle in spring, summer, and autumn if that is what you are implying. As I remember, we had some foul weather in each of those seasons."

"When you had the bike and lived in Alston, you stored it during the winter in the garage, on a fancy pulley system you installed. No hernias from lifting the bike up and down to its storage hooks for you. Correct?"

The word 'pulley' prompted the flicker in Mettler's eyes, a sudden anxiety, it seemed. He understood the line of questioning. It was momentary, but it provided a telltale that mattered. He knew its implications.

In the solicitor's briefing before the interview, Sammie had said they would explore whether Dennis Lewis had ever been to Mettler's home.

"Yes, I stored it out of the way."

Sammie looked at a piece of paper taken from the file she had opened.

"At university, you were a member of a vintage car club. We have evidence of that. So, you would know about hoists and pulleys, for moving engine blocks and so on. Can you confirm that?"

Mettler seemed confused, then slightly amused. "That was quite a while ago. I enjoyed the club, but I recall little about it now."

Sammie went on, "Oh, we think you do. You knew enough to install a pulley but not enough to do so properly. But I'll come back to that."

She pulled another piece of paper from her file, saying, "We have been doing a lot of work on your activities."

She showed the document to Mettler and his solicitor. "A sales receipt for a four foot long, fifteen cubic feet Indesit chest freezer, bought by you on June 6, 2008, one day after the choir concert at Carlisle Cathedral. Delivered the same day, it says."

She smiled. "Does that ring a bell, as one thing you did in the two days after the concert?"

"Now you mention it, and we are talking about ten years ago, I did, yes."

"Why did you buy a freezer?"

"To store frozen food, of course."

"Where did you position the freezer?"

He looked at her, hesitating, his eyes suddenly worried again. That provided the second reveal. His hesitation was a breakthrough, as he thought about lying, Sammie saw. In the viewing room, John Kent gave a small sigh. They needed to push now.

"I wanted it in the house but, as I recall, it was first placed in the garage. I never did get it moved from there, afterwards."

"That's right. Your former cleaning lady recalled seeing it there, locked. You bought one with a lock."

Mettler said nothing in response. It was a statement. He waited.

Sammie continued, "We have forensic officers now examining your old garage, a search team in your office at the Cross of the Redeemer and others in your current home. We are checking your bank records and your credit cards. Other police officers in the Yorkshire Constabulary are helping us go through the junkyard where the Volvo you drove at the time was recently scrapped."

She sat back, waiting. After a long ten-second wait, she said, "Aren't you going to ask why?"

He sounded exasperated. "Obviously, it's because you think I was somehow involved in the disappearance of Dennis Lewis. The other officer, Chan, asked me about that earlier. But why you are doing all this, I still don't understand."

Sammie shook her head. "We are beyond the boy's disappearance. Now we are tracing back exactly how you disposed of Dennis Lewis, Mr. Mettler. We are past the kill stage now. Harriet?"

"Doctor."

He repeated the correction he had made to Louis earlier.

Sammie responded, "A professional title that I associate with a healer. Not one I want to use with a man I believe murdered a fifteen-year-old boy. Harriet?"

Louis thought that Calder would build on Sammie's swipe at him; he knew the points she would cover next.

But she didn't; she waited a moment or two, her expression somewhere between disappointment and bewilderment. Then she looked at Fielding and spoke to him. "Geoffrey Bergon's Nunc dimittis arrangement. I have always liked that piece, until recently. I would never have known it without the BBC usage, the story of a spy betraying his country over many years. Now..."

Her gaze swung on to Mettler. "Now I wish I could forget that link. Now I see it as the theme music for a crime about a choir director who betrayed his faith for many years."

From Mettler's expression, it was a verbal slap in the face. Harriet left no time for objection or any rebuttal.

"We have your breviary. Compline, the night prayer; do you say it regularly? *Save us, O Lord, while waking, and guard us while sleeping...*

She looked at him, waiting.

In the viewing room, Louis said, "They are really pushing it."

Kent said nothing, but Linnie murmured, "They have hardly started. Watch Harriet."

Harriet Calder was a straight player, Louis thought, no nonsense, certainly not a bully. The last few seconds had him not so sure about that last point.

Mettler picked up the line. "*...that awake we may watch with Christ and asleep may rest in peace.* That is the opening of the Nunc dimittis."

He sounded tolerant as he finally gave his answer. "I try to."

She continued, "The reality is that mornings and evenings are crowded, with other aspects of life. You do your daily offices when you can fit them in. Right?"

He gives her a quizzical look. "I try to be faithful to my daily devotions, whether alone or with others, or simply with the prayers in my breviary."

She said, "It took time to work it out, but you did see Dennis Lewis, didn't you? Before the concert, somewhere. A place you chose, I'm sure. Methodist Central Hall."

Mettler looks at her dismissively, saying nothing.

Her voice took on an abrasive tone.

"I asked, did you see Dennis Lewis on the fifth of June 2008 at Methodist Central Hall?"

"No."

"After the concert, perhaps. Did you see him then?"

"No."

"Two denials. One more and I'll hear the cock crow, eh?"

A biblical reference, the taunt that he was lying, clearly angered the man. He just closed his eyes briefly and sat back.

Harriet opened her own file and withdrew a sheet of paper. "For the record, I am showing Dr. Mettler a copy of a church bulletin found with the body of Dennis Lewis at Crosshill Farm. It is a Methodist Church bulletin for services in the period mid-May to Mid-June 2008.

"On the back, in handwriting identified as belonging to Dennis, there are three words. In this area are the words Nunc dimittis. In this area is the word Compline."

She asks, "Do they jog any memories for you, Dr. Mettler?"

"No."

"Not Nunc dimittis, which you know so well, given our discussion now and the choir concert with Valerie? The piece you performed."

"Well, yes in that context. Yes. But I know nothing about something you found."

"How about Compline, which Dennis Lewis wrote down after he phoned you, perhaps?"

"I never spoke to the boy. You have that wrong. Please stop this badgering."

They could hear the tone change. Firm denial. Too firm. And Fielding was not intervening, both detectives noticed. He knows his job. As soon as they move off Dennis Lewis, he will be pressing Harriet and Sammie for a re-direction or a break.

Harriet leaned forward a little, compensating for the move backward by Mettler. "If someone used the words Nunc dimittis and Compline to Dennis, he would probably have asked how to spell them. He was a keen student. And he and Valerie were friends."

She stared at the lawyer, challenging him. "And Valerie was depressed and hiding something. It disturbed Dennis enough to want to help her. We suspect he thought it was another person in the choir bullying or abusing her in some way. Dennis was concerned enough to talk to the person he thought could help him fix the problem, the person in charge of the choir. Perhaps at a meeting agreed at short notice in that person's busy day."

Peripherally, she could see that Mettler was locked on her now. She added, "Someone who would drop the word Compline into the conversation. We looked for anything, anywhere which was a service for Compline, even the snobby public schools lost in the traditional rubbishy rituals they get up to. We checked other churches, other denominations and, you know what, it made no sense. There wasn't a Compline service anywhere between Maryport and Carlisle that day. And it's a service later, not early evening."

Mettler was now looking at her with disdain. The jibe about public schools had revealed this woman's animosity; they would know he was educated at one.

Harriet said confidently, with emphasis, looking into Mettler's eyes. "It made no sense until I realised it wasn't a service, or an observance of the Daily Office. It was simply a lure."

John Kent was intently focusing on them. In the silence of the viewing room he said, "Louis, did you see that? Fielding's eyes showed his surprise then his understanding. Mettler's eyes showed nothing. He was already there."

"I was watching Mettler, boss, so no. Thanks. I'll re-run the recording later."

Calder spoke more aggressively now. "He might be aware of Evensong, living across from St Mary's, but not Compline. Dennis wanted to talk to you about his friend. You tied it to a vague event he could see you at before the concert. 'Something I perform as part of my daily prayers'. Was that it? You would be free then. To talk alone with him. That's why he probably traveled from Maryport well before the concert and that's when you killed him."

Mettler says, "This is preposterous. Mr. Fielding, can she say these things?"

He didn't get a chance to respond.

Sammie spoke up. "After the choir concert, after everyone went home, you had to deal with the body, still at the deserted hall, probably hidden somewhere. Not easy, doing that, we know. We see it messed up; the things people try to do. They decide to cut them up and find they are too squeamish to finish the job. A bloody awful mess, literally, in the bathtub.

"You came up with the idea of the freezer. Keep him frozen until the hue and cry over his disappearance goes quiet. Then, weeks later, once you found your site, once you knew that no one would be walking the land at Cross-hill Farm, you took your opportunity. Thaw him out a bit and hoist him up."

She looks at Calder. "The bindings around Dennis were to keep him constrained for storage, or for some perversion, some bondage thing prior to death. Are you into bondage, Mr. Mettler?"

"Don't be ridiculous."

"It was just a straight storage and movement job then. Except, frozen and a lot heavier, the hoist gave way at one end. It wasn't strong enough. Down falls poor Dennis's head and bangs into the edge of the freezer. But you got him out, into the car, into the field, into his new home, didn't you?

"That's a question, by the way. Did you store Dennis Lewis in a freezer in your garage in Alston and eventually transfer him to Crosshill Farm?"

"No."

Sammie looked at Harriet. "That's 'no' number three, isn't it?"

"Number four, at least. He puts Peter to shame."

The biblical reference that had so annoyed Mettler earlier; Jesus's prediction that Peter would deny knowing him three times before the cock called out the arrival of sunrise.

Sammie reached into her folder and brought out two more documents.

"Statement from a former neighbour, Hugh Kelly, who bought the freezer you sold. It had a crack in the top edge, which is why you sold it so cheap, he told us. He sealed it, but with the cold, it never stayed sealed properly and his wife worried about contamination and germs, so they sent it for disposal."

The solicitor jumped in. "You don't have the freezer?"

"No."

"What we have," says Sammie, "is a tiny fleck of plastic found in the forehead, stuck to the bruised area of bone. One we couldn't tie to any standard implement used to kill someone. It is being analysed, to see if it is the same as a sample from the same make of freezer, of the same age.

The solicitor responds quietly. "Again, sergeant, this is all speculative, circumstantial at best. Plastics are not that unique."

Harriet suddenly leaned forward, getting into Mettler's face.

"What gets me, Dr. Mettler, is the extent of the damage and suffering inflicted on the Lewis family. As a preacher myself, I am also dismayed about the far broader damage to come. You have been a church musician for over twenty years. In that time, you have brought joy to thousands of congregants and given wonderful performances. Once this gets out, people who see you as a beacon of their faith, part of their journey in the love of Jesus Christ, will think twice."

Sammie saw Mettler's throat swallow hard, his head rising in indignation at the slur on his professional life and his role with the church, a picture of both anxiety and anger.

In the viewing room, Chan picked up on it, too. He knew intuitively that Mettler had been caught unawares by that one. He looked to see Kent's reaction, but he was focused on the screen. It was Linnie, at the recording controls and the microphone, the veteran of many of these sessions, who asked.

"Boss?"

"Tell them to go for it; flat out."

Linnie murmured the instruction into her microphone

and Sammie's head nodded slightly as she and Harriet exchanged glances.

Harriet continued, with her eyes fixed on Mettler.

"They may leave the churches you were at. They may leave the faith entirely. Remember the Messiah performance three years ago? At your church? It was packed, I heard. People talked about a future one being televised. As if, now.

"Doubters, on hearing about your crime, won't even join the Cross of the Redeemer, tainted by Dr. Mettler, the unrepentant child killer, the man who molested a young virgin then killed the friend who tried, in his innocence, to help. Everything you have done in the last decade is totally, utterly worthless. Every piece of religious music you have performed or directed is contaminated now."

Her contempt was filling the room. She leaned even further towards him as she spoke, seeing the anger rising. Her voice dropped in volume.

"So, tell me this, Oliver, an evangelical whatever you are to a plain old Methodist. Did you pray properly for Dennis when you buried him, or did you just dump your rope bag of meat and bone in the hole? Did you forget how to do that, pray? Were you too busy hiding your awful crime?"

The fist came out of nowhere, hard, with a crunch as it hit Harriet's face. Mettler jumped to his feet, his own chair toppling, his face purple with anger.

Arthur Fielding saw Calder fall, her chair tilting back and rotating sideways, her legs flying up as a shoe came loose and sailed in an arc. He felt Sergeant Livermore's hip bang his shoulder as she raced around him to tackle and restrain his client.

The most significant element for the solicitor, however, was Oliver Mettler's voice, yelling at full volume.

"No, you self-righteous Methodist cow, I didn't dump him in the hole. I buried him, and I prayed for him, and asked for forgiveness from God. The whole thing was an accident."

By then, the room was filling with police officers.

29 ARREST

As they helped Calder up, she held her hand to the side of her face. Chan caught Harriet's look at Sammie, now holding Mettler's shoulder and wrist, restraining him. The man had gone limp, as if he, too, was shocked at his actions.

Sammie beamed at her, the smile of victory, but Calder's face showed only pain. Intuitively, Louis felt only part of that was physical. He had just witnessed a side of Calder and Livermore he hadn't seen previously. Calder particularly. If he got into trouble, he wouldn't want to face her. Her interview skills were formidable.

John Kent entered the room with two uniformed officers, glanced at Mettler, then at Fielding, who was clearly disturbed. Kent signalled for the uniforms to relieve Sammie, as one brought out handcuffs.

"Interview terminated at 3.32 p.m. by DCI John Kent on entering, as Oliver Mettler has assaulted Sergeant Calder. Take him away, Sergeant Livermore, and arrest him on that charge now. Place him in custody."

Kent reached over and switched off the recording. "Are

you all right, Mr. Fielding?"

Fielding nodded, then said, "I need a few moments, that's all. And then time to makes some notes."

"You can stay here." Kent's eyes fell on the second constable. "Bring Mr. Fielding some water, or tea or coffee, please, as he wishes."

He turned, following Calder, with Sammie and Louis now helping her, out of the room.

Fifteen minutes later, Mettler was in a holding cell.

A station first aid officer had checked over Calder. Procedure called for her to be taken to the hospital for a check-up. For some minutes, Harriet talked quietly with John Kent alone.

Louis Chan, now back in their work area, spoke to Sammie as she sat drinking a juice, destressing.

"It was amazing, the way you two did that."

"Harriet took him over the top. It hurt her to do it, and I don't mean just the punch. It hurts her to act aggressively like that, particularly about aspects of the church."

Louis responded, "But she is a natural, finessing everything into the last go at him. Well, you both did."

Sammie replied, "Louis, both you and Howard did very well today. Howard, I have known him for years. I'm glad you are on my team, both of you."

"We should celebrate."

"We will, the three of us. Harriet won't be up to it."

"He gave her quite a punch. She will be hurting."

Sammie didn't respond. She knew Harriet better, about what hurt her. But these two needed the celebration, the recognition.

~~

After the X-rays and checks for any signs of concussion, Kent assigned Louis Chan the job to take Harriet home from the hospital. Sammie was busy with the follow-up documentation while John Kent met with Chiswell and the communications team. Charging a noted musician with the murder of a boy ten years ago would make national and international headlines. When it became known that it was tied to a prior sexual assault of a choir member, it would gain further notoriety.

Mettler was to be interviewed further tomorrow. Arthur Fielding agreed to that.

Chiswell was happy with the development. "They still need to keep up the pressure for any hard evidence. Tomorrow, John, make sure that Mettler gives us some of that himself. It will be a lot easier if he leads us to it."

Kent just nodded. His boss was always one for stating the obvious.

"And hopefully we will protect Miss Carmichael's good name."

That got another nod. Fleetingly, John Kent wondered if Norm was after an autograph or a signed photo of the star. He doubted that Chiswell was into selfies.

In the car, Louis stayed quiet. As much as he wanted to be back in the middle of things, he felt it was a privilege to take Harriet home. A uniformed officer was behind them, driving Harriet's car. They would return together and by eight-thirty, at the latest, Sammie promised, they would be in the pub.

"It's not the first punch I've taken, Louis. Liven up a bit. Thank God the chair rocked back; it took a lot of the energy of the punch."

"I'm thinking about how you did it, boss. Going back over your words, the way you built it. John had said we needed a confession, and you got one."

"We all did it, from you onwards. I hope you see that. It was teamwork. And it's not 'boss'; it's Harriet. Not for the first time."

Chan shook his head firmly. "You should be leading this team. We all think it. You'll be 'boss' to me, as far as I'm concerned."

He sighed. "But I am glad DCI Kent made me do the first interview with Mettler. I really feel part of the team now, not an add-on. And as part of it, I can give you all the bitching it takes until you take the DI job."

Harriet responded smugly. "No, you can't. I asked John, got him at a weak moment. I can go back to my old job now, thank you, once I go back on duty. Back to Keswick and away from that vile example of a man."

After Chan left, and Harriet changed into more comfortable clothes, she sat with Susan for a while drinking tea, loosely bringing her up to date.

Susan said, "So, the man who molested Valerie also killed the boy. He'll probably have a boatload of excuses."

"John and Sammie are handling that. I'm glad it's over for me. Apparently, the killer has a temper on him."

Susan laughed out loud. "You don't say?"

"I mean, he exploded in anger at Dennis Lewis much the way he did with me. He killed Dennis in anger, he said, as he was being taken away. John will be the one to break the news to Bernice and Eamon, his parents. Once the charge is made, he will go over, taking the police chaplain with him this time."

Susan pondered it a little. "I am thinking of the man who assaulted Valerie, and of Duncan. Duncan Aster wasn't evil if that's the best term to use. He abused me, but he was basically a good man. But both men were petrified about losing image, losing their status. It drove their actions afterwards, and eventually drove Duncan to his death. The lack of humility, the inability to come to terms with their guilt."

Harriet was reminded of her session with Dominic McCluskey in Haverigg Prison. She hoped that Susan was right, that Aster's actions had been impulsive, not carefully planned.

"Well, it will send the person we have arrested to prison, at least. But the damage is done; it is the healing that people need to focus on now."

Susan continued, "What I was going to say, what I was leading to, is that I see none of that in Chris. He's a priest, but he has none of that image, that condescension. He is at the other end of a spectrum."

Harriet smiled. "He is, with a lot of others, thank God. It's good to hear you say it. I've been watching. I'm not around much, but you two seem good together. It is a pleasure to watch."

Susan takes a deep breath. "And, as I said, I am going to his church on Sunday."

"At St. Anselm's?"

No, he is at St. Cuthbert's. I was cornered by two women at St. Anselm's earlier. I thought I would surprise him. The car dropped me off there, but he was with someone dying, they told me. But he is coming here when he finishes."

Harriet was tiring, Susan observed. "Well, it's over with. Once your bruises fade, you can get back to your normal life."

Harriet gave a wry smile and a shake of the head, which she instantly regretted.

"Back to Keswick, yes. Over with; I very much doubt that."

She didn't elaborate, just seemed lost for a moment or two. "Enough of that. You have only a few days here. You and Chris need to spend time together. Focus on him, not me. St. Cuthbert's indeed."

"Why 'indeed'? Where is it?"

"To a city girl like you, in the middle of nowhere. It's small. They will be packing the gunnels."

That made Susan's face show even more confusion.

"Gunnels. Gunwales. A naval term. The church will be full of women. Probably some from his three churches, the ones who act like doting mothers to their young bachelor vicar, and their daughters, the ones who swoon over him. They will all want to see the woman who he has fallen for."

"I'm still going. I'll wear the suit I wore when I spoke at the conference."

When the doorbell rang, Susan went to answer, hoping it was Chris, back from his bereavement call. It was Kerri.

"I saw the car, so Harriet's home. How's the face?"

Susan took a breath. "You had better come in. It is, 'how are the faces' today."

PART 3

Aftermath

30 RETRACTION

Sammie had just bought the drinks for Howard, Louis, Linnie, and herself when her phone rang. It was the custody sergeant in the cell block.

"There was a call here from a Reverend Lambert, wanting to visit Oliver Mettler tonight. I told him that people in custody don't get visitors, only their solicitor. He said he was his priest, so I gave him five minutes on the phone and told him to check again tomorrow about a visit."

Sammie thanked him but didn't give it much thought. Given Mettler's blurted confession and paltry excuses uttered as he was taken away, she could see the need.

After she closed the call, she said to her team, "Mettler's priest wanted to visit him, a Reverend Lambert. Perhaps he needs it, before we interview him again."

It was Louis who pursed his lips. "He's in charge at the Cross of the Redeemer. It's logical, I suppose, for him to be Mettler's priest. But he is the man's boss, too."

Sammie realised she knew that name from the file. The events of the day had made her miss it. She was tiring.

She thought for a moment then raised her glass. "Here's to Harriet. We are going to miss her."

The glasses chinked as they moved on. The following day, Louis's observation was to come back to haunt her.

Before the morning briefing, John Kent called Sammie into his office when Tim Hutton, a crown prosecutor, arrived. As they seated themselves at the table, John said, "I had a call this morning at seven-thirty, from Arthur Fielding. He simply said that he had spoken by telephone with his client and no longer represents Oliver Mettler."

Sammie saw Hutton's eyes look at the ceiling as he grimaced. She asked, "Is there a conflict?"

Had Arthur Fielding identified a conflict of interest? If so, professional standards would require him to withdraw from the case.

Kent was looking at Hutton. "He didn't say. He just informed me. Tim?"

Hutton asked, "Has Mettler talked to anyone since his arrest, do you know? Other than Fielding?"

Sammie suddenly realised. "His spiritual advisor asked to visit him yesterday, late in the evening, a Reverend Lambert. The custody sergeant explained he couldn't do so but gave him a few minutes on the phone with Mettler. Lambert is the CEO of the church that employs Mettler, in Bradford."

The lawyer said, "I smell a retraction in the air, if he is changing defense counsel. Given his confession, the statement from Carmichael and the assault on Calder, that will be an uphill road if ever there was one. But it feels that way. John, you should go and speak to him, ask him about the news from Fielding, see what he says. I'll wait."

Kent sighed. "We have the morning briefing next. I'll put that off for fifteen minutes."

During the wait, Sammie brought the prosecutor up to speed with the developments in the case. When Kent reappeared, he said, "Mettler confirmed it. He is waiting for his new solicitor but couldn't give me a name. He said he would say nothing until he had met with the person."

He looked out of his office into the MIU operations area. "We had better get on with the briefing. The teams need to get on with other work."

Hutton stood, ready to leave. "You will be charging Mettler, though?"

With the murder of Lewis and the assault on Carmichael before the detention clock expires, he inferred. Mettler was already charged with assault on Calder.

John Kent confirmed it. His final words were, "I hope your suspicion is wrong, Tim. I want the path forward on this one largely resolved today, from my end, if I can."

Hutton nodded, but his face was questioning that comment. "Once the new defense counsel gets here, let me know."

During the briefing, Howard Mooney broke away to answer a call on the dedicated investigation landline. It was his role to do so. He wasn't on the call very long and returned, saying nothing until they finished, and the teams moved to their assigned duties for the day.

Howard said to Sammie and John, "That call was from Mettler's new lawyer, a Cynthia Needham. She and a colleague are on the train from London and should be here by eleven o'clock. She wants to meet with her client before he is interviewed again or charged. She will want a prebrief on the assault charge and the others to be made."

Kent gave it only a moment's thought. "I'll brief her. Sammie, you and I will meet with Mettler before laying additional charges. I have a funny feeling our CPS friend is right, Mettler is going to wriggle."

That's not funny at all, thought Sammie.

The legal duo from London stood out; conservatively well dressed in dark suits, the larger male, a Richard Campona, was clearly the aide to the slim woman in her late thirties. Cynthia Needham met with Oliver Mettler, while Campona looked at the charge sheet for Calder's assault, with Sammie watching him.

He looked at her. "We will want the interview transcript as soon as possible, please." He made an entry in his notebook after checking his watch. Sammie thought that if she burped as she replied, he would write that down, probably in square brackets; he was the diligent sort.

She looked at him and said nothing.

In the interview room a little later, John Kent took the seat opposite Oliver Mettler as Sammie sat opposite Cynthia Needham. As they sat down, a tall, uniformed police officer stationed himself against the wall, within pouncing distance of the suspect. They were taking no chances of a second swing at a police officer.

Once on record, Sammie asked, "Dr. Mettler, at the end of the last interview you stated you killed Dennis Lewis, but that it was an accident. Would you explain that to us now, please?"

Mettler said, "No comment."

She responded with, "Will you please confirm your earlier statement, that you killed Dennis Lewis."

"No comment."

"Did you, on May 26, 2008, and June 2, 2008, assault sexually Valerie Krestman at your home?"

"No comment."

Sammie glanced at Kent.

John Kent asked, "Are you married, Dr. Mettler?"

Mettler glanced at Needham, who gave a slight nod.

"No, I am not married." He looked puzzled.

"Were you married in 2008?"

"No."

"Were you in a relationship with another person in 2008."

"No. Why do you want to know?"

To get you moving, talking, thought John Kent.

The solicitor said, "Don't ask questions, Dr. Mettler. DCI Kent, move on, please."

Kent said, "Earlier, you gave 'no comment' answers to my colleague's questions about your first interview in this room. When you were escorted out of here yesterday, I was right behind you when you said that Dennis's death was an accident. Do you realise this is the time when you can explain that, and help us understand? That the charges we will lay next may be significantly influenced by such an explanation?"

"No comment." He looked at Needham to check, who nodded.

Kent said, "I am not asking for that explanation, sir. I am just asking whether you understand that you have the opportunity now to help us, and yourself, to allow appropriate charges to be laid."

Needham spoke up. "My client understands his rights, DCI Kent. He has given his answer."

Kent nodded, saying nothing for a moment. He then moved on.

"Can you confirm you owned a blue Volvo estate during the period June 2007 to February 2010?"

"I did, yes."

"Did you transport Dennis Lewis somewhere in that vehicle?"

"No comment."

John Kent looked at the clock. "John Shelburn Mettler, we will now take you to the charge desk to formally lay further criminal charges against you. You will be detained in custody pending a bail hearing. Do you have anything to say now?"

Mettler's eyes filled with tears as he said stiffly, "No comment."

The lawyer spoke up. "For the record, I wish to meet with you, DCI Kent, and a representative of CPS before you proceed further and lay charges."

Kent looked at her, impassive. "Providing it is short. We need to move on."

Needham said carefully, "It will be a very short meeting, I assure you."

"Interview terminated at 12.07 p.m. Officer, take the prisoner away."

As the room went quiet, Sammie switched off the recorder.

Ten minutes later, Needham and Campona were on one side of the table, with Kent and Hutton on the other.

Without preamble, the defense solicitor said, "You will be charging my client now with what, specifically?"

"The murder of Dennis Lewis, and two sexual assaults of a young woman, then a minor, Valerie Krestman, as she was, now Valerie Carmichael."

Needham pursed her lips. "Do you have a formal statement from the sexual assault complainant?"

"We do, yes."

"But no agreement to release her name?"

"We didn't expect one, nor did we ask."

"Do you have any forensic evidence or corroborating witnesses to these alleged assaults?"

"Not yet."

Kent was interested that she was focusing first on the assault charge.

"I take it you will be charging my client with these assaults today, then. However, I advise you not to proceed currently with the charge of the murder of Dennis Lewis. My client denies it. He claims his statement yesterday leading to his outburst was coerced under extreme pressure after an assault on his faith. I will be looking into this allegation further, but I do not rule out a complaint to the Independent Office for Police Conduct against Cumbria Police, the Major Investigation Unit, and specific police officers."

Her voice was even and factual. "Should you proceed with the murder charge now, and our complaint is proven, we will seek extensive financial compensation from Cumbria Police for any damages to my client's reputation. As I understand it, at least you have a complainant on the lesser charge. On the second, other than my client's own words under duress, you have nothing."

She stood. "Thank you for your time. Please let Mr. Campona know when further charges will be laid against my client. I would like him to be present."

With that, she picked up her briefcase and moved, waiting for one of them to open the door for her. Campona moved swiftly to do so, then followed her out.

When alone together, Tim Hutton pursed his lips. "I don't think, as you put it, this one will be 'largely resolved' from your end today. Superintendent Chiswell will be reaching for his antacid medication when he hears about the threat. But the way she worded it, she didn't put a foot wrong."

John said, "What do you think?"

Hutton sighed. "You had better find some forensic link between Lewis's death and Mettler. Until then, charge him with sexual assaults against a minor. Between that and the assault on Calder, we will be able to hold him in remand. 'Outburst', she said, a rather vague description of punching out Sergeant Calder."

John grimaced. It was what he expected.

Hutton went on, "I remember her from that meeting on the Aster case. How is she doing?"

"I'm just about to call her and find out. And tell her the bad news; alert her to it, at least. After I have spoken to my boss."

When John Kent spoke to Harriet at home, he first asked about her face, which she dismissed quickly. "Sore, badly bruised with a thumping headache, and the colour starting to come out. I will soon match Susan. What's happening?"

Once he told her, Calder's first reaction was, "But we often get empty threats of lawsuits after arrests, don't we?"

She was surprised at first, given the dramatic and painful memory of the interview yesterday, that MIU had only laid the sexual assault charge.

John responded, "Tim Hutton, you remember him?"

"From the meeting about Aster. Yes."

"He has done some checking. Cynthia Needham is a partner in a firm in London, Wolstenholme & Partners. They focus on serious crimes, murder charges particularly. Darcy Wolstenholme is representing a Russian oligarch at present. He and his two other senior partners represent other big money clients, including a drug gang leader the Met are trying to put away. Overall, a tough bunch who normally have wealthy clients, some tied to organized crime."

Harriet said, "I don't see a choir director, even one with the public image of Mettler, having that sort of income.

He's not in the same league as, say, Valerie Carmichael, in terms of earning power."

Kent added, "Needham is a junior partner at the firm. She probably comes a bit cheaper. You are a right, though. But the Cross of the Redeemer has money – and some monied members of the congregation, I understand. We think they are backing Mettler. CPS need us to get some solid evidence for the link between Dennis and Oliver Mettler. I have given Sammie two more officers, and Chan and Mooney are full-time on it, particularly focusing on the Volvo we found. I'll let you know of any progress."

Harriet paused. "Well thank you for that. After yesterday, that he now denies it… it shouldn't shock me, but it does. We are both used to constant denials of responsibility after arrests but this one, how he can live with himself? I don't get it."

Kent said quietly, "He has lived with it for ten years, Harriet. It is just a different facet of the same denial. You rest and get better now."

He closed the call.

Susan had moved into the kitchen to give Harriet some semi-privacy as she took the call, but she could hear her friend's responses. When she went back to the lounge, she just gave her a querying look.

Harriet said, "I expect Valerie will get a call today confirming that Oliver Mettler has been charged with the assaults on her."

Susan responded, "But not the Lewis family, about Dennis?"

Harriet shook her head. "No, not yet. And that worries me. One more disappointment for Bernice and Eamon."

She paused. "The man who assaulted Valerie now has a new lawyer, a Cynthia Needham, from London. I–." She stopped herself. "I had better not say any more, really. It's becoming more complicated. I'm going to take another ibuprofen."

"Why do people change lawyers – generally?" Susan asked.

Harriet sighed. "Most times, it is when then they plan to fight the charge and don't think their current solicitor is up to the task. Sometimes it's the other way, they choose a different lawyer when they want to plead guilty."

Later, Susan looked up from her laptop after doing some checking. "Do you know anything about a case involving a Sarah Tinley, from Wiltshire? Where's Wiltshire?"

"It is a county down south, near Oxford. No, I can't say I do, I have enough of that at work, really."

"A man was prosecuted for the rape of Tinley, but he got off. Apparently, according to this article, the trial was notable for the harsh treatment of the victim on the witness stand, causing the judge to take issue at one point with the barrister and his briefing solicitor, a woman called Cynthia Needham. The victim tried to commit suicide afterwards, but her mother found her in time."

She saw Harriet putting it all together, but all her friend said was, "I shouldn't have even mentioned her name to you, at this stage."

Susan glared as she closed her computer. "I don't like the sound of this woman Needham."

31 SUNDAY

During the two days following Mettler's arrest, Harriet received calls at home from fellow police officers and people from the Methodist community with good wishes for her recovery. Given the bruising, Harriet had informed the Methodist district office that she was unable to meet her circuit schedule for the next two Sundays. A preacher with her face bruised and battered didn't quite fit, she said.

On the case, there was no news. When Sammie called her to see how Harriet was doing, she mentioned that there had been another brief interview with Mettler. They wanted more details about his car usage around the time of Dennis's disappearance.

"Needham didn't object. She turned up, talked to Mettler. We got nothing useful. I got the impression that she had schooled him well in when to give a 'no comment' and when to use a vague answer."

Harriet just said, "I'm not surprised. He is good at vagueness; we know that."

On the Sunday morning, Susan said, "I'm a bit nervous

about going to St. Cuthbert's, and being at the service. Followed by this fraud that Kerri and her cronies have perpetrated in the afternoon."

The capacity problem for the people wanting to find out about the woman in the Reverend's life had been solved by a brain's trust, led by a Bassenthwaite man called Seymour Lovett, a regular at St. Anselm's.

"Seymour is as rich as Midas, acts as thick as two short planks, and has a heart of gold," explained Harriet. "It's his birthday today. On Thursday he suddenly announced an afternoon tea party for himself at St. Anselm's, for friends from all three churches. Kerri said that he is paying for everything, catered.

"His deeply thought-out strategy is that the men will attend for the food and a natter, and the women will want to poke and prod you, kick your tyres and turn your crank."

"He likes cars, does he?"

"British cars, yes, currently a big old Jaguar. He is in denial about the car firm's change of ownership over the years. He's never owned 'foreign stuff', he claims. He was the man at the service on your last visit who concluded that you were a Mountie, seeing as you knew me. A deep thinker, as I said."

Susan responded, "And the self-appointed chair of my welcoming committee."

At 10.30 a.m., Susan was in St. Cuthbert's, a small, old church near a bridge over the River Derwent. As Chris drove closer, pointing it out, Susan concluded that there would be a few people there, and some nosey sheep. There weren't any houses around.

She was wrong about that.

Nervous about her face, she had dressed in her suit and made the best of it. Kerri had apparently spread the word about the bruising, so she received an equal mix of good wishes and stares during the service and the subsequent coffee chat. Eunice, a sort of Kerri equivalent at St. Cuthbert's, looked after her and lead her through the process of their Sunday morning service.

The only awkward point arose during the Eucharist, when Susan didn't get out of her pew in the sequence to go forward for communion. Neither did anyone next to her. Chris beckoned forward the next logical person and the traffic jam was averted.

Afterwards, one young teenager, clearly planning to marry Chris at the first available opportunity, tried to disguise her hostility as she asked if 'wedding bells were in the offing', but her mother promptly escorted her to the kitchen before Susan could answer.

It was on the drive back to Bassenthwaite that she took a call and said, 'Yes Valerie. Not easily, but I can listen." A minute or so later she thanked her and said she would call her once she was back in Canada.

As she put the phone away, Chris didn't ask any questions. They were beginning to see the need for that, each of them.

Harriet was at Bassenthwaite Methodist Chapel, simply a member of the congregation in a service led by a young man, James Lee, his second time doing so. Six of the congregation were not regular attendees there, they were Lee's family and two friends.

As Lee worked his way through the service, Harriet was happier than she had been for quite some time. James had approached her four years ago about a sense of ministry. She had encouraged him, introduced him to the man who helped him further and, on occasion, she had dealt with his doubts and concerns. As a service, it was no great shakes, but it was special for everyone.

Contrary to Susan's fears, the afternoon tea party at St. Anselm's Church was a pleasure. Seymour had bought a large 'welcome' card printed with a view of Bassenthwaite Lake, which he had people sign. There was a joy to it, the surreptitious glances at her and the smiles when she was with Chris, talking to someone.

She looked at Harriet on occasion. At one point, as the two bruised women talked, Harriet said quietly, "They assume I was the matchmaker so I took every bit of credit."

Susan responded, "Seymour said we 'look a right pair together with our faces'. Is that a compliment?"

"With him, yes, that's best."

Harriet had watched the media coverage following the assault charge made against Oliver Mettler for the sexual touching of a minor. Valerie's identity had been protected by the court. A couple of people at the party had asked her if her injury was tied to a police investigation. She hoped that the MIU team found hard evidence soon, so they could lay more charges.

Susan was also thinking along similar lines, concerned about Harriet. While her host and friend said nothing, or made light of her injury, it was obvious to Susan that Harriet was troubled by the experiences, and particularly the failure to charge Mettler for Dennis Lewis's death.

But Susan would be leaving, going home soon. Chris was driving her down to Heathrow. They had decisions of their own to make. Yet the meeting with Valerie Carmichael had drawn her into this aspect of Harriet's life, too. Somehow, it bonded them more closely.

32 IOPC

It was the middle of the following week when John Kent called Harriet, simply asking if he could come over. There were one or two things to cover.

Harriet went straight to it. "Mettler's solicitor is following up on her threat, a complaint to the IOPC, isn't she? Should I come to Penrith?"

He paused. "No. We'll come over. Did Susan Carlson go back to Canada?"

"Yes, she left here on Monday and flew back yesterday. It's been a lot quieter so far this week, for me at least. Not you though, I'm sure."

"You could say that. We'll see you in a bit."

As the call disconnected, Harriet wondered if her assumption that 'we' meant John Kent and Sammie was right or not.

The previous day she had spoken by phone with Bernice, explaining she was returning to her role at Keswick, making light of her own injury.

Bernice had said, "Sergeant Livermore told us Mettler hit you, losing his temper. We know the man is tied to

Dennis's disappearance in some way, but mustn't say anything, she said. How are you, really?"

"Oh, fine. I'll be back at work in a few days. And you and Eamon, and the family?"

"Not sure, to be honest. Empty, waiting for someone to be charged. And Harriet, don't try to make light of your own hurt in this. I saw it when you were in the pulpit at the funeral, and I am sure to be injured now must be awful for you."

"Thank you. After what you and Eamon have been through, it's... how is Eamon doing?"

"He's doing better, strangely enough, after all his worries about not preparing Dennis for the real world. We have talked with Valerie twice. Once she came to see us, no fanfare, just her in a little car she has. That helped him a lot, for some reason. She's still feeling dreadful about it, and she shouldn't."

"No. She was a victim, too."

"We can never thank you enough. You and the team. It is very close, I feel, the answer to all this."

It wasn't the easiest conversation, but for a police officer, it was an appropriate sort of closure, she thought.

When John Kent got out of his car, it wasn't Sammie with him. It was a woman in uniform, her boss Inspector June Robinson. She knew then it was no closure at all. Her doubts hidden from Susan a week ago were becoming real.

Kent didn't beat about the bush as they entered, and Harriet offered coffee. "Let's all go in the kitchen, make it as we talk. We have some news, not good news, either. Cynthia Needham came to Penrith this morning."

Harriet arched her eyebrows as he added, "They are going after us, with a complaint to IOPC. After you, specifically, I am sorry to say. We are fighting it all the way."

June Robinson took the coffee spoon out of Harriet's hand as she stood there frozen for a moment. She gave Harriet a sympathetic look and said, "Bull in a china shop, this man. Sit down. I'll make it."

Clueing in, Harriet said anxiously, "That's why you are here, isn't it? I am going to be suspended."

Robinson scowled. "Let Ferdinand hoof his way through this, then we'll talk. One step at a time."

As Harriet moved and sat across the kitchen table from where Kent had plonked himself, he said, "Needham's complaint to IOPC is about inappropriate interview pressure forcing a false confession."

Harriet responded, "A complaint against who? Me, obviously, and Sammie and you?"

He looked apologetic. "Against Cumbria Police and MIU. But only you are named specifically. I wasn't in the room. Sammie's comments were on facts and timeline, with the odd minor insult. Yours included his failings as a church official and the betrayal of his faith. That is where they see the opportunity."

Harriet looked away, her eyes filling with tears. "I'm sorry you dragged me into this, John."

She stood, moving to the Welsh dresser, facing it and the wall as she grabbed a couple of tissues, wiping her eyes and then blowing her nose.

"What happens now?"

"Nothing, until the complaint is processed. Tim Hutton and I met with her. You will be named in the body of the complaint, which isn't public, but not in any media brief, we agreed. Tim pushed hard and Needham agreed to that. The details are confidential, of course, but word will get around. And, once it hits the news, we can't guarantee that some rag or scuzzy website won't name you – or any of the team, come to that."

He sounded lost. "I've got everyone I can working the evidence, the car, his home. They are sampling everything for any traces of Dennis that tie him to Mettler. Beardsley gave me free rein on that. But we aren't there yet."

Harriet sat back down at the table still holding the tissues. "They want the interview expunged at trial. His outburst, the confession. I see that."

She focused on Robinson. "Are you here to suspend me, I asked?"

"No. You know the regs well enough. Suspension is only applicable to misconduct when a temporary relocation to another role has been ruled inappropriate, or in the case of gross misconduct. You are no longer tied to the MIU team, or the role involved. You can come back to Keswick when medically cleared. Or we can extend your medical leave until the cows come home."

"But if they claim gross misconduct..."

"Beardsley is adamant he won't suspend you. First, IOPC must assess the complaint and find if it merits their review. They could rule it out then. And the DCC will take the responsibility for keeping you on if they choose to proceed. He doesn't want your record marred by this, he says."

"That's something. Please thank him if you would do that. I'd like to come back as soon as I can. I planned on it."

It seemed the appropriate point for Robinson to pour the coffee.

Harriet said, "I don't even know how the IOPC operates now. It seems like no time since they replaced the IPCC."

The Independent Police Complaints Commission, its long-standing precursor.

Robinson responded, "And hopefully we won't have to, if they do the right thing and say there is nothing to answer. If they say there is, they will have people investigate. That also could conclude there is no case to answer. If there is, IOPC refer it to the Cumbria's Police Commissioner, and then back to the Chief Constable."

Kent muttered, "It could drag on for months."

Harriet shook her head and took a deep breath. "This lawyer will file the complaint today, I take it?" She put down her mug.

John Kent nodded. "She said so. Straight after our meeting and another with her client. Then she was heading back to London. She'll probably do the media announcement there, to get more attention. You know how that works."

He paused, contemplating something. It came out as a rush. "I'm sorry you are on the receiving end of this. It should be me, and I mean to make sure that, if IOPC chooses to investigate, I tell them that. It was my strategy, and I gave the order to go all out with him. But I'm not sorry I brought you into the investigation. Not sorry at all. And I'd steal you from June to replace Cotton in a heartbeat."

Inspector Robinson shook her head. "He's still lumbering about, breaking the bloody china."

But Kent looked stoic. He had a lot on his plate.

At 4.00 p.m. that afternoon, outside the offices of Wolstenholme & Partners in London and just in time for coverage on evening news slots, Cynthia Needham gave a press briefing announcing that the firm had been engaged to defend Oliver Mettler. They would be seeking his release on bail at the earliest opportunity. At this time, they would not say more, other than that they would vigorously defend his innocence on all charges.

She sounded reasonable, looking quietly resolved. She explained that this was a complicated matter. They had filed this afternoon a complaint to the Independent Office of Police Complaints against Cumbria Constabulary and a police officer within the Major Investigation Unit regarding the treatment of her client inside Penrith Police Headquarters. No, she would not say more, other than she expected him to be exonerated.

As more questions were hurled at her, she turned and re-entered the building.

"I don't mind that error," John Kent said to Ken Gilles, the Cumbria Police Communications Director, as they switched off the coverage, "I don't want that corrected. Let her run with it. It may help protect Calder."

That the officer in the complaint was a part of MIU. He looked at Sammie, who gave a single nod. She was on board.

Gilles grimaced. "Calder's name is out there already. You know that."

John shrugged "We do what we can."

Sammie said angrily, "What I can't take easily is this Needham woman. If Mettler had simply taken a swing at Harriet for pressing his hot buttons, I could see it. But he admitted killing Dennis, even saying what he did at the farm. How could, in any ethical sense, Needham not run with that? I think Fielding would have."

Kent didn't bother to answer.

Harriet had vacillated a little after the visit of Kent and Robinson, then decided to give the internet and the media a miss. She headed off late afternoon to St. Anselm's, to chat with Kerri, who was over there, and hide away with a cup of tea.

As Kerri made the tea, Harriet walked around the church. "Where's the little bible, the one from Duncan Aster? I don't see it in the collection."

Tourists visiting the Lake District had started the collection, dropping off bibles in different languages and editions. Word of mouth had made the collection grow. Duncan Aster's bible had ended up there.

It was the pause in the response that gave Harriet the answer, as Kerri brought in the mugs.

She asked Kerri, "Chris or Susan?"

Kerri said softly, "Susan has it. She offered to buy it before she left. I told her it was a gift to us and would happily be passed on as one. She asked me not to say anything to you or Chris."

Harriet's smiled.

Kerri continued, "I wondered, you know, Harriet? Perhaps it's for Chris?"

Harriet was thinking that Kerri's partial answer worked for her, and she would leave it be.

Susan had first bought the bible for Duncan Aster, her priest at the time, as a present, well before the event which wrecked their relationship and Susan's life. The gift card Aster had kept in it, with Susan's original message, had been sent back to Aster's Bishop. Harriet had organized that. When Susan visited Keswick the first time, after the service for Colin Kavanagh, Harriet had asked if she wanted the bible back. Susan declined, saying it was behind her.

Harriet intuitively felt the bible was not for Chris, given its baggage, but you never know. The fact Susan took it with her, though, pleased her.

Neither woman said anything else for a while, enjoying the silence and company, each thinking about the younger couple. In that tender moment, Seymour Lovett barged into the church. Like a blunt force trauma, he asked loudly if 'The Reverend' was taking the service next Sunday.

Kerri, irritated at the interruption, said "He is, at least he should be. It's in the bulletin. Do you want to see him? Give his office line a call and leave a message if you do."

Seymour seemed to be less than his normal hearty self. Kerri flashed a look at Harriet. Sensing the moment had gone, she said, "I'm off. Thanks for the tea, Kerri. Good-bye, Seymour."

Lovett suddenly asked, "Harriet, are you thinking of coming back to the true faith? Seen your errors, have you?"

Harriet gave him a stern look of disbelief. "You want to argue faith and doctrine with me, a Methodist preacher?"

He shook his head lugubriously. "No, not really. That sort of thing cheers up preachers, I thought. You look like you need it. I do. I hope Willard has the sense to marry that Susan and get her back here. He won't find another like her, y' know? I thought she was a right cracker from the time she made us all hold hands and say that serenity prayer for Colin Kavanagh. And it's about time that priest took a wife, with half the women in this parish swooning over him."

He gave Kerri an accusatory look. Harriet got out before Kerri exploded at the insult.

33 AZIKIWE

Ten days later, Susan Carlson said the Serenity Prayer to herself mentally as she connected online to Harriet.

"What happened, Harriet? I just heard."

Harriet sighed. "Chris shouldn't have said anything. There is nothing that can be done about it. I must wait for the police complaints commission to decide whether to investigate, or not. They should let us know soon."

"Not that! We talked about that. I just had an email from Kerri. She is very angry. Your church district has laid you off, she said."

There was a momentary silence. "That's not quite right. Rumours and gossip have been spreading, saying that I used improper pressure to force a confession from Mettler. A church in my circuit asked me 'to take a rest for spiritual reflection' after a family there made a fuss and refused to attend if I preached. Two other churches want to show support for me."

Susan interrupted. "Good for them."

Harriet pressed on. "I met with Reverend Wescott, at the District Office. He has overall charge of the lay preacher scheduling. Other churches are uncomfortable, too. Neither of us were happy that I had become a point of divisiveness for our congregations, so we agreed I would take a leave of absence."

"For how long?"

"I'm not sure. I had been away with the bruising, anyway. If the IOPC chooses to investigate MIU and me, it could be a long time. If not, it will be the District Committee that will decide when I should go back."

Susan's self-promised serenity evaporated as her voice changed, angrier. "Going after you and the team I met there. Unbelievable. Bloody unbelievable. Have they interviewed you yet?"

"No. Sammie told me that the only person contacted by IOPC they knew of was Linnie, a civilian member of MIU. She recorded the interview."

"And now people in your churches are doubting you, after all the years you have served them."

"I was part of that decision. And some people there are very supportive. They call me but, obviously, I can't talk about it. And it isn't at all unbelievable if you are a police officer.

"It hurts, I'll own up to that, hurts a lot. Part of me wishes John Kent had never brought me into this mess. Then I feel bad, because we did it, both of us really, to help the victims. In my case, the Lewis family; in yours, Valerie. I just need to roll with whatever turns up. What's new with you?"

Changing the subject, thought Susan.

"I'm meeting tomorrow with James, in Hamilton. Chris is still astonished I have a bishop I talk to. This Cross of the Redeemer, are they behind it?"

"Well, not specifically, but who knows? We know they are funding the new law firm, the one who made the announcement. These lawyers don't work cheap, and they are known for being very aggressive in their defense tactics, as you pointed out to me. But no mention of this to the bishop, please?"

Susan parried the request a little. "I'm seeing him about me and Chris, that's the reason. Just want to talk it through. With him being clergy and me being… well, you know my beliefs."

"I am sure the bishop will reassure you on that front."

"Chris and I meet online or by text several times a day, but I miss him. I want him to come over here for a visit."

As they closed the call a minute or so later, Susan said to herself, "My love life is the primary reason for meeting James, anyway." She hadn't exactly told Harriet she was going to talk about her as well.

Within ten minutes, Susan was making another call, this time in response to a promise made in the UK. She felt the need for absolute care in the choice of every word she said. As a counsellor, it became a learned behaviour. It didn't intimidate her in the least to be calling a television personality widely known across the UK. It had been scheduled days ago, by mutual agreement.

"Valerie, I am sorry I didn't call back earlier, when I got home. It has been so busy. You know about that, I am sure. How are you feeling?"

"As you would expect. Still deflated, guilty, angry, embarrassed, you name it. I have someone looking into the type of therapy support you suggested."

"Anger is understandable. Where is the guilt focused?"

"I let Dennis's parents down very badly. I went to see them, and they were so good about it, concerned for me. It should make it easier, but it makes it worse, somehow. If I had made the connection between my own problem and Dennis's disappearance and spoken up sooner... ten years, they have suffered."

Susan responded, "You are going to need to let go of the 'if only's'. Find the person and work with them."

"You know, I still can't thank you enough for what you did. That interview could have been a lot worse without that. I have been thinking about you, how to thank you. Is there anything, anything at all I can do? Honestly, expense to me is not the same as expense to you. I want to show my gratitude."

Patients often do, thought Susan. "I'll think about that, Valerie, but I didn't do it for money or reward. Helping you has helped me, if you can believe that. It is part of the reason why I work with other women who are alcoholics and addicts. In helping them, I see how I was, and how I never want to be again. I take it you saw or heard about the statement by Mettler's legal representative?"

"I did, but I don't understand it. Given my own experience with the Cumbria Police, I can't credit it. I assume it is one of these attempts to mitigate charges in some way. The police aren't saying anything. But I hope they lay the charge for Dennis's murder soon."

The TV star paused. "I wasn't going to say this, but I will. I thought about it after my talk with Bernice. At some point, I am going to make public that I was the girl assaulted. There could be other women abused by him. I need to speak out, if for no other reason than I am well known and at ease with public visibility and the media."

Susan thought through her response. "Think about it carefully first. Once out in the open, it can't be closed off again. In my case, I was initially angry at the man who abused me. Over time, I came to see that a lot of my problems were the system he was part of. It protected my abuser because he was a priest."

Valerie was silent for a moment. "Is Mettler's church involved then? Is that why the lawyer is accusing the police of misconduct in some way?"

Susan answered slowly. "I can't speak to that. I assume you still have a lawyer, a solicitor who can look after you; that person with you, perhaps?"

"Felicity, yes. She is more a general counsel to me but has been my solicitor since... since I became known. I trust her."

"Have her check out the law firm Wolstenholme & Partners, and a Cynthia Needham. See if they will be involved when it comes to any trial proceedings on the sexual assault charge. Get her to prepare you. I have no clue how the court system works over there. But I doubt it will be a kindly police officer asking you questions. Be prepared."

Susan pressed on. "The police officer who asked me to speak to you. You never met her. She was part of the interview team and was assaulted by Mettler during the interview. It is one of the charges. I can't say more, other than I am thoroughly shocked by some developments. Felicity may have some idea about those or have contacts who can inform her. Be strong, be kind to yourself, but be sure of your ground before you go public on this."

There was a silence for a moment.

"I'll talk to Felicity Murray right now, get her on it. I don't like the sound of this."

Susan asked, "One thing I would appreciate is, if you do go public, can you let me know in advance, so I can watch the coverage?"

"Of course. I'll make sure you can do that. It is the very least I can do."

Susan finished with, "Let's stay in touch. You are on a road I know well, and I am glad my friend put us in contact."

After the call, she thought about fantasy holidays in the Carribean with Chris, knowing that it would be only that, a fantasy. But she hoped her gentle steering would help the situation with Harriet, at some point.

~~

The following morning, after an overnight 'snow event', Susan Carlson, in toque, boots, mittens and a quilted, waterproof coat, took a GO train ride from Toronto Union Station to the city of Hamilton, at the west end of Lake Ontario. On arrival, she trod the mix of plowed and uncleared sidewalk sections along a familiar route, down James Street to the Anglican Cathedral.

Susan had studied for her Diploma in Addiction Studies in the city, at the university, so knew the area well. But the walk down James Street now brought back the memory of the canon hearing in early December last year, and her first meeting with Harriet Calder. She smiled at the memory of that pre-snow day, with Calder commenting on the cold wind. You should come back now, Harriet, she thought. Then we can talk about being cold.

Miriam, her AA sponsor, had picked up on it at their meeting after Susan's return. "You seem a lot closer to Harriet now than you did before you left."

Susan was honest. "I am, I know her better now, because of the mess I got involved in. I keep thinking, what should I do next?"

Miriam said, "You pray on it, and sort it out bit by bit, a day at a time. Going to see your bishop buddy is part of that."

She smirked. "A bishop, and now a priest for a boy-friend. Not considering holy orders yourself, are you?"

Susan flashed her a look. "That's about as likely as you deciding to marry an old rabbi."

In the office of Bishop James Azikiwe, Susan felt supported both by him and, beforehand, by Audrey Lille, his assistant. Susan whispered the primary reason for her visit to her on arrival. Audrey was overjoyed.

In his office, Azikiwe said, "It is wonderful news, Susan. For you and others, but for me, also. Is it too early to say more? I have a cathedral available if you need one."

It was his expression rather than the questions which made her laugh. "Too early by far! But you sense my hopes, the way I dream a little. But my question?"

Azikiwe turned serious. "I won't fob you off with humour on that one. There is no basis I see preventing you and Reverend Willard developing a full relationship, with marriage and a life together, as you put it. Nor will your absence of commitment to our church be an impediment."

"I can't become a token Anglican, or even an avowed Christian; you know that. I believe in the love and words of Jesus Christ, but –."

She stopped, unsure of her next statement. Azikiwe smiled.

"Stop overworking it. You were baptized in Christ, like it or not. You have faith in God, and you live it. Reverend Willard – Chris, I should say – has no urgent desires to become Archbishop of York, does he?"

She smiled. "No, not that we have ever talked about such a thing. He has his cluster of three churches. He calls them his benefice, St. Anselm's and two smaller ones. He seems happy there."

"I'll be candid; you asked me to be so. The Church of England is more old-fashioned than the Anglican Church of Canada, but not by much. Both organisations are far too stuffy about wealth, parentage, and other parameters that affect promotion to senior levels, unfortunately."

She smiled, "Old Edmonton money, were you?"

He pulled a face. "You know better! There is not a lot of money in a household where the dad worked as an Air Canada passenger agent, so no. I'm something of an aberration in my position these days."

She said quite seriously, "And I thank God for that."

He pressed on. "If you were from an 'old school' C. of E. family, the ideal partner in the eyes of decision makers more influenced by church politics than God's will, it could help his career. But you aren't. And you speak your mind. And sometimes that is challenging. You haven't told the Bishop of Cumbria that words like priest and bishop nauseate you, have you?"

It was one of her comments to him when they first met.

She smiled. "No, nor would I. And through you, Chris, and Harriet, they don't any longer. Apart from one or two I can't even name."

"Are we clear then? Don't let your perspective on churches, or Chris's vestments, or our rituals, blight your love and relationship. Enough. You said you wanted to talk about Harriet, too?"

Susan lost her smile. "I do. And you being a priest matters a lot, there. I think she is in trouble, more than she realises, perhaps. Not legally, I hope, and I'll explain that. But she has been 'placed on leave' from her post of lay preacher with the Methodist Church. There are a lot of rumours circulating about her, all false."

Azikiwe's face clouded over. "Tell me, please."

~~

It was shortly before six p.m. in Keswick when Harriet

took a call on her personal phone from Audrey Lille.

"Harriet good evening, are you at work or at home?"

"Still at work until seven here, another hour. I'm guessing that Susan talked about me to the bishop. Is that the reason for your call?"

Audrey said, "Yes. You could put it that way. Look, the bishop wants to talk to you. Are you free for a video call when you get home later? Would 8.45 p.m. your time work?

"I'll be home, yes. But he shouldn't. You must all be busy with preparations for Christmas. I know what it's like, remember?"

"Busy or not, he will talk to you then. I will send a link for you to connect. We are thinking about you, with love. I'll let you go."

Audrey closed the call and Harriet shook her head.

Later at home, when the screen opened on the call, Harriet saw the smiling face of James Azikiwe and a surprise, a second window already open, with a young female priest she vaguely remembered from the visit to Hamilton for the canon hearing so long ago.

"Harriet, it's good to see you. This is Jean Ames, who you probably won't remember from your visit. Jean is our communications director."

Harriet responded, "I remember the face. You waited outside the bishop's office while he slid Susan and me in for a cup of tea, ahead of the canon court officials."

Ames laughed. "So, it was obvious. Yes. I'm pleased to meet you."

Azikiwe said, "Jean will stay a couple of minutes only, then we will talk alone. I talked with Susan, and she told me about her visit, the good news and the bad. And about your lost role, too."

Harriet said nothing for a moment. "I see. Susan… worries too much."

James Azikiwe responded, "Whether too much or not, we will see. Jean was formerly a local news reporter before she found her calling. And now, with others, she deals with the intractable issues of communications for our diocese. She has a passion for the subject, particularly regarding the perception of our churches by young people looking for a spiritual home. They, after all, are our future. But this is about you. What happened, Harriet?"

She paused, unsure what to say. "I'm taking a leave of absence. My circuit of churches is clearly divided over a rumour that, as a police officer, I forced a confession from someone inappropriately. I didn't, I don't think, but it got rough. That's the truth of it. I feel in limbo. Somehow the damage is spreading as people gossip.

"Those who doubt me talk to others. People who have faith in me call me in support, but I can't tell them anything except repeat that I agreed to take a leave of absence. Some are missing me, and I am missing them."

She gave a grimace at the screen. "Yes, we all wish to attract young people to Christ. These days, police officers aren't popular with many of them unless they need us, and a lot of the gossip is online, I gather. I am also surprised by the reactions of some others, including some clergy in my district, keeping their distance."

She paused. "You asked, Bishop. Police officers have plenty of experience of this."

Azikiwe nodded slowly then said simply, "Jean, tell us what you found."

As Reverend Ames started speaking, the video system showed the priest centre screen.

"Bishop Azikiwe asked me to look at the internet traffic on this story, about you and this gossip, Harriet. Putting it bluntly, you – and probably your Methodist committee – are listening to half the story, and from the wrong people. I don't know you, but in your explanation now I see the hurt.

"I'll send you a summary, with some quotes. I hope they help. Many young people – and older people, I should add – are focused on the sexual assault of an unnamed woman by this man Mettler. And that Mettler also physically attacked you. There is speculation about who the woman is.

"There is a strong, adverse reaction from young women to the announcement by the lawyer, Needham, about a complaint made against Cumbria Police. Your name comes up as a woman who took on the conservative establishment of the Cross of the Redeemer and got to the truth about a man with a big reputation."

Harriet looked surprised. "I didn't. I was just part of a team that conducted the investigation."

Jean Ames smiled. "For every slight you or members of your committee perceive, I can find women in online Christian groups who support you and your police team, saying that churches must change, stop actively or tacitly supporting abusers and think of the victims. These are the quotes I mentioned earlier."

Before Harriet could speak again, she added, "And it's a distortion. All gossip is a distortion to some degree, what you heard and what I found. What matters is that in your faith journey, you are on part of the road that is rough-going now. Bishop James will doubtlessly talk about that after I go, but there is one more thing I want to say, a personal comment."

Harriet sat back, instead of trying to interrupt and correct the misconception. The woman was a powerful speaker.

"My brother is a pastor in a church in Canada not too dissimilar to Cross of the Redeemer. He became one before I found my calling. Where we differ is this; his church is for all who can see the light – their interpretation of the light. If you do, they will sweep you up, enfold you, support you. If you don't, well…"

"Your ministry, like ours, is for everyone; no matter what. We bring Christ's love to all, without reservation. To all who hurt and suffer. Including each other. Including you. We are here for you. Bishop, I'll take my leave now if I may, and send Harriet the file?"

As Azikiwe gave his affirmation, she told Calder to stay strong and, within seconds, there were only two people on the call.

Harriet took a deep breath. "She'll have your job one day, Bishop. That… that was a motivational speaker if ever I heard one."

He smiled but gave no direct reply. "Harriet, when I last saw you in person, our parting words to each other were that we would pray for each other's ministry. I still do, for yours. I will not have you doubt yourself, or doubt that you have a calling. It may be directed differently at present, but I hope it will strengthen through this, not diminish. I pray for that. Forget denominations. Forget distance. In these difficult times, I – and Jean – will be here for you, as she said. So, if you wish, tell me not about the facts, but what is truly troubling you and then we will pray together."

As Harriet Calder finally spoke openly about her anger and bafflement, her disappointment with some in her own church, and her disgust with her treatment by Cynthia Needham, Azikiwe didn't interrupt. He heard a ping at Harriet's end as he saw on his own system that Jean Ames had sent the file with her findings.

A little later, his door opened quietly as Audrey put her

head in. His eyes gave a flick – no, he wouldn't finish in the alloted time. She would adjust his schedule accordingly, he knew, as she closed the door as quietly as she opened it. The Bishop of Hamilton-Brant was first and foremost a priest, now dealing with a person who needed spiritual help. Administrative issues must wait, even in the planning for Christmas services.

34 SILL

The following day, bolstered by the unexpected support from Canada, Harriet turned up to work in Keswick in a brighter frame of mind. Within an hour, it got even better as she received at last the call from the IOPC.

June Robinson had sent her a text fifteen minutes earlier, saying she was on her way over to the Keswick police base from headquarters. Robinson walked into the room as Harriet froze, concentrating on the IOPC call as PC Keston and PC Harris talked about the next job they were assigned. Robinson told them to pipe down.

Seeing Robinson's face, Harriet gathered her boss knew the outcome already. She smiled at Harriet, raising her thumbs.

The male IOPC officer on the line said, "Sergeant Calder, the claims by the counsel for Dr. Mettler against the Cumbria Police and you specifically are without merit. We have rejected them. We informed the complainant today."

It didn't matter, but Harriet wanted to know. "I don't understand why you called Linnie – Mrs. Linnie-Morton –

for interview, not me."

"We wanted to verify formally that the video recording of the interview provided to us had not been tampered with in any way. She swore to that. The recording showed the events covered by the complaint clearly. In our review, it was a forceful interview strategy, but our conclusions were that your actions did not deviate from police standards."

Harriet said quickly, "My rep says I should ask for a letter to that effect, specifically addressed to me, with a copy sent to my personnel file."

"Which we will be happy to provide. Can I ask how your face is doing now?"

"The bruising has faded, except for a spot near the corner of the eye socket. That will take a while longer, I am told."

"I am glad to hear that you are on the mend. Best wishes to you."

As she put the phone down, Robinson said to the room, "The case against us, and Harriet in particular, has been rejected by IOPC. It's over."

As Pam and Donnie came to congratulate her, Harriet wondered if that statement was true; she still had her church role to sort out. But it was the big item of the week, or so she thought then.

That evening, Harriet called Reverend Wescott with the news of the IOPC decision.

"Well, that is very good news, Harriet. We will take it to the next District Committee meeting. I will have Carol Kent present it as she is more capable of explaining the issue than I. If there are questions, I mean."

Harriet got the impression he was less happy about presenting it himself. She decided to test the water.

"With it being Christmas soon, there is a lot to do. Do you want me to cover for anyone before the committee meets?"

There was a short silence.

"I think it best, Harriet, for you to continue your leave of absence until the committee reaches its decision. The IOPC may have made their own, but the world doesn't change overnight. People still talk. We don't want to create new problems over the Christmas period, when attendance is high. I'm sure you understand."

Harriet thought that she did. She said coolly, "I'll wait to hear, then. Thank you."

She closed the call feeling deflated, despite the positive news of the day.

~~

Two days later, at 6.12 a.m. Harriet's phone rang. It was Louis Chan.

"I couldn't wait. Were you asleep?"

"I'm up, Louis, having my first cup of coffee. How are you?"

"Over the moon. The results came in an hour ago. I drove into the office and looked at them. We took the rear end of Mettler's Volvo apart and things like carpets had already been stripped, but under a piece of vinyl moulding by the rear door sill we found a sizeable stain on the insulation. It's blood, Dennis's. They say that the DNA results are unequivocal. I wanted you to know."

Harriet let out a long sigh. "Thank you, thank you. I appreciate it."

Louis seemed nervous. "I shouldn't have, so if John calls, it's between you and me, OK?"

"I won't drop you in it. Sammie said you and Howard

haven't stopped."

"How could we? But we have hard evidence now. That's what I wanted, the truth for the family. What you did was great."

"Thank you. It wasn't great, but it was necessary. Go get some coffee and we'll talk again soon."

As she closed the call, she gave a small prayer of thanks.

Later the same day, Cumbria Police charged Oliver Mettler with the murder of Dennis Lewis, bringing him from prison, where he was on remand, to Keswick for an interview before laying the charge.

John Kent and Sammie Livermore entered the interview room together. Cynthia Needham had spent about ten minutes alone with Oliver Mettler before signalling that they were ready. Sammie had thought it would take longer than that for the lawyer to bring home the damning nature of the DNA evidence. It may be a single forensic item, but the presence of Dennis Lewis in the vehicle was solid.

In the viewing room Howard and Louis, having spent so long working on the search for the pieces of the vehicle at the scrapyard, had spectator seats.

"He'll crumble, watch!" said Howard.

"No, he won't," replied Louis.

Linnie asked, "Have you two got money on this?"

"Not money; a pint, that's all."

Linnie smiled. Howard was paying, she thought, but stayed silent.

John Kent began with, "We have undertaken a forensic evaluation of the vehicle you owned at the time of the concert, Dr. Mettler. Traces of dried fluids were found in an area of moulding where liquid could have entered."

He paused, to see if the man would speak up, accept his guilt. No-one said anything.

Kent continued, "I am told by experts that the DNA found there unequivocally belongs to Dennis Lewis. The area was protected from rain and sunlight and was porous, and there is no doubt about that analysis. So, when did you have Dennis Lewis in the back of your vehicle?"

Mettler spoke without prompting. "No comment."

Kent sat back suddenly, implying surprise. "You continue to deny that you killed Dennis; after both a confession you later retracted and the hard evidence that I have just advised you about. This is your chance to set matters straight. It could affect the charges laid and the eventual sentencing recommendations. It's time to talk, Oliver; it really is."

Mettler just stared at him.

Kent focused on the lawyer. "Did you explain to your client the role and importance of DNA evidence, Miss Needham?"

Most defense council would take such evidence as so strong, the client really needed to re-evaluate their claim of innocence.

Needham pursed her lips. "I did. It may be present, and if so, may be relevant. Or not. We will see."

Louis saw Sammie give a small shake of her head, deliberately or involuntarily, he couldn't say. Her back was to him. Needham caught it, he saw.

The lawyer added, "And we will have our own experts examine the results, including the chain of custody of all retained samples."

It was gratuitous, a challenge.

Kent said, "You are entitled to do that. But with the IOPC's decision communicated this week, the confession by your client will also be evidence."

Needham gave him a stare, not acknowledging the point at first. Then, having thought through her response, she said, "We will challenge its validity on other grounds, the medical condition of my client under extreme stress."

In the viewing room, Linnie muttered, "All she needs to do is to sow the seed of doubt in the mind of a couple of jurors already uneasy with the idea that a pillar of the church could ever do such a thing."

John Kent focused on Oliver Mettler, assessing the man, his expression.

"DS Livermore, take Oliver Mettler to the charge desk. Charge him with the murder of Dennis Lewis before he returns to prison. Also lay the charge of unlawful manslaughter, for good measure. Interview terminated at 3.17 p.m."

He stood up and turned, leaving the room without a word to anyone.

Louis looked at Howard. "Needham said, 'may be relevant'. We had better make sure our documentation is faultless. This is going to drag on for months, isn't it?"

Closing the communications system, Linnie said, "At least. Ever the optimist, Louis."

Just as Superintendent Chiswell entered the viewing room, to see people standing in the interview room.

"Over with already? That bad?"

Mooney said, "DCI Kent has left, sir. He probably went back to his office. It sounds as if Mettler's defense will contest the DNA relevance and the confession, this time on medical grounds."

Chiswell grimaced. "That bunch of experts will cost them a fortune. It cost us enough getting the DNA results. I'm glad DCC Beardsley approved it, but... still, a lot of money."

So was Norm's Caff, thought Louis. And Dr. Kulis.

35 BAIL

The media coverage of the case increased dramatically after the charge against Mettler became public. This time, Needham made no comment to the press, but was recorded entering and leaving HMP Durham, where Oliver Mettler had been remanded. Her attempt to get bail at that time was unsuccessful, partly because of his demonstrated violence against a police officer.

Sammie and Louis Chan were the police officers from MIU who next got to see Cynthia Needham in action. They attended the next bail hearing for Mettler, where she chose to represent him, rather than use a barrister. Bail is not primarily about the severity of the crime, although it plays a part. It is about risk to members of the public.

Needham showed no sign of combative behaviour. She argued that Mettler was a citizen with a home, a community that supported him, and no prior criminal record. The case was complex and would take time. He now had two people, members of his church, who would give sureties for his behaviour, should any conditions be applied to the bail.

She also wanted him examined by medical professionals for the possibility that he suffered from an anger disorder. Yes, as the prosecution had stated in previous hearings, Dr. Mettler had struck a police officer and allegedly struck a young male. The defense would address those issues appropriately at trial, but their client was under great duress when he hit the interviewing officer. They needed to assess whether there was an underlying cause. Proper psychiatric evaluation was best achieved if he had a normal environment and access to appropriate professionals.

Ten minutes later, Oliver Mettler was freed on bail, with restrictions. He was limited to his home and workplace, and direct travel between the two. He could not be alone with any female other than his lawyer and family members, and he had to report into the authorities in person, twice weekly. His passport was confiscated. Specifically, he could not contact or be in the presence of members of the Lewis family.

The media clip showed him leaving the Carlisle court with Needham at his side, hand on his elbow, guiding through the flurry of reporters and others waiting. He was whisked away in an anonymous limo.

Sammie telephoned Harriet. "Tim Hutton and Cynthia Needham agreed to the bail conditions. But he is out. Bernice seems stoic and Eamon is angry."

Harriet responded, "It still blows me away that he confessed, yet we now have this turnaround. I was sailing backwards, but I heard him so clearly. That he now denies it again."

That's Needham, I expect," retorted Sammie, "He just wants out of jail. It'll be months before the trial. Ken Gilles says that the Church of the Redeemer has put out a release that Mettler will now advise the current choir director and organist on programming, but not lead the choir or play an active role at church. Apparently, he had three other event contracts in the works, but each has been cancelled by the organizers, or they have hired a replacement. Have you heard any more from your church, on preaching again?"

"No. I am waiting for the next committee meeting. That's tomorrow evening. I think my circuit will want me back, but it is what it is."

No, it isn't, thought Sammie. It's hurting you a lot. But she stayed quiet.

"I'd best get on."

"And me," replied Harriet, glad to get out of talking about that subject.

~~

The following afternoon, Dr. Yvonne Kulis walked into Norman Chiswell's office and joined Sammie and John Kent at the meeting table as Chiswell moved from his desk. She had completed a mental health assessment interview on Oliver Mettler that morning at Trafalgar House Police Station, in Bradford. She was providing her initial feedback.

"The bottom line, then. I don't see anything which supports Needham's anger disorder claim. He seemed surprised by my questions at times, I think, because he focused on his presumed condition and expected questions on that theme. There were some that were relevant and visible to him, others more embedded. The fact he didn't have his solicitor with him didn't seem to phase him at all."

Chiswell interrupted. "It certainly didn't go down well with Needham, despite her own claim. She opened that door."

Kulis just shrugged it off. "What I do see is evidence of NPD, Narcissistic Personality Disorder. He is very self-focused, has no empathy for others, and there are clear signs of extreme arrogance and other indicators."

She smiled. "At one point I asked him about his favorite UK choral directors. He went on about some, then I asked him why he hadn't included Jane Glover in his list. He had only mentioned male conductors. Mettler was lost for an answer but made a remark about her being quite good."

"I responded 'Quite good? She has conducted just about every major orchestra and the Huddesfield Choral Society. She's a Dame Commander of the British Empire for her services to music'. He hated it, but he didn't show any visible signs of anger. In fact, he thought for a moment then apologised; he hadn't thought of her, or some others he then mentioned. A reasonable comeback, really."

She saw Sammie looking uncertain, so she explained.

"He lashed out at Sergeant Calder not because she challenged his musical skills or capabilities. Momentarily she crushed his sense of superiority. Conducting choirs supports his ego, his fantasy about himself, strokes his own self-admiration."

As the faces at the table showed their understanding, she added, "Basically, he has a God complex. He will fight tooth and nail to preserve that. He has money behind him now and a very combative lawyer on his side. He will persist to the bitter end unless his vision of himself is broken or removed in some way. If that happens, he will become a shadow of his former self. But until that point is reached, he will fight.

"I went back through the video recording and the transcript. Calder's attack on his faith and that question of 'did he pray or not' was exactly the breakpoint. It was like a knife sliding into the chink in the armour, hitting the nerve. It surprised and wounded him so unexpectedly he lashed out, and spoke out, before realising he had lost control. On that note, not that it is my mandate to comment, I am rather surprised that Sergeant Calder has returned to community policing. She is a very strong fit for MIU or Organized Crime Division, I suggest."

John Kent just gave a sigh.

Half an hour later, Norm Chiswell and Dr. Kulis gave a shortened version of her findings to DCC Beardsley and Tim Hutton. Beardsley focused on the implications for the trial. After a moment, he said, "Dr. Kulis, it sounds like you will need to be an expert witness for the prosecution, to counter this 'anger disorder' play by the defense."

It was a tacit understanding that costs would go up. Norm nodded sagaciously, in agreement.

Beardsley thought a moment. "How did Calder find that breakpoint? Was it part of the interview plan?"

Kulis looked at Chiswell, saw his uncertainty, and answered. "In a broad sense, yes, to pursue the 'Compline' link. But specifically, the focus on 'did he pray or not?', that was all Calder, on the spot. Insight from her own background and intuition, I suppose."

As they left the office, Kulis glanced at Beardsley's desk as she stood. The Deputy Chief Constable had jotted down only three points: 'God complex', 'costs', and 'Calder'.

In Keswick, Harriet Calder was unaware of all this, busy with her own work, and her own problems.

She had received a call from Reverend Wescott. The committee meeting was now postponed until the second week of the New Year.

Harriet was about to ask what this meant now, but he spoke again. "I want you to continue your leave of absence, Harriet, until the meeting. It's best that way. For once, you will be free to spend Christmas with family and friends without having to work around church commitments."

As she closed the call, she felt the loss heavily, and a deep disappointment that a member of the clergy couldn't see how being sidelined from her role at Christmas would hurt her, rather than be accepted as an unplanned holiday.

36 MID-MORNING

The following Monday, around nine forty-five in the morning, Harriet was taking a probationer to make an enquiry at a home in Keswick. When June Robinson called them, she said, "You need to get back quickly and link in. Apparently, Communications just heard that Valerie Carmichael is to be on television, on the 'Mid-Morning' spot soon, talking about Mettler."

"What! She must know how much of a problem that will cause. She has a lawyer."

They changed their route, to return to the Keswick Town Council only a few minutes away. The new police officer, driving and overhearing the discussion, said as Robinson closed the call, "A bit of excitement in your day, Sarge."

She gave him a baleful look. "More like a never-ending bad dream, you mean."

In the TV studio, Andrea Plante, the main presenter, had announced a surprise addition to the advertised guest list. She was now seated across from two women, side by side on the facing couch.

"Valerie Carmichael, welcome back! It's wonderful to have you on the show again, but this one is special, and I want to warn the viewers that this piece does not concern your role in 'Ruston' or have anything to do with acting. You are here as the result of a real event, a profoundly serious and tragic matter, indeed. And with you is Felicity Murray. Welcome also, Felicity."

Valerie appeared comfortable. Felicity Murray, sitting next to her, seemed tense and alert.

Carmichael responded. "It is good to be back, Andrea, and for my friends out there, Felicity is my solicitor. She will hopefully keep me legal, but she is here because, as a woman, she feels as strongly as I do on this one."

Andrea was in full frame now. "The term, 'this one', as Valerie will tell, is about abuse and victims, and their re-victimisation. Watch these clips."

They replayed connected excerpts from the announcement of the arrest of Oliver Mettler for assaulting a police officer, to the police briefing that announced the murder charge against the man. Finally, they showed a brief clip of Mettler's lawyer citing the complaint to IOPC. It had been carefully edited for clarity of story line and impact.

Andrea said, "Valerie, speak to it."

Valerie's face filled the screen. "The complaint made against Cumbria Police by Oliver Mettler's lawyer, Cynthia Needham, was dismissed by the IOPC some days ago. There is no case to answer, they say, and I believe them.

"Oliver Mettler stands accused of the murder of Dennis Lewis, an assault on a police officer, and two sexual assaults on a minor around the time of Dennis's disappearance. They haven't named that person. They don't do that. It's the law. But that was me. I was fifteen, and Dennis Lewis was my friend."

A snapshot of Valerie and Dennis in their teens, provided by Valerie, was floated on screen for several seconds as Andrea said, "It must be awful for you, I am sure."

"I can't say more about that part, Andrea. Felicity tells me I can't say anything which would jeopardize the cases being brought before the courts. I am being careful about that."

"But why come on 'Mid-Morning' now? Tell us about Dennis."

"We were friends from being at primary school together in Maryport until the day he disappeared, at age fifteen. We were simply the best of friends growing up and it will emerge, he turned out to be a better one than even I thought. My heart goes out to Bernice and Eamon Lewis and Dennis's sister, Aileen. They have been through so much."

She looked at Felicity, checking, it seemed, before going back to her camera.

"I thought what happened to me and the disappearance of Dennis were totally unconnected. Some weeks ago, in the renewed investigation after the discovery of Dennis's body, Cumbria Police interviewed me and, I have to say, it proved to be a remarkable experience.

"I have played minor roles in other series, including police dramas, before I got the part in 'Ruston', but this was reality. Andrea, they treated me with such respect and consideration, it floored me. The interviewing detective, a young man, was so good. Abuse is an awful experience to relive, but the man and woman who took my statement were above reproach. That is my major reason for being here, to reach out to anyone in my situation. Don't hesitate and deny it, as I did. Don't be put off through fear, like I was. Talk to the police."

Andrea, now the devil's advocate, said, "But we have heard enough stories of the bad experiences that assault victims have undergone when they did that. At the hands of the police and in the courts."

Valerie nodded. "I have heard them, too, and I am not discounting them. I am just telling you about my own."

Andrea focused on Felicity. "Would you agree, Felicity? You are a solicitor; you have probably seen more of this than Valerie."

Felicity responded, "I have, and I have seen a spectrum of responses from police officers. Times change though, and the police are far more sensitive and supportive now than they are given credit for. But I agree with Valerie, Cumbria Police were exemplary. What may be less so, I am afraid, is the next stage."

Andrea asked, "What do you mean by that?"

"What is concerning me as Valerie's legal counsel is the legal team defending Oliver Mettler."

Andrea Plante asked, "Why?"

Felicity shook her head. "We are talking about serious costs here. And lawyers that are used to hard courtroom tactics. This is the team that defended Furness in the Sarah Tinley case."

Andrea took over as the camera returned to her, addressing the viewers. "That was the trial two years ago of Adam Furness for sexually assaulting Sarah Tinley. We covered at that time that Sarah and other witnesses were subject to rather harsh cross-examination, causing several admonitions from the judge.

"The solicitor for the defense of Adam Furness was a Cynthia Needham with Wolstenholme and Partners. She is the same solicitor engaged by the church, the Cross of the Redeemer, to defend Oliver Mettler. We will come back to that in a moment. But Valerie, you have something you want to say first, I know."

She looked at Valerie and the camera moved to a shot of both guests.

Valerie said, "I'm giving notice now. I'm not taking the sort of treatment I have seen given to other abused women during preparation for trial and in court. Will we, Felicity?"

Andrea spoke up, her voice taking on that dusky tone she was noted for in emotional situations. "I think you have a lot of people out there who will be wanting you treated well."

Valerie responded. "And I love my fans. I think of Sarah. I think of other woman, perhaps with no support, carrying their hidden hurt, being questioned in court-rooms. In Britain, it's done relatively politely, of course, but they are still dissected, as Sarah was. I am saying I am with them. We have had enough of dry old male barristers in wigs picking at us, urged on by solicitors no better than sharks. And, from what Felicity tells me, I think there is a rather nasty shark circling around this case right now and Andrea, I have no intention of becoming sharkbait."

She looked defiant as she deliberately made the implied insult.

A silence of more than a second is expensive and is a seldom-used element of daytime TV, but it has uses. The camera stayed focused on the two women for several moments, their faces firm.

Andrea said, sympathetically, "When you can, when you feel up to it and not tripping over legal hurdles, will you come back on, Val, and tell us more? Will you do that?"

"I will, Andrea. You and I are friends, and 'Ruston' is my life at present, and ITV is where that show lives. When I say more, it will be here, with you. And to the remarkable woman who told me that helping others will help me recover, I know you are out there. Thank you again, from the bottom of my heart."

Andrea Plante's face filled the screen. "After the break, our own Rod Leicester, outside the Church of the Redeemer, Bradford, with more on this story."

The ads came on.

In the meeting room in Penrith Police Headquarters there was a moment of silence. Ken Gilles filled it with, "Exemplary. I couldn't buy that if I tried. Lil, we must go and set up to deal with the calls. They will be swamping us."

He called out, "Sergeant Calder, I'll be talking to you shortly. Don't go out of contact."

John Kent sat still for a moment, then looked searchingly at Harriet and June Robinson, on the videolink.

Harriet said softly, "I had no idea." Her thoughts were on Susan Carlson, wondering what she had done.

Howard Mooney said, "It wasn't me, boss." He was beaming with pride.

John Kent responded, "I never thought for one second it was you, Mooney. You are safe on that one until you start giving autographs to people. Then I will lift your warrant badge."

He looked at Sammie. "My read is Carmichael was careful, other than slapping Cynthia Needham in the face. We need to check with Hutton."

Sammie smiled. "God, I wish I could have done that with Needham. Valerie deserves a medal."

Harriet said, "If no-one has alerted the Lewis family, someone should reach out. I don't know how they will react."

Louis Chan said quickly, "I'll call them now."

As the ads finished, other than Louis, they refocused on 'Mid-Morning'.

Rod Leicester was a familiar face on morning television. The camera framed him with the Cross of Redeemer church entrance behind him.

"A few minutes ago, I was able to interview Reverend Charles Lambert, Andrea, at the church behind us, the Cross of the Redeemer. He was very welcoming, and here is a clip from that interview."

It showed Leicester inside an office in the building, with a man in a light grey clerical shirt and clerical collar under a darker grey suit.

"Reverend Lambert, thank you for taking time for an interview and for the personal tour of your church. Earlier, you showed me several awards and certificates won by your choir over the years, led by Dr. Oliver Mettler."

The clergyman spoke clearly, in a soft voice, at ease with the video camera and interview. "Yes, we have a first-rate choir which brings a lot of joy and pleasure. Dr. Mettler has led them for many years and is highly regarded here."

"Is regarded, or was regarded, may I ask, given the recent charges?"

Lambert paused. "I think that is a decision made in each person's heart, is it not? When Dr. Mettler was taken in by the Cumbria Police it was a great surprise to us, of course. When he was charged, we followed our own procedures and suspended him from certain duties. He is to have no contact with our choir members. Another person is leading the choir at present.

"We support him as we can, of course. He is still a member of our church and a valued employee, much loved by those who know him. It is a painful time for everyone. We pray for Oliver, the Lewis family, and all who are involved in this terrible situation."

Rod said, "The Church of the Redeemer is paying for his defense, we understand?"

Lambert nodded. "We are, to some degree, supporting that, yes. Dr. Mettler is currently paying a significant part of those costs from his own resources. Legal costs are expensive, as you know, and these are very serious charges. We have agreed to assist, to ensure he is able to defend himself."

Rod continued. "Was it your church's insistence to change solicitor from a firm in Carlisle to one in London; one with, if I may say, a reputation for hard tactics?"

Lambert frowned. "I won't comment on that, Rod, about choice of defense expertise. Dr. Mettler is entitled in law to plead his innocence and present a defense. I will leave it at that."

The scene returned to the view of Rod, holding a microphone, outside. "There you have it, Andrea. I was pleased that Reverend Lambert gave me an interview. We weren't turned away with a 'no comment'. There are clearly a lot of good people here who think well of Oliver Mettler and are shocked by his arrest. They want to help him, as it was said, because he is a member of their community."

As Andrea Plante segued to the next item on 'Mid-Morning', John Kent said, "The bit at the end of the interview with Carmichael and her lawyer. 'To the remarkable woman...' Now who could that be?"

He left it hanging.

Harriet said, almost a groan, "I know. I need to talk to Susan Carlson. I saw it, too. She needs her backside kicking, I suspect. This whole media thing could have gone right off the rails and made prosecution a nightmare."

"Ooh," said Sammie. "Is that the vicious copper from Keswick? Did the IOPC get it wrong, d'you think?"

John smiled. "Carmichael was careful. I suspect her solicitor coached her on exactly what to reveal about the case. Let us know what Susan says, please? And give her a big hug from Sammie, who is sitting here smiling her face off."

"And me," said Howard. "I mean, say hello from me. I hope she comes back."

As they closed the videolink, Ken Gilles came back in.

"John, to have that sequence set up with the pair, then Rod in Bradford, this was planned. Carmichael didn't 'drop in'; they must have worked on this, timing it for after the murder charge was made. There is no sign of the BBC or other networks having it. Carmichael gave her own corporation an exclusive. Our phones are humming now, but the Chief is pleased as punch with the way we are portrayed.

Kent said, "Well, at least the Chief Constable is happy. I doubt Cynthia Needham will see it in the same light."

Ten minutes later, Harriet was talking to Susan.

"We don't get ITV over here. Valerie organized a special link on the internet for me to watch. So yes, I saw it and loved it. It's only six a.m. here, I could have been asleep when you called, you know."

"I guessed. If I was wrong, I would have been your speaking alarm clock; rise and shine. What did you tell Valerie? Will you tell me?"

Susan thought for a moment. "Nothing until she told me that she planned to go public with her role in this. Then I told her she should be very careful about doing that. And for her to get Felicity to check the legal aspects, as she would be a witness, and Mettler seemed to be getting some new lawyers involved."

"That's all?"

"More or less. Yes. I never said anything else, because I don't know anything else, do I?"

Harriet said, "You seem to have prior knowledge of

witness lists before any trial procedures have started? I am amazed."

"Well, she will be called, won't she? For the part of the trial dealing with the murder, and to confirm he molested her. It's obvious. Give me that, at least. She was on the ball on that one, giving notice to the shark lady."

Harriet relented. "Sorry. You are right, she will. Unofficially, you are MIU's hero of the day. Sammie sends a big hug. And Howard Mooney would give you one, too. Perhaps you have another admirer, there. He wants you to come back."

Susan smiled. "I would like to come back. Not for him, though. Any news on your lay preacher role?"

"I won't hear further until the New Year when the committee meets. Given the increased visibility of the Mettler case as of this morning, I doubt that I will be back any time soon."

Susan's face showed her obstinacy. "I think they need to suck it up and let you get back to it. I'm not buying your 'I was part of the decision' excuse any longer. I'm going to tell Chris to come over and give you a big hug."

Harriet smiled. "Have him do it when Kerri's here; I want to see her face as he does so."

37. SOLWAY

The initial public reaction to Carmichael's appearance on 'Mid-Morning' was a wave of negative criticism of Oliver Mettler and, by association, the Cross of the Redeemer. Cynthia Needham, leaving court in London on another matter, was swarmed by the media but made no comment.

The following Thursday, the viewing statistics for the Ruston episode, one recorded long before the announcement by Carmichael, had the highest rating in the series history.

By the same evening, the Cross of the Redeemer put out an announcement that Dr. Mettler would have no direct or indirect involvement in the activities of the church during this 'distressful time for all involved' and would not attend there at present for work or services.

More locally, parishioners from several Cumbria Methodist churches called the district office, asking for the immediate reinstatement of Mrs. Calder. Two members of Windermere Methodist Church were interviewed by the

Westmorland Gazette. It also asked for an interview with Reverend Westcott, but he was not available to comment.

Even in vindication, Harriet's absence on leave was a continuing problem for the church.

~~

Louis had been assigned to dig into the background of Shannon Nichols. Neither John Kent nor Sammie had forgotten that she, too, had given the impression of not being completely open with Harriet. Acting on it had been delayed, with both the search for DNA evidence and the preparations for trial.

The rain was lashing the windows as Louis made his findings known at the briefing. He had followed up with Nichols by telephone a day earlier, just to get her recollections of the final committee meeting with Oliver Mettler, the one closing out on the fundraiser.

"I asked about it and – remember Harriet said her voice changed, that she lost the 'I'm here to help' tone – well, I got the same response, I felt. She missed the wrap-up meeting of the concert committee, claiming she went on holiday."

John Kent responded, "Harriet said she is a poor liar if caught unprepared, at least. Do we know where she was?"

"I checked. She was in a retreat, at a place in Norfolk. One she organised very suddenly."

Kent pulled a face. "These things happen with priests, I suppose, but..."

Louis pressed the point. "I felt she was uneasy in her answer, though."

Kent nodded. "Sammie?" He wanted her input.

Sammie looked out of the window. "I think Louis and I will go and see her tomorrow; the forecast is for sun and cloud then. We can talk outside."

Louis looked a little surprised at the reasoning.

John Kent said, "Harriet said the dog acted like a lie detector, I recall. Good thinking."

They called Shannon Nichols when they were fifteen minutes away. She was walking home from the church, excited about all the preparations for the forthcoming Christmas services. Louis said, "We can meet at your home or the church, if you want. But Harriet said you liked to walk your dog and we could do with a stretch of the legs."

As they arrived, Nichols emerged in walking boots and carrying a retractable dog leash, with Bel beside her. As Louis shook hands with the priest, he introduced Sammie. "This is Sergeant Livermore, my boss. She is leading the investigation."

Sammie gave a short 'hello' but looked serious; enough to make the priest's face change from the welcoming smile to a more sombre expression.

As they set off, Sammie walked behind, leaving Louis alongside Nichols to do the questioning.

"When you were interviewed by Sergeant Calder, you told her that you and Oliver Mettler didn't stay in touch. Why?"

Shannon Nichols didn't answer him immediately. First came the temporizing statement.

"It was a defined project. The organising team went their separate ways. And he is a member of a different church, in Yorkshire."

Louis looked at the road ahead, at Bel, beginning to see what Calder had spotted. "Yes, I see the logic of that. I just thought a celebrated choral conductor is a useful contact for future events the cathedral might hold. We all network, don't we? We keep contacts because you never know when something else will come up and it could be useful."

Nichols shrugged. "I didn't, anyway." After a pause she added, "Given the events in the news, I am glad I didn't."

It's there, in the tone, Louis thought. He exchanged a quick glance with Sammie, then said, "We are going to need you to come over to Penrith sometime soon, to make a formal statement about the committee meeting where you arrived late, the one when you mentioned Crosshill Farm. It is an important piece of evidence in the case, how he knew about the burial site."

Nichols muttered, "Disposed of, is what you mean. Not buried properly. At least, he has had a proper burial now, the poor boy. I will do that, make a statement. Can it be after Christmas, though, given our Advent and Christmas services? There is so much to do in preparation."

"Of course."

It seemed to relax her. Bel seemed happier again.

Louis waited. Nichols filled the silence with her own comment. "I feel bad about talking about the farm at the committee meeting. It has bothered me a lot, a sense of guilt. I pray on it."

As they rounded a bend, two people came up the same path towards them, waving at Nichols. Bel pulled out on the extendable lead, running to them, tail wagging.

One said, "You've got visitors, Shannon. Lovely day to be out!"

Nichols looked a little lost, giving them a quick smile. Sammie spoke up, deflecting the expectation of an introduction. "You know Bel well, I see?"

"We often meet on this path, don't we, girl, with her mom? Here, or at church, sometimes, not during services, obviously, but at some of the social events."

It was a long enough chit-chat to allow the two police officers to pass by, leaving Nichols to close out with her parishioners.

As they moved on, the priest said suddenly, "I am so sorry your colleague was hurt. That he could do this to her."

'He', Louis noticed. He glanced again at Sammie who, sensing the moment, said, "Sergeant Calder had some colourful bruising, I tell you. And he called her a 'Methodist cow' as he hit her."

Nichols winced visibly.

Louis was looking at Bel sniffing away at something a few yards ahead, when he said, "You missed the close-out meeting of the committee for the fundraiser, you told me. You went on holiday."

"Yes, I did."

"Anywhere nice?"

Nichols said, "Yes. Norfolk, to see friends there. It was a timing conflict."

Chan stopped so suddenly, it took Nichols by surprise as she faced him.

"Bel is so attuned, you know? Look at her ears. Now she's looking back at you. The holiday wasn't a visit to friends, and it wasn't planned. You went on retreat at very short notice. We have the booking details. Why did you need that?"

Nichols went beet red with embarrassment at being confronted about the lie. Bel gave a small bark, a pathetic noise, really. "Things had been so busy, I needed a break, some peace. I needed peace."

From behind her, Nichols heard, "Its time you told us, Shannon."

The priest swung around. "About what?"

Sounding irritated, Sammie said, "About Oliver Mettler." She stared hard at the priest, who was now look-ing frightened. Bel came running up, agitatedly pawing at

Shannon Nichols' leg, as the priest reached down, hiding her face, buying time to make her response.

"I don't – I can't. It was nothing. I–."

Chan said quietly, sympathetically, "Nothing. Enough to make you miss the final meeting of a project you had worked on so hard for months. Enough to make you go on retreat. It doesn't sound like nothing to me. Sergeant?"

On cue, Sammie moved forward, face-to-face with Nichols. "It sounds like something to me. Y'know, I've got a big bust. I hated it when I was in my teens. So has Valerie Carmichael. So have you, Reverend Nichols. It makes me think."

The priest's eyes widened. "He told you, didn't he? Is that what this is about? It was nothing, an accident. It was a misunderstanding."

Sammie asked quietly, "What was?"

"We had made coffee. We both went to get the milk out of the fridge at the same time, and he reached past me and accidentally caught my breast with his hand."

Sammie raised an eyebrow. "Were you alone, or would one of the others on the committee be able to verify that?"

Nichols almost recoiled. "We were alone, thank God! Look, I don't know what he said –." She stopped, stroking the dog's head now, calming her, trying to calm herself. "I'm not involved. I don't want to be involved."

Chan dropped down, patting the anxious dog, rubbing her jaw, and whispering calming sounds. Then he said, "You are already involved, Reverend, like it or not. We need a formal statement, as I said. You may be called as a witness because of that fact alone."

He stood up straight, his head higher than the priest's. "And you may convince yourself that it was nothing, but we disagree. You see, Dennis's death arose from a series of actions beginning with what, Sergeant Livermore?"

His eyes were on Shannon, but his hand moved closer to hers at the junction of the lead and the collar, as Sammie said quietly, "We can't say what happened precisely, as that is evidence to be presented in court. But Oliver Mettler was alone with Valerie Krestman during the first rehearsal. Think about that."

As the tears came and Bel bucked, Louis steadied the animal. Sammie put an arm around the priest. She said, "Let's head back, and you can put Bel inside at home, or leave her with someone. Then you are coming with us, quietly, to Penrith, to make a complete statement. Either that, or I'll send a car and officers in uniform to get you. You don't want that, do you? With everyone around here knowing who you are. And so close to Christmas. Let's get this over with for you, quickly."

On the drive there, Shannon asked if she needed a lawyer. Sammie told her, "Not unless you want one. It's a formal witness statement we need."

Shannon said, "The touching. It was a surprise, and totally unexpected. I didn't give him any basis for it."

It fits, thought Sammie. "But it troubled you, I think? You went on retreat."

Shannon responded, "He was apologising too profusely I thought, overdoing it. I felt manipulated. We hardly knew each other. I gave him a look and shut it down, then walked away. That was it. Absolutely nothing tangible. It disturbed me. I was never alone with him again. I missed the last meeting because I knew the concert had been a success. I didn't want to be around him."

Sammie looked at her, sensing it. And when he touched you, you had a romantic hope about the man momentarily, until you felt manipulated. Part of the reason for the retreat was the guilt associated with that failed hope.

"Did you suspect his role in Dennis's death, once the body was discovered on Crosshill Farm?"

"No. Never that. It was the earlier meeting with Sergeant Calder which brought him back to mind. Awful as the man's acts are, I won't accuse him of something based only on my perception. Him or anyone else."

Chan was driving. He called back. "We are simply taking a witness statement, Reverend Nichols. That will be just the facts about Crosshill Farm and your observations."

That seemed to calm the priest a little.

Once they had the statement and reported the bigger picture, like it or not, Tim Hutton would want Nichols on the witness stand in court. Under oath, they would get the full story.

Sammie could see another reason for Nichols' reluctance. The priest was happy, safe in the Solway Plain, away from it all. She could be the 'bundle of fun' there, not have to face the visibility of the Mettler media coverage, or her fellow priests who may gossip about her.

She said softly, "There may be other women out there, too intimidated to come forward. That's why Carmichael spoke out. No others have appeared so far, but if there are any, they are still hurting. A decade ago, you looked into his eyes and saw his manipulation. Your words."

Sammie bit back the thought 'And you did nothing'. She thought about Harriet for a moment, what she would say, then added, "Think on it, and perhaps on the value of atonement."

Nichols could interpret that however she chose: Mettler's atonement, or her own. The conversation in the car died as each person was lost in thought. They all knew where they stood now.

38 BEARDSLEY

On the Sunday after Christmas, two days before the New Year, Harriet received a call in the evening at home from DCC Beardsley.

"Are you working tomorrow, Sergeant Calder?"

"Yes, sir. I have the early shift at Keswick. We have a larger community team assigned over the holiday."

"I'd like to see you here afterwards, say at 4.15 p.m., in my office. Come to headquarters and straight in here. And no mention of this to others, please."

"Is there a development, a problem, sir?"

"On the Mettler case. No, I wish there were. And no, not any problem for you. I just want a word, that's all."

He closed the call, leaving her in the dark.

An hour later, Sammie called her. "We had a development, a late Christmas present, really."

Harriet's first thought was of Beardsley's call. Assuming a link, she simply said, "What?"

"We took a formal statement before Christmas from Shannon Nichols, about the committee meeting where she mentioned Crosshill Farm. She came back yesterday and revised it.

"Mettler touched her, too, her breast. Something like he did to Valerie, but Nichols shut it down immediately. We have charged him."

"What did Mettler or his solicitor say?"

"That's the thing. John telephoned her and gave a summary of our intent, then asked her how her client would respond. She immediately told him their position hadn't changed; her client would not be commenting. We had sent Mooney and Chan near his home on stand-by. They took him to a station in Bradford to charge him there. Just do it and leave, they were told."

She didn't wait for Harriet to work it out. "We think Mettler will be far more concerned about this charge, given it involves a priest, than Needham picked up. He will worry about what the people at his own church will think. By the time Needham thought it through and called John back, Mettler had been charged. She's not happy about it and is now interrupting her holiday, on her way to Bradford to see him."

Harriet responded, "It'll give him a few hours to sweat about it before the team coach can fire up his resolve. I see that."

"I'll let you know how it goes."

So, Beardsley's call wasn't linked, Harriet concluded.

~~

"Thank you for coming after your shift, Harriet," said the Deputy Chief Constable.

I didn't have much choice, Harriet thought, looking suspiciously at the smiling face of Reverend Shelagh Amos in the other chair at the table. Her presence was a surprise. Harriet decided she was about to be lumbered with a particularly sensitive piece of pastoral work, and Shelagh had involved Beardsley to make sure she would do it.

He began with something she didn't expect: the topics of religion and her husband's death.

"I was a DCI in Organized Crime when your husband died, Harriet."

She nodded, suddenly recalling him then.

"I had my eye on you at the time, as a possible for us, at some point. You were doing well in MIU back then. You did well there again, last year, and again more recently."

Harriet knew then the reason for the visit. "John Kent spoke to you?"

He looked at her. "Not specifically. Hear me out. I know he wants you. It's more than that."

He paused. "I'm C of E. Always have been, but I keep my church personal and my professional side separate. I grew up where religion and policing were hand in fist, a recipe for favoritism, and I detested that. Still do."

"I'd just been promoted to superintendent in the South Territorial Area when the word came you were studying to be a preacher. It struck me then; I wondered how you would do. As you know, John Kent trying to get you into MIU is not the first time that people have talked about promotion. But we have always respected your position, haven't we?"

He waited for an answer.

"Yes, sir. And I am grateful for that. I love my work as a police officer, and my –."

She stopped herself. "My work with the church, my church. You know the situation, I gather?"

She glanced at Amos, almost a glare. "I miss that now."

Amos jumped in. "You miss your ministry."

Beardsley continued softly. "The Chaplain and I talked last week. She put it in a different context, one which I want to go through with you. Shelagh, you start. This was your take on it."

Shelagh Amos sat forward suddenly in her chair, her face becoming serious.

"Your work with the Methodist Church. What do you do there, do you think?"

That puzzled Harriet. "You, of all people, ask that?"

Amos ignored the rebuttal. "I also talked again recently with Dennis Lewis's parents. You, Livermore and the MIU team are held in high esteem. You particularly, not just because you are a good police officer, but the way you treated them."

Harriet said nothing.

The chaplain continued, "What do you think your work in MIU brought to them, besides the perpetrator of the crime being caught? What could you bring to others? Have you given it any thought?"

Harriet gave her a combative stare. Beardsley sat silent, watching them.

Amos was not dissuaded, she pressed on. "Eamon told me about his discussion with you; about his own feelings of guilt and what you said to him then, during his interview. And how they both felt when they met you again at Bassenthwaite Methodist. They came over to see you there before Christmas, I know.

"One of the hardest things for police officers to deal with is people who are spiritually hurt, the dying, and the bereaved. You do that and do it well. You are a first-class investigator, John Kent says. How many combine those skill sets? And get the chance to use them together?"

Harriet responded, "They are best separated. DCC Beardsley just said as much."

Amos shook her head. "Not the same thing at all. You know the boundaries between the two worlds, as do I. We have talked about that in the past. You have the experience.

"Sometimes, people in ministry like you and me, we fool ourselves that we know God's purpose for us. We like what He revealed to us, even when it proves to be hard or wearisome; we sense the purpose. We convince ourselves and stop listening, stop asking for direction."

"All I am asking is for you to consider the possibility you are being closed-minded about other opportunities. And to pray a little on it. Warren?"

Beardsley came back in. "What I say now is in strict confidence. There are going to be changes soon across the constabulary. You know from experience that happens from time to time. I would very much like to see you become an inspector in the Major Investigation Unit. It is bigger than the issue of John simply wanting to fill a vacancy. If you take it, you can have Livermore as your sergeant, with the specific mandate of bringing her along, and Chan. You will have that responsibility for all your team, as you do now in Keswick, but Livermore and Chan stand out to me. As you did, all those years ago. I know you are in a dilemma. All I can do is provide an option to consider."

He smiled. "I've given my sermon. Please think about it. Let me know within a month, so no rush."

He looked at the clock and the door. Clearly, he had other items to deal with.

Harriet stood, her mind in turmoil. "Well, thank you, sir. And you, Shelagh. I will. Give it thought, I mean. I really appreciate your consideration."

As she left the room, she was struck that, in the days before and after the celebration of the birth of Jesus Christ, it was clergy in the Anglican Communion, here and in Canada, who still saw the importance of her call to ministry, rather than those in her own church.

Compline

39 FIELDING

Two weeks later, DCI Kent appeared at the police base at Keswick Town Council around four o'clock. They were back in 'low season' mode, with just Harriet and the three constables, Keston, Clarke and Harris. As Harriet saw him, he gave her a nod, a small smile, and asked, "Is Inspector Robinson here yet?"

Harriet responded, "She got here ten minutes ago. In the office."

The small office attached to the operations area filled several functions, but when Robinson visited, she took it over. Earlier, June Robinson had called, simply saying she would be dropping by.

Ten minutes after he entered, Robinson called Harriet in, saying, "Pam, cover for Harriet, please."

As Harriet entered behind her boss, she found John Kent logging into the computer system. "I want you to see this. As of yesterday, Arthur Fielding is the solicitor of record again for Mettler. He asked for this interview, held this morning."

He stood back as the two women watched the screen.

Harriet was struck that Mettler had the same suit on, cleaned, as at the interview where he hit her. He had lost a lot of weight, noticeably in the face, and seemed tired.

John Kent had given the interview to Sammie and Howard Mooney, with Sammie leading. As they went on record and identified themselves, Sammie said, "I gather that you want to make a statement, Dr. Mettler. Please go ahead."

Mettler spoke in a clear, seemingly emotionless voice; not robotic, simply that he was now past caring.

"On the fourth of June 2008, I received a telephone call from a young man, Dennis Lewis, wanting to speak to me about his concerns and seek my advice. All he would say is that it related to the choir about to perform the day following at the cathedral.

"My first response was to put him off, but he was quite persistent, saying it was a sensitive matter. When he said it related to the soprano soloist in the choir, I wanted to know what he was talking about. I suggested that he come to the rehearsal hall to see me before the concert.

"I would be there, I said, on impulse, for a private service of Compline, to give him the sense of something routine occurring. On reflection, I don't know why I did that, rather than just tell him I would meet him there. I worried he had found out about my intimacy with Valerie."

Sammie was making notes to herself, Harriet saw. They would need to go back over a lot of detail.

"He turned up early. I had just got there myself and had opened the side door I told him to use. No-one else was there. I was due in an hour and a half at the cathedral. The choir was scheduled for a final sound check. I was quite stressed, as you can imagine.

"He told me he was sure that someone in the choir had

been upsetting Valerie deeply, and he was worried that it might be bullying or something even more serious. I tried to talk him out of it; to be careful about slander, to realise that young women can get somewhat fanciful, that something innocent could easily be misconstrued.

"He suddenly said, 'It was you, wasn't it? I just realised.' I denied it. He called me a filthy bastard. Then he punched me in the chest.

"I am prone to occasions of intense anger; I realise that. I have demonstrated that trait here, unfortunately, what that does to me. I hit him hard, as I did your officer. The hall has structural pillars. His head hit one as he fell, his forehead. He was dead when I checked him.

"I lined a cupboard with garbage bags found there and put him inside, locking it. After the concert, I returned to the hall. In the end, I found some plastic sheeting and rope in a storage area. The boy was not yet in rigor, but it was starting, and I knew he would soon be hard to move, not solely because of the weight, but the shape. I bundled him and tied him up before transferring him to the boot of my car."

He paused, collecting his thoughts.

"The day after the concert, I bought a freezer on sale with a guarantee of same day delivery. In the middle of the night, I transferred the body from my car into my garage. I lined the freezer with more plastic and placed him in it and locked it.

"I realised the body would be difficult to remove. So, as you worked out, I used my bike pulley. A month later, when I thought that the body could be buried, I used warm water to loosen it from the sides and bottom, winched it up and the pulley gave way. One of the joists had a weakness, a crack, but I didn't realise that at the time. His head hit the freezer top near where he hit the wall.

"I had heard about Crosshill Farm at a committee meeting when Reverend Nichols apologised for being late. I went there twice during the period I had the boy in the freezer and found the area by the knoll I thought to be suitable. It was close to Maryport, too. If his body was discovered, I thought, it would appear to be a local death, far away from Carlisle.

"I buried him there after sunset, in near darkness. There wasn't anyone around the whole time. I prayed for him and for my own forgiveness. It was an accident in a short tussle, a blow from me after a blow from him.

"My subsequent actions were guided by panic and my unwillingness to face the consequences, but also to let me continue my important role as a musician, which is my life work. I am deeply sorry for the boy's death and the distress it has caused his family and others."

He stopped. Fielding just said, "Oliver?"

Mettler added, as if remembering something he was supposed to say, "I know you will need a lot more detail. I can't handle that now. I will give what I can during other interviews, but not now. No matter how you may regard me, the last weeks have been traumatic."

He sat back.

"Sammie said, "Just a couple of questions now, Dr. Mettler. First, throughout your statement you used 'boy', 'him', 'young man' and 'body', not his name, Dennis. You used that only once, at the beginning. Why is that?"

Mettler blinked as he thought through the answer. "Depersonification makes it easier for me."

"Final question from me, at present. When he fell after the punch in the church, did you consider seeking help, to call an ambulance or find another person to assist?"

It was an important element; he did not seek help immediately, despite claiming it was an accident.

Mettler thought about that one a lot longer, staring at the table. Eventually he looked up at her.

"No. He never regained consciousness. I think he died within no time at all. I am not good at things like taking pulses, but when I did, his was undetectable and his eyes looked dead."

Sammie looked at Howard, who said, "Just one. Earlier you said you demonstrated your anger here, unfortunately. What did you mean by that?"

Mettler looked puzzled at the question for a moment. "That I shouted and hit the police officer, Calder. I regret that."

Howard wanted to know if the man had any sense of remorse. He had not heard it, so far, regarding Dennis, despite the formal apology at the end of his statement. Mettler hadn't said anything about the assaults on Valerie Carmichael or Shannon Nichols, either. It struck Howard that there was no real apology offered to Harriet Calder either.

Mettler focused on Howard. "It was hard in prison, on remand. And now, although I am on bail, I feel that I am in hiding, after the television coverage of Carmichael."

The uniformed officer noted his hands clenching into fists. He moved forward, placing a hand gently on Mettler's forearm nearest to him.

Sammie said evenly, "We will have to take you back into custody now. I am sure Mr. Fielding explained that."

Mettle nodded but said nothing.

Arthur Fielding said, for the record, "My client is struggling at present, for the reasons he stated. I request that the interview be terminated at this time. I think you have enough for now."

Sammie, finding Arthur Fielding a lot easier to deal with than the Wolstenholme superwoman, said, "Interview terminated at 12.12. p.m.""

Harriet looked at John Kent, who pointed at the screen. "Watch. There is a little more."

As Mettler was taken away, Fielding asked, "And how is Sergeant Calder's injury to the face? I had no chance to ask."

Sammie responded cryptically, "The face healed well, but the bruising over the last couple of months is deep, the effects are still lingering."

He said, "Indeed. Please give her my best wishes for a full recovery."

He left the interview room as the recording went blank. John Kent leaned forward, closing his site access.

Robinson said, "The trial will be about sentencing provisions, then. It could be over with by Easter?"

Kent nodded his agreement. "We hope so. I have people making sure our evidence stays watertight, as we learn more, but his confession simplifies things a lot."

Harriet felt as if a great weight had been lifted. Then she caught the MIU chief's expression. He said, "If I could have a word alone, Harriet. As I walk back to the car, perhaps? Nothing to do with work."

As they walked outside and had some privacy, he said, "Have you heard from the District Committee yet? I know they met yesterday."

Church matters, not the case, she realised. "No. I am expecting a call; today, I hope."

He said carefully, "Carol resigned from the committee last night. I wanted you to know. If you call her, I doubt she will breach any confidentiality about her role, but it may be useful for you."

Harriet was surprised. "Did she resign over me?"

"Yes and no. Give Reverend Wescott a call first, I suggest, find out where you stand. Then talk to Carol, see what she says, or can share, I mean. She knows I was going to raise this with you."

When Harriet called Carol Kent a little later, she answered cheerfully, and there was laughter in the background.

"Hi, Harriet. Sorry. Emma and I were just sharing a funny experience."

Emma was their older daughter, Harriet knew.

Her voice turned more serious as she said, "John told me he was going over to Keswick."

"I'm sorry to hear about you leaving the committee. It's a surprise, I must say."

In the background, Harriet heard a door close.

"Thank you. It was time to move on. Look, I can't say much. What exactly did Reverend Wescott tell you – about you, I mean?"

"I thought he would call me, but John said to call him. I did, just now. He says the committee wants me to take a longer leave of absence, let the gossip die down completely about Mettler and Valerie Carmichael. Then he and I will meet. He gave me the impression the meeting would take place in later spring or early summer. That's a long time away, Carol. I'm really feeling it, I tell you."

Carol Kent heard the contained anguish and anger. She stayed silent for a moment, to give Harriet time to calm herself. "I informed the committee that the IOPC decision vindicated you as soon as you told us. As if you really needed vindication in the first place. I can't decide whether that is a more an insult or a farce. For some parishioners who called me, your departure was a real disappointment, I tell you. At the meeting yesterday, I reminded them of my earlier report and recommended that you should have your circuit position restored immediately."

"Well, thank you. Some didn't accept that, I'm sure. Wescott told me the discussions were 'difficult', to use his term."

Carol Kent changed the subject. "Roger Kearns, in Ambleside. A compound fracture of the leg, remember? He has been off for four months. He's just turned fifty-two."

"Yes, I heard."

"Do you know Lorna Unwin in Brampton?"

"I've not met her. Someone said she was a good preacher."

"She is. Only thirty-one, but she has been off with post-partum depression. Not sure when she will be ready to take up her ministry again. I mention them, because like you, they both hope to return to their former positions."

Harriet suppressed her immediate thought; I am not ill or injured. But she was tainted with being a police officer.

"Go on."

"The EDI commitment. You follow and support that, I think?"

The equality, diversity, and inclusion agenda of the Methodist Church in the UK.

"Yes, I do. As do you, I know. We need to reach out to everyone."

"I do, but I'm like my husband. You know exactly where you stand with John, don't you? I do, anyway."

Harriet agreed. "Even when he dragged me into the Lewis case, he told me it was to make sure I didn't get the choice. So yes, John's straight, a good boss. And I see now where you are going with this."

Carol Kent said, "Good. I think you were given a non-answer by Charles Wescott. I don't want to be part of a group giving non-answers to people. There may be new people with the calling to preach; I hear that. It doesn't mean that you or others have lost that call, I told them. I can't say more than that. I have probably said too much, as it is."

As it sunk in, Harriet went numb for a moment. Carol had a lot more insight into the strategic plan implementation of the Methodist Church in the area. It was working hard to achieve greater diversity of backgrounds, gender inclusiveness and age range among its staff. Harriet hadn't considered the impact on existing people that much. Roger, Lorna, and she were all established lay preachers, but white and presumably heterosexual. It seems that they, and probably others over time, were being placed on hold to make way for change, she concluded.

She saw the future; uncertainty and a reduced and more occasional role, filling in for absences or illnesses of others in the circuits, a second-tier function. It would be dressed up in some way, of course, as mentoring, or another reason.

Taking a deep breath, she said, "Thank you for being honest with me, Carol. I won't breach the trust you have shown with this discussion. I'm really sorry you are not part of the committee any longer. It sounds as if they need your voice."

"It was time for me to go. I have done eight years, in one committee role or another. Time to make way for someone new, more in tune with…. I'd better not say."

Carol was in the same boat as the preachers she mentioned, she intimated. At least in her case, she had made the decision.

Harriet said, "I'm going to miss you. But not those calls to cover for someone at short notice. They always seemed to be when the weather was bad."

"I'll miss you, too. By the way, John will never say it,

but he thinks the world of you. Take care now and stay in touch."

After she put the phone down, Harriet thought it was unlikely they would stay in regular contact. Calling up DCI Kent's wife for a social chit-chat was not really on the cards.

Harriet slept on it, spending some time that evening praying for guidance on her path forward. She thought sleep might be a problem, but she slept well.

The following afternoon, after her shift, she made a brief call to DCC Beardsley's assistant. Beardsley called her back an hour later.

That evening, Harriet composed an email to Reverend Wescott. It started out long, became tangled, and was heavily revised. Finally, she rewrote it completely, and it ended up being very short indeed.

40 LUHAR

It was five weeks later, as March loomed. They had an unexpected bout of freezing rain early that morning. The MIU morning briefing was special; everyone had to be in headquarters first thing, they were told. Typical, Sammie thought, when the road conditions made it that much harder.

Still, people turned up. That none of the bosses were in the room as they gathered was a giveaway. This meeting wasn't just about casework changes.

When Kent appeared, they were surprised to see Chief Superintendent Dunn from Organized Crime enter beside him, talking with Norm Chiswell. Behind them were two female officers alongside DI Ken Nolan. Superintendent Chiswell was looking stoic.

Dunn took the pole position. "Good morning. We have some changes to announce this morning before you begin case review. First, the appointment of John Kent to the rank of superintendent in Organized Crime, effective immediately. It is well deserved, I'm sure you will agree."

The people in the room were stunned.

He continued, "The new head of MIU is DCI Fara Luhar, transferring from Organized Crime Division. Some of you know her, have worked with Fara at one time or another. Joining her is DI Harriet Calder, who has been in and out of here in the last while. Now she's back permanently. She and Ken will be the two team leaders and you will be reorganised accordingly. John?"

For some, they heard the word permanently emphasized.

Kent moved forward. "I know this will be a surprise for you, but I have been in MIU for a long time. I need to move on and so does MIU. It's time for new blood and, you will be pleased to hear, additional staff. What they will do, how you will be structured, will be for DCI Luhar to sort out. Anyone who has worked with her knows she can do that. You are in good hands.

"I'll miss you; we have achieved a lot together, and I thank you for that, for your dedication. But I'm glad to say also that Harriet Calder is joining you. I finally prised her out of Keswick. For those of you who have worked with her, you will know why I said that. She will be a strong addition to this team."

It was a wisecracker that broke the tension. "She takes a good punch."

"Thank you, Neville. Never short of a quip, as usual."

He turned to Luhar. "Fara, It's all yours."

Dunn looked at Chiswell, as if inviting him to say something. Norm's expression was impassive, but those who knew him could see that the man was unhappy with the changes, that they must have been imposed on him. Eloquent as ever, Norm suddenly said, "I'll leave it to DCI Luhar, then. Let's get on, everyone."

With that, he led the way out of the room followed by Kent and Dunn.

DCI Luhar said, "I'm glad to be joining you, I know this is good team and John's shoes are hard to fill. But I'm looking forward to the easy stuff as he takes on some professional criminals."

The tension started to ease immediately as Fara, a large woman of Indian ethnicity, gave a dazzling smile at her own joke. Several groans were heard.

"Case review. Let's get going. First, DI Nolan on the warehouse arson death. Livermore, you are next, on the Halford case, until you bring your new boss up to speed. Apparently, she wants to work with you, if I provide a bodyguard every time you two interview someone together."

Over the laughter, Sammie said, "Yes, boss," and smiled at Harriet.

Later, when Sammie could talk to Harriet alone, all she said was, "Gotcha! But what did it? Not my lunch at The George, obviously. You ran screaming from that one."

Harriet certainly wasn't going to mention the meeting with Beardsley and Amos. Or the feedback from Carol Kent. She just smiled. "A mix of things. A different Christmas experience, for one."

She paused. "I have resigned from my lay preacher role. Something had to give. Talking to Bernice and Yvonne Kingsley, I feel I am valued here, I suppose. That matters. I went to one of my former chapels last Sunday to see my replacement take the service, and it was OK. She did well. I was happy for her and told her so. She was nervous at first, saying she had big shoes to fill, but together we made it clear to the congregation that all was well."

"But you will miss your church work, I'm sure."

Harriet nodded. "Oh, I do already, a lot. But this place will keep me busy."

With that less than subtle hint, Sammie said. "On that note, I had better get out to the interview I put off for an hour when we were given the drum roll about everyone being at the briefing."

A minute or so later, Detective Inspector Harriet Calder looked around her obviously unfamiliar new office and then out at her team, with Linnie pointing out something to Chan. Howard was on the phone, and Sammie putting her coat on, ready to leave. On impulse, she opened her purse to touch the small bible received in yesterday's post and pulled out the note written by Susan Carlson.

Harriet,

I wasn't sure why I took Duncan's bible home with me this time. Somehow, I knew it shouldn't stay on that shelf; discarded, in a sense. I think Kerri thought I wanted it for Chris, but that wouldn't be me. But I didn't tell her that.

So, it has been here with me these last couple of months, every now and again reminding me of my impulsiveness at different times of my life, for better or worse. It reappeared when I first heard of Bassenthwaite, and then met you, and through you, Chris. Now you, your part of the world and people there are so meaningful to me, and I can't wait to come back.

I don't think of bibles as Catholic, Anglican, Methodist, or anything else these days. With your recent experiences we talked about, perhaps you may be thinking more along the same lines and can find a use for it, if not for yourself, with someone you know. It is given with love, anyway.

Yours, Susan.

As she folded the note again and put it away, her new boss walked into her office. "Harriet. We have one just come in, a body in some rocks out near Eskdale. That will be all bloody uphill, no doubt. You have it. I think I'll go out on this one with you to begin with, not to play at being your mum, just that we are both settling in. Alert Mooney and Chan, and be ready in ten, OK? We'll leave Sammie handling the Halford case, I suggest, for now."

With that, DCI Luhar was out the door.

EPILOGUE. WINDOWS

"Oliver Shelburn Mettler, on 26 March this year you came before me and pleaded guilty to three crimes: the unlawful manslaughter of a fifteen-year-old boy, Dennis Lewis; the sexual assault of a minor at the time who has authorized her identify to be released, Ms. Valerie Carmichael, formerly Krestman; and the sexual assault of another person, Woman B, whose identity is protected.

"In sentencing you today, I have taken account of the submissions by the Crown Prosecution Service and your own counsel. I have also listened carefully to the statements of the impact of those crimes on the Lewis family and the assault victims."

It was Wednesday, April 8, the day when Passover began, only days before Easter Sunday. The case was reaching its conclusion, much as June Robinson had predicted. Sammie sat in the row behind the CPS barrister and his junior, with Tim Hutton next to her. Across the room she had exchanged looks once with Arthur Fielding, who was similarly placed behind the barrister for the defense. He had given her a small nod of recognition, but no sign of his state of mind.

In the dock, Oliver Mettler looked anxious. He seemed physically better than months ago, as he went through the series of interviews after his confession. Behind her, Sammie knew that the Lewis family were seated with Valerie Carmichael, her own solicitor, and Valerie's parents.

She had wondered if Shannon Nichols would appear, anonymous, in the public seating. The priest had been granted anonymity after lodging her revised witness statement, which was a relief, Shannon said. There was no sign of her, though. The only priest there was Reverend Lambert from Cross of the Redeemer, unaccompanied. The church had fired Mettler immediately after he confessed, but she knew Lambert had continued to visit him in prison. She respected him for that, despite his church's engagement of Needham.

The last news she had of Needham was that she had left Wolstenholme & Partners. Sammie had a call from a detective in South Wales asking about her; the lawyer was defending a wealthy investor at Bristol Crown Court in a tax fraud case.

She refocused on Judge DeCourcy, as he turned the page of his sentencing report. He was not that old. Sammie knew he was on the rise in the Crown Court system; a sharp intellect and former barrister in London, he was part of a new generation of judges with a foot in the modern world.

"Despite the pre-sentencing submission from an expert witness for your defense on the contribution of Suppressed Anger Disorder to the death of Dennis Lewis, I give it little weight in this case. Not in general, I say. Where social reports and medical histories align to show relevance, it must be considered. In this case, it was presented simply as a justification for a totally unexpected response. I wish to dispel the impression that, without an established medical history, any clinical anger disorder holds much sway in a matter as serious as homicide. In that regard, I gave greater credence to the expert witness for the Crown, who identified the possible contribution of narcissistic elements in your personality."

Although quiet and impassive so far, Sammie saw Mettler's fleeting facial change, a rejection of that statement. Judge DeCourcy put down his notes and focused, to Sammie's surprise, on her.

"Cumbria Police are to be commended on their investigation in this case. They never closed the file in the search for Dennis Lewis, or his killer. They used modern police methods, including extensive forensic analysis and criminal profiling, to bring these charges."

Turning his head to look at where the Lewis family were sitting, he said, "Nothing in these proceedings will assuage the pain and suffering that the Lewis family have experienced, nor those of the women also assaulted. I am aware of that. But hopefully it will bring closure to a long struggle for answers and to see justice done."

His gaze finally fell on Oliver Mettler in the dock.

"Dennis Lewis was a young man with the zeal to help his friend, holding a youthful innocence that other adults would feel the same way. You betrayed the trust he placed in you first by luring him to a private meeting and lying to him there. When he saw the truth and hit you – without any serious impact, I noted – you hit him hard enough to cause his death. For over a decade, his family were left with no explanation for his disappearance. You went to elaborate lengths to conceal his body and even when arrested, denied repeatedly all culpability. Dennis understood innately the importance of doing the right thing. You do not and did not do so until forced to face your heinous behaviour.

"In determining your sentence, I find your actions meet the criteria of highest culpability given within the guidelines for unlawful manslaughter. You chose an isolated, private meeting place where Dennis could not seek help. You lured him there with an esoteric deception, the prayer service of Compline. I sentence you therefore to twenty years and four months in prison. That is not the maximum sentence available to me but is close to it, as your solicitor can explain to you. Appropriate deduction for time already served in custody will be applied administratively, as will the relevant sentencing surcharge for the victim support fund.

"A sentence of that length will exclude you from automatic probation eligibility. After serving a major component of your prison term, you will be required to satisfy a parole board that your release on licence presents no further risk to others. I also place on record that, were it not for the supportive forensic evidence of an impulsive blow leading to the death of Dennis Lewis, other elements of the crime would have met the sentencing criteria for murder, with the prospect of an automatic life sentence.

"Dennis would not have contacted you if you had not first betrayed another trust, that of Valerie Krestman, when you sexually assaulted her. You also admit the sexual assault of Woman B in that period. You left these women with the sense of violation and shame that can shape their lives adversely and sometimes destroy their future. In this case, both women rose above that, I am pleased to note.

"For the crimes of sexual assault by touching, I sentence you to five years of a custodial sentence in each case, to be served concurrently. You will be placed on the Sex Offender Register for life. Take the prisoner away."

It is over, thought Sammie Livermore, standing up and looking around after the court adjourned. Across the courtroom, Bernice Lewis gave her a small wave of acknowledgement before heading to the exit with Eamon, Aileen, and the Carmichael group.

Tim Hutton spoke briefly to the CPS barrister before turning to Sammie. "I really thought your boss would come with you."

Sammie shook her head. "DI Calder sent me, as she decided to take most of the afternoon off."

Intuitively, he saw the reason. "She is still brooding about the loss of her church role, I suspect. This case would only bring it back."

Sammie nodded. "I think so. I know she spoke to Bernice Lewis yesterday evening. I think the Lewis family understands her absence now."

~~

Harriet Calder was in Bassenthwaite, but not at home or the Methodist Chapel. She was at St. Anselm's, with Chris Willard. He had been unaware of the reason for her escape from work that afternoon but had called her for another reason.

"I was wondering, Harriet, if you are around later, have you time to pop by St. Anselm's around four?"

What's wrong with the lovebirds, was her first thought. She resisted the impulse to ask why and agreed to drop in.

When she got to St. Anselm's, Chris was alone at the church. Two visitors, tourists by the look of them, were just leaving, walking to the road.

"Come, sit with me here, Harriet; my thinking spot."

He moved to a row near the back, on one side. As she sat down beside him, he pointed at two windows. "About now the sun is just right, through the stained glass."

Harriet asked, "How are the plans going? Susan told me she is coming to live here. You decided that last week, I know."

He smiled. "Yes, Bishop Azikiwe will marry us in Hamilton, we decided. Her family will travel there from North Bay. They seem happy with me – and that Susan will have an Anglican wedding. In fact, they are amazed that she will be married in a church, and in a cathedral, no less. Then after our honeymoon in Nova Scotia, we will have a blessing here at St. Anselm's with my own bishop and congregation. I met 'her James' when I was over there. Bishop Azikiwe thinks well of you, I might add."

Harriet smiled, thinking, I know that. And I of him. But she said, "And the logistics?"

"We still have a lot to sort out and it takes time. Susan's work visa, residency, her licensing level with the counselling authority, all that sort of thing. Applications have started. A woman she met in York, in charge of addiction services in Tyne & Wear, is helping to find a slot in addiction work around here. And there are other bureaucratic details neither one of us ever contemplated."

"But we are getting there slowly. And from time to time, I sit in my thinking spot and pray and reflect on both my good fortune and the challenges ahead, watching the light through those windows. You know their meaning, the context, obviously."

Harriet looked at them. Two lancet windows of stained glass, long, and with arched tops. Each had a figure, one male, the other female. The texts 'Consider the lilies of the field' and 'How they grow' appeared in scrolls in the lower panes.

Getting the drift now of his request to visit, she replied, "Plant your leeks early, d'y think? No. So Kerri blabbed about me still missing my ministry, despite all the work in MIU?"

He smiled at the joke and ignored the question. "I think you meant to say, 'Do not worry, place things in God's hands', didn't you?"

Harriet dipped her head, accepting the point. She said softly, "I'm missing it more this week, with Easter here. More than last Christmas, as you can relate."

"I understand, and I do feel for you, which is why I called. Ministry has been a major part of your life. But let go of the anger and doubts, Harriet; focus only on your trust in God. I remind myself of that as Susan and I deal with the bureaucracy."

He gave her a look, assessing her. "The gossip this morning via Seymour is that another lay preacher has just been assigned to your former circuit of Methodist churches. She's from Brighton; 'down south, would you believe', he said, and only twenty-three. Who knows anything at twenty-three, Seymour asked, seeming to forget that I was a curate about then."

Harriet laughed. "I hadn't heard, I've been so busy at work. Oh Seymour! I should phone him up and tell him my replacement loves old French cars, with them being so superior to British ones."

She paused, briefly bowing her head again. "What I should do is go to hear this new preacher and support her; pray for her. What happened to the one I talked to a couple of months ago? Did he say? Bassenthwaite Methodist wasn't part of her circuit, so I wouldn't see her there."

"No. I have no idea, nor should I pry."

He took her hand and gave it a squeeze. "I'm going to

leave you here, to enjoy my spot for a while. Pray for her, and for your inner peace. I have yet another sermon to finish. But come to the office and interrupt me if you want, in a while. We can make tea and raid Kerri's fig biscuits."

"Thank you. My church doesn't want my skills at present it seems, and Cumbria Police do. I don't know if I will find an answer, though."

He responded gently, but firmly. "But consider the message in these windows, as the sun moves and the light changes. It may help. You may find it less important to have that answer this afternoon, or any time soon. Give it a try."

He stood and moved away, leaving Harriet Calder sitting there, gazing at the windows as the sun dropped lower across Bassenthwaite Lake and the hills beyond.

NOTES

Some of the places in this novel that are real are used entirely fictitiously. Any portrayal of a particular place or organisation as part of this work is fictional. All persons and events are the product of the author's imagination and are used fictitiously. Any resemblance to actual persons living or dead is entirely coincidental.

Several Cumbrian churches mentioned are real while others are fictitious. St. Mark's (Methodist) and St Mary's (Church of England) are in Maryport. In Bassenthwaite, there are passing references to the Methodist Chapel and a greater mention of a church on the east side of Bassenthwaite Lake I call St. Anselm's, located where the real pre-Norman church of St. Bega sits. Carlisle Cathedral and the Methodist Central Hall nearby are real places, as is St. Andrew's Church, Penrith.

The Cross of the Redeemer church in Bradford, Yorkshire and the Langdale Circuit of the Cumbria Methodist District are entirely fictitious. Christ's Church Cathedral is in Hamilton, Ontario, Canada, but the Anglican diocese of Hamilton-Brant is fictitious.

The original idea for *Canons*, the first novel in the series, was that it would stand alone. It was only later that the idea of a trilogy developed around the main characters and, for the second novel, the plot of a missing person 'cold case'. *Compline* took shape.

In approaching the story, I had the benefit of feedback on *Canons*, and some reactions to a thematic trilogy on the topic of investigations based on clergy abuse. Many readers clearly enjoyed the plot of *Canons*. Others, familiar with the Catrin Sayer novels, were far less comfortable with the topic or, indeed, a book which spoke of such failings within a church denomination or its clergy.

The challenge as a writer has been to capture emotions and perspectives of both the victims and perpetrators of such crimes without adding to the 'cringe' factor which makes people turn away from the topic. In the period between the two novels, the Independent Inquiry into Child Sexual Abuse in the UK finished its task and produced its reports on institutional failings – not only of churches, but many other organisations. It is a global problem, and the findings of the Inquiry are of broad applicability.

I thank my wife Gill and my friends Fred and Ellen Grigsby for reading early versions of this book, my friend Jack Soule for once again copy-editing the text, and the various readers of Canons who responded positively to the story and gave me the encouragement to continue into *Compline*.

ABOUT THE AUTHOR

Allan Jones lives in Ontario, Canada. He was born and grew up in Merseyside, England. By profession an industrial chemist, he worked for many years as a consultant on international chemical regulation.